I0669328

Lofty Issues

mac black

The question has to be asked: was Alexander *really* a villain?

It is worthy of note that Alexander Findlay, one of the few Scottish pipers to survive the horrors of the Great War, returned from the battlefields as an injured hero. After that ordeal, shouldn't life have become kinder to him? Admittedly, straying from the straight and narrow was wrong, but his untimely death shortly afterwards in the centre of Glasgow seems so unfair: and his legacy? He may have been a hero, but his ill-gotten gains became a shameful family secret.

Are the Findlays up for a challenge 'from the grave'? Will there really be a worthwhile prize?

The story involving six generations of the Findlay family gradually unfolds when Tom visits the loft *"looking for the 'jeely pan'..."*

Front Picture copyright © Allan McQuarrie Black
Cover Design copyright © U P Publications 2021

Copyright © 2021 Mac Black

Mac Black has asserted his moral rights

A CIP Catalogue record of this book is available from the British Library
ISBN 978-1-912777-14-3 FIRST EDITION

Also published as an e-book by U P Publications
ISBN 978-1912777-30-3

3 7 9 0 1 6 8 5 2 4

U P Publications, St George's House, George St, Huntingdon, Cambs, PE29 3GH UK

www.macblack.info
www.uppbooks.com

Lofty Issues

mac black

2021

The Findlay Issues...

(as researched by David and Tom Findlay - Nov 2009)

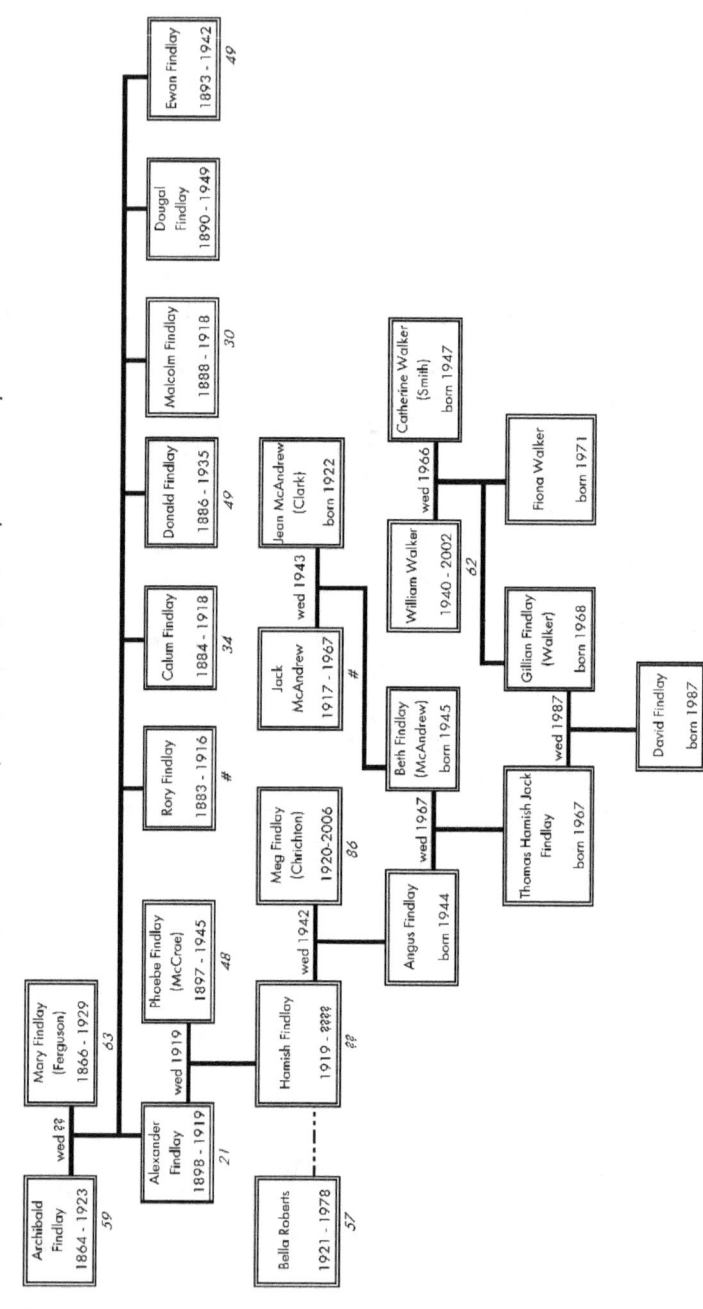

1

2009
Good morning, Mr Sunshine...

Tom Findlay would not have described himself as a grumpy person, but maybe on that particular Saturday it was the world that had chosen to be against him. He was outside. It was only early morning in Glasgow, but he was hot, tired, and irritable, as if he'd already suffered an exhausting day of work.

Snapping at Gillian at breakfast had not been clever. Wisely, he'd immediately apologised, but...

Blooming heck!

Now the simplest of tasks seemed too much.

In his hand was a vehicle key, grabbed as he passed the hall table, but the two keys lying there were almost identical, so... which did he lift? Was it for car – or van? He should have tagged them long ago for easier recognition.

Parked on the driveway in front of him, the two vehicles were in full glare of the early-morning sun: the family car – looking clean and shiny in the bright light, and the works van, less so – in fact, long overdue at the carwash. He pressed the remote. The indicators flashed and...

The flipping van! Surprise... Surprise... Stuff it!

He should then have gone back inside, simply walked to the far end of the hall, swopped the keys, and so been able to travel in the comfort of a shiny, clean and much more comfortable car – but no!

"God, I'll roast in here..." was the mumbled grumble as he eased into the driver's seat – quickly followed by "Damn!" as he noticed that he'd successfully transferred dirt from the van's bodywork onto his first-time-on summer-lightweight-cream-coloured chinos.

Not a good start...

"Sunglasses! Why didn't I bring them? I'll never see in this blooming glare – and the spare pair's in the car!" but he did nothing about it. He chose to moan, out loud, and feel sorry for himself, as his day worsened rapidly!

He had not slept well. It was freak weather for Glasgow and, even with the bedroom windows wide-open last night, much too hot. Not surprisingly, Tom left his bed early, feeling lousy and definitely lacking enthusiasm. He now sat, reluctantly, in a dirty van, impatiently drumming his fingers, overheated and in a filthy mood – and why? Was it a late start to work? An emergency call-out? No...

Mother had summoned him!

If only I'd answered the phone myself, I'd have told her where to go...

Oh, no he wouldn't – and at the time he'd been glad when Gillian answered – it stopped the ringing!

The visit was requested only an hour ago, and immediately accepted by her. "Of course, we can, Mother," Gillian said. "No problem. Tom will be delighted." He could have done without it, but he wasn't asked. So many other things I ought to be doing, he told himself – but the way he was feeling, it was unlikely any of them would have been tackled anyway. He'd have most likely slunk back to bed.

Mother had a task for Tom, but wouldn't say what.

Something to make me feel even hotter and stickier – something overly physical and demanding – that's guaranteed! Or else she'd have landed dad with it.

"I'll tell him when you get here," was all Gillian was given.

A surprise? Well, I hope it's a pleasant one, Mother!

Oh, for goodness sake! Where are you, Gill...?

He lowered the window but, being almost as warm outside as it was in, it made little difference.

God – the heat!

The weather was most unusual for the west of Scotland. Only 10.20am and, as predicted last night by the BBC TV forecaster, another scorcher had arrived. '*Saturday will be a repeat of the last two days...*' the tall bloke with the hairless head and the English accent had stated confidently. But when he added, '*...so if you are out and about, be sure to use* *sun cream,'* Tom had smiled wryly. He just couldn't take to this bloke. Gillian waited. Tom had developed an annoying habit of talking back to the TV, and of course the response came... "Yea, that will be right, pal. This is Glasgow. Glaswegians are hard men! We like getting burned – we're masochists!"

Gillian locked the front door. Her mother-in-law awaited. She walked along the path and, with a puzzled look on her face, passed the car. She opened the passenger door of the van. Her eyebrows rose as she started to say, "Why are we not using the...?" but the words faded with the glare from her darling husband. She got in.

Tom started the engine and switched on the radio. "OK! Let's get it over with," he mumbled grumpily.

He could already feel the frustration building, and that was only *thinking* of what he was about to face, so he needed soothing. His daily programme 'Good Music for Early Risers' was essential today! He liked that.

Bad enough his having to be nice to Mother for the next hour, but before that he'd have to cope with the Cross and its never-ending streams of traffic – and traffic lights – traffic lights that had always hated him!

If a car ever passed him in the street, with the windows wide open and the radio blaring, Tom would be first with the criticism. Today he was the offender – and he didn't give a damn! Anyway, his, was 'Good Music'.

At least the side roads were deserted. Since the new bollards were installed, fewer drivers were attempting to dodge the Cross. In fact, their van appeared to be the only vehicle locally going anywhere today, until they reached – Crow Road. There, it all changed. He had to be quick to squeeze into a slight gap in a virtually endless flow of vehicles in two lanes. Of course, being Saturday and hot and sunny, it seemed everyone was wanting out of the city – via the Cross!

Surprisingly, at first it seemed better than anticipated. He arrived in the correct lane, and was moving, so a silent *thank you* was said to the Traffic-Light Gods for once being kind to him on this road. They would reach Bearsden in no time at all. The thought *almost* made him smile. He would find out what the task was, have it completed and be back home by lunchtime. The international on TV was best viewed from the comfort of his own favourite chair.

Blast! We've stopped!

Any chance of a smile vanished because the traffic flow was much worse than normal. He'd been lucky earlier. Patience was required now. Sadly, Tom Findlay lacked that. He felt uptight and had begun frenziedly tapping his fingers in time with the music, until he realised it was a tune he disliked intensely – and immediately stopped.

Damn this! Crow Road, red light, long queue...

The distance from their home to his parents' in Bearsden was certainly not far by car; in fact, a few years back when his son was still at school, once on a cool dry day, he'd walked there with David. Today, if he'd had any energy, or enthusiasm, it would have been quicker walking! He must stay calm... He took a deep breath, sat up straight, and forced himself to grip the steering wheel a bit less aggressively.

Ruddy lights!

For Tom, hearing music he liked could usually make a journey seem less exasperating. Today, he was later than normal and sitting in a queue at traffic lights that showed green for a ridiculously short time, when he realised disturbingly – his early morning music programme was about to end – the thing that kept him calm in situations like this.

Oh!

He disliked 'talk' radio.

The other lane... It's inching forward. They're moving... Why... why are we not? What's wrong with the idiot in front? Get going, for goodness sake!

He hit the horn – and got a rude hand-signal back!

'Coming up next...' announced the female voice, 'Saturday Review – a round-up of world news.' She made it obvious that in the past week, important events had occurred, but her bright tone hinted of fun and excitement to come – a programme not to be missed. 'So, stay tuned!' she purred. Her voice was meant to keep you on this channel, obviously.

Tom was cajoled – for the moment.

His mind rattled over his own week – what a carry-on! Snag after snag, never mind the ridiculous heat... The wrong type of panel for one job, then short of cable and, of course, the old biddy who forgot the appointment. That really messed it up – her wandering off for the day – leaving him standing like an idiot ringing the doorbell of her empty house... Should all have been routine, not a mess to face next week!

He reached to change the radio programme, but...

The lights! Green! Us, this time! ...Yes! No, blast it! Why is this queue so slow?

That's when he had the idea that if he kept moving forward and made contact with the car in front, and kept pushing, it would nudge the ones in front progressively, and take up the ridiculously large gaps – and get him closer to these ruddy lights! Thankfully, he resisted the temptation...

Meanwhile the female's voice was advertising yet another programme. Yatter, yatter, yatter...

He would have to find suitable music and was about try, when the outside lane started moving. Tom sat up, but it was only closing the gaps in readiness... Suddenly there was music – from the car on his right – not his radio.

It was AC/DC –– and at full volume!

The windows of the old Mini were wide open and Tom rapidly assessed that the driver, in a torn t-shirt, was not someone to be messed with – someone who didn't give a damn about the world around him. The engine was being continually revved, annoyingly, but probably necessary to keep the engine running. Next to him was a fierce-looking shaven-headed passenger – smoking, who then challengingly blew smoke out of the window – directly at Tom! He glowered at the smoker. The smoker glowered back. Tom suddenly realised that it was a woman, but just as her smoke was about to be blown his way again, the Mini's engine cut out, and the music stopped. She swung round and started berating her driver. What a pair. She wanted her music – *now* – and her language was choice!

But there were more important things...

The lights! Red and amber! This is it. Here we... Go! We're off! Yes, keep moving – but why so slow? We'll miss the...

Must change lanes! ...Whoops – sorry pal!

Tom had taken advantage of the Mini's pause and swung over into the gap, but it had restarted, and the wheels burned rubber to catch up. Maybe it's fortunate that a Mini has not much of a front end, or Tom might have removed it. The tough-looking driver, now racing up behind, realised that too – and he was after Tom!

Oh-oh!

'...then, after the early evening news, we have Gregor Simpson, giving seasonal guidance for the...'

The female voiced droned on, but Tom wasn't hearing, focussed on the next set of traffic lights at the top of the hill – and the threat from his newfound 'friend' in the Mini, who seemed out to get him.

The brassy blast of intro music for the news didn't help Tom's blood pressure, but he focussed!

Don't change! They are still green! Can I do it...?

Must accelerate! Stay green, please... Please, please, please... but will we...? Yes... Yes...

YES! MADE IT!

Not only did he beat the traffic lights, but the Mini that was on his tail turned left!

Phew... and suddenly he was relaxed. Tom's urge to change programme had gone. With the Cross behind him, life was different. 'News' was starting, and he was listening – actually listening, and he almost smiled. What a lovely day!

But never believe a purring female announcer! She inferred that good news would follow – it was anything but!

A male was speaking, calmly with confidence that comes from knowing everything. It was only the facts, but to Tom it seemed that the civilised world was going to hell in a handcart: The demise of Michael Jackson; the demise of Farrah Fawcett Major; and, according to the World Health Organisation – with Swine Flu about to obliterate everything on four legs, *and two* – the demise of the human race!

Tom's day didn't seem quite so bright now...

'...and finally, to complete an action-packed programme, we'll discuss Cristiano Ronaldo's transfer from Manchester United to Real Madrid for eighty-million pounds.'

"Eighty-million ruddy quid!" Tom nearly choked. He was well aware of that individual's world-famous skill, but his was a different world so, thank you very much...

That was it. He'd had enough.

He'd lost the urge for music too, so he reached over and switched off...

"Don't ask if *I* was listening to that...!" was Gillian's immediate reaction.

2

1919
Under a special Umbrella...

On that miserable winter's day, Alexander Findlay could have chosen other ways to reach his destination, but he did not and, for him, it would prove to be the wrong route...

An ordinary morning in Glasgow city centre ...well, that's how it began ...the first of March and cold but, like every early morning in this city, already buzzing. Even in dreadful weather, it seemed people always had to 'shop' and under the Hielanman's Umbrella there was constant activity.

Hordes of good citizens, and others, were on the move. It was Saturday.

Every Glaswegian knows Hielanman's Umbrella, the affectionate nickname given to the long, high tunnel, formed by a rail bridge over one of Glasgow's busiest thoroughfares, Argyle Street. Always busy, it was a well-used access, connecting important parts of the city, but in miserable weather it was a shelter, a dry haven for drifters with little purpose in going elsewhere. If they wished they could remain all day in that temporary home, ignored by pedestrians hurrying along crowded pavements.

However, being in that long, dark tunnel was neither quiet nor peaceful. It was a huge sound box, magnifying all noises. A major rail terminal was overhead. Its routes, with many lines to and from the south, bridged the nearby River Clyde. Rumbling trains, trundling slowly, contributed to the clamour in the tunnel's vast space below, and polluted the air above with the smoke and soot.

Dragging heavy cartloads of assorted goods were horses, neighing and straining, their shod hooves clip-clopping and echoing from the surfaces, metal shoes slipping on the cobbles. That morning, steam from the horses' hot flanks and nostrils emphasised the coldness. Occasionally, the crack of a whip demonstrated who was in control.

Along the middle of the street, tramcars rattled by, blue flashes from overhead wires brightened the dark underside of the bridge for brief moments, crackling and sizzling, and contributing to the lively clamour.

Four-wheeled motors venturing to travel along this route struggled to maintain pace, powerless to compete with the many surrounding carts and trams. Now and then, frustrated drivers sounded their horns to add to the noise.

Inside the tunnel, pedestrians rarely tried to cross the street. That action was not safe. The mass of traffic, in both directions, rarely stopped long enough.

On busy pavements, people jostled along, reluctantly accepting that they would have to leave the overhead protection eventually. When exposed that day, it was an impatient wait in sleety rain, until burly Glasgow Bobbies brought traffic at the busy junctions to a halt for a few moments, and permitted them to continue.

Yes, it was just an ordinary Saturday...

Stepping from the shelter of the close and striding hurriedly along Dover Street exposed Alexander Findlay to the awfulness of the March morning. The fog had gone but it was now bitterly cold and wet, threatening snow any moment.

His threadbare jacket, scarf, and cap were inadequate clothing for the conditions ...but that was the least of Alexander's concerns! Anyway, his heavy, winter coat was serving a better purpose – on the bed helping to keep Phoebe warm. His wife was not feeling well.

He had slept badly – a troubled conscience – so he rose early and lighted the fire straightaway but sadly, although well alight, it made little difference to the warmth of the icebox they lived in. He'd left her alone in the house and with his encouragement, being too cold for her to sit around, she had returned to the warm bed.

This morning, something more serious than a pregnant wife feeling unwell had his attention, something that clearly should never have happened. It preyed on his mind all night. He was returning to the scene of the crime ...it was not far.

Why did he not walk?

He probably would have if the weather had been better, and used another route – and that might have changed the outcome. Instead, he was going towards the city centre on an electric tram. He sat gazing vacantly at the condensation on the windows and through bleary eyes watched sleety rain stream down outside. His head hurt, the injured leg throbbed, his clothes were damp and cold – yes, the miserable weather matched his mood perfectly.

It was not warm inside the tram but it was dry and, with few people on the vehicle, he could have sat anywhere. Nevertheless, even if travelling a long distance, he always wanted to be near the door. He preferred the long seat. Though draughty, it was easy to vacate quickly if he chose. It would be a short journey and it felt claustrophobic sitting farther inside the body of the tram. He would never go upstairs – the smoky fug encouraged coughing. When full, it was possible to get on and off without paying because the conductor was so busy, but no chance of a free ride today with so few passengers. With his mind elsewhere, Alexander handed over the fare instinctively. The conductor, with little to do, sat down on the seat opposite and stared morosely across the passage.

Alexander worried – is he looking at me? Can he tell what I have done? Of course not, but though Alexander knew that, it still unsettled him – the guilt was uncomfortable and though, deep down, he knew that returning to the scene was unwise, he felt compelled... He was nearing his destination and wanted to get off as soon as possible, but would wait for the shelter of the bridge.

Nearly there...

The police officer on point duty waved the tram through the junction. Without losing speed, the vehicle clanked its way under the bridge with wheels screeching, adding more noise to the existing discord. As the speed changed and the tram began to slow down, some passengers rose for the next stop.

Alexander was already on the platform. Now inside the tunnel the noise increased, and the pains in his head began again. He closed his eyes – but that did not help.

It would have been wise to wait until the vehicle stopped fully, but he was agitated and eager to alight. It would also have been wise to observe the surrounding traffic. He should have noted the tramcar overtaking a slower-moving fully-laden horse-drawn cart.

The tram was still moving quickly when he jumped and staggered... He stumbled forward awkwardly, arms flailing as he struggled to stay upright, and winced at the sharp pain from his bad leg.

His sudden appearance startled the carthorse. The carter had to react quickly to prevent the poor, blinkered creature from veering sideways onto the busy pavement. The man dragged hard on the reins as Alexander jumped aside. If the wheels hit the kerb, it could tip the load! It did not, but the angry carter's ripe words rang out, adding embarrassment to Alexander's agitation. He was wrong and he knew it.

The incident unsettled him. He'd endangered others and, worse still, he could have been hurt! How would his pregnant wife have coped?

Alexander was in the middle of the busy road. That was not sensible. The tram behind was at a standstill too and its driver was also shouting at him.

Annoyed and embarrassed, desperate to get away, he lost concentration, turned and looked back, shouting a delayed response, bravely glowering at shouting drivers... Grumpy buggers!

Anxious to distance himself he darted out from between the stationary trams onto the other track – straight into the path of another tram speeding towards him...

What the... I can't...!

"No! Aaaaaah...!"

Had he been able, the desperate driver would have veered to avoid the dark shape that appeared and stood frozen in shock. Wheels screeched piercingly and sparks flew from the rails as the brakes did their work – but the rails control the direction of the vehicle. The poor tram driver could do nothing to avoid the inevitable. He would explain later that a rare gap in the traffic had created an opportunity to accelerate and make good progress for a change.

Suddenly, in the city, it was no longer an ordinary Saturday.

A major hold-up in its busiest area and, much

worse – for the young man struck down, lying on the road – a tragedy. With traffic at a standstill there was almost a respectful silence in the tunnel, but not quite. Overhead, the trains continued to rumble...

The end for Alexander Findlay was most likely instantaneous and sadly, by a careless action, his short life of twenty-one years was over.

In his favour, it was never his intention to mess up the day for the good citizens of Glasgow, and in fact, he had no wish to draw attention to himself. Alexander's desire had been to remain a 'nobody': a 'nobody' with a guilty secret.

Was his death avoidable? Would the Grim Reaper have found him in another way on that special morning? Had he left home five-minutes later on a different tram, would anything have changed?

Some might claim it was justice, in his state of mind – inevitable and predestined – but death surely should not have been the outcome. It was certainly a young life wasted but, although Alexander's time in this world was brief, he experienced a loving relationship and, heroically, survived warfare.

It was regrettable for that normally honest and decent person, that villainy played a part and that a foolish action weighed heavily on his conscience. However, to be fair to his memory, his misdemeanour was a single spur of the moment act that hurt no one. Ironically, had he survived, he would probably have got away it!

3

2009
If you can't stand the heat...

When she told him, he relaxed. He wondered why he had been so uneasy about the task. It might make him warmer for a very short time, but nothing like as bad as in the van. It wasn't complicated – at least, that was the first impression...

"Tom, I need the jelly-pan," his mother declared, giving a false smile in the hope of encouraging him into rapid action, "...so would you please be an angel and go up to the loft and fetch it for me? I need it now, desperately!"

"Easy," Tom had smiled...

That request was made over an hour ago, and he was still searching in the loft's stifling heat, without a clue as to where it could be. There was so much darn stuff. And he thought it had been hot in the car! Before climbing up his father mentioned that some rearranging was done in the loft recently. "Extra insulation – for free, couldn't resist. To help the fuel bills. Bit of a rush job though – glad for your Uncle George's help. Just be careful up there, your mother is relying on you."

Tom had wondered why his father hadn't fetched it himself because surely he should have known where to find it. Getting too old to climb the ladder, he had concluded, but now he knew differently... Dad was being smart! He'd known what the loft was like.

The upstairs bedrooms were now protected from heat. The added insulation on the loft floor prevented heat that permeated the roof tiles from going any further. It stayed in the loft now. Tom found that out the moment he poked his head through the hatch – the heat hit him!

The rooms below were pleasantly cool even with today's scorching sun – but the loft was like an oven. He was cooking rapidly!

As for his father's 'rearrangement'...

"Easy to find, Tom. You are so good at that sort of thing," Mother had said. "I bought fruit yesterday, collected some from the garden too. All sitting ready, so I'll have to make jam soon. Fruit goes off so quickly. Not so good if it's left for any time. The pan will be in the middle of the loft. You'll find it easily."

Find it easily...! Hmmm... He had not, and had been up there considerably longer than comfortable, but it would have to be found! He dared not go down without it.

Mustn't step through the ceiling...

He would never live that down. It would not be the mess, or even being injured that disturbed him – it would be David's comments. He would mock him for the rest of their working lives.

'Old Avacare!' was what his son had started calling him at work. Not to his face though. The nickname surfaced a few weeks back, and the others now used it whenever they thought he was out of earshot – he'd heard them. Yes, he was a stickler for health and safety, and proud of it because the electrical business was his. If he saw one of the team using an unsafe method, instinctively, out it would come, "Hey! Have a care! Don't do it that way!" He took safety seriously.

Yea, thanks David. Old Avacare indeed....

Tom remembered how from four years old, the Mister Men were David's favourites, and that gave him the idea to make up names for people whenever it took his fancy. He was still doing it seventeen years later! It had become second nature. Everyone suffered – including him now.

Where is that pesky jelly-pan...? Oh God, what a lot of rubbish! But just a minute! It's not *Mister* Avacare he's calling me! *It's Old Avacare!*

David could be really annoying, but was a good worker. Tom recognised that. He was also secretly proud of his son's drawing skill. The caricatures he did were very good. Quick-fire sketches of his workmates – house owners too. They were usually left on rafters in the loft when a job was finished and one of these days, someone would complain, but they were good drawings. Stuck on the office wall was a special set, showing the whole team and, like any good cartoonist, David could exaggerate certain features. For his old man, it was the nose and the belly. "Nothing like me," Tom had tried to pretend...

The pan, where is the wretched thing?

Used to have trouble at school, David did, doing caricatures of a teacher when he got bored in a class. Got caught often, and warned about it, even had it recorded on his report card and then discussed at the parents meeting with an embarrassed Gillian and Tom. Afterwards they found out that over the years, the headmaster confiscated the drawings but kept them, because he thought they were excellent. He'd filed them away, secretly hoping that this young lad would be the first from his school to achieve a place at Glasgow Art College – but that never happened. When David was leaving the school, he cheekily did one of the headmaster, which was confiscated as usual – and ended up proudly displayed by the headmaster, on the wall behind his desk...

Tom took a step.

Whoops! Have a care! Tom couldn't see very well and placing a foot on a joist was essential. If he lost his balance...

It was years since Tom was last in the loft. It seemed even darker than ever: a large loft and a very small skylight. Even on that bright, sunny day only the minimum of natural light entered, and, with so much rubbish piled high on the limited flooring, it was surprising that he could see anything at all, and it had never been as hot before. The floor surface, that was laid many long years ago, was non-existent for walking on or even to stand on – totally covered by assorted unrequired items and he knew that stepping on joists that were barely visible was asking for trouble – only slight surface bumps showed on the insulation. Everything was haphazardly stacked on very limited floored area. There was no question, it was a mess! How would he ever find that jelly-pan?

It was obvious that the stacking was unstable. Moving the wrong thing could cause the whole lot to collapse – and the heat was getting to him! The darkness too! Was he hallucinating? There should be electric light. Even a torch would help. Someone could be hurt in the dark – and guess who it would be! He remembered how the day began in the van earlier – could it get worse?

Permanent lighting was needed. Being a professional electrician he knew that years ago he should have done the work for his parents. His dad wouldn't dare to try – not after what happened with the toaster – a wizard at theory and design, but not the handiest with practical stuff.

Tom took another tentative step.

Yes, I will do the wiring... but it needs flooring too. There never was much of it! "Extra flooring? Totally unnecessary!" his dad decided years ago. "Rubbish will not be accumulated. We'll throw stuff out! Ridiculous how people let these things get out of control. It's fine."

Hmm... Yes indeed, Father.

"Are you all right up there, Tom?" shouted his dad from the foot of the ladder. "You know what your mother is like. She's getting impatient."

"Haven't found it yet, Dad. Be a few more

minutes."

"I'll tell her you won't be long."

He had made some progress – he'd cleared a corner to stand on, and allowed the skylight to let in the bright sunshine. The stacks were a bit safer too, with boxes sitting on the insulation. He hoped he'd balanced them safely over the joists.

Ten minutes later he realised it was a bad idea to have moved things absentmindedly from in front to behind him – when he turned around and found himself blocked in, and had to move everything back again!

"Tom..." Oh no, Mother's turn... "Tom, Tom, are you all right?"

"Yes thanks. Just a few more moments, I hope."

"That's what you said to your father, Tom. I cannot start without that pan. I thought you'd be quicker. Please try and concentrate on the job in hand."

"Yes Mother..."

Do not swear, Thomas Findlay, he told himself firmly, but he could not resist – when he was sure she was out of earshot. Only natural, when hot and frustrated on a ruddy impossible jelly-pan hunt. Why couldn't she just buy the blessed stuff in jars from the supermarket like everybody else?

Tom had grown up in this house. He knew it well. A long established detached stone-built villa, constructed diligently in the thirties, with biggish rooms, high ceilings and a large loft, quite unlike modern houses. Such properties also had spacious gardens – great for the young, high-spirited boy he had been at the time.

The Simpsons lived next door – Uncle George and Aunt Mary. There was no blood relationship, but he had reached forty-two still calling them that. No youngsters in their house – deliberate or otherwise he knew not.

It should have bothered them to have a noisy kid, over the wall, who encouraged pals to come round and play boisterous games in the big, back garden, but it had not. In fact, the Simpsons liked it.

What the...! That donkey, bought on that first holiday in Spain – years ago! There it was, legs sticking up in the air. They'd kept that?

Tom was beginning to feel aggrieved. There was no chance of seeing the rugby on TV. He hadn't chosen to spend his Saturday morning like this – and he was suffering! The others certainly weren't.

Gillian, who came with him today just to visit her in-laws, was downstairs happily having coffee, maybe even a lovely cold beer. All three sitting in the garden under the sunshade and enjoying each other's company, while he was in the loft – stewing! He had made a face earlier when given the task, but all his lovely wife said was, "Tom, get on with it! Just don't get your new trousers any dirtier."

His mother spoke very sweetly to him today. He knew it was only because she wanted a favour, but still, it was nice – and a novelty, but "All that fresh fruit sitting on the table desperately crying out for the jelly-pan," had emphasised the need for speed. So, where the hell is that blessed...? Maybe I could nip out, and buy another pan? God! How could anyone accumulate so much rubbish?

"Tom... Tom, can you hear me?" It was Gillian now.

"Yes darling?"

"What's taking you so long? Your father poured out a cold beer for you over an hour ago. You told him you would only be a few minutes more. He's had to drink it."

Oh great, very nice ...and thanks for telling me.

"It's been a little awkward, dear," he shouted to her.

"You've been up there for hours. What are you doing?"

"I am looking for the ruddy jelly-pan – *Gillian*! What do you think I'm doing?" he exploded, and then regretted it.

"Oh well, if you are going to be bad tempered about it..." and off she went.

It was a perfect moment to come across an old toy: Little Teddy – moth-eaten and one eye missing, the very one that he used to take to bed with him as a child, to hug and love. Imagine, this dear little teddy bear still being kept. Such a tender moment... All the anger drained from him as he lifted his little friend and smiled. Then...

The damn thing snarled at him! He almost fell over as he hurled it to the far end of the loft – but losing his temper didn't help. It was too damned hot and there was too much rubbish!

And where in heavens is that blasted jelly-pan?

Then he felt guilty... Some of these items would be his grandmother's. Granny Meg – a happy lady until well into her eighties. Passed away many years ago, her humour and excellent memory remaining with her until she died. Would she have thought it clever that her one and only grandson lost his cool like that? No.

She'd lived on her own for a long while, but nearing the end of her life Granny Meg moved, to be with his mum and dad. There was bound to have been some of her stuff in this lot but, as he had not been involved with her house-clearance, Tom had no idea what was kept

He tentatively reached out to move the old Hoover. Why the heck was this kept? It doesn't work!

He pulled at the handle – it was jammed. Pulled harder! ...Whoops!

Two cases nearly toppled, but he was quick and grabbed them. He imagined a 'domino effect' if they had fallen over ...but look!

There it is!

A copper handle was peeping-out tantalisingly from under some old dustsheets, the handle of the much sought-after, the one and only – jelly-pan.

He tried to pull it out but it felt heavier than it should. Difficult to see why in the partial light, so he reached in. It was heavy for good reason. He lifted out an old iron without a flex, two glazed, chipped, flower pots, an Oxford English Dictionary, and an old photo album.

Maybe it was the relief of completing the task – maybe just heatstroke – but that is when he made his momentous decision!

Lighting to be added urgently, and this loft to be given a good clear-out. It has got to be done – and I am the boy to do it.

Exactly. Positive action – and then he looked at the mess again, and reality kicked in. Hmm, but certainly not today...

Would such a commitment be too much to take on? No, it was needed, and his mother and father were pushing on a bit. They would never get round to it themselves.

So, when? Soon – or after they've kicked the bucket?

Another hesitation at that thought, and then a smile slowly formed. Yes... it should be done, but not as a one-man job. David could help, with a bit of encouragement. Give him something else to do rather than wandering off to some pub and getting involved with yet another different young female. Gillian might help too. Clearing so much rubbish needs teamwork – when the weather's cooler because Gillian and David could never cope with the heat. Of course, that's been no problem for me!

A stamp of approval from dear Mother would be necessary before removing any items, but with his usual powers of persuasion, he would win her over. He felt confident and he felt good – current task completed and future decided – he could return triumphantly to civilisation and enjoy cool air, and a cold beer if there was any left.

He turned, and bumped against the cases again. The dictionary and the photo album bounced on the insulation. Photos fell out. He replaced them then became curious. He needed some light, so he made his way back gingerly to the hatch opening.

The album was not one of his dad's. It was old and the photographs were loose, He opened it carefully. If it were Granny Meg's there might be some of him, for she'd photographed him many times when he was with her. Would he look as slim and youthful as he remembered? He looked at his waistline. Are David's cartoons true...?

Opening it carefully, he found he was not the star. The photos were of times long before his. He did not recognise his grandmother at first – she looked so young. The man beside her must be his grandad. He had not seen this album before, but then again, he had never seen his grandad either, been only vaguely aware of his existence. He had never questioned it, that his grandad had vanished to Australia not long after the marriage and – if he was remembering correctly – gone off with a certain Bella Roberts...

There were many other unknown people in the photos, probably family and friends of hers, he guessed. A nice little bit of family history which could be useful. Now, there's a thought...

We need a family tree! We don't have one.

Curiosity about previous generations had always been there, but doing something about it was never attempted. Wandering around graveyards and searching through library files never appealed, but with this to help...

This could be a starter. People trace families nowadays using the internet? Yes... but David hogs the laptop. Anyway, even if I did get on it, how would I manage? Me... On the computer? No... But David is good! Could he be conned into emptying the loft – and maybe into doing the family tree as well? If I show him these photos, I could maybe tempt him – for both...

He placed the old album back in the jelly-pan and, holding it in one hand and the ladder with his other, he carefully began his descent – a broad grin spreading right across his face,

Old Avacare! David, you are a cheeky bugger! We'll see who the smart one is.

Then he missed his footing!

"Wow! ...Ohhhhhhhh... OUCH!"

4

1898-1913
A talented young lad...

Over the length and breadth of the British Isles, anticipation was growing. People everywhere were looking with optimism towards the end of a troublesome old era. Two more years and the world could move forward into a glorious new century – a chance to wipe the slate clean, a fresh beginning, a time to let a bright, new world emerge; like previous New Years – only better; a perfect time for new resolutions to be declared by all countries and all leaders. Worldwide peace could be agreed and there would be no more fighting – ever. That had to be the way forward, surely...

Alternatively, life could remain on its downward spiral.

Reality for the British was that war in Sudan was likely to continue and, in South Africa, the Boers would probably restart trouble for Queen Victoria's loyal troops.

Why does there always have to be fighting? No one ever has an answer to that. No matter, reality would not prevent the ordinary folk, the good citizens of the British Isles, from wishing for that idyllic world to appear, one day...

In Aberloudie, most of the inhabitants could be considered 'ordinary'. They did not seek problems beyond the family and the village. Here, news from outside more normally arrived by word of mouth, saving the need to read any newspaper.

"Aye, it's a big world out there..." could be heard often in Aberloudie, and it was not considered a disadvantage to be ignorant of happenings beyond the village boundaries. However, they were not totally ignorant of current affairs, oh no. News had reached Aberloudie from Glasgow that horses there might be losing their jobs. Glasgow Corporation Tramways was starting to use electricity. That was the current gossip.

"Whatever next...?" came the comment in Aberloudie when that news reached them. "Oh me oh my, but that's the big city for you... Always the changes..."

It was obvious that catastrophes and disruptions occurring in the big wide world, or even fresh activities in the grand city of Glasgow – or any other large city for that matter – were unlikely to be of great consequence in Aberloudie. In fact, they tended to be of no consequence at all. There, no matter what these big events had been, or were about to be, within the boundaries of the village, life carried on as normal.

Normality, for the Findlay family, was the regular

reproduction of the species.

The local news, that Mary Findlay had given birth to yet another wee baby boy, was currently circulating. The little boy's father, Archibald Findlay had been hoping that this time his wife would present him with a wee girl, but no; another suitable boy's name would have to be decided – and remembered.

Archibald did not believe in a father and son having the same name, and in the Findlay family, they already had Rory, Calum, Donald, Malcolm, Dougal, and Ewan – always good Scottish names for the Findlays. Mary liked the name Alexander. Scottish kings were called that, so it must be a good Scottish name, she claimed. Archibald was happy to go along on that suggestion. Up until now, he'd had to come up with all the other boy's names.

It would have been nice to have had a daughter, though. They had a long list of girls' names ready, names that they'd been desperate to use each time previously. Maybe the next time, thought Archibald, but wisely at that precise moment he did not pass that suggestion on to an exhausted wife.

So, in Aberloudie, 1898 was the year for little Alexander Findlay's life to begin. His place of birth was well north of Glasgow, and it had changed very little in the many years that the current Findlay family had lived there. Practically, the family was already struggling to survive and, if it hadn't been that Rory was fourteen, and Calum thirteen, old enough to travel about and find work and earn some money to add to their father's meagre income, penury could have been on the cards.

As it was, Alexander, the seventh son in this all-male brood, had almost become one mouth too many to feed. He had certainly turned out to be one body too many to clothe. New clothes solely for this young fellow were way beyond their means, but the Findlays never threw clothing away. He was not the first to become grateful for hand-me-downs, but it was to his disadvantage that most of the others before him had already enjoyed that privilege. As he grew, being seventh in line, the hand-me-downs, by the time they reached him, were barely holding together, and quite unable to keep out the cold unless they were worn, at least, doubled up.

Not many children attending school in Aberloudie were likely to be considered as intellectuals in later years. Heaven knows, he tried really hard, but no matter how dedicated the schoolmaster was, the local youngsters he handled were rarely of a high standard as raw material, and Alexander stood out.

The master had been pleased with this young fellow, and later could claim to have guided him in the right direction. This one was a cut above the others. At least, he showed interest in learning. He might not become academic – but the conscientious teacher recognised that this boy had talent.

Aberloudie schooling concentrated on the well-established Scottish principle of Three R's, and, though Alexander's arithmetic was not spectacular, his ability to read and write was well ahead of the others. Over the years most of the books owned by the master, those that could be of interest to a young boy, were avidly read by the star pupil, and some over and over again.

Although the master was a good all-round teacher one particular skill that he lacked was that of drawing, but he could appreciate it in others. During classes, he always encouraged the children to attempt to draw, both as a break from the rigours of his teaching and for their own good – it could be fun.

It became apparent early on that the youngest Findlay boy was considerably better than his classmates, so the master took pleasure in encouraging development of this talent. As Alexander grew older, he became more proficient. Eventually, he was able to observe and capture a likeness of any subject. In fact, he developed far better than the master could ever have hoped and probably, had he lived in Glasgow, would have been given an opportunity to continue studies at an Art College. Unfortunately, there was little chance of that. This was Aberloudie. To send their son to study in the city, no matter how talented, was way beyond his parent's means.

He would be a successful artist one day – his teacher was convinced of that but, to have success, he would have to leave Aberloudie. It would happen one day, the schoolmaster was certain, and when it did, in addition to what he had already learned academically, his developing drawing skill would hold him in good stead.

Drawing was not Alexander's only talent.

When it came to playing the bagpipes, there was no one in the region could better him.

The instrument Alexander played was old and had been in the Findlay family for two previous generations. How the Findlays acquired bagpipes was unknown because his parents' memories told only of hardships. They knew that the pipes were 'handed down' – a little bit like the clothes – but unlike the clothes, they were still in excellent condition.

His father, Archibald, had been taught by his dad when young and both had been braw pipers in their day, renowned in the area, so playing to the highest standard had become a family tradition. Alexander was now the expert.

Several years before, when Archibald decided to give up, his hope was to pass on his playing skills to his eldest son, Rory. A high standard was expected of him, and Rory did try hard, but it was not to be. His level of achievement was low. Not surprisingly over time, he lost the urge and became reluctant to play, but when Rory stopped, his brothers were unwilling even to try. Alexander being too small wasn't given the chance, and as his father felt too old to start again, the pipes were put aside.

They lay unused for many years, stored under the bed.

For all his life, Alexander had admired his big brother, Rory, envying the additional attention he used to get from their father because of the bagpipes so, one day, he asked his father about the abandoned instrument. The lad claimed that he was now big enough to hold the pipes, and proved it, but could he inflate them? The proof was in the noise... It was an exciting moment for the family – and the neighbourhood, when the unholy wails and racket rang out that first time.

He proved willing to learn. In fact, he was eager, and that did his father's heart the power of good. The learning process brought the youngest son and his father much closer. He became devoted to these pipes and, at a young age, became a highly proficient player, proud to restore the Findlay piping tradition. His success also permitted the guilt of failure to drop from brother Rory's shoulders.

As Alexander improved his technique, playing gave him confidence and the instrument began to feel an essential part of his life. The bagpipes were hand-me-downs, like the clothes, but this time, it felt different. They had reached him, without being held, or blown, by five of his elder brothers: that made him feel very special indeed.

His other talent continued to develop as the years progressed.

With a lump of charcoal in his hand, and a clean piece of paper, he delighted the villagers by producing appealing images of them going about their daily tasks. The neighbours bartered food for the sketches and used them to decorate cottage walls. Alexander was pleased to contribute something to the family larder. As he grew older, his fame spread to the other villages. He began to draw new scenes and portraits of fresh groups of faces, and, to the benefit of the rest of the family, the bartering of food and drink for the sketches continued.

His drawing skill brought him to the attention of the local Laird, a man of some aspirations himself. His wife, Daphne, and eldest daughter, Catherine, were well aware of the talent of this handsome, young, local artist, and made Alexander welcome at Aberloudie Big House.

It was clear to everyone who entered The Big House, and especially to the Laird's good lady, who was there day in and day out, that the hall lacked something – a majestic portrait of her husband! The young fellow could be the one to correct that, so the Laird offered money to Alexander for his artistic services. Unfortunately, it came as a minor disappointment that painting in oils, hoped for by his new patron, was not Alexander's forte.

Should that mean that the hall must remain devoid of a portrait? Of course not, declared Daphne and Catherine. So, after due consideration and persuasion by them, though with some apprehension on his own part, the Laird decided to proceed – and he was not disappointed. The sitting was pleasant. While he worked, the young fellow was capable of discoursing in an interesting way with his subject. The hours passed without becoming tedious, though, until Alexander relaxed, several failed attempts were a bit unsettling for the Laird. It all worked out in the end and the result was a very flattering full-length portrait, with the Laird wearing kilt and glengarry, done in charcoal and achieved after only hours. Even without colour, once framed, it would look magnificent in the entrance hall.

A job well done, so, money changed hands and Alexander felt good. This was a new experience for him. No bartering of food involved and, for the first time, he earned real money.

"The young lad obviously has talent," the Laird commented later to his wife. "Maybe I should give him further support. I could claim to be a patron of the arts." He had heard that sort of thing happened elsewhere. It should improve his standing in Glasgow, he predicted, and, could lead to more business in the big city.

Willingly, and generously, he paid the young fellow a retainer for future work, and a commission followed. He would be drawing each member of the Laird's family. Special paper was obtained for the young artist, paper brought back from the city by the Laird himself.

For Alexander this was a very busy time because, in the Laird's family, there were three sons and two daughters, plus his wife and the Laird himself – and the dog.

To achieve the family portrait initially, due to family members failing to be together at the same time, each was drawn individually so it became a 'family' in stages. Alexander used ingenuity, creating gaps, which as each sitter became accessible he filled progressively.

Getting the dog to remain still for long enough to achieve an acceptable sketch was difficult, but, even harder for him, was to concentrate successfully on the art work while working on Catherine's portrait. She teased him and flirted, prolonging her spell as the model. In the privacy given them, who knows what else might have happened if he had been willing, but he was a good boy and, though tempted by her suggestion to misbehave, he resisted.

On completion, there was again a generous payment, achieved without having to break sweat doing carpentry like his father. The other males of Alexander's family found it hard to believe that he was being paid good money – for simply drawing. No questions from his mother though. She was most appreciative, proud of her youngest son's talent, and grateful for the extra income.

Most of his earnings he donated, generously, to the family purse, but as he had earned it, it seemed only fair that he should keep some for himself. That money, which he put in the pipe-case, would remain hidden – savings for his own future.

5

2009
Oh, to be appreciated!

He opened his eyes to find he was lying on the floor on his back, staring up at an open hatch and an extended Ramsey ladder. His immediate conclusion was that, possibly, he had used the wrong technique leaving the loft. Quick – but painful! Next time he'd settle for step by step...

The jelly pan had made its own way downstairs with a clatter, no doubt accumulating a few more dents on the way. The clattering had not disturbed the enjoyment of the three who were still relaxing happily together in the garden.

He lay for a moment feeling sorry for himself, before very carefully moving one arm, then the other, followed by each leg in turn. Thankfully, all parts seemed to be continuing to function, creakily perhaps – but that was normal. Raising his head gingerly, he could see that most of the photographs had tumbled out of the album and had spread all around him on the landing. The album lay open by his side. Surprisingly, it looked none the worse.

"Tom, why did you throw the jelly pan down the stairs? You are getting very lazy in your old age. It's not a new pan you know," shouted his mother from below. "It isn't easy to buy a pan of this good quality nowadays. It should be treated with respect and a little more carefully – but thanks for getting it..." and she went back into the garden.

Though her words sounded a touch grudging to him, he muttered, "It was a pleasure, Mother," but that might have gone unheard.

He pushed himself upright with difficulty, then stood, felt the twinges, and was glad it was Saturday. Would he be fit for work on Monday? He would have to be. There was a long list of jobs to do before the holiday. Bending with a grimace, he gathered the photos and replaced them roughly between the pages, no way of knowing where they'd come from.

He fancied going through them carefully at home but that would mean permission from Mother, later, when she was more likely to say ok. Meantime, where to leave the album?

Back in the loft? No thank you!

Leaving it on the wooden chair in the spare back bedroom was a wise move – not on the bed as he'd been about to do for, even after hitting the floor, the album was still covered in dust. His mother's displeasure at a mark on the bedcover he could imagine.

With the loft ladder, and the hatch replaced, it looked as if nothing had happened. He went downstairs and met the other three returning from the garden, still laughing and chatting away. What were they finding to talk about – nonstop?

"You took your time, Tom," said his wife, with a critical frown. "Oooooh... You are all sweaty – and why are you limping? And your new trousers!"

Tom gave her a look – he could not handle sympathy. Women!

He turned to his father. "Dad, rather than stack all that rubbish in the middle of the loft, shouldn't you have thrown it out? It is all rubbish, isn't it?" If his dad agreed with that statement, he did not have the opportunity to say.

"Rubbish? Rubbish!! All these things are memories – OUR memories," was his mother's snappy response. "The trouble with you, Tom, is that you have no sentiment!"

His dad was glad he hadn't offered his opinion. He knew better. He realised that any comment by him could make it worse – for both Tom and him. He remained silent.

"Oh, Tom... How could you?" added Gillian. "I have to agree – what a suggestion! What were you thinking?" she went on. "You never ever have a sentimental thought in your head, do you?"

Tom wanted to return to the loft to safety – on his own. Why had they turned on him? "I only said..." he sheepishly started...

"Well, don't then!" came in unison from mother and wife.

His dad stood there, sensibly looking at the ceiling. That dominant women ran in the family, was the thought passing through the heads of both males simultaneously.

Tom sneaked back upstairs and felt much better physically and mentally after a cool shower. He decided that when he joined the others he would expose his sentimental side. It was in him, somewhere, desperately wanting out. A bit impassive earlier, he realised, probably due to the shock of the fall. Now recovered he would stand up for himself and, feeling quite perky, downstairs he went.

He waited until after lunch, when everyone was together in the kitchen feeling rested, before trying again.

"How would it be if, up in the loft, I helped to move the heavy items for disposal, and you could maybe give the stuff an affectionate once over – before I throw it out?"

The reaction was not positive but neither was it unfavourable. Had he sounded sufficiently sentimental? At least he had their attention, so he kept going.

"A lot of the stuff you'll want to keep, obviously, but perhaps in the process, if there happened to be any ...like ...junk exposed ...I could get rid of it for you?"

Nothing again! Was it wise calling it 'junk'?

Disappointing... How much sentiment did a guy have to expose? By the looks on the faces of his wife and his mother, they were certainly not seeing him any differently. Was he being overly tentative with his words: speaking as if he didn't mean them?

Frowns had appeared...

"Oh," his mother started, "I don't know..." so

Tom bravely soldiered on.

"...And together we could maybe lay some more flooring, make it safer. David would be willing to help, I'm sure – and we could add lighting, it certainly needs it up there."

Now that was more positive – much improved! He felt he could not have phrased it any better, but silence followed again. Had he failed?

His intention had been to mention the photograph album at that point and get permission to take it home but, from the look on his mother's face, he could forget about that! No, not the right moment. No rush anyway – the family tree could wait another week. The album would not be thrown out; they didn't throw anything out of that house!

He'd just leave it where it was, in the upstairs back room. It was rarely used these days, but even if they did go in, they probably wouldn't notice it lying there.

Anyway, if he suggested borrowing it just now, they'd think that everything he'd been saying was for his own selfish reasons. He had tried. He'd said his piece and got a cold reception, but neither had there been outright criticism of his last proposal from either his parents or his wife.

It wasn't until they were leaving that Tom's mother grudgingly mentioned that she was pleased that he would be doing work in the loft. That surprised him. They had heard. Was it progress? He had tried hard, and meant what he'd said but neither his mother nor his wife would have heard the words as sentimental and well-meaning. Tom could tell. It was so obvious that they were convinced he had an ulterior motive.

Why, oh why, he asked himself, do I always feel under-valued?

6

1913
To the woods, young man...

Sophistication was not a natural attribute of village life in Aberloudie, but one of the young women of the village, Sarah Stewart, had acquired a little more culture than most – there were family connections with the big city. Over the years, she had become a close friend of Alexander's, but, although their ages were similar, the Stewarts were of a social class above the Findlays and of most of the villagers – although not quite the status of the Laird and his family.

Sarah knew of Alexander's success up at the Big House and encouraged him artistically, but her enthusiasm stemmed from a touch of vanity. As a willing model, she was the subject of many of his early figure and portrait sketches. For Alexander and Sarah, it was a chaste and proper relationship. For her, being the centre of his attention felt good – and thrilling, having onlookers stop to watch Alexander work his magic when drawing her. She liked to think they were admiring her too.

An aunt that she visited, who liked to see Sarah regularly, lived in Glasgow. They took shopping trips together. On one visit, for a change, they went to view what was on display at the new Art Galleries. Many of the paintings surprised her – some were very daring; the ones that took her attention were focused mainly on the female form – bare-bosomed women. Viewing this art was a new experience for Sarah. She was shocked!

Her aunt found her reaction to be funny. What a prudish niece!

Having always lived in the big city and been around socially a great deal more than most of the inhabitants of Aberloudie, including Sarah, her aunt knew the ways of the world. It was not in the least unusual for a model divested of clothing, to be drawn or painted, she explained to her niece: classic, in fact...

"How could a lady have the confidence to do such a thing?" asked the young girl with flushed cheeks, "...especially if it's a male artist?"

"Oh, anything is possible in art these days, my dear," was the reply. "These people have a laissez-faire approach to the human body and nakedness, though, goodness knows what else could be happening when clothes are removed! Though, Sarah darling, I'm sure that is nothing that you need bother your pretty little head about."

However, Sarah's little head was bothered. This was exciting; it gave her an idea. She knew an artist. Just imagine if he...! If she...! Would Alexander be shocked? She would have to ask...

It might not have seemed like it when in Glasgow but one could say, with considerable justification that, on home territory, Sarah Stewart was a forward young miss – in Aberloudie she felt quite daring. Not everyone in the village had the chances she had to visit the city regularly. Even fewer would have seen what she viewed at the galleries. Had Alexander? She couldn't wait to find out. As an artist, he would know, surely. He would be able to talk about that sort of thing in a sophisticated manner, without embarrassment...

Alexander had never visited an art gallery or seen originals of drawings or paintings as Sarah described. He wasn't sure initially what to think. There were some pictures in the schoolmaster's books like that, he remembered, described as Classic poses.

"Have you ever thought of doing that sort of drawing?" she asked tentatively, "...Of a female without part of her clothing?"

"No, of course not!" he replied with a large grin.

Sarah asked if he would like to do drawings like that.

"Hmm, suppose so..." he replied, but with only a little enthusiasm.

"I know someone who would pose for you."

"Oh... who?" and he seemed more interested.

"Me – and I'd... I'd remove my bodice, if you wished."

He hesitated. The only people he'd ever drawn in the past who hadn't been fully clothed had been his brothers – for a bit of a laugh, and anyway, they'd had on their vests.

He felt awkward. He had never even considered that approach to drawing. If he had, he would never have dreamed of asking someone to sit for him ...especially not a girl.

It didn't seem right but this was her suggestion, and he was an artist and that's what artists do – apparently. Sarah said so. He was also a hot-blooded young male, and willing to try anything once – so it took little persuasion!

The answer was yes, but how? Not the sort of thing that could happen in the middle of the village.

...And so, it looked as if Alexander's sketching was destined to become a little more artistic, a little more adventurous, and – as onlookers would not be welcome – a little more secretive. Where could they go? Neither knew of anywhere indoors, if it were to be secret, therefore, it would have to be a quiet spot in the woods. They would be safe there.

It was dry, it was sunny, it was warm and it was perfect!

Sarah encouraged him to sketch her from a variety of angles and in the dappled shade of the trees beside a pool off the stream. It was a bright, sunny, summer's day and he achieved differing effects for each drawing. He transformed the skirt she wore into a diaphanous drape and, although it pained him to do so, he altered the facial features to create anonymity for the partly unclothed young miss. When completed, each drawing displayed a beautiful, but different, person.

Alexander had created a delightful assortment of woodland nymphs.

With clothing replaced and primly worn once more, Sarah was first to leave the clearing and slip off home. Alexander went for a long plunge in the ice-cold pool – he had to cool down. Seeing, for the first time, the naked breasts of his friend had been a very enjoyable artistic experience, though in truth, enjoyed more than just as an artist – she did have a lovely body...

How the Laird became aware of the sketches Alexander never found out for certain, but the only one who could have talked about the 'nymph' drawings was Sarah, herself. Who knew whether she'd shared her secret with someone who'd shared it with someone else, who'd shared it again, the way secrets seemed destined to circulate?

He certainly told no one, but the young artist did not grumble too much at the offer of a nice sum of money for all of them. How could he resist?

...And the drawings changed hands.

It was on a confidential basis, because obviously the Laird had secrets too. They were destined for a very personal collection.

"You're a lucky young man," said the Laird, "having the services of so many beautiful models. One day you'll have to introduce me to a few of them..."

He did not ask who they were, or if they were local, though Alexander thought there was a chance he might have recognised the views in the wood, but he hadn't. He just liked what he saw, and he saw only the semi-naked figures.

Alexander was afraid that he might have guessed who the model was but, how could he? When they were handed over, and the money changed hands, the Laird's parting words were that if he sketched any more, and they became available for purchase, he would be interested.

Alexander felt guilty at receiving a large sum of money and keeping it. Being party to the Laird's secret vice was also disturbing. He could not tell any of his family what he had been up to, or offer this recent money, so, he gave some to Sarah. She was delighted and said it had been fun for her, and suggested that, provided no one else found out, she would model again, especially now there was a buyer.

Yes, she was willing – and eager!

It would have been churlish to refuse. Here was a pretty girl who was very happy to oblige, so, on the next hot day, they met at the same quiet spot in the woods and she disrobed again.

With the same care of Sarah's anonymity, another set of drawings was completed. Having retained the memory of the previous night's enjoyable dream involving Sarah and, with anticipatory thoughts, an unsteady hand was evident this time. He had to concentrate very seriously on drawing, and less on the model.

Afterwards, for him, the naked, cold plunge was

an absolute necessity!

However, this time Sarah did not return home. She came back to the pool, saw him strip off and jump in, and decided that she required cooling too. Knowing she was in the company of an artist, and that exposure of naked flesh was apparently a non-event for that sort of person, off came all of her clothing, and in she went.

Thank goodness the ice-cold water had the desired cooling effect on Alexander's physical wellbeing, or things might have really got out of hand. As it was, it remained artistic and platonic for artist and model, but opened up a new vision for the woodland nymph poses – *total* disrobing.

As both artist and model were all for it – and it was warm enough – sketching began again the moment they left the water...

The message from the Laird intimated that he wanted a meeting with Alexander.

Again, somehow, he had become aware of recent sketching, and offered more good money for further drawings; the artist had more – many more than the intended purchaser expected.

Four sketches of partly clothed 'nymphs' delighted him immediately, and then he was shown the five drawings of young ladies – *wearing no clothing*.

The Laird's eyes sparkled and he jumped at the chance to buy. This time he paid more handsomely, and very willingly.

Not long afterwards, Sarah delivered a note to Alexander, from Catherine, the Laird's daughter, the one who flirted with him. She was a close friend of Sarah's and she wished a favour.

She cannot want to buy them, he thought, and was correct – she didn't!

She pleaded with him to sketch her, in the same way he sketched Sarah – naked. There was one stipulation – Sarah should chaperone. It seemed reasonable enough, he decided. There would be none of that flirting nonsense if Sarah were present too ...but this was incredible – another beautiful young female volunteering to disrobe. What had he done to deserve it, and how could a fledging artist refuse the offer? Wasn't life wonderful and what a coincidence, her father being interested in art too.

Wait a moment. This was supposed to be a secret! The Laird knows, now his daughter knows... Is there anyone who doesn't?

"Sarah, who else have you been telling?"

"Me? No one..." and, as she said it, she looked so innocent that, against his better judgement, he did not argue.

"Does her father know, the Laird, does he know about Catherine wanting to...?"

"Of course not! Don't be silly!" was Sarah's retort.

This lack of secrecy disturbed him somewhat, mainly because he could not imagine what the reaction would be if his family ever found out. Even so, although Sarah was proving to be a gossip, it had its benefits. It was becoming profitable, and giving him some wonderful experience of 'life drawing'. He was becoming a real artist, so why stop?

Of course, he'd do it...

For the sketches of Catherine, the birch woods would be the backdrop again, and for the accomplished artist he was becoming, Alexander forced himself to pay just as much attention to the composition of the trees and the shrubs, as he was giving to the beautiful unclothed figure in the foreground.

As before, he avoided showing the correct facial detail and the sketches displayed lovely girls, but none recognisable as Catherine.

He had explained to her, before he began, that he would be selling these if someone wished to buy them. She was happy about that. She didn't mind a little secret fame as long as only she, Sarah, and Alexander knew that she was the model.

The knowing look from Alexander to Sarah indicated that he knew secrecy sometimes couldn't be guaranteed.

However, being secure in the knowledge that this part of the wood was rarely visited, they relaxed and enjoyed the experience. Three young people laughing and joking with one another in the way youngsters do, except that two were clothed, and one was totally devoid of apparel – and loving it.

Unknown to the trio, that sunny afternoon, the Laird was close by, venturing into the quieter part of the woods with his shotgun, on the lookout for wood pigeons. When he came across some, the loud bang as he fired made his presence known – and caused considerable guilty panic!

Frantically, Catherine replaced her clothes, and drawings and charcoal were hurriedly packed.

Two young girls shot off in one direction, the artist in the other – all three going well away from the direction of the sound.

Although it had been a surprising conclusion, it was not a wasted day. Under Alexander's arm was more almost-completed work – an investment for the future.

Sarah was not at fault this time. It was Alexander, himself, who made contact with the Laird and cautiously offered his patron the new drawings. One look was all it took – he grabbed them. There was no question, he liked them, and eagerly paid on the spot. Alexander prayed that this man would never find out that the shapely nude figure, the one causing eyes to sparkle, was his own daughter.

What was happening to these drawings, his minor masterpieces?

Alexander was curious. Could they be part of a collection of naughty drawings gathered for this man's own pleasure, or was he selling them on to someone else ...though should that be of the artist's concern?

No, he concluded. It was generous payment. He should settle for being happy that these anonymous drawings of fictitious people could give pleasure to someone, somewhere...

Next time Sarah met Alexander, she asked if he would like to meet another model, an unnamed lady. Sarah didn't say 'young'. Neither was she willing to disclose who but, she told him, this was someone who would take great pleasure in removing her clothing.

The difference, for this sitting, she would pay him and retain the sketches herself.

Obviously, his fame had spread – although it shouldn't have.

Finding the person who arrived with Sarah to be the wife of the Laird, was a shock. The previous time she'd posed, she was with her family, and on that occasion she was elegant and aloof, sitting demurely in the large sitting room of the Big House – fully clothed.

Sarah had guided her to the meeting place but, as introductions were unnecessary, she hurried off and left them to it.

This time, in the middle of the birch wood, as this 'lady' slowly and sensuously divested herself of every part of her clothing, Alexander wished Sarah had remained to chaperone.

He felt threatened.

It was almost as if she were trying to arouse the animal instincts in him. He struggled to avoid looking, and told himself that she was a model, an object to draw, just another woman, like his mother – but she was not!

Looking at her lie back on the tartan rug, languidly raising her arm to rest her head and cause her mature bosoms to move gently, was bad enough, but to see her flutter her eyes at him...

That caused a little flutter somewhere that had nothing to do with drawing. It was a matter of application, so, like the dedicated young artist that he was trying to become, he began to sketch.

Concentrate!

And success! Three tasteful impressions were created, but, whereas his other two models valued the anonymity, this lady appreciated his skill and wanted a flattering likeness. To him, this was a lovely-looking woman requiring no artistic flattery, and he began to feel sorry for her: the blatant narcissism.

It was awkward for Alexander having a model whose age he reckoned to be midway between his own and his mother's and, never mind being Catherine's mother – she was the wife of the Laird!

It should not have been happening and even though he was behaving impeccably, he could not help but feel guilty when three beautiful sketches were completed, and handed over. He had succeeded in maintaining his detachment as an artist but now, as a gentleman, he looked at his feet as she stood there before him, admiring her own likeness, with a smile on her face – and not a stitch of clothing.

It was an over-generous payment and, in the circumstances, what else could he do but accept. However, he did something that later he regretted: at her insistence, he signed his name as the artist...

Alexander should have known that the Laird would find out – and he did! He should also have been able to guess that, when it happened, the shotgun would come out, and this time not for pigeons – her husband would come looking for him, and he did.

It turned out it was not the first time that the Laird's good lady had misbehaved!

When she returned to The Big House that afternoon, after being absent for several hours, she was being secretive. The Laird saw her carry the drawings inside; he saw where she hid them; he looked, and he saw what they were...

Obvious! His wife had behaved in the same shameless way as she did with their young gamekeeper four months before: a gamekeeper who was no longer an employee. It was the only conclusion he could draw. That had been in the woodman's shed – no drawing involved then – she'd been caught 'in flagrante' with the young man. Now she was 'at it' with a sixteen-year old artist! Even worse, he, the Laird, had been buying that artist's drawings.

Just how long had they been 'at it', was the question!

"By heavens – I've been patronising a young stallion..."

As the husband, he did the 'right thing' – at least, what he considered necessary under the circumstances – he confiscated the drawings. The money used to buy these was his money – although payment could have been special favours! He made the best of a bad job – and made the drawings part of his collection.

"That scoundrel of an artist," he said aloud, pronouncing the artist '...guilty!'.

It stood Alexander in good stead having six large, older brothers who believed their little brother's protestations of innocence and, it was thanks to them that the Laird's shotgun was not fired in his direction.

The siblings stood grinning in the background as an embarrassed little brother gave his explanation to the Laird. Unconvinced, but intimidated by the brothers, that man departed feeling even more frustrated.

At least his parents were not present to humiliate the young innocent further.

His brothers would stand up for him, Alexander knew, but his mother and father would hear the gossip eventually. He hoped that when they did they would believe his version, but it seemed wise for him to leave the village. Life could never be the same.

He felt guilty telling the lie to his parents that suddenly he had the urge to make his own way in the world. His father gave him an address for Glasgow, his mother showed a tear of acceptance. Though he would be going with feelings of sadness and trepidation, at least he would take away a small fortune – thanks to his 'art', and the Laird.

As he left, he was dressed in the hand-me-down kilt and, under his arm, a tightly-tied bundle in which he had his few other usable clothes: his barely wearable suit, a woollen balmoral bonnet, pinched from one of his brothers who'd laid it down and wouldn't realise until later it had gone, and two shirts he claimed as his.

He put charcoal and unused paper into the pipe-case, beside the bagpipes – he could not leave without those; he was an artist and he was a piper, and though he could consider himself very good at both, sadly, that day any pride he'd had was left behind...

7

2009
Have a well-earned rest, but hurry back!

It was time for Gillian and Tom's visit to sunny Spain, a summer vacation of two weeks that had become an annual event. Making use of Gillian's sister's flat was both convenient and more economical than a fancy hotel and, by co-ordinating their holidays with Fiona's, Tom and Gillian had the full use of Fiona's home, an arrangement that had worked well for the last five years. This year Fiona was having a three week visit to Australia,

Tom's business wouldn't be closing, so for two weeks David would be at home to take over the reins. He liked being the boss, and was eager for them to leave him to it. Tom was less enthusiastic this year because the BBC weather man, the English one with the shaved head, had forecast that a deep depression would travel slowly across Spain for four of their precious days, centred over their holiday destination – though Tom found it hard to believe that the long-range weather forecast could be correct.

Gillian had packed excitedly, and was looking forward to going, but planned to use a new tactic on her husband this year. When it came to meals, unless she played it craftily, self-catering could again mean the onus was on her. She would be left to decide a menu, to shop for the food, to prepare it and then serve it to a hungry Tom. Tom's role on previous self-catering holidays was simpler – he just ate. Wisely he had never complained in any way about what she served up. This year he would not be getting that opportunity. They would be *eating out a lot* – Gillian would be making sure of that.

They'd gone.

Back home in Glasgow, David had his feet up. Saturday and time to relax. Mother and father were on their way. They left early for the airport, and he was now in charge of the business. He was confident and eager to get into action on Monday with the freedom to do everything his way. There were a couple of things to check before Monday, otherwise the weekend was his, and he had plans for this evening. Sophie Stephens would be tonight's target...

The phone rang as he was about to have some lunch.

"Hola! It's me, David, just checking ...anything I can help you with? Have you remembered that the...?"

"Dad, everything's fine. Enjoy your holiday."

"But, what about..."

"Everything is fine, I said Dad..."

"Right then, speak to you tomorrow, hasta la vista, Baby."

A phone call to check that all was ok with work – from the Spanish airport where they'd landed only moments ago! That was a bad sign...

This hadn't happened in previous years even though David had been younger and less experienced – Dad hadn't given a toss back then – and on top of that, before they left, he'd said that he had every confidence in his son's management and organisational abilities. Obviously there would be no problems in his absence – he'd said....

Dear, oh dear. Relax, old fella!

The reality was that if David had a problem, David solved it. He was a big boy now, and would never have dreamt of burdening his father, especially on a holiday.

No matter, even after being told on Saturday that everything was under control, Tom phoned again on Sunday. Silly, because with the business being closed at weekends, nothing happens on Saturday or Sunday. On Monday, and Tuesday, the phone calls came again. It was annoying but David was tolerant of this apparent lack of trust. He had to be – that was his boss in Spain.

To be fair, the old guy is getting on a bit. Could be a mid-life crisis! Forty-two, David smiled to himself.

Tuesday evening, David did some thinking. He couldn't just ignore phone calls and possibly lose business, but if his dad continued to phone for the next ten days the wrong thing might be said. So, he devised a simple plan...

From early Wednesday, the office answer phone sang out a different message: *Dad's in Spain, being a pain, but David's here to help you!*

David chose to let the phone ring out and respond only if requested by a client. The new message raised a smile with anyone phoning about business. David responded promptly when required and no callers complained about inattention or had a bad response. The only unhappy chappie was the gentleman on holiday who heard the same words every time he phoned: *Dad's in Spain...* It was frustrating for him. Tom made many attempts on Wednesday to get through, but each time, out of cussedness, refused to leave a message for his son. The next day he relented. David smiled as he heard it.

"OK, clever clogs, you win. Hasta la blooming vista!"

In Spain, Gillian found her husband's antics amusing. She'd told him he shouldn't phone, but he hadn't listened. He'd lost face this time; his son had got one over on him and he could do nothing about it.

Tom knew the daily phone calls had been meaningless but had hoped it would ease his conscience. He'd abandoned his son at a busy time. Would he have to remain feeling guilty?

Of course, the pitiful weather could have been

making things seem worse.

"Cheer up, Tom..." Gillian laughed, and as a consolation poured another generous glass of sangria. They sat there together in the flat looking out at the dismal weather. The jug was almost empty.

"...It can't pour down forever," she offered.

She'd only said it hopefully, but it could not have been a better moment for the rain to stop – as it did – and for the sun to come out in strength – as it did, and become what Spain was supposed to be like. The clouds broke up and the roads and walkways started to dry and, suddenly, it started to feel like a proper holiday!

David – and the business – totally forgotten...

Fiona's flat did not have air conditioning. Tom found it difficult to sleep in the humid Spanish night-heat, but scoffed at his wife's suggestion that the afternoon siesta was his problem... However, maybe it was lucky he was wide awake in the early hours, or he might not have been able to converse with a chatty sister-in-law in Melbourne – in the middle of her day.

Out for a few drinks too many with her friends, Fiona had failed to remember the considerable time difference. Twice it happened. Each time, she was full of slurred apologies when Tom pointed out it was the middle of the night in Torremolinos.

"Get your own back," suggested Gillian.

Unfortunately, Tom's attempt backfired...

Now was the chance to catch her out, he decided.

Early afternoon in Spain, a perfect time, the middle of the Australian night, but there was no answer. A disappointed Tom hung up without leaving a message. The following day Fiona noticed that the missed call was from her own number back home at the flat. Oh dear, there must be something seriously wrong for her sister to make contact in the middle of the night! She rang back immediately.

Unfortunately, the time zones were again different. Her call coincided with Tom and Gillian having fallen into an exhausted and really deep sleep. Not a problem for Gillian – the phone was at Tom's side of the bed...

It would not have been a proper holiday without the odd marital upset. This year's dispute began in the bar, but not due to strong drink!

Gillian's plan to eat out all the time had been abandoned, partly due to the continuous rain. Organising and preparing meals to have in the flat had given her something to do, and it hadn't turned out too bad.

However, the bar round the corner had a new barmaid. Early that first week, Gillian had seen her, a pretty young girl. In passing, after buying food for lunch at the supermarket, on her return she noticed Tom sitting inside, chatting away to the girl. She returned to the flat and the meal was ready when Tom returned. "New girl in the bar, I see. Looks nice," commented Gillian. "Seems to like you."

"Can't speak very good English," said Tom. "I was trying to help her with a few words."

The bar had been a favourite on previous visits, although normally frequented more by Tom than Gillian, and a quick beer while Gillian did the shopping had become part of the early routine for Tom.

It was the third morning, after dodging heavy downpours to and from the little supermarket, when Gillian took the urge to pop in and join him in the little bar. She arrived at what looked to be an overly intense English lesson by the way he was gazing into that barmaid's eyes. There was no question – flirting was flirting in whatever language! The lesson ended, promptly, and Gillian did without a drink.

"You were at it, Tom Findlay – and don't try blaming the barmaid!" Gillian declared as she ushered him out.

"Of course I wasn't! I told you, she's desperate to learn English."

Next day Tom had to do a lot of crawling – Gillian found out that the barmaid was from Liverpool.

That little misdemeanour gave her the opportunity to claim a special memento of the holiday, a new necklace. Tom would be going home with a lot less Euros than expected, but at least forgiven – almost...

With the weather on the second part of the holiday becoming more normal, warm and sunny, Gillian decided to make up for lost time and they became highly active. When it came time to leave, she was still surprisingly fresh. She had really enjoyed herself and did not want to go home, but for

Tom it had been too much. He was exhausted. He hoped he'd maybe get some proper sleep at home.

At the airport, the response from her husband to her question about their next holiday destination – was a glare...

For Tom, it actually felt good to be going back, and he appreciated the return journey being uneventful. At least they did not suffer any strikes at the airport, or had the airline making 'liquidating' headlines, or any last minute breakdowns to prevent their flight leaving on time. For those little things, they were both extremely grateful.

Tom, back at work, was surprised to find how easy it had been to get out of the habit. He used to be eager and energetic, encouraging the team to do a good job, working with them, and showing an example, approaching physical and mental tasks with equal enthusiasm – yes, *used to* – only two weeks ago!

A holiday intervened – broke the rhythm. In Glasgow, it felt cold by comparison to the holiday weather in Spain – and freezing, compared to that unforgettable jelly-pan day in his folk's loft!

He survived the first working day, yes, but it was good to be home and to sit down. He'd worked at his own steady pace today – a lot slower than the speed Gillian forced him about on holiday. Evening meal over, it was his chance to settle in the easy chair, and have his usual five minutes' snooze. He'd missed that. A siesta is not the same...

"Tom! I hope you are not forgetting your

promise..." Gillian took great delight in catching him just before he dropped off. Snoozing after the meal had become a bad habit, she considered.

"What...!"

"Your promise to your parents? New flooring, new lighting..."

"Oh that? Yea, yea..."

"...Your mother, she asked on the phone this afternoon, Tom!"

Gillian had won – he was awake now.

"Don't keep going on about it. I just haven't had a chance..."

"...To get David to do it for you?" she added. "Am I correct?"

"No! Well, not quite. I was going to ask him, but he's not likely to say yes, is he? What would he rather do? Go out with his pals to a club or a pub visit – or help me clear out that loft? I have no chance!"

"Don't be so negative, Tom. You work together successfully during the day, don't you? Look, I will help as well, if that's any use... In fact, I will speak to David. I'll make him an offer he can't refuse."

Her suggestion to her son that 'helping Dad could be fun' received short shrift, so she tried another tack – that his father probably could not do the job without him. David smiled and shook his head, but she was not giving up.

"Your grandparents would really appreciate you being involved."

"Mum, I'd love to but..."

Obviously, to win him over, she would have to up the offer.

"The tickets for the Red Hot Chilli Pipers ...for four of you... You are still going?"

"We sure are."

"Your dad will pay for them!"

"A deal!"

"Oh... right!" she'd done it, but at Tom's expense. "For goodness sake, David, don't tell your dad what this is costing him. He'd burst a blood vessel. I'll have to pretend I overspent at shopping."

Yes, a costly negotiation, she realised, but at least now it could be a team effort, and that very evening the project got under way.

"This is great, David, to have your help. We'll have the job done in no time," said Tom, "and I'm sure your grand-parents will appreciate what we'll be doing."

"How could I refuse," said David.

"I very much appreciate it. Are you still going to that concert with your pals?"

David nodded.

"Tell you what, I'll pay for the tickets."

"Wow! Thanks Dad!"

At the other side of the room, sitting knitting, Gillian smiled.

"Putting lighting in the loft should be first," Tom proposed, "for safety's sake."

"I agree!" David responded.

Tom hesitated. David wasn't arguing?

"Yes, being able to see what we are doing to start with," said David. "Can't be too careful. Safety first!"

"Oh... yes," said Tom.

When properly lit, additional flooring would be next. Ordering would be David's task – on internet. To him, that would be a piece of cake. If his father were to try – a mountain-face to climb.

"How much will we need?" David asked.

"Ummm ...about, ummm... approximately..."

"You've no idea, have you?"

"Nope..."

David had no idea either, but he made a guess and hoped that the quantity ordered was reasonably near the needs. Anyway he didn't have to worry about cost. His father was paying that as well.

Gillian was not there on that first Saturday morning to encourage them, but father and son worked well together, and made progress.

The wiring was straightforward; second nature, being what Tom and David did for a living – and what a difference additional lighting made! With extra illumination, they still had to work with caution when adding flooring. A little bump against any of the stacked heavy items could have had serious consequences.

Tom could visualise his mother's face if something fell through the ceiling! Luckily, anything they did dislodge was lightweight and the thick insulation acted as a cushion.

They were both very careful.

Tom was cautious on the ladder – his previous exit was fresh in his memory. Every time he went up or down the old 'Ramsey' he used two hands, two feet, and held on tight. It was slower than his last exciting drop but, arriving at floor level with no bruises was much more pleasant.

No problems on the ladder for the 'boy', Tom noticed. Up or down in an instant. Yes, David seemed to move so much faster than he did – for everything, another thing to make Tom feel his age.

Much easier with two involved. It took a large part of the day but, after happily slogging away together, the flooring was almost complete. Had David guessed correctly for the material? Not a chance, but he had erred on the side of caution so, when they ran short of wood, it was an excuse for a break. Tom needed it. Nothing like his last visit in the height of summer, but it still felt too hot for him. Maybe he was just unfit. David had no problem.

Together they had made it happen. A much larger safe-working area of flooring now existed. So far so good. Sad thing was, Tom realised, that when all the stuff was unstacked it would probably fill all the floor-space again.

Some of that rubbish would have to go!

Downstairs, Tom explained their achievements to his mother – their excellent progress. Beth immediately was appreciative and said so and, to Tom, it sounded like praise for him – until she added, "Keep pushing him, David!"

David looked slightly uncomfortable at that – they had done it together. His dad forced a grin; for him, that treatment was normal. Anyway, the next stage could be stormier – the question of 'Disposals'.

Do not say 'rubbish' or 'junk', Tom reminded himself.

Beth Findlay would be the one to make decisions, so they invited her to join them in the loft. There, she could instruct them what should stay and, more importantly, what should go. Unfortunately, that plan was doomed to fail...

The long Ramsay ladder was wobbly and daunting for someone lacking confidence. Only the brave should climb – and not look down. The view was an open staircase that showed a very long drop. Of course, the higher the climb – the farther to fall.

Beth made a tentative attempt but four steps was the best she could do before she threw in the towel and backed down, not too surprisingly. A valiant attempt by a woman of advancing years.

Angus was willing to climb, and he probably could have succeeded but, "Too dangerous at your age, dear," said Beth. Tom suspected that she did not trust him to make the right decisions in the loft without her...

"Gran, if Dad and I were in the loft and you two on the landing and we tell you the item, could you decide from down here to keep it or dispose?"

"An excellent idea, David. Why didn't you think of that Tom?" she asked.

Tom and David went back up the ladder. Beth and Angus, the decision makers, stood at the foot. Tom picked up the iron, the first bit of rubbish – a safe choice. The stamp of approval would be a formality.

"No flex on this iron, couldn't possibly be used,

Mother," Tom shouted down, and held the iron so that it could be viewed by the two on the landing.

"What do you think, David?" shouted up Beth.

Tom bit his tongue.

"Yes, I'd say it should be thrown out, Gran."

"Thanks, David. Throw it out then, Tom."

David sympathised. He shrugged his shoulders as his father grimaced. It was not going to be easy, but they carried on.

Even with the new lighting in the loft, it was difficult recognising exactly what some items were. The folded-up thing, was it a rubber sheet? Ah, a punctured, double size, inflatable bed...

"You ask her," Tom said to David.

"Not much use keeping this, Gran, could never be used. It can't be inflated."

"All right, David. If you think it should go," she replied, and Tom smiled sadly.

"I'll throw it down then, Gran. Stand clear, Grandad!" David warned, and Angus should have gone farther back.

"Watch out!" David yelled, but too late.

The rubber bed opened up as it dropped. Grandad was surprised to be underneath it. Beth thought that funny but Angus was not quite so amused. He dragged the useless bed down the stairs, happy to get out of the line of fire.

"Golf clubs..." shouted Tom.

"Golf clubs?" shouted back his mother.

"Yes, golf clubs," repeated Tom. "Whose are they? Old wooden shafted ones – and in an old golf bag too."

"Your father must have brought these from the other house, but I don't remember him having golf clubs, or that he ever played golf... Angus!" she shouted to her husband who was halfway up the stairs again. "Golf clubs..."

"Golf clubs?" Angus shouted back.

"Angus, you're just repeating what I'm say again. You must try and stop that. Try to listen! Anyway, come back up here this minute and help!"

"Of course, dear... you did say – golf clubs? Ah, uhmm... yes, they are mine," he shouted, as he trudged up, "...from a long time ago... It would be nice to keep them," was added meekly.

"Keep them," instructed Beth to the loft.

Angus paused on the stair. He remembered acquiring these clubs long ago but had never told his wife, or anyone else for that matter, how. His first affair... Unusual for him to remember something clearly... They'd belonged to the girl's father. She became quite emotional, he recalled. The clubs came between them. Angus remembered being a 'love god' back then. Ah, yes ...happy days. Her dad offered the clubs – but not to encourage him to take up golf.

"...You can have them, but only if you bugger off," her father had hissed. Angus remembered the girlfriend being furious. "You'd rather have me than silly golf clubs, Angus," she'd whispered desperately in his ear, "...wouldn't you?" But, free golf clubs! Now, he felt embarrassed and guilty. He'd get round to using them... one day.

He was lost in thought until suddenly he realised

his wife was standing, arms folded, giving him one of her funny looks.

"Harrumph..." he coughed, and brought himself back to reality: the clubs... Perhaps he should have left them in the big hall cupboard. They would still have been gathering dust if he hadn't moved them to the loft last year. No one would ever have found them in that cupboard – anything put in there was lost forever...

"Did you hear me, Angus? You are in a little world of your own! We are putting them aside for the moment," said Beth.

The day continued but there was a great deal of indecision and, consequently, lots still to do when time ran out. Beth and Angus went downstairs feeling they'd done a great job. Tom was less satisfied. At this rate it was going take an awful lot of weekends.

At least a separate pile now existed for disposal. Tom and David manhandled these items down the ladder carefully, probably more tenderly than the rubbish justified, and then sat down to consider how successful they had really been.

An iron without a cable. A toaster that had lost some of its chromed surface and was last used about 1976.

An air-raid warden's tin helmet, bashed with holes in it. "Goodness – bullet holes, Grandad?" David had asked. "Eh, no," was the embarrassed reply. "Your Gran wanted a plant-pot... drainage!"

A bundle of ancient 'Woman's Own' magazines. An old wireless set. Two dead birds. Seven emaciated mice. Some part rolls of carpet of a pattern no longer used in the house. Vintage linoleum, amazingly that had been lifted when they bought the property, and retained – just in case...

The demoralising fact was that the enormous pile remaining in the loft did not look any smaller. However, Tom and David had actually enjoyed doing 'manly things' together as a team, away from the day-work – so they pronounced the project a success.

Tom remembered the photo album. It was still in the bedroom. No one had touched it.

"This might interest you," he said, and pulled out a photo of his grandmother, and immediately had David's attention.

David knew his great-grandmother as an older woman. It was only after her death that he learned that her husband skipped off to Australia. These were photos of her as a young and developing woman. Many of the prints had writing on the back – though not all relevant to the photographed subject, it appeared.

"I was going to borrow this," Tom told him. "It could be of use."

"Huh! You'll have to sneak it out of the house."

"Don't worry, I'll ask first, or better still, David – you ask." Tom knew his mother well.

David carried the album downstairs.

"Ah, yes, my mother's isn't it? Just a bunch of her old snapshots," his grandad said, giving it only a passing glance. His gran did at least look at a few of the photos but made no comment.

Tom explained how he found it, and how he'd fallen down the ladder that day and dropped it. His mum and dad did listen and hear what he said, but Tom would have liked if they'd asked if he hurt himself!

"Gran, could we possibly borrow these photos for a while?" David asked. "Dad's about to research the family tree. This could be very useful."

"Yes, of course you can ...but Tom," and Mother looked straight into his eyes, "Please be more careful this time. Look at the muddle you already have them in – and remember what you did with the jelly-pan. You can be so careless, you know."

Tom's smile was a touch forced as he put the album very carefully into a borrowed plastic bag, and handed it to David to carry – safely.

The loft clearance would continue the following Saturday but, to be honest, for today, Tom had had enough of his mother. He was delighted to be leaving.

8

1913/14
The call of the city...

By no means was the city of Glasgow standing waiting with a welcoming committee for Alexander, but at least in his hand he had the address of one of his father's relatives, a certain Thomas Stout, Esquire.

The information was old, so Alexander considered himself fortunate to find it correct. Otherwise, it might have meant sleeping under a bridge, or in a park. He had heard stories about Glasgow lodging houses and decided beforehand that he would prefer suffering the cold night air outside.

Thomas Stout left Aberloudie for Glasgow a long time ago, to better himself. As a second cousin to Alexander's father, Thomas and Archibald played together when young and went to school together, so they had known each other well. Thomas now lived with his wife near the centre of the city; two up, in two rooms in a tenement and life hadn't turned out to be a great deal better for him than the one left behind.

A stranger, knocking unexpectedly at the door on a dark evening, would not normally have been invited into the house, but someone who was able to prove he'd come from Aberloudie was. Thomas welcomed the young man as if he was a close family member, though his wife, who was Glaswegian, was not quite so pleased. Someone appearing so late seemed odd to her.

She guessed correctly that it was in the hope of a bed for the night. She knew Thomas would offer it, for sometimes he was too kind for his own good! Anyway, they had no spare bed and their wee house already felt crowded with two of them, but she smiled indulgently all the same.

Thomas liked a good gossip. To learn that nothing major had changed in the village since he left eight years ago had been reassuring. That was how it should be, he said, Aberloudie was not a place that should ever change.

It was fortunate that Thomas Stout had a fond and good memory of Archibald because he remembered only vaguely of the existence of the sons – so many of them. There had been no reason ever to return to Aberloudie but he'd never forgotten his cousin, or his wife, Mary. He had always thought of her as a fine fertile woman, so unlike his own dear spouse Ina – who had borne him no children. Aye, Mary Findlay had always seemed to be expecting yet another wean. She was a braw, big lass and could fair produce the boys, an awfu' lot of them...

Cousin Archibald had been a fine player of the bagpipes, known throughout the area as the best. It pleased Thomas to learn that this boy, Alexander, the seventh son, had gained the skills of his father.

"Aye, nice to have family traditions continuin'," said Thomas.

Thomas and his wife were not rich. In fact, they were exactly the opposite. Their visitor's request to stay with them for a while was not a surprise, but... his offering to pay? That was! Without doubt, it would mean overcrowding, but there was no hesitation in accepting. It would be nice to eat heartily for a change.

Alexander was extremely grateful to be having a roof over his head from that very first night in the big city and delighted to pay for the privilege; he was sure that if the Laird had known of his good fortune, he would have been pleased too...

It had been a long day and he was exhausted, and even though the old moth-eaten armchair in which he spent the first night was most uncomfortable, Alexander slept soundly.

In the cold light of day, the place seemed less appealing.

Alexander accepted it for what it was. With eight males in the household in Aberloudie, his mother had always insisted on tidiness, and she kept the home clean. It was so different here. Thomas, being a shoemaker working in his own home, was very untidy, and bits of leather and parts of shoes were everywhere. The small rooms were a mess.

However, it was a good arrangement for both the Stouts and the young man.

Thomas Stout's clients were usually locals, and poor like him, so he made only a very modest living, so Alexander's payments were heaven-sent for the couple. For Alexander it was much better than sleeping rough.

With some bedding they supplied, he slept each night on the floor in the main room – once he cleared a space of leather cuttings. He rarely had the chance for sweet dreams, due to rolling over in his sleep and landing on a chunk of leather. One night it was a loose tack. He enjoyed many a rude awakening but it was, at least, a home and it wasn't all bad.

Here, for instance, the toilet on the stair landing, shared with another two families, often meant that when he had to go, the wooden seat was warm ...and having running water at a sink inside the house in the tiny scullery – that was a novelty too.

These two factors by themselves, made it seem to him that Glasgow was highly civilised. In Aberloudie, they had an outside water tap – it would freeze up, and a visit to the lavatory was a long walk to the hut at the bottom of the vegetable patch. Rarely, was that seat ever heated!

"Are you lookin' for work?" Thomas asked.

"No' really," was his response. The raised eyebrows of Thomas and his wife demanded further explanation. "Ah can draw," Alexander said simply.

He had never done physical work because people paid him for his sketches, he explained. The looks from Thomas and Ina were of amazement and disbelief, so, Alexander displayed his skill by quickly sketching the pair of them as they sat.

That impressed them.

The wonder and admiration shown towards him in the early days began to wear a bit thin. His being around during the day, an additional body in the limited space and apparently doing nothing but sitting still and scribbling, did not seem proper to Thomas and his wife.

'Everybody should work – if they can get a job,' was a simple creed they lived by, and Thomas suggested that Alexander should be doing something to bring in the pennies.

"What about playin' yerr bagpipes?"

"You want me to play ye a tune?"

The offer was refused rather quickly. Thomas and Ina were pleased to encourage him and have him display his talent – but out of earshot! They suggested instead that he should go into town and play for the crowds. Hordes of people would be there that he could entertain. They would give money to listen.

"Och aye, I could be trying that," he said and so a visit to the city centre was planned.

They lived in Anderston, not far from the main parts of town. So... wearing his kilt, with his brother's Balmoral bonnet – for collecting the money, and gripping the handle of the pipe-case tightly, he set out to walk along unfamiliar streets. His pace was more of a march than a walk – the natural way of moving when he held the pipes – and with the lilting melodies in his head keeping him in step, he was able to ignore the disturbingly increasing hum of city life.

It was a new experience for him. He remembered Sarah, several months ago in Aberloudie, telling tales of Glasgow, but it seemed so different to him now, being part of it.

There were not many motor vehicles about, but the ones he did see were much noisier than he had expected, and smelly as they went by... Many tramcars clanged along, almost as noisy as the motors and to Alexander, as they passed, the sparks coming from the overhead electric wires looked dangerous. Restricted to the rail tracks, it was obvious that, if one tram broke down, all those following would have to form a long queue.

As the traffic trundled along, the pedestrians were crazy. They were weaving in and out between the vehicles, seemingly without looking. Everyone appeared to be in a rush. He could not understand how they succeeded in reaching the other side of the road without being knocked over. He was extremely careful.

As he strode along the unfamiliar streets he realised he was missing Aberloudie: the fresh country air, the woodlands, and his family and friends. The real Glasgow was smoky and smelly, and he knew nobody other than Thomas and his wife, Ina, but this was where he would be making his fortune, was it not?

It was getting busier.

Where shall I stop? What tunes should I play? Bright and cheerful ones? Get the feet tapping, and see the smiles on faces as they recognise the music and appreciate my skill!

Alexander was sorely disappointed!

Admittedly, there were a few coins but where he chose everyone was on the move – off to work, returning from work, going to shop, returning laden, and the look on some business men's faces implied that listening to his music was beneath them. Argyle Street, with masses of people jostling and dodging along, but no one caring enough to stop and listen.

It must be the wrong place to stand. He would try another...

He went farther along Argyle Street and chose to stand outside the Arcade – a popular place to visit, with shoppers entering and leaving all the time. It was a congested area. He stopped next to the entrance and placed the pipe-case in front of him. Blocking part of the pavement made the area a little more chaotic, and did the trick: pedestrians were still on the move, but more slowly. They would hear him now. He started to play, this time with more success. Several people did stop, then a small crowd gathered and coins began to land in his hat – until a policeman appeared! A shopkeeper had complained that the gathering crowd was causing an obstruction at his doorway. Alexander was told to move along or else!

He could not give up now. He had tasted success...

Northwards he headed and arrived at a large

open space with statues and imposing buildings surrounding it. Crowds milled around. By chance, he had found George Square, but he'd arrived at the wrong time. Someone had beaten him to it...

The Square was busy. The man on a soapbox stood right in the middle, spouting forth, a good orator and obviously confident. He had the attention of a large crowd and, though heckled every so often, he was perfectly capable of holding his own. He even seemed to be enjoying it.

The crowd was being lectured on the wrongdoings of the German nation, behaviour that, in the opinion of this gentleman, could almost certainly lead to a war. He was working the crowd well and every so often shouted at them, "Do you want to go to war?" to which the response each time was a loud, and clear, "Noooo..."

Alexander stood and watched, interested in the man's rhetoric.

From the expressions on the faces of many of the people standing there, the smiles, the nods and backchat, it looked to him that they could be having fun at the soapbox man's expense, but each cheeky comment received a similar response. It took expertise to control this crowd. Alexander guessed he was probably on the same spot every week.

Although the orator was warming to his subject, and the crowd was paying proper attention, if Alexander had started playing his pipes it would have been easy to have drowned out the speaker, and drawn attention to his music. Other than the obvious rudeness that prevented Alexander from doing that, there was another important factor – the orator was a big man!

It was the wrong place again, so, he tried the nearby Railway Station.

Minor success this time, a few coins once more, but everyone in too much of a hurry. He was disappointed. There was little purpose in trying to continue, he decided, so he would return to the house. Unfortunately, the good citizens of Glasgow were not recognising his pipe-playing talents.

Thomas Stout was hard at work when he got back, pleased at having received some more shoes to repair. He was busy cutting and shaping leather, determined to uphold his reputation for a quick turnaround. The lad returning so soon surprised him. From the disappointment shown on Alexander's face, it was obvious that the young fellow had failed.

Pressured though he was, Thomas stopped. He sympathised and offered words of encouragement – then came up with another suggestion: "Why no' go out in the early evenin', the queues at the theatres, catch them standin' there, when they are no' in a hurry..."

Alexander had been easily convinced. After careful guidance from Thomas and with the destination clear in his head, he had walked to the far end of Sauchiehall Street and was now outside a big theatre.

The target was people out to enjoy themselves, already relaxed and in a light-hearted mood. Most had partners or friends, and all were looking forward to tonight's theatre entertainment – a high quality variety show – and standing in a long queue waiting for the opening of the doors.

Perfect, and this time there was no competition for his music.

Placing the pipe-case at the pavement edge, he took out the instrument, inflated the bag, tuned the drones to perfection, and the melodies began. He marched back and forwards, his kilt swinging jauntily. It did the trick.

This time they were hearing him – an expert piper, and they were listening in the open air – the best way to hear the bagpipes! Not only was it a captive audience, it was an appreciative one, standing tapping feet and absorbing the sound. After playing the first selection, going along the queue with Balmoral in hand and hearing the 'chink' of the coins dropping in, put a big smile on his face. Here was a crowd that willingly dipped hands into pockets.

He moved farther along the line and another selection of tunes from his wide repertoire entertained a fresh group of waiting theatregoers. This time he gained applause after playing, and more coins as he walked along. All very rewarding and pleased him immensely – then suddenly the mood changed!

Without thinking, he had placed the pipes back in their case on the pavement as he walked along the queue – then noticed the two boys. They were not queuing: they were hovering, and moving too close to the bagpipes, and then they bent down and made to grab them!

Collecting rapidly abandoned, he had to be quick!

The speed of Alexander, and the reaction of the crowd supporting him, alarmed the two young thieves. He was running towards them shouting loudly... A hesitation ...and they missed the chance. Leaving the instrument, they ran off.

The pipes! Were they damaged, was his panicky thought? No, but the drones had been disturbed. They would have to be re-tuned.

At that point, the theatre doors swung open and the queue began to shuffle forward – no longer his captive audience. That was it. There would shortly be no one to listen. He gave up the idea of playing and went back along the queue to continue collecting where he left off, cap in hand again, but this time, carrying the pipes in their case with him.

He was less successful. The queue had reduced to stragglers, so it was time to give up, but it had been a good start. It was time to go home. For his brilliant idea, Thomas would be getting a big thank you ...and a little of the money. On his way back, he was feeling much happier, until he realised he was being followed. The two rogues from earlier were on his tail. Alexander guessed – trouble.

If it had been only two against him, he would have stood his ground and fought, but another three joined them. It was dark and no one else was there to help. Alexander did the sensible thing – he ran!

When he saw yet another three coming the

opposite way, towards him, he panicked. He was nowhere near home. At the first chance, he turned and ran in a close entrance, and went for the stairs. Laying his pipes down safely, he closed his eyes and thought of the fighting tricks his brothers had taught him but, what chance had he against so many. He hid, standing on the steps for a height advantage, breathing deeply, and waiting for the clatter of feet as the group followed him in – but they didn't. He heard running footsteps, then shouting, as one of them passed the end of the close, then another ran by, and a third. None stopped. He waited a few moments and then ventured a cautious look. The gang of three was chasing the original five, who were going back quickly the way they'd come. It looked like two separate gangs. An invisible boundary crossed? The five had trespassed perhaps?

He smiled. Whatever the reason he was no longer the target. He'd been lucky; the pipes were safely in their case, and he still had the money, but before he left the close he made sure the way was clear, then ran as fast as he could all the way back. It was a relief to reach the safety of his digs without further mishap, other than to be struggling for breath.

That night he slept soundly, even with bits of leather in his back when he turned over.

Another inspiration came, but this time, Alexander's own idea. After a good night's rest he recalled the fanciful dream which had sparked a thought when he wakened and, as they sat together at breakfast, he shared it with Thomas and Ina. It would be a variation of the previous night, but more of a novelty. He would be returning to the theatre queues, this time without the bagpipes.

It would be a performance of his other skill: drawing.

Thomas and Ina looked at him blankly...

He was returning to the previous night's venue. Undaunted by the lack of enthusiasm from Thomas and his wife, and with a new self-confidence, he was about to do something he knew he could do well. His face was shining after a good scrub and this time he was wearing a suit. In his hand, a new sketchpad and, in his pocket, pencils bought earlier in the day.

Different people would be standing in the queue tonight, and every night. On his face was his winning smile and he intended using it extensively, essentially being as mannerly as he could.

"Surr, would you mind if I sketched yerr charmin' companion," he asked a well-dressed man, near the head of the queue. "That is, if she'll give hurr permission too, of course...?"

The man asked his wife. She smiled her assent, and Alexander performed his magic with the pencil. This brought smiles from both.

"Could I buy that for my wife?" the man asked Alexander.

"I hudnae intended sellin' it, but..." he replied in his best voice and, with a smile to accompany it and hide the lie, he accepted the money offered. It really tested him, trying to appear reluctant while feeling wonderful inside, particularly when the couple behind, who had been watching, also wanted a sketch. In this way, he progressed along the queue.

He made a lot of money in the time it took the queue to pass him because he could draw very quickly, and still achieve excellent likenesses. He went home that night feeling very happy indeed, and so it went for several months. He was making better money than his father ever had, without doing hard physical labour.

He played the bagpipes less frequently so the instrument case proved a very good place to keep his money. He was spending very little of it and it was mounting up, but then he began to feel uncomfortable about all the cash he had saved. Was it safe, keeping it in the special wooden piggybank, underneath the bagpipes?

That was when the Post Office Savings Bank beckoned. He did something about it, and rested easier at night knowing that, instead of his money being hidden in the pipe-case, it was safe in a bright new banking passbook.

He was onto a great business, even though only successful in dry weather. Most people in the queue became grumpy having to stand outside under umbrellas when it rained, and no one was in the right mood then for his quick portraits. Anyway, his paper got wet...

Although each evening he was meeting a different crowd of people queueing, it was the same staff in the theatre every night and they liked what he was doing. The novelty of his sketching took some of the pressure from them, at least on dry evenings. It helped pass the time for normally impatient theatregoers and slow-moving queues.

It was a wet evening when life changed for Alexander...

Being soaked, and doing no business, the artist stood near the theatre entrance looking miserable, hoping that a break in the clouds might occur and permit him to perform his usual pleasurable task. Having seen him regularly work the crowds outside for many weeks, the Theatre Commissionaire invited him inside, out of the rain and into the foyer. He couldn't be permitted to sketch patrons inside the building but Alexander was grateful to be in more comfortable surroundings.

That is when he glimpsed Phoebe for the first time. She worked in the ticket office, and it was not the first time she had seen him. Every night, since he had started, she had looked out to check that he was there. She had a soft spot for this friendly man – with a lovely smile, she thought.

When the patrons were all inside, seated, and with the front doors closed, the Commissionaire went to do other things. Alexander sat on in the foyer, dreamily watching the girl in the ticket office. He opened his sketchpad. When she left her little room, Phoebe was handed her perfect likeness on paper, with a little note from him begging her to go out with him.

9

2009
She has gone to heaven, but...

David drove the van that Saturday evening. Having
worked the whole day in the loft the pair of them
were feeling good about going home. Father and son
were tired, without doubt, father being the more
exhausted. They were hungry too and arriving home
to an empty house was a big disappointment.

What? No Gillian?

Having left her at home that morning, and her
being both wife and mother, they would have
expected her to have had a meal ready as they
walked in the door.

Was that not how wives and mothers were
supposed to behave? Full and steaming plates
should float in, as if by magic, so that two,
exhausted, cooking-shy males could plonk
themselves down at a dining table to get stuck-in and
concentrate on the sole purpose of eating. It would
have been the perfect start to a Saturday evening for
two out of three of the Findlay family members.

Not so tonight!

For Gillian it had been hectic. Her day had been spent at the hospital, not because of any problem with her health – no – the panic had been for Gillian's mum. During the morning she was taken in for observation, pains in the chest – and not for the first time either. She could count herself lucky that her daughter had been visiting.

That was why a tired and exasperated woman – the afore-mentioned wife and mother – was in transit and standing, squashed on peak-time public transport, wishing she had used the car. Taking a bus, to get between Jordanhill and Hyndland had seemed the right thing to do, when she was enthusiastic earlier in the day but, sadly, now that she was trying to return home, attempting to be environmentally friendly had its drawbacks.

She was thinking desperately of what was in the fridge, or the freezer, something that could be quickly conjured into a meal for three. Maybe they will have... Huh! Stupid thought! There was little chance – no, correct that – no chance of her son or husband even considering entering the kitchen to take responsibility for a meal.

One day I'll let them starve, she decided as she hobbled up the path ...damn these shoes! She searched her handbag but, annoyingly, could not find the key, so rang the doorbell.

As she tottered in, David recognised the importance of not getting on her wrong side.

"Had a good day, Mum?" he tried cheerfully.

"No," she curtly replied. "Granny Walker's back in hospital. Is the table ready?"

He decided to avoid confrontation. "Not yet, Mum, that's what I was about to do," which seemed the correct thing to say, and he set about it.

"Evening, darling," came Tom's voice from the front room easy chair, the introductory music for television's early evening news fading to expose the newsreader and today's headlines. "Have you been having fun too?" he shouted, as he fiddled with the remote. The voice of the newscaster stopped as he played the usual game of changing channels.

"Not particularly," she replied through clenched teeth.

David noticed his mother's reaction, and hoped, for his father's sake, that the old man would not be stupid and mention food being late.

"Would you look at that!" came from the front room. "Who'd be stupid enough to try that?" Tom was concentrating on the TV.

It had been a very trying day for Gillian. Cath Walker stubbornly not wanting to be bed-bound again in the hospital and Gillian having to encourage her to remain 'in the best place'. Successful in the end, yes, but it had been frustrating. By comparison, the males had had it easy.

Table prepared, David returned to the settee – at least he helped a little and it seemed best to be out of the way to let an exasperated mother cool down.

His dad was sitting, channel hopping.

The photo album, brought in from the car by his father, was lying abandoned on the coffee table – his dad's enthusiasm already lost. David lifted the plastic bag. As he turned it over, the loose snapshots fell out – almost the entire content of the album. The photos were well and truly out of order now.

"Oh dear, David," said a grinning Tom, "That is going to make your gran very unhappy. Wonder if food's nearly ready?"

"I wouldn't ask..." David warned.

Tom gave a sigh and stood up.

"I'm starving."

Nothing interesting on the news and with David now looking at photos and Gillian preparing the meal, Tom decided to leave them to it. It did occur to him that maybe he should offer help in the kitchen, but decided he could avoid that if he was doing something else.

"Yes, that's it..." he said, and left the room. As he passed the kitchen, he shouted in, "I'm going for a shower, dear. I could do with freshening up. I've had a long, hard day."

That was probably the wrong thing to say at that precise moment because Gillian stopped and gazed at the pan of cold water in her hand. She had the means to cool him down and save him having to climb all those tiring stairs! She resisted ...but only just.

David, in the other room, tensed, and waited for his mother's reaction, but there was only an ominous silence – and then the clatter of pan lids told him that his father got away with it.

He returned to the photos. Long gone relatives in shots taken many, many years ago. Most appeared to be snapshots from an old box camera, but one photo he lifted looked more formal. Taken by a professional! Someone would have had to spend hard-earned cash to have that – a pretty, young girl, obviously wearing her best outfit, and posing in a studio beside a table with a large plant in a pot. Could that be what an aspidistra looks like? Don't see many of those nowadays...

In another, a man in army uniform stood in front of a row of bell tents. Other soldiers nearby were sitting or lying around, looking very tired and dishevelled – all 'old' young men. Taken after action, David guessed. The figure in the foreground was the only one smiling but his smile looked forced and especially for the camera. He had a set of bagpipes under his arm. With horses and wagons in the background, David presumed it to be during the First World War...

Although the photos were almost all loose, they were still in good condition, but it would be impossible to put them back into the original order. No colour snapshots either, just black and white, and brown and cream – to do with their age, or the type of film?

He looked at the backs of a few. Were any dated? Yes, some were. One showed his earlier guess about which war to be correct. He put dated ones aside for starters and then noticed that many had several words written on them, but the words seemed unrelated to the photos ...strange?

The one in his hand showed '...**and put them in the right order.**' Another, '**I'll keep it simple,**' and on yet another he read '**How'd you like some fun?**'

How'd you like some fun? Now that was the sort of message you'd find on the business cards stuck inside the few usable public telephone boxes in railway stations or subways – invitations from sex workers!

Surely, these were not... No!

The words made little sense. Incomplete simple phrases in most cases, all done by the same hand. In ballpoint pen? Difficult to say.

"Dad!" he shouted, but no answer. "Dad, where are you? Come and look at this."

"He's upstairs, David. He won't hear you," shouted the harassed mother who was attempting too many things at once in the kitchen, where smoke was coming from the oven. It was beginning to irritate her eyes, but the cause was not obvious to Gillian.

"Is something burning down there? I can smell burning!" shouted Tom from upstairs, out of the shower and standing dripping on the landing. "Is everything all right? It's not my meal, I hope!"

Another crack, mate, and it will be, thought Gillian, whose eyes were starting to stream.

"David! Could you come through and open the window, please? It would be helpful if you could solve the smoke problem. We don't want to worry your dad, now do we?" she added sarcastically.

David found the little bit of bacon from a previous occasion being well over-grilled lying in the base of the oven, and became a minor hero in his mother's eyes. Eventually, the smoke cleared, and Tom appeared.

"Feeling better ...darling?" his wife asked. The insincerity was obvious – even to Tom!

It was a hastily prepared meal, using frozen products from the little stock of emergency foods snatched by Gillian from the deep freeze. However, chilled solid as they had been, these items defrosted quicker than the atmosphere as the three sat eating.

Gillian was not in the mood for small talk. The panic with her mother during the afternoon, the smoke-filled kitchen and streaming eyes, and Tom, skiving off as usual when she could have used his help, gave no reason to be cheery.

In the silence, it occurred to her that she would have to phone Fiona. It could wait until later – when she was in a better mood and she could choose the correct words. Merely mentioning the words 'unwell' and 'mother' would set her sister into panic mode! Fiona might rush over from Spain, possibly for nothing.

"We will be keeping your mother in for checks," they'd said. Gillian sincerely hoped that was all it was. It had been like that – just checks, for her dad. That was seven years ago. He did not recover. But Dad was seriously overweight, she recalled – Mum is not. Yes, she will be all right...

During the meal, David asked how bad Granny Walker was. He liked both his grandmothers, always had. When he was younger it was a source of extra pocket money sometimes, and that had been handy.

Gillian hesitated, still feeling frosty and unwilling to talk – but at least David had tried to help earlier – and he had found the smouldering bacon – so she spoke to him.

"False alarm, they think," she told him, "...but they were not certain, so they kept her in. And how was your day ...David?" and that was said pointedly to exclude a husband who, anyway, was quite happy to be just munching away.

"Yea, we did all right. You might be interested in photos we brought back. Found them in the loft, well, Dad did – must be Granny Meg's. One shows her in a wedding dress, with Grandad Findlay, I guess. They look young. Some are her parents too, I think, but they are all out of order. You'll probably make more sense of them than us."

"Grandad Findlay, hmm, that's interesting." She was still talking only to her son. "He was always a bit of a phantom figure... Hamish was his name... We could look at the photos in a moment – while your father makes us a cup of coffee." Speaking directly to her husband, she added, "...And washes the dishes, and cleans the pots and pans – and puts them all away!"

Tom decided to humour her and made no comment. Obviously in a grumpy mood – taking it out on him for some reason. Must be her time of the month, was his guess.

When eventually he completed his chores and came through with hot drinks, Tom found the other two fully engrossed in the task, kneeling on the floor with the photographs scattered all over the carpet. They were scrutinising both sides of each photo, selecting those with writing on the back, while attempting to guess the subjects' identities.

They were making very slow progress but judging by her enthusiasm, Gillian was having fun, her earlier coolness gone.

Forgiven... Tom guessed but, for what?

His wife and son sat happily in the middle of the floor amongst the photos, but Tom's favourite chair beckoned and, as normal, he joined it.

"Thought you were meeting your mates, David," said Tom.

"Maybe go later, but Mum and I have, sort of, got involved in this..."

"Yes, Tom, and guess what we've found. It's a message, from your grandmother," said Gillian, looking up at him. "I recognise her writing. Now isn't that spoooooooky!" She made a face as she handed it up to him. "Woo-hooooo..."

"Love from Meg," he read aloud. Tom had liked her. Gillian handed him some more. 'Join the treasure hunt...' one said. Tom hesitated then read another, 'Dear family – remember me?'

"Well, would you believe it?" he sighed. "Good old Meg." She was still at it! Dead and gone for many years, his grandmother – the one who used to play tricks on him, and who helped him play tricks on his mum and dad when he was young. He looked again at words on the first card, and turned it over. The picture was of her, when she was young, an enormous grin on her face, looking straight out at him – laughing at him, again!

David was reading the others silently. Each phrase made only a little sense. "Are they meant to be put together perhaps, to be sorted into sensible sentences?" He directed the question at his father but, from Tom's glazed expression, an answer was unlikely, so he talked to his mum. "Maybe there is a correct sequence, but how would we know if it was correct?"

"Trial and error?" she offered.

To Gillian and David this sort of thing was a challenge. Not for Tom. Physical stuff he would slog at, but thinking? No. Tonight, his plan had been to sit in front of the television and slowly drift off into dreamland for half-an-hour, and then have a beer – but that now seemed unlikely.

Switching on the TV would have been his choice but, after the frosty treatment from Gillian earlier – for no discernible reason that Tom could think of, that seemed unwise. Anyway with the noise they were making he would never be able to hear it. He was unlikely to be able to doze either, he realised. He would have to settle for a beer. The others could play detectives if they wanted to. Anyway, they would soon get fed up.

Tom got up, left the room and went for that beer. But David and Gillian didn't get fed up, in fact, they became more engrossed but, juggling the phrases was not bringing success and David was having doubts. How could they know what was correct? There was no one to tell them – and then Gillian's keen eye spotted a possible link! Some photos had a tiny number inscribed at a corner.

So, photos without writing on the back were put aside. They sorted the remainder. Those with writing and a number in one pile, and those without in another. The twelve with numbers were placed in numerical order and... Eureka! There it was! A message!

"Tom! Where are you? Success!"

Beer in hand and a sceptical smile on his face, Tom returned,

"Ah, perfect timing." Gillian smiled up at him. "We've got it! Have a read of that."

"Right then..." was said with a smirk.

> *"[Dear family – remember me?]*
> *[How'd you like some fun?]*
> *[Join the treasure hunt...]*
> *[I'll keep it simple...]*
> *[Find the words on the back]* "

He stopped and looked at the other two. This felt odd...

> *"[of the other photos]*
> *[in this album,]*
> *[and put them in the right order]*
> *[to obtain the first clue.]"*

The smirk gradually left his face as he continued.

> *"[Are you game?]*
> *[Of course you are!]*
> *[Love Meg.]"*

Tom's comfortable chair sat unoccupied because he was kneeling on the floor beside the photos, reading each card again, silently this time.

"I don't believe it!" he said, but he did! "Good old Meg... Wonder when she did this. She was a joker! Unwell before she died, but I remember when I was young, she was lively – enjoyed a good prank and this was the sort of thing she would do. Had you involved too, David."

Tom straightened up, looked at them both and declared in a serious voice, "Right then, a clue to find? We will have to get on with it." However, by 'we' he meant Gillian and David, not himself. They had deciphered these instructions and could not possibly fail to do the same with the other bits. Right! He was not needed now and had every confidence in them – but Tom didn't leave, he was curious.

Eventually he said, "Ok. Let's see." They were getting nowhere. "I'll show you. These are the ones with the words? This will be easy-peasy!"

This was certainly no ordinary Saturday evening. All three at home together, crawling around the floor, laughing and giggling just like kids, looking at old photographs and trying to imagine what a clue would look like, and Tom – at this time usually asleep in his armchair – actually awake!

Though the target was the hand-written words, they could not ignore the photos, each being carefully lifted, and studied. For most of them, what they were seeing was guesswork, but they thought they recognised Tom's gran at different ages.

Many were presumed to be Meg's family, based

on a similarity of features. There were different groupings. Sometimes it looked as if they were taking turns with the camera – some shots well composed, others, less so and, from the clothes worn, many photos, possibly, taken on the same day.

One, probably was of Meg's parents sitting on their own on a park bench. In another Meg had joined them. One, of a younger boy who may have been her brother, and an older sister looking like young Meg. Some, a little more dog-eared, were of an even older generation, and there was one of Meg in a wedding dress... Her errant husband, Hamish Findlay, did not look like a rogue in that photo.

An unusual one showed someone called Bella Roberts. The name was on the back. What made it unusual was not the smiling, full-length study of a pretty, young woman – it was the addition, drawn in ink on the photo itself, of devil's horns on her head, and a forked tail trailing at the back. The reverse of that photograph had her name and a date, and a single comment. "Grrrrr..." Intriguing ...but they were searching for a clue. As a treasure hunt, it would be one clue at a time, leading to another.

Gillian and Tom were more intrigued by the photo images. It was David who was looking at the words and trying variations, determined to be the one to create the correct combination. He was getting eager for success. *[Iron it out? It is]* was on the photo he was holding.

"Should we be looking for an iron?"

"Hope it's not the one we threw away this

morning," said Tom flippantly, "the one with no cable. If it is, where will it be by now? No, it couldn't be that: but then again!"

Tom was quickly tiring. He had really no idea how to play these silly games. He felt he was getting too old for this sort of thing.

To David, it was a challenge. He stared at the words. [**a fair**], [**drive or just**] and [**go for a**]. All simple little snippets, but meaningless on their own. Meg didn't drive, so couldn't be anything to do with a car – or could it?

Tom hoped the others had sharper brains than his, but so far another eureka moment had not yet come. Anyway, why was he torturing his tired head like this?

The search continued until, in the bundle, Gillian found one they'd missed, [**way, isn't it?**] Was that the last? No. David picked up [**Should I**], were there more?

"Golf clubs!" Tom said suddenly. "Could it be anything to do with golf clubs? We put that set back in the loft, today, David; the ones that your grandad said were his. Could it be to do with them maybe? If it's a treasure hunt and she's made it simple, it would be things she could reach, to attach the clues."

"And you think she climbed into the loft and put a clue with those golf clubs? You could hardly get up and down that ladder today. How would she? No, no chance," said David.

Tom, deflated, at least had tried. Meanwhile, Gillian was continuing thinking, shuffling the photos around to give different combinations – and she came up with something that made more sense than anything that they had guessed up to now.

"How's about this," she offered, "Should I / go for a / drive or just / iron it out? It is / a fair / way isn't it?"

"Wow!" said Tom and David in unison.

"Well done, Mum. A driver, an iron, a fairway – they are all golfing terms. Yes, Dad, it could be the golf clubs right enough!" David made his comment seem grudged but, in truth, it gave him a nice feeling inside that Dad could win, now and again.

Tom felt good but found it hard to believe – that he'd guessed it! Although they wouldn't really know until they actually proved it was the hiding place.

It was getting very late, even for a Saturday night, but it had ended well – though not if it was the wrong conclusion. None of them wanted to think of it not being the golf clubs, because they had no idea what else it could be!

"Roll on next Saturday," said Tom with boyish enthusiasm. "We'll find out then."

For him, that loft had become a little more interesting and next Saturday morning he would show his mocking son – by running up that ladder like a young thing!

That's when David remembered. He was supposed to be at the pub – he'd promised to meet Jennifer!

10

1914
'Your country needs you...'

Phoebe and Alexander were going steady for almost four months when the news broke – the assassination of an important person, Archduke Ferdinand of Austria – someone neither had ever heard of.

Alexander found he could not avoid being aware of happenings in the big wide world and did not have to buy newspapers to know. He lived in the city now.

The posters displayed beside newsstands told him, whether the news was pleasant or nasty. Always there, impossible to miss and, this time, reporting dreadful news that would affect millions of lives; the date was 28th June 1914.

The city of Glasgow was so different from the village of Aberloudie but sadly, in the future, the differences would not prevent a great many of the inhabitants of both places from suffering painfully.

War had arrived.

Alexander and Phoebe continued working in the evenings, and were happy to be seeing a lot of each other during the day, but Alexander was asking himself, was he really working?

Calling his daily occupation 'work' made him feel guilty; he was only drawing. It was true that he enjoyed doing it, and that he was earning money at the same time, but was it working, or just a form of begging.

No, surely not begging. He offered a product that people were willingly buying from him... That wasn't begging but would his good fortune last? The selling of drawings? If he were to be married, he'd need a weekly wage and a regular reliable income, particularly if they were to have a youngster.

Phoebe and Alexander were seriously considering marriage, although when had not been decided. So far, they'd agreed it would be soon, until Alexander presented his bride-to-be with a personal bombshell. Because of one pointing digit and hypnotic eyes, he would be joining the army!

Lord Kitchener, on iconic posters stuck to surfaces all over the city became, for Alexander, very personal, and very uncomfortable. 'JOIN YOUR COUNTRY'S ARMY' the posters said, but one finger pointed, and two eyes stared – directly at him!

Alexander Findlay took it personally!

Sorry, canny do it, Alexander said to himself each time he passed a poster; *Ah'm committed, already promised – me and Phoebe – we're tae be married* ...but Kitchener was persistent!

Certain streets where he had already seen the

posters displayed, he avoided, but they were plastered everywhere. He tried averting his gaze as he slunk past, but the eyes and the finger followed, even when he'd walked away – he'd checked! So, he stopped looking back over his shoulder. This was successful for several days but then, one morning, stopping, bravely staring straight back – he knew – it was useless to resist. The eyes, the pointing finger – they had won. There was no doubt – he was wanted. His country needed *him!*

Phoebe cried. She did not want him to go. Life had become so enjoyable; particularly the comforting thought of marrying, and setting up home together, and a family, but she knew it would be disloyal if she tried to dissuade him.

The feeling experienced by Alexander was not unique. Most young males were responding to the call with little thought of the outcome.

The homeland was in danger.

They would be protecting their loved ones and their way of life – and they laughed and joked as they willingly stepped forward to sign the dotted line.

Humiliation was the outcome for those who ignored the call – no one wanted that.

For the next two years, this would be in keeping with the mood of several million other young men across Britain, including Alexander's brothers. All signed-up for the honour of fighting for their country and, for many, the more dubious honour of dying.

Alexander and Phoebe made a promise. With a smile, he promised to survive if she would wait for him and they would marry when the fighting ended. It would not be long, he said. Phoebe removed her necklace and handed it to him, a good luck charm that he must return to her – when it was all over. She held back the tears until he was out of sight.

In joining Kitchener's Army, Alexander was able to offer the unusual talent of a musical skill, an ability to play the bagpipes really well, and for the Scottish Regiment that he was joining this was valuable, and greatly appreciated.

What is it about the sound of the bagpipes that stirs something deep inside the mind and spirit of a Scotsman? The feeling may not be one ever experienced before. The sound of bagpipes, plaintive and mournful, or bright and irresistibly foot tapping, making a kilt swing jauntily. It is a very special sound. It may bring a tear to the eye, but it can strengthen the will to succeed, particularly in battle. The skirl of the pipes helps Scotsmen summon the extra courage needed for the fight, and Alexander was the man with the bagpipes.

Before joining, he was not particularly brave, or even tough, but these qualities somehow surfaced naturally in the heat of battle, battles that were hard fought and bloody. Without exaggeration he was not only a good piper, he was a piper who became a brave fighting soldier too.

Remarkably, Alexander Findlay was one of the few military pipers to survive and return to civilian life at the end of hostilities. For his pain, genuine pain caused by twice being shot, he received a Distinguished Service Medal. Twice he was 'Mentioned in Despatches.' Agony though it was, the bullets had caused wounds from which he recovered, although the second gave him the legacy of a limp.

Twice he'd pushed hospital staff to release him, maybe earlier than they should have, because during his recovery the feeling of deserting his mates never left him. Returning could not come quickly enough. It was to the same regiment and tired comrades and muddy battlefields. Sadly, both times, he re-joined the fight to find his comrades, his friends, vastly reduced in number.

When standing in the trenches, during those lonely frightening times, it was nice to remember his Phoebe, longing to return to her. He treasured her necklace and carried it with him at all times. He tried to remember the feeling of a soft warm bed, or even dry socks – but could not. The cold mud, it was hellish...

The Conflict began on 28th June 1914 and ended on 1st November 1918.

The Casualties were 36 million.

The Dead were 17 million. What a waste...

THEY said – The Great War to End All Wars... but THEY lied.

11

2009
Pieces of Eight...

After her initial misgivings, Cath Walker settled down in the hospital and became a well-behaved patient, well behaved except towards one nurse that she could not quite take to, the rest were great. The experience was not too bad, she would tell her daughter later.

It was for four days, but even though she began to enjoy the company of those in the other beds – those who were not in too much discomfort and happy to chat all day – she had been delighted to learn that on Tuesday afternoon she could go home.

Now, she was back in Hyndland, enjoying her own surroundings again. Being a caring daughter, Gillian had dutifully visited each day since the return, and she was pleased to see an obvious improvement. By Friday, she assessed that her mum was making a good recovery and would be able to cope over the weekend by herself. Her mum concurred. There would therefore be no visit on Saturday, unless she felt unwell again, in which case she would use her mobile to call Gillian. She and Tom would come over as quickly as they could.

"My mobile number's on your telephone, Mum. Fiona's is there too, OK? And I have added Tom's, in case you can't get me. Just remember to put on your glasses though, or you will never see what you are dialling. You have your medication?" Confirmed... It was sitting where it should be, on the sideboard, and would be taken exactly as instructed.

"I'll phone Fiona and tell her you are progressing nicely. If you feel well enough, you could give her a ring yourself. I am sure she would love to hear from you. Keep smiling, then. Bye."

Gillian would not be going to her mum's on Saturday for a very good reason. It was earmarked for visiting Tom's folks – provided there was no emergency. The loft would be the place to be and she wanted in on the act, to be present to find out if their deductions were correct.

Granny Meg had been mischievous, there was no question, but nice with it. Gillian remembered her fondly and hoped this final bit of fun would enrich memories, particularly in the minds of Tom and David. They had adored her.

David was surprised but pleased with his Mum's enthusiasm to join them. He assured her, that since he and his dad nailed down the extra flooring last Saturday, three of them should be able to move safely in the loft – without standing on each other's feet. Though the whole surface was not covered, it would be safe for her to go up.

Tom was not so eager – but he wasn't bothered either – he was sure his wife would never even manage to climb the ladder...

"I am looking forward to this for a change," said Tom, "...but remember, the main reason for the visit is loft clearance. We must not be side tracked – too much." That is what he said as they left Jordanhill but Gillian was sure, for the two males, any enthusiasm was to do with Meg's clue! "Gillian, how would you like to return the photo album?" Tom added. "You could explain to Mum and Dad what we did last Saturday night. You are good at that and they like you. Oh, don't forget to mention that I guessed the clue!"

"And what are you...?" Gillian started to ask, but stopped. Why bother...

Delegated to return the photos – while they go straight to the loft, huh! They are trying to delay me! It was so obvious but she did not want to appear churlish – even though that would give them a head start.

As she expected, when they arrived and after the briefest of hellos to Beth, Tom and David shot straight upstairs.

Gillian watched them go and had to bite her tongue but she did as requested and stayed, holding the old photo album. The photos were now replaced neatly – nothing like the original sequence, because no one knew what that was.

"Come through to the kitchen, Gillian dear," said Beth, "and we'll have a seat."

Gillian would rather have gone upstairs. She could hear the noise of the loft ladder being lowered, but she had to do this first. She smiled at her mother-in-law and handed her the album. Beth seemed surprised to have it returned so quickly.

"...In a much better state than last week," she said. "That is, better than when Tom took it. Tom can be such a messy worker ...but you will know that better than anyone, Gillian dear."

She is doing it again – being catty about Tom, but Gillian smiled sweetly, thankful that Tom was already in the loft with David, and didn't hear the comment. He would not have been pleased. Gillian never understood why Beth always chose to put down her only son, but little use in defending him. Anyway, she had a task, recounting last Saturday's discovery to her mother-in-law – the challenge from Meg.

"Meg? ...She did what?" exclaimed Beth, "Created a Treasure Hunt? I don't believe it! How clever. You must tell your father-in-law, dear!" The two women went through to the sitting room where Angus sat reading. "Gillian has a tale to tell you, Angus," said Beth but, before Gillian could open her mouth, Beth had recounted everything Gillian told her, ending with, "It was in this photo album. Isn't that amazing, Angus?"

To Gillian, Angus seemed less than amazed. Almost as if it was exactly as he expected, although his eyebrows did rise a little. It was his mother after all and he must have known what she was like – a touch eccentric.

"She didn't give up, did she..." he smiled. "She had me take this album up to the loft. Couldn't go up herself, obviously, and asked me to put it with her other stored things. I didn't feel so nimble that day but... I didn't look at it – but what did I do with it? Oh, I remember, I put it in the jelly pan."

Gillian had given up trying to rush away. Tom and David had probably discovered the clue by now and would suddenly appear looking smug and smart. So, she took the chance to relax and talk and tell of the silly fun they'd had last Saturday. She recounted how three adults were giggling like children, crawling around the floor amongst all the old photos. She made the tale so interesting and challenging that Beth became eager to go up to the loft and be involved.

Angus managed to dissuade her. "Oh no... If you succeed getting up, who will be getting you down again?" He remembered that she took cold feet the last time – after four rungs! That argument did not apply to Gillian. She was definitely going up! Being a mere female was not going to stop her, so she left them and hurried upstairs. She could hear the footsteps above. She hoped they hadn't been successful yet – she wanted to play her part.

She stopped at the foot of the ladder. She could hear Tom and David still moving stuff around so the search was still on. She looked over the bannister at Beth and Angus. They had come into the hall and were looking up at her, so she gave them a nervous smile, for the ladder looked daunting... but slowly, she stepped on it, and climbed. Her first time, fearful and not daring to look down, and glad that Angus had dissuaded his wife. It was easier when she had head and shoulders through the hatch. She coped with the climb and was pleased with herself, but then realised that it might be harder going down.

Don't think about it, she told herself...

Tom and David had been busy, but at other things. The golf bag sat where it lay last Saturday and easy enough to remove from the stack, but they had delayed touching it until she stood beside them. It would be all three together, they said. All for one and one for all! How could she ever have suspected otherwise...?

She'd never been in the loft before but she could imagine it must have been pitch black before, with no lighting.

"Tom, you've done a great job here," she said, and he beamed happily. He was not used to compliments, not from his wife. He did remind her that David helped – a little.

Tom lifted down the golf bag and laid it on the floor. The three stood around it. "Go on, David. You look," he said, and watched as each club was removed carefully. They were all of wooden shafted clubs, not seen on a golf course these days.

How could anyone hit a ball with these? David wondered. They would be embarrassing to play with, and as for the old golf bag... No thank you.

In Tom's head, the clubs together with the old bag looked super. They could fetch good money as antiques. Hickory shafts. Nothing fancy about them but in his opinion, you could keep your hi-tech, modern, steel, titanium, and graphite; these were the real thing, and, looked in tip-top condition. In fact, he thought, I wouldn't mind having a game with them myself.

Gillian stood, wondering what the other two were thinking.

All the clubs were now out on the floor, but there was no thrilling discovery. That was a little disappointing. Nothing attached to them. No little notes. Tom now wondered if he'd been wrong.

David tried to look inside the long bag, but it was difficult seeing to the bottom, even with the new lighting. Again, nothing. There was a front pocket. He opened the flap and, one by one, took out the golf balls, six of them. They started to roll on the floor. Gillian grabbed them. She could visualise treading on one and falling full length!

Several wooden tees were next, and finally – right at the bottom of the little pocket, a folded piece of paper,

"Aha! Told you so!" said a grinning Tom. "Hurry up, David, tell us!" This fully-grown adult was stepping excitedly from foot to foot – like when he was six. He and Granny Meg would be waiting to trick someone with their latest ruse – and that was the little dance he'd done then. It had also signalled a desperate need for the toilet! He stopped quickly when he remembered that.

David unfolded the paper very slowly, a combination of wariness, that it might tear in the process – and the enjoyment of making the other two wait! A dramatic deep breath, then...

"There is Mister Silver and hero, young Jim! And the Pieces of Eight – talking bird,

In tales of treasure. Adventure galore. But my own tale is much more absurd.

My treasure was stolen from under my nose. The present, a book, left behind

Gives the clue that you need in the search for your treasure, a treasure I know you will find..."

David looked up, a puzzled look on his face.

"What's that all about?" said Tom.

"Right, we've begun," said an enthusiastic wife, "Something to think about. I don't know what it means, but we did not expect it to be easy, did we? It's a treasure hunt!"

"How are you getting on?" shouted the voice from down below. "Have you found anything?" Beth was standing on the landing, with a cup of coffee in her hand. The aroma was drifting up into the loft.

"We've found the clue but we'll need your help," shouted down Gillian. "Anyway, a good time for a break. Do you agree, fellas – I smell coffee? Yes, we are coming down..." and without any hesitation and with her mind on the new information – and the coffee, she stepped onto the ladder and down she went.

Last Saturday evening, it had been a novelty with three of them surprised and delighted at Meg's inventiveness. One week ago they were simply curious. Now, they had moved on – they had become Treasure Hunters but first they would enjoy coffee and home baking – a perfect combination!

Angus was not surprised at what his mother had done. She was bright as a button until the end, but when had she prepared the clues? While staying with them? He had noticed nothing at the time, well, nothing that he could remember. She'd had no major physical problems, other than tiring a bit quicker – although she had admitted to stumbling a bit when out walking, so Angus reckoned that made it likely she hid the clues around the house.

The five of them – sitting around the Bearsden kitchen table, each with a fresh mug of coffee and a warm pancake covered in thick, homemade, strawberry jam – were now ready to contemplate the clue they had discovered and this time Gillian read out Meg's words.

Angus listened and began to smile. "I can tell you why she wrote that," he said. "Bella Roberts stole my father. They'd left my mother before I was born, so I never knew either of them. My mother had some photos and that is all, but her special wedding present to him – it was a book. She never forgave him for leaving it behind. Hmmm..."

He stopped. He sat and pondered.

They waited.

If he had been smoking a pipe, the smouldering tobacco would have extinguished and been relit at least twice. Get on with it, thought Tom. David's the same! What a pair. Has to be a blooming drama!

They were patient and, "Yes, that's it," he said eventually. He was smiling broadly. "It is about her special book. Have you ever read Treasure Island?" he asked them.

"I haven't," said David. "It's been on telly, but I didn't see it."

"Me neither," said Gillian, "...but I vaguely know what it's about. Pirates, isn't it?"

"I read it, when I was at school," said Tom, "...but I remember being at the theatre and seeing it on stage – with you, Mother, you took me. I can remember it very clearly – Captain Hook making people walk the plank, and the big green crocodile swallowing an alarm clock, and then there was Tinkerbelle, the little fairy..."

"Tom," interrupted his mother, "that was Peter Pan!"

"Oh, well there was a Black Spot somewhere – now that was serious... If you were given that by pirates, heaven help you!"

Angus interrupted.

"Yes, this is a link to 'Treasure Island,' I'm sure. She gave it to my father when they married, but he never read it, and that annoyed her. Then he left her – of course that annoyed her more, but he didn't even take the book, and that annoyed her even more again! As soon as I could read, she made me read it, just for spite, I think, but I enjoyed it. I enjoyed reading."

If Angus was right, the hunt was now on – for a book!

"Well Dad, any idea where the book might be?" Tom asked, although he guessed what his father was about to say.

"...In the loft?"

There was still doubt in their minds of how Meg

might have accessed that space, but... That was forgotten as three of them went back up the ladder – with the original objective of loft clearance also forgotten, for the search was on. They found many things because there were many to find – but not a book called Treasure Island and that was a disappointment.

After a while getting nowhere, Tom remembered, and chose to remind the other two, that the real purpose for their being there was to reduce the quantity of unwanted goods.

"...So, let's do it. Anyway we might just stumble across the book."

"Of course!" Gillian and David responded.

However, that is not what happened because curiosity took over for all three and, as each began to find interest in the diverse items lifted, the main objective was forgotten again.

Old magazines, thought Tom at first, lifting the bundle. These can go, but... They were very old. Sixty-three sections, held together by staples, many rusted through, and barely holding the pages together. Printed 1920, twice monthly. Harmsworth's Universal Encyclopaedia. Fascinating that these booklets were almost ninety-years-old.

Yea... I'll be that age soon... Oh, oh! Must stop thinking like that!

Angus later said that he had no recollection of where an encyclopaedia like that might have come from, but he was interested. "Bring them down, Tom – something to read." He would look at them in his leisure time – he had plenty of that.

Gillian's discovery was a bundle of dusty knitting booklets. She sat on a box and started looking at them, then suggested that David carry them down to his gran. He did and, for her, the patterns brought back memories; how she enjoyed that period in her life, she told him.

When he returned to the loft and mentioned that Gran was gazing nostalgically at designs she had used long ago, Tom gave a shudder. He remembered those dated patterns. He hoped sincerely that she would not start knitting jumpers for him again!

Eventually the team did get round to doing some clearance.

It was fortunate that no one came to the front door because it would have been difficult to gain entry. Items proposed for disposal now sat in the hall awaiting Beth's stamp of approval, but that would be a while away – only when she gave up reading the knitting magazines would anything else be considered.

"Mother won't want to hold on to any of this stuff," said Tom, but the look from Gillian and David questioned his confidence...

Time would tell, but the best that the old yoghurt-maker could do was to support the coffee table with the missing leg. Then there was the vacuum cleaner – it was a danger to society with a burst bag and a frayed cable, and it sat in a defunct footbath, which should have been able to vibrate but stopped doing that years ago. A fizzy drinks maker with no canister to make drinks fizzy, was of little use either. There was also a box of very old soft toys. A sad-looking one-eyed teddy bear sat at the top.

In the judgement of the loft clearance team, all should go – but who could know what Beth would think!

Of course, items for disposal were not the only things that blocked the hall – two white, chipped, kitchen chairs that had been already condemned by Beth sat there too. Gillian had been surprised by that and looked closely at them, and disagreed with her mother-in-law's judgement. To her mind, they had potential, but she kept that thought to herself. She proposed to salvage them and, once successfully renovated, Beth would get no chance to claim them back.

Though it was sitting in the hall, the old wooden standard lamp was not for disposal either. Its discovery in the loft had caused ructions because it had been put in the loft – without his Beth's knowledge. It would be going back to Jordanhill with the chairs – and Tom was landed with the job of sanding and varnishing it

Traditionally, it sat in a corner of the front room, mostly unused because table lamps were preferred, then one day, a while ago, Beth noticed it missing. She asked Angus if he knew where it was. "Oh, you must have thrown it out ages ago," he suggested. "Don't you remember?" He had never liked it, and it wasn't being used, however, not being brave enough to throw it out, one day he'd put it up in the loft. After bluffing it out with his wife, he erased it from his memory – until being discovered that afternoon by Tom.

Tom felt guilty after overhearing the rollicking his father received. In no uncertain terms, Angus was told by his wife that, when renovated by Tom, and after a new lampshade was purchased for it, the wooden standard lamp would be returning to where it should be – in the front room.

"The moment Tom returns it, the furniture will be fully rearranged and you will be redecorating the room for me," Beth told her apparently contrite husband. "I think we could do with a new carpet too. I'll teach you to hoodwink me!"

"Sorry, Dad. Didn't mean to land you in it," said Tom afterwards.

"Oh, don't worry," replied Angus. "I know your mother well. Just do me a favour – do not rush the job. With any luck, if you take long enough, she'll forget all about it again..."

It was Gillian who called a halt to the day. Tom was extremely relieved. Having climbed the ladder and the hall stairs so many times, he was tired, and it seemed to get stuffier and more airless in the confined loft space as the day had progressed. Anyway, that was it and overall, it had not been a wasted day. Something was achieved, even if the 'Treasure Island' book had failed to surface.

Tom had already one foot on the loft ladder, about to descend, when David accidently knocked a small brown suitcase from the top a pile.

It crashed on the flooring, and the catches gave, the lid burst open and an assortment of books spilled out, books that Tom recognised – his father's old reference books that were always kept downstairs in his study, but one book was not his father's – *Treasure Island by R L Stevenson.*

David lifted it. It was not apparent at first, but as he riffled through the pages, he found it. *Yes!* In his hand – the next clue!

A tired cheer reached downstairs, and to Angus and Beth in the kitchen, it sounded like the team upstairs might be staying a little longer in that confined space.

12

1918
The war is over...

The war did end. They buried the bodies and, all over the country, long lists of names of the dead were carved on blocks of stone and marble. Scarred memories would remain forever with the wounded. Families survived but, in many cases, without male breadwinners. Fathers and sons, brothers, uncles, and friends – all gone. Life for many families would never be the same again and, sadly, the fight would continue for those who did return – a fight for survival.

On his release, Alexander went back to Aberloudie to visit his mother and father. There was sadness everywhere. The Findlay family had suffered in the same way as most others, and he was broken-hearted to learn that three of his brothers, Rory, Calum, and Malcolm, perished. Donald, Dougal and Ewan had survived, though Dougal was still in hospital recovering from a serious arm wound. They had all been foot soldiers, like himself...

The Laird had been an officer, but status didn't help him. He was killed in battle too.

For Alexander, like many others who fought at the front, returning to civilian life was not comfortable. Yes, he came back alive, but every night suffered the dreams, very bad ones, as he tossed and turned and talked in his sleep. The man who returned had changed. Having his discharge record folded in his back pocket became a habit: not to remind him of where he had been, but at the worst moments to convince him that he was no longer in that hell. The piece of paper gradually became tattered, but remained always on his person.

At bad times his head would feel as if it would burst and he would give a sob of despair. He went to the war taking pleasant, loving memories of life, and came back with nightmares. Thankfully, one person stayed strong in his thoughts, and during his worst moments helped him believe that there could still be a future – Phoebe, his beloved Phoebe. As promised, she'd waited. She was his reason to return.

Phoebe had her dark moments too, not the physical danger that he faced of course. That he might not survive was her fear. Would she ever see him again? Alexander placing the necklace in her hands – the one she'd given him – was the fulfilment of a promise, and the end of not knowing.

Now, they could have a future together.

They were wed two months after his return, a simple affair at the local Registrar's and to celebrate they held a little party in their tenement home. Phoebe's parents were there. Alexander's brother Donald and his wife came down from Aberloudie, but his parents did not. They sent apologies – they could not face the journey to Glasgow, but Thomas Stout and his wife, Ina, who lived nearby, managed to attend. Most of their new neighbours, and several of Phoebe's friends from work, came too and overfilled the room and kitchen.

It was good that the neighbours were there because the noise and chat had to spill onto the landing and neighbours do not complain when they are helping to cause the noise.

They all shared the enjoyment of that special day with the smiling couple though, that afternoon, not everything was shared. Someone had a secret – Phoebe. Only she could sense that she was pregnant. Alexander will be happy, she told herself, but I mustn't tell him yet, not until it's certain. It's only two months after all, it might be a false alarm...

Life went on.

Almost every evening Phoebe was in the tiny ticket office at the theatre, enjoying what she did; a trusted and established employee, greatly appreciated by her companions. She planned to continue doing the job for as long as she could manage and would save her earnings. Having a little money put away would be wise. With a baby on the way at some point she would have to stop – and who knew what the future could hold.

Since his return, Alexander had developed a deep mistrust of authority and of the people and the systems running the country. Somewhere he had learned of a bank collapsing years ago, and of a great many people losing all their savings.

That was not what he wanted. He had a wife to care for, and there would soon be a wee one too. Money for the future was important, so he decided it would be better to make sure that his stayed in a safe place, a safer place than the Post Office Savings Bank – so he withdrew his life savings.

...And where was the new safe place? Why, under the bed in the case with his bagpipes, of course! What could be safer than that!

For Alexander it was difficult returning to the old routine – sketching people waiting in theatre queues. This time it was giving little pleasure, and although once more he was making money using his talent, the smile and charm had become forced.

There was an alternative, though a poor one – the bagpipes. He could try them again, even though he remembered that first experience in the Glasgow streets many years before. A failure, with few people interested – all too busy to stop and listen.

Playing on the battlefield had been very different. His mates did not ignore him there. He was appreciated. No choice on the battlefield – they had to face the hardships and the fight – together. During battle, people *heard* him when he played; they told him – his pals and the officers who lived – the pipes were important to them, and they wanted to hear him. It helped them face the prospect of death.

The experience left him scarred and hardened. He'd survived, but many had not. If he played, it would be for them: his fallen comrades, and yes, he would play again! If there were no coins, it would not matter. If people walked callously by, he would not be saddened.

I will be playing for departed comrades...

Once again, Alexander took the pipes to the centre of Glasgow and as expected earned little. People walked on, he was ignored, but he was not playing for them. His thoughts were elsewhere. At least the marching gave him satisfaction, even with the limp.

He played his favourite tunes – tunes learned from his father, when he was a young lad and life was much simpler, a time that seemed an eternity ago.

Music engrained in his memory, and in his heart: *Salute to Inverary* – *Welcome back again* – *Waking of the bridegroom...* and sometimes, depending on his mood – *The March of the McDonalds*.

As for being ignored. Though people tried to pretend they could not see him, their jauntier steps gave it away.

People were walking differently – in time with the pipe music – and that made it almost worthwhile, but the good feeling only lasted a short time.

He was restless.

Alexander had brought back a gun. It was against the rules, but he knew he was not the only soldier who successfully smuggled home a handgun – a Webley Mk VI revolver. It had not been his, it belonged to Harry Graham, an officer who befriended the lone piper, and who had known him from joining the regiment at the start of the conflict.

Harry was another sad memory...

It happened one night when Alexander returned to the front for the third occasion. One moment Harry had been standing beside him in a trench, both having a smoke, laughing sadly as they remembered together the various blokes who'd joined when they did, and the next moment he was dead – killed instantly by a sniper's bullet.

It could have been him!

Alexander had only the vaguest notion where the sniper had fired from but he put his own life at risk by raising himself and firing back. Emptying his rifle's magazine in that general direction had been with a mixture of fear, shock and rage – and frustration, knowing that there was little chance of hitting the hidden figure. He was unlikely to have gained revenge for his departed friend. Two weeks later, hostilities ended...

He retained the empty pistol in memory of that friendship. He had known Harry Graham since the first week he joined the regiment; he'd been an officer who'd lasted longer than many others; barely twenty-one when killed, just about the same age as himself.

Inside the wooden box that housed Alexander's pipes, was a small compartment. It appeared to be part of the shape of the case and had a lid, but was not obviously an accessible space. It had been useful in the past, like before the war when he hid his money, and then his Post Office Bank book.

When he returned to civilian life, it was in that secret compartment that the gun had nestled, wrapped in a cloth. It had been a good hiding place that went unnoticed. No one stopped him. It remained hidden there when he came home, beside the bagpipes. His medal was there too, modestly kept out of sight.

However, that was not where he secreted Phoebe's necklace, the one she gave him before he left home. That was too valuable to him. It never left his person.

A month after being wed, one day on his own and feeling a bit more unsettled than normal, he removed the gun from its hiding place. There he sat with it in his hand, thinking of that horrible moment and how unjust life and death could be. He could still picture his friend as he slid down into the mud, beside him, dead! Alexander even imagined that on that fateful night he had heard the hiss of his cigarette extinguishing as it hit the watery surface.

His head was hurting again and, not really thinking, he tucked the gun in his belt, hidden by his jacket. Why did he do that? It was not for the thrill of having it on his person; in fact, his action caused more of a sad feeling – or at least that is the way it started, but it became routine from then on. Every time he left the house he took the gun, though always without bullets and quite safe.

Alexander was in a depressed state and convinced that life was dealing him a bad hand. Before, he had thought that what he did each night outside the theatre was begging. Unfortunately, now he was *convinced* it was, and he did not like it. He had tried without success to obtain other regular work. He knew that he lacked experience of skilled work, but he was getting annoyed at foremen glancing at his artist's hands and declaring him 'too soft' for labouring tasks.

He'd had to force himself to return to sketching. Four years ago it was fresh, and the means of his accumulating a reasonable sum of money, but now it was being done devoid of enthusiasm.

His carefree confidence had gone. He had become afraid of the future – afraid of not being able to support a wife and baby. He wanted a better life for himself, and Phoebe, and his unborn son, and he knew he was failing her when she needed him most. She needed him to be strong and supportive. The baby could arrive any time, and all he could do was think pityingly about himself.

And his problems were all in his head: he was not rich, but he was certainly not poor, and at least he was not drinking all his money in a public house on a Friday, the habit of many male Glaswegians.

Not only was there self-pity, the bagpipes were being neglected. He shook himself. Here was a task, a necessary one, and something physical that would also occupy a confused brain, so he took the pipes apart. The wise words he'd heard from his father so many times came to mind – *the musician must care for his instrument.* No matter how much he was disillusioned about playing them, they still needed care. The bag could dry out, and that was bad.

He disconnected the chanter, carefully took the reed from the stock and laid it on a safe surface. Similarly, the drones, placed with the reeds on the mantelpiece out of harm's way. These important parts created the sound and he had experienced how fragile they could be. Carelessness ruined them many times.

Seasoning. The magic liquid was poured into the hide bag – his father's method had always worked well, but was a sticky process. Then, soak and drain! He hung the bag at the sink where it would drip for a while.

Something had been achieved, but today being indoors was becoming oppressive. He had to get out of the house.

It was foggy and damp and had been for several days; normal for Glasgow in winter, but somewhere, up above the clouds and the fog, there was a sun, he told himself and, if it would shine, the dampness would go and make his leg feel less painful. He was only twenty-one, but felt forty years older.

The old overcoat was becoming a bit threadbare, but it still kept out the cold, and it was all he had. He put on the scarf that Phoebe knitted for him – it helped – and, though breathing cold foggy air was not pleasant, he could keep himself warm by walking into town.

At times like this, he longed for the tranquillity of

Aberloudie. It would be nice to go back home, he thought – but it couldn't happen. If he were to return, how would he earn a living? He did not want to make life harder for Phoebe. His wife and the baby would be dependent on him.

He walked along a quiet street. He knew it would be busier in town, it always was, and he could lose himself amongst the milling crowds. As he reached the Central Station he could have entered but he kept moving to stay warm. Under the Hielanman's Umbrella and over another two busy crossings and he was at Buchanan Street. The scarf was over his mouth in a vain attempt to prevent his lungs filling with foggy air.

And it was crowded in this part of the city. At the busiest spots, people jostled to hold direction and, though he was going nowhere in particular, it annoyed him having to dodge others on crowded pavements. Today, many things were annoying him.

The fog was patchy and very thick at times, forcing drivers of motor vehicles and trams to go very slowly. With the tram-tracks in the middle of the road, anyone alighting, or stepping off the pavement to board a tramcar, had to take great care. It was a dismal day. Gloomy-faced carters and bedraggled-looking horses hated being where they were because for them, in the fog, it was difficult to know where that was! There were lengthy queues at stopping points for public transport and people waited impatiently, shuffling about to keep a little warmth. Wherever they were destined, in this weather their journey would be long and slow.

Alexander just kept moving, but he was now questioning why he came out!

The clanging gave indication of a tramcar's approach but, in the fog, until the large glowing shape came closer it was difficult to tell from which direction. He let one pass before attempting to cross Argyle Street. He listened for vehicle sounds and looked for lights, and was ready to move rapidly if surprised, but the strain of peering into the fog was not helping his throbbing headache and now that he had slowed pace he was feeling the chill. Though he had his overcoat buttoned and the scarf still in use, it could not stop the cold and damp reaching his body.

He had no intention of purchasing anything but going into one of the large department stores would take him out of this nasty weather for a time – but not the stores in Buchanan Street. They were posh and not for the likes of him – these places were for moneyed people. He was remaining in Argyle Street, crossing over to the Royal Polytechnic, the Poly: a large warehouse that was more suitable for ordinary folk. There, he could wander without feeling uncomfortable.

Inside, he walked around, forcing himself to appear interested in the assortment of items displayed on counters and in cabinets; up the stairs, viewing the variety of goods on each level and back down again. He felt warmer, but not better in himself.

He'd stopped and looked longingly at warm overcoats. "Could I help you with your choice, sir?"

was the question asked in the Gent's Department. Alexander had hurried away from that disappointed sales assistant who'd guessed, from the look of the coat the man was wearing, that a replacement was sorely needed – it had seemed a sure sale!

Leaving the confines of the store, Alexander cautiously and hesitantly crossed back over the street again, and arrived outside the Argyll Arcade. Years ago, when he arrived from Aberloudie, this was where he had attempted to entertain the great Glasgow public, and had an early taste of disappointment.

He entered the wide passage of the Arcade. Was there anything here to hold his attention? Initially, he resisted the lure of the many jeweller's windows, for what was there to see that he could buy? Nothing, but the Arcade was more pleasant than being outside. In there the lighting of the multitude of large glass windows made it surprisingly bright, even though it was open at both ends and the fog swirled through. These lights made it seem less cold too. He slowed and forced himself to look at each window for a moment and, as he did, the next window always seemed to sparkle brighter than the last. For those with money who wished to purchase expensive jewellery this was the place to visit.

Ah... Here was a window to gaze at for hours if you had little to do, and it was so different from the others. Who could resist admiring the display in the Clyde Model Dockyard? Young or old this was a place to linger. Alexander looked and wondered how anyone could have the skill and patience to achieve the incredible detail of the miniature ships and trains in that window. If he'd had money to spend, this would be where he would spend it.

I will buy toys for my little son. Will Phoebe give me a son? I would like that, but...

The window display sparked an idea – subjects for drawing, other than portraits. He could go to the Broomielaw in the future, sit at the quayside and draw scenes of the river. But could he sell drawings of boats and the workings of the Clyde? No, he concluded, I would be wasting my time.

He moved on. More jewellers. He was becoming mesmerised by the dazzling displays of precious stones, and didn't like the feeling. He was also despising the type of person who could walk into one of these shops and afford to buy the stuff, the type of people who were better off than he was. Everyone was better off than he was! Helped by the cold seeping into his bones, he felt bitter and jealous.

He was approaching Buchanan Street and almost at the other end of this shopping parade. There had been no change to the weather in the short time that he had been wandering. Visibility outside still poor, and fog continuing to swirl.

He stopped yet again, reluctant to leave the protection of the space and stood looking at the last window, full of shining, sparkling objects.

Imagine having a timepiece like that... A fob watch... That was something he had never owned ...and the jewellery! If he had been rich he would have surprised Phoebe with one of those sparkling rings, but she would have been shocked if he had. Probably cause the baby to be too early! That at least was a good reason not to buy one, he decided wryly, but again he questioned how anyone could pay that money.

His gaze focussed beyond the window display and took in the activity inside the shop, or maybe, the lack of it. Normally the centre of Glasgow was busy, or very busy, but it was a foggy Monday. No one out today who does not need to be. So, why am I?

To be in this fog was not pleasant and was certainly a deterrent to shoppers, especially those looking for fancy jewellery – or whatever else they sold here. Inside the shop, no customers, only one plump, middle-aged man standing bent over the counter, loosening the top of a small canvas bag. He was opening it and pouring out what looked, to Alexander's eyes, to be uncut diamonds, big ones. Alexander continued to watch, fascinated. With the aid of an eyeglass, the jeweller did a magnified inspection, with each little piece of glass handled carefully and, Alexander thought, lovingly – and there was still only one person in the shop.

What if I...? Somehow, Alexander Findlay was unable to stop himself as he stepped into the shop entrance and opened the door. A tinkling-bell sounded as he went inside. The plump man looked up for a moment and removed the eyeglass then, laying it down on the counter, gently swept the precious objects together in one well-practised movement, and looked up again – to find a handgun pointing straight at his nose!

"Jist pit them a' in the bag again," grunted Alexander. The man did not hesitate. "...And turn around," was the next grunted instruction, and the man did so. Alexander grabbed the bag, pushed the useless gun back into his belt, opened the door and ran out as the tinkling bell sounded feebly again.

He hurriedly dodged, and weaved, and pushed passed the various people meandering aimlessly around in the arcade, and made for the entrance. Walking quickly, he found himself outside in the busy street. He hesitated and then halted, suddenly realising what he had just done.

"Stop him – stop!" came from behind. It was the jeweller who had realised he was no longer in danger. He had rushed to his doorway but did not want to abandon his shop.

"Stop! Thief!" was the yell. "Look – that's him, there!" and the hand pointed at Alexander, standing frozen to the spot.

A few other voices started shouting. Some onlookers near Alexander took notice, and came towards him. He backed away and started moving again, the pain in his leg causing him to limp. The bystanders were tentative with the uncertainty that occurs in these circumstances. He dodged them with head lowered, and kept going, as another cry rang out from the jeweller.

"...And watch out, he's got a gun!"

The warning caused a few Glasgow citizens, who were about to be brave, to shrink back rapidly and give him free passage. He ran off, thankful for the fog – then came the sound of the police whistle. That made Alexander move faster. Taking his life in his hands, he ran over the road, frightening a horse and a dozy carter who were both having difficulty seeing and had strayed to the wrong side of the foggy street.

People kept stepping in his path. A few disgruntled curses came his way as he almost knocked over several who were determined not to change direction or give way. He reached the next corner, went along the lane and just kept moving – anywhere to take him away from the scene.

He was back on a busy street and slowed to a fast walking pace to avoid attracting attention. Must keep moving, he told himself as he crossed another busy road, gradually working his way towards the Central Station. He could not see anyone following, but he could see little anyway in the fog.

Why? Why? Why? The word kept repeating in his head. It had not been an act of bravery this time, had it? He had just been bloody stupid! What would Phoebe say? No, she must not know! She would never forgive him...

Back at the Arcade, the 'poor distraught' jeweller had gone back into the shop to think. There was no getting away from it – the old ticker was beating a bit faster than normal, otherwise no harm done this time. He smiled. This sort of thing had happened before, many years back and though he had taken a bit of a beating then, in the end, he had profited, and with any luck, he could pull the same trick again, so it was his sincere wish that the idiot of a thief wouldn't be caught.

He had lost ten of his best uncut diamonds but, with a little adjustment to a few pieces of paper, as far as the police and insurance company were concerned 'ten' would become 'twenty-five'. A phone call to a friend at the Glasgow Herald was about to ensure he would receive some good publicity too.

"There is little use in having friends if you don't use them to advantage," he muttered to himself then, looking up, saw the shape at the door.

"Ah, yes, Constable, I'm coming..." He hobbled over to unlock the door for the police officer. He had to make it look good! "It's the leg, Officer. He could have broken it... I shall have to sit down. Give me a minute... It's been such a shock!"

Alexander was still furtively looking around, as he had been doing ever since he slowed pace. As usual, the concourse of the Central Station was busy, with everyone apparently in a hurry. No one seemed interested in anyone else in a place like this, being concerned only with moving on. That was exactly why he was there.

The fog had aided his departure. In there it was less thick and though still bitterly cold, after the rush to leave the scene and the panic, he was hot and feverish. He looked around once more, ready to sprint off again if anyone appeared to be still chasing. No, he had not been followed into the concourse so, thankfully, he would make his way homewards at a slower rate.

As he walked along, he smiled to himself, and then started laughing aloud. What have I done? He felt invigorated! It was wrong but – God, I feel good!

The elation was momentary. Suddenly, he could not stop shaking and the explosions were in his head again. The horrors of his previous four years were back with him – the images, restarting. Earlier in the day had been a mild attack, a warning, and he should have recognised the signs. This was much worse. He couldn't drive the memories away. Maybe they would always be with him. It had not been as bad as this for months. He felt dreadful...

Shaking hands struggled to open the door with the key, and his sight had gone strange. Phoebe was back, and she could not help being concerned when he entered. He looked as dreadful as he felt but he insisted that he would be all right – it was just a bad turn and wasn't new. It would go away. He lay down. It would pass...

...And after a time it did. Lying on the bed, he was relieved when his head cleared – but then he thought of what he had just done.

I, Alexander Findlay, am a thief.

He had never stolen anything in his life – now, he would go to jail! What about Phoebe – and the baby? Oh my God! It was wrong, he knew, but with these guilty feelings was also an exciting tingle... The diamonds! He had just stolen diamonds! In his pocket – real gems! They would be worth a lot of money, probably a fortune!

"We need food," said Phoebe. "Will you be alright if I leave you for a short time?"

He did feel better, but hid the fact. He nodded feebly. The moment Phoebe closed the outside door he was on his feet. Wishing he had never taken it, he quickly returned the gun to its original hiding place once more, in the bagpipes' case.

What about the ill-gotten gains, the wee bits of shiny glass? What should he do with them? What would happen when the jeweller gives the police a description? That man saw his face – did anyone notice the limp? ...But he was not the only person in Glasgow with a limp. What if the jeweller had been in one of the theatre queues? Could he even have sketched his wife?

The police could be appearing soon and they would take the house apart, so he would have to get rid of the diamonds – and quickly! Selling them was for the future, he decided, although he didn't know anyone who'd buy them. A good temporary hiding place was needed now.

He was not thinking straight, but he would have to be quick – before Phoebe returned. It couldn't be beside the gun? If they found the weapon... Where could he put them? The tartan cover for the pipes, still lying loose at the back of the chair caught his eye and suddenly, he had the answer!

The bagpipes, inside the bagpipes! No one would think to look in the bag. It was still drying out and, if he put them there now, the pieces of precious glass would lodge in the creases. They'd stick, and with the bag left hanging there in full view, who would notice?

The instrument, that had been carried by him

during some of the worst moments of his life when comrades were falling around him, was about to become his salvation – ten uncut diamonds would be inserted in a set of bagpipes!

One by one, he dropped the stones through a drone hole. He had to hope that, with the chanter replaced, the diamonds would not move or touch the reed. They would stay there until he could decide what was best to do. Next week, if the police stayed away, he would retrieve them.

Then he had second thoughts.

Maybe they should have been thrown away. If he'd got rid of the evidence then no one would know. It would not clear his conscience, but...

No, he decided, that would be stupid if they are worth good money, particularly after all the trouble and, when sold, he could buy things for Phoebe that she would like – a nice thought that made the theft seem more acceptable. But if he were to sell them he would have to find a contact, someone he could trust that could help him find a buyer.

He had given himself plenty to worry about! That night he cuddled very close to Phoebe...

At daylight, Alexander rose, exhausted. It felt like he had not slept a wink. The bad dreams made it seem that way.

Tired though he was, he felt compelled to leave the house; he had to get out. He had to find out what was happening at the Arcade. He had heard that a criminal always returns to the scene of the crime, and he recognised the feeling because he was that criminal!

He also knew that if he did not go out immediately, he might never cross the doorstep again. He had to go. It would only be to look around the area. He would be very careful, of course, and if anyone did recognise him he would be ready to run again – but that was unlikely, he told himself.

As for the gun, never again. He wished the pistol was not in the house, but when he thought of his dead friend and the reason for having it, he left it where it was.

Phoebe must never find out!

He was agitated, but had to maintain the pretence and play calm, so a kiss for a dear wife... She was feeling unwell and back in bed at his insistence, but smiled at his affectionate pat of the bulge that was beginning to show – then her expression changed to apprehension...

Why that strange look, he asked himself, it was almost as if she knew...

At the end of the street, he jumped onto a tram that was starting to move away. His leg gave a twinge. The fog, which lingered for many days, had cleared but was replaced by a horrible sleety rain that had very quickly dampened his clothing, so he appreciated the shelter of the tram. Not many people getting on and off today so, the tram speed increased and, with limited stops the journey seemed short.

The centre of town was not far. As the vehicle slowed down under the bridge at the Central

Station, he stood up and stepped onto the platform, ready to jump. He intended to dodge through the traffic and walk along the pavement on the far side. He would decide there which way to go, and he would have shelter under the bridge.

He jumped too casually, and stumbled, painfully jarring his leg and startling the horse pulling the fully-laden cart alongside the tram. Annoyed at himself for almost falling over, he had to move smartly to avoid the horse. The carter yelled a curse as the horse and cart veered towards the pavement and Alexander leapt aside to behind the stationary tram. He had to get out of reach of that man's whip. He expected to feel its sting on the back of his neck as he swung round onto the other tram track. He glanced back. Made it!

He turned, relieved, a smug grin on his face – and then heard the frantic clanging...

Yesterday, Alexander had been afraid that the police would be visiting his house in the near future. His fear proved correct because they were, but he could not have imagined the reason would be for anything other than his theft...

Phoebe refused to believe what the police constable said, though he could not have been more gentle or sympathetic in conveying the unpleasant news.

The officer was much older than Phoebe, soon to retire and looking forward to the moment, because he hated this part of the job. His sergeant considered him the best when it came to announcing bad news to relatives, so nowadays landed him with the task whenever he was on shift. After countless number of times, he should have been hardened to it, but no, he had not. He knew that this sad duty would never be easy for anyone.

"No, no, no..." she insisted, "...it can't possibly be my Alexander! He only went into town a short time ago, for a walk. He'll be back in a moment, you'll see..."

The police officer hated it when they refused to believe.

"No, no... He can't be dead," she continued to insist, but he was, though it took a visit to the City Mortuary to convince her...

Alexander Findlay's death made the newspapers the following day, and initially it was to be a simple story: an accident that delayed traffic for a long time – just an unfortunate incident involving a Glasgow pedestrian.

The words were to be run-of-the-mill, until an enthusiastic young reporter discovered that the dead man was an ex-soldier, with a past – a glorious past. After some personal research by that reporter, enough detail was obtained about the dead man to add the essential personal touch to the story and he knew the details would delight his editor. 'It is having the personal touch that brings a story to life!' the young reporter was often told, '...even for death.'

The new front page became a double heading. UNTIMELY DEATH OF WAR HERO; and CITY JEWELLER ROBBED AT GUNPOINT, with the two stories sitting side by side!

When they had approached her for the personal details, Phoebe had been too upset to talk about her husband. Anyway, Alexander never told her the gory details of his time in uniform, she had no real knowledge of his war years; so, the newspaper reporter obtained information from Alexander's regimental record and printed that – a few important extra lines, together with a grainy photograph.

That day was one of the few that Phoebe bought a newspaper and learned a little more of her husband's bravery. It had been plain to her, when he was alive, that her Alexander suffered the after-effects of his war; he had been unable to hide it, but he had been silent about being a 'hero'.

Reading a copy of that same newspaper was a certain jeweller, *'who had suffered terribly at the hands of a villain'*. He was delighted to see the write-up his friend had manipulated for him. His hope was that it would encourage some extra custom along the way and, even if only out of curiosity, bring people to look. It might help sell the goods, and that would make him very happy.

He glanced at the article next to his heartfelt story, then looked a little closer. The face – seemed a bit familiar, a bit of a resemblance to ...but no, it was a grainy photograph, and anyway the man, knocked down by a tramcar and killed, he had been a hero; the person who robbed him was a vicious criminal...

For many weeks after his funeral, Alexander's bagpipes remained where he had left them – in bits. Phoebe could not bear to move them. Seeing them caused tears. The pipes had always been a large part of Alexander's life, sadly however, they were also a reminder of his misdemeanour...

...And she knew! Alexander talked in his sleep!

One day, she plucked up courage and decided to wash the tartan cover and improve its appearance. It did, but only slightly.

The bag still hung over the sink in front of the window. It could not remain there forever, so tearfully, she lifted it down onto the table. She replaced the tartan cover, and then brought the drones and reeds over. She had watched her dear departed do this many times during their short marriage. The reassembly of his bagpipes was done with care, exactly as she affectionately remembered him do.

She could not play them, nor did she want to, but neither did she want anyone outside the family to have them. They held a terrible secret that she learned from her husband's sleepy ramblings – one that she was having difficulty accepting!

He could not have... She had tried to convince herself that it did not happen. Why would he do something like this when all that money was in his pipe-case? That, she would never know.

Much later, when she was able to think of her husband without bursting into tears, she realised how fortunate she was financially. If Alexander had saved his money in a bank account, she could have been destitute. She would have received very little of it. She was only a wife, a female, an expectant mother, with few legal rights to a husband's possessions. Ridiculous though it seemed, such was the law of the land.

As it was, all his money was there for her, in hard cash, in the bagpipe-case. When she counted how much, she was amazed. They had been quite frugal in their way of life together and he, personally, had spent very little. He had been earning a lot each evening without even bothering to count it, and it was stacked away with the bagpipes.

Good for you, Alexander... Thanks! If only...

She was still working and intended carrying on as long as she could. It kept her mind occupied.

...And the bagpipes? They would remain under the bed. That was what Alexander would have wanted. He had loved these bagpipes. As she thought of that, she remembered, now and again, being foolishly jealous of how he had cared for them. He had tended them so lovingly – but they were only bagpipes.

Now, the one person who would be given them in the future, and would play them proudly, would be the son she was about to have – Alexander's son – and she would be calling him Hamish.

13

2009
Give us a clue...

'David, my boy, you are in the wrong job,' his grandfather had often told him. "You are a born actor." To which his dad's mumbled comment usually would be, 'He's a blooming ham!'

David was certainly hamming it up now!

In his hands – 'Treasure Island', and the folded paper that was found between the pages. He was in control and in his grandparent's loft, putting on a special performance for his mother and father – and milking it!

Tom was in no position to criticise though. Moments before, he'd been the ham! As the folded paper fell to the floor, "Take care, young man!" he'd wailed dramatically. "If it is the Black Spot – Heaven forfend! Misfortune will befall every man-jack of us."

Gillian gave a few claps of ironic applause. "Maybe we could have two spotlights installed?" she suggested with a sigh. "Now, please... Enough nonsense!"

"Should we charge admission?" said David. He sat on the stool and unfolded the piece of paper teasingly, "...And sell ice-creams."

"Give me it! I'll read it!" Tom grunted, reaching for the paper.

David jumped back and knocked over the stool.

"Grow up – both of you! That's enough." said Gillian despairingly.

"Is everything all right up there?" shouted Angus from the foot of the ladder. "Has someone fallen?"

"Sorry, Dad," Tom shouted. "It's David being an idiot..."

David decided it was time. He would read it out. When his dad tried to see it, he hid it.

"David... Please. Just read!" Gillian instructed. She was getting irritated by the pair of them.

"Right then, are you sitting comfortably? ...Then we'll begin."

"David!" There was now menace in Gillian's voice.

So, at last...

"Pass the time with a little rhyme.
The clue you'll see underneath this tree.
Do not be fooled, there's only one,
But searching's such a lot of fun.
It's a tree for gullible people..."

"Hmmm, yes..." said Gillian, nodding intelligently.

Beth and Angus were waiting patiently at the foot of the ladder.

They'd come upstairs sensing that events were moving forward. Sensibly, Angus had fetched chairs. The search above might take some time, so they were sitting, reading magazines during the silent spells.

"Down there, did you hear what David said?" Tom shouted to his parents.

"What?" was the reply from down below – obviously not...

David stood at the opening and read it aloud once more, looking down expectantly at his grandparents – only to see two blank faces staring back up at him.

"No matter," said Gillian. "Anyway, we'll have to stop soon. I'll go down and get cleaned up a bit." She started down the ladder.

"We'll carry on a little longer," said Tom.

"Agreed. We can't give up yet," said David. "We've hardly moved any of this lot."

"There's so much damn rubbish!" Tom added in too loud a voice. "We could get rid of so much more if your grandmother would stop interfering!"

"What was that, Tom?" came the voice from below.

"I'm bringing the clue with me, Beth," Gillian shouted down diplomatically, and as her head vanished, "We'll have it solved, by the time they come down, I'll bet."

"You must be ready for a cup of tea, Gillian," said Beth.

Tom gave a sigh of relief. Thank goodness his mother hadn't heard him properly.

"Tea's just what I need," said Gillian. "It is dry work up there," and the chat continued as they went downstairs.

The two males in the airless loft heard the offer – tea. They hesitated, and looked at each other. It was tempting – but they would soldier on. It was a male thing, martyrdom...

"Wow! Look at this, David!" exclaimed Tom. "The old Dansette Record Player – and a pile of records! LP's and 78s!"

"A Dansette Record Player? Oh, come on now, Dad... A bit old hat. Does it play CDs? Does it download stuff from the internet? Could I have it in my pocket when I'm waiting for a bus? Can it pick up Sky TV? Could I...?"

"All right, you're not interested– but this would be a treasure to some people," mumbled Tom, enthusiasm dampened, "...Me for one."

"Chest expanders and dumb-bells! Whose were these – Gran's or Grandad's?"

"And look! The tape-recorder. Wo-ho-ho! Wonder if it still works?" Tom's enthusiasm was renewed, "...and old tapes. I am taking this lot home. Bet you won't recognise anyone on these recordings, David."

Downstairs in the kitchen, the kettle had boiled and Angus was making the brew. The clue was laid aside for the moment. Gillian lifted mugs from their wooden peg-holder onto a tray.

Beth moved the jelly-pan off the table and onto the dresser. "Must ask Tom to put this in the loft again," she said. "I hope he leaves it somewhere more accessible so that next time he'll find it quicker. Imagine forgetting where he put it the last time! He really should try and remember – and look at the bashes!"

Gillian was about to point out that poor Tom was not the one who put the jelly pan away last time, but bit back the words – Beth was getting a little confused. Anyway, no use falling out with mother-in-law over a silly comment. Tom could defend himself.

Beth had been busy and, yet again, the jelly pan had served its purpose. A large quantity of jams and jellies was the result. Their own garden had yielded a good crop of usable fruit this year, to add to the sizable quantity purchased.

If asked, Beth would claim that jam-making was her forte, but to be fair to Angus, recently the jam and jelly-making process would not have been a success without his very active involvement.

The bought-fruit was carried home by him. He washed and sterilised most of the empty jars that Beth used on each occasion over the years: jars that he fetched annually from the loft. It was also Angus who'd been to the supermarket, doing a 'bulk buy' for the enormous quantity of sugar that his wife needed for the process, and rushed out several times for jam-pot covers when Beth realised that there were more filled pots than available covers.

Stirring of the bubbling concoction was a shared duty, though Angus felt he did more than his share. He didn't enjoy the stickiness of the outside of the pots when the jam had been poured into the jars – by him – particularly when it ran down the sides and had to be cleaned off – by him. Oh yes, he also had to prepare the labels, printing the appropriate names and dates as shouted out by Beth and, like jam-pot covers, it seemed no matter how many were bought, there was always a shortage.

Privately though, he had to admit that he would not have been doing anything else of importance anyway. However, the serious consequence, at the end of this now traditional process, was Angus testing and consuming it. He had no complaint about that.

"You haven't yet tried any of my efforts, have you Gillian?" said Beth, producing an over-generous quantity of newly-made pancakes on a fancy plate and nodding towards the fresh jam.

"You really must have worked awfully hard," commented Gillian, having a mouthful, "...the jam, it tastes delicious."

"Oh, I manage," sighed Beth. "I just have to roll my sleeves up and get on with it. What else can one do? I often ask myself, who else would do it?"

Angus raised an eyebrow, and sipped his tea.

They had more pancakes – too many, and some more tea, and sat relaxed, until eventually, Gillian went into the hall.

"Wake up, you two – rest break over," she shouted up to the remaining members of her family. "That's it for today." It was time to go.

Tom laid down the record he was holding, having been waylaid by these and concerned with nothing else for the last half-hour. All the records still looked in good condition even though old. Obviously now obsolete as far as being able to purchase. The one in his hand was ancient: a long player, 33 rpm, undamaged with its cover in perfect nick. Perry Como fans must still exist ... Would it sell on eBay?

There were lots waiting that he had only glanced at. A stack of vinyl discs, 45rpm, and ...wait for it – a pile of old 78rpm, and none broken. Wow! They could be worth a fortune.

Could he sell 78s on eBay? No, too heavy for posting. It might be easier at a car boot sale. The queue would be right round the car park when the word got out about these... Look at the titles – classics from the sixties. David won't have heard of them. When they were bought, even I was a baby...

The Dansette Record Player and some of the records, he would take these, provided there was no objection from dear mother. It would be fun to try them at the weekend, and have a real live good-old Top of the Pops.

Why ever did they stop 'Top of the Pops'? Now that was a telly programme to watch... Come to think of it... Whatever happened to the old TV sets Mum and Dad used to have, a black and white, and an old colour one? Oh! He looked at the stack in the middle of the floor and there was a horrible feeling in the pit of his stomach! Please God, don't tell me they are still in the middle of that pile!

14

1929-1944
Just have a wee go, son...

Hamish was turning out to be a disappointment to his mother. She made it plain. No matter how hard he tried, he could do very little that was right in her eyes. At least that is how he felt.

In Phoebe's mind, her now long-gone much-loved spouse, Alexander, the father that Hamish had never known, had become a mythical figure.

"Your father was a wonderful man, you know, and you'll never be a patch on him. He was a real man; a man who fought for his country."

After all the years without him, the tales of heroic deeds that she would tell to the young lad were of pure fiction and each tale a little grander with the telling, and it did nothing for the morale of the young boy to be compared to this ever-more-perfect departed spouse of Phoebe's. Aspiring to be as good as a father should be normal in a lad, but what use was there in trying to match the standards of a man so wonderful?

Tough though it was, he suffered in silence,

appreciating the strain his mother was under and the struggles she'd endured for him. Many years of crushing comments were tolerated before he became brave enough to talk back. He was almost twelve when that happened.

"My dad might have been a hero, but I'm not, and I dinna want to be – an' you canny make me!" he told her one day – and then felt bad at having said it.

That was when she realised what she had been doing. It had been silly of her. Her husband may have been a war hero, but he was flawed, like most men – as he had proved. From then, if she felt like talking about 'her Alexander', she avoided comparing.

Was it too late to let Hamish know she really loved him? She feared it might be, and losing one dearly-loved male had been hard enough.

"Oh, Hamish, please forgive me!"

Wrong though she'd been, good did come from it. Unintentionally, she had toughened him up; he was certainly not a 'mammy's boy' and thankfully, Hamish appreciated her new attitude.

Life after Alexander had not been easy for Phoebe...

After he died, she'd had no urge to discover more of her young husband's army life. The limited knowledge from the newspaper article was accepted as sufficient, and those few printed words enough to spark the imagination that fired the tales told to Hamish.

The bitterness that pained her came from

Alexander's thieving; only once as far as she knew, but it was wrong, very wrong. On top of that was the way she learned of it. It made her feel guilty – stealing his secret thoughts!

Talking in his sleep had happened ever since he returned from the fighting. He would mumble fearfully in the night about things that she did not want to understand, that she would never repeat – certainly not to Hamish – and the night before he was killed was the worst. That night, he was really troubled...

But it was a blessing Phoebe had been aware of the hiding place. Those hidden savings made life for her and Hamish a bit easier. Phoebe dreaded to think how bad it might have been without that money. Of course, there were the diamonds too, but they were where Alexander left them, still in the bagpipes and would remain there, untouched, as far as she was concerned. She wanted no part of that.

Anyway, what could she have done with them – taken them to the police? His thieving would have become public, and how would she have faced her neighbours, or Hamish's pals and their parents? What would they have thought? Maybe she would tell Hamish one day, she decided, when the lad was old enough to know what to do.

She used Alexander's savings sparingly but though a sizable sum it did not last long. Inevitably, when there was little remaining, life became very difficult for the young mother bringing up a child on her own. A young son at school, needing clothes to keep the cold out and food to keep him healthy, very often meant little for her.

These were hard years for both, and out of necessity, Phoebe tackled all sort of work. Occasionally, it was back at the theatre, but only at holidays because they employed someone else when she left to have her baby. The jobs were menial, but mother and son survived. She coped, with a little help now and again from parents who could ill-afford any niceties themselves – she really appreciated that.

When there was no money left in the pipe-case, there was no longer a reason to open it, so it was left under the bed holding the bagpipes containing the diamonds. It became a well-hidden secret about which Phoebe felt only shame. She could talk about it to no one and even when it seemed the right time to share the secret with Hamish, she hesitated.

To her son, his father was a hero, and she was the one who'd told him that. To her, Alexander was also a thief.

Would telling Hamish about the diamonds implicate him? Worse, she would be saying she'd been lying all those years! What would he think of her then? It might even lead him the same way as his father – into a life of crime...!

Hamish had always been eager to be older, and for his body to catch up with his brain. The young lad appreciated how his mum had struggled, and his wish was to reach the age to leave school. He would start work and help her and only then would life become more pleasant for both of them.

Time passed too slowly for the boy, but eventually, the day did come and, at last, he was working. No longer a young lad in his mother's eyes, he became the breadwinner with a job in the shipyard. Now, a man, and learning all about adult life.

Was this the time to share the secret with him? Phoebe was undecided. Surely no one would be looking for these diamonds after all these years. They'd be given up for lost, she was certain, probably worth a lot of money, money that would be of benefit to both of them. Should she tell Hamish?

Yes, I will!

Now... she could have been forthright and said to his face, but she thought that there might be another way; if he were to find the diamonds for himself... as if by accident?

"Why don't you have a wee blow at your daddy's pipes?" she suggested.

"No, that's not for me," was the response.

"He would have been really proud to see you now, an' you workin' too. The big lad that you are – with a braw pair o' lungs; that's what he always said was needed to play the bagpipes."

"No, I am not doin' it. At work, they'd just laugh at me."

"But son, you never know, you might like playin' them. Maybe if you just opened the box..."

"I said no, Ma!"

So that approach did not worked. However, she had no intention of giving up and would try on many occasions after that. "Just a wee go, son. You could be great – like your da!" but he continued to refuse to be persuaded.

After he started working Hamish continued to live with his mother. She had always been there for him, with advice – and criticism. Over the years, he had tolerated her chatter, good and bad, but, after being in the job for a while, he stopped listening to her. No, not quite correct ...he stopped *hearing* her.

His job, when he began in the shipyard, was riveter's mate. That involved heating rivets to red-hot in a brazier, and skilfully tossing them to the riveter. With a pneumatic hammer, the riveter crashed home the little bits of metal that would hold the ship together.

In no time at all and despite using wads of cotton-wool in his ears, Hamish could hear very little. At home, communication with his mother became stilted.

Fortunately, by the time he became a fully-fledged riveter, he had also become an expert lip reader, and that is when he became friendly with a girl in the next close, very friendly. She had lovely lips, and soon they began to talk of getting married. Well ...Meg Crichton talked about it. To be honest though, she wasn't sure that when Hamish nodded 'yes' he'd actually been looking and understood – but he hadn't actually said no, had he?

So Hamish Findlay, qualified riveter, became a man committed to marriage.

'World War Two' interfered temporarily when he received call-up papers. He did not volunteer like his father. When conscripted, he simply conformed – to then be told that someone who cannot hear the Regimental Sergeant Major yelling in his ear was not wanted by the army – or any of the other branches of the forces.

Hamish was not sure whether to be angry, disappointed, or relieved. They would not let him fight, so, it was back to the shipyard. There, he had a job.

"The yard'll soon be buildin' warships, so, I'll be doin' ma bit for the war effort," he told a very disappointed mother.

"Your father, he wasn't rejected, you know..."

That slipped out, so it was fortunate for Phoebe's relationship with her son that Hamish was looking elsewhere at that moment. He did not 'see' her say it.

At least Meg was pleased that he was not going away. Wedding plans could continue and give her something to look forward to, something other than the depressing news about war. She was a tracer in the shipyard, so she and Hamish shared the common bond of shipbuilding.

Along with the many hundreds of others who worked in shipyards on the upper part of the Clyde, it was a relief arriving at the gates each morning to find the yard had not been targeted on a previous night's bombing raid and that it was still there for their war effort to continue. In the future, the inhabitants and buildings farther downriver would not be so fortunate.

Though working with a riveting team was noisy, and grimy, and uncomfortable, Hamish was grateful to be part of it. Pleased to go home dirty and tired each evening and be able to tell himself that he was as good as his father.

His mother's attitude had softened towards him. "My Hamish, he does a real man's job," she was now telling the neighbours...

Meg's work was considerably less physical. Looking out at the cold wintery Glasgow weather from the comfort of the Tracing Office made her appreciate how easy it was for her, and how good her work was. A wage earner and eager to wed, she was putting away money for the future, for when the family would come along. She wanted her wee ones to have a good start in life.

Hamish was less enthusiastic. He could not remember agreeing to be wed! It was two years before he submitted totally and eventually, they did marry and, in 1942, the knot was tied.

They rented their own wee room and kitchen, only two streets away from Phoebe. However, although it was nice to have money in the bank, as the war had progressed they found almost everything limited by rationing. Money did not help when all the coupons were used, so Meg's savings were barely touched.

They had a wedding meal at home, splashing out on the food, and everyone reckoned that the corned beef on the sandwiches was the very best that Fray Bentos had ever packed into a tin.

On that day, Phoebe managed to surprise

Hamish. As part of her wedding present to the happy couple, his mother passed on his father's bagpipes.

"Thanks. Just what I was hoping for, Mother," he said, but did not mean it. For a moment though, he actually wondered that if he did try to play the bagpipes, would he be able to hear them – but he never did get round to putting that to the test.

Meg said, "What a lovely thought, Mrs Findlay," and did mean it.

When all the visitors went away and it was only Hamish and Meg left in their own wee home, the bagpipes were put in a safe place, under the bed where – as far as Hamish was concerned – they could stay and gather dust!

The war continued. Hamish was not fighting in a far distant land, he was living at home and working in Glasgow, however, there was an occasion, during September 1944, when it seemed that the enemy had found out, and targeted him personally.

It was late in the war and visits by enemy bombers to the area had become rare, so the air-raid siren sounded only occasionally. One night, when it did, it was stormy and cold and, due to the continuing blackout, very dark. Meg and Hamish were in bed together.

Being deaf, and a sound sleeper, Hamish was utterly oblivious to the siren sounding – he would have slept on. It was a blessing that Meg's hearing was good because, if Hamish had been on his own, he would have been a goner – his side of the bed was flattened!

None of the tenants, who then huddled together down in the cold washhouse, were harmed but, with an unexploded stray bomb up above – as the Air-Raid Warden informed them, they'd have to move. With other endangered residents from adjoining buildings, they were herded out and moved a safe distance away, into the local church hall.

However, it was not a bomb – a chimney-stack had collapsed! Badly maintained, it had blown over in the gale and crashed through the roof, landing partly on the bed – Hamish's side.

But, a bomb or not, returning to their own top-floor home would not be possible for a long time. It was open to the elements and uninhabitable, so they finished up along the road in Phoebe's place, and crowded though it felt, with Phoebe, Meg, and Hamish all together, they were at least safe and dry.

Salvaging some of their goods from the damaged tenement on the following day was awkward. Thanks to help from the Fire Brigade, and the Police, they succeeded in saving a case of clothes from the wardrobe, and some personal items. These were crammed into a battered and dusty case.

The bits and pieces included: a photo album, some cheap jewellery, a wooden piggy bank that Hamish made years ago, the trusty alarm clock that was still ticking away, and a second-hand copy of Treasure Island that Meg had bought for Hamish as a wedding gift – a book that he had yet to read.

As for the bagpipes, they were surprisingly undamaged, still in the case that had never been opened since Phoebe closed it many years ago, safe under Meg's side of the bed. Hamish wanted to leave them there but Meg disagreed. She asked a firefighter, very nicely, to lift up what remained of the bed to retrieve them.

"Sentimental value," she whispered to the man, as Hamish reluctantly carried them out...

For Meg and Hamish, sleeping together had been normal. It continued at Phoebe's but now, with his mother in the close vicinity, intimacy for the young couple was awkward. In their own house, even though Hamish could be tired after a hard day's work, a little coaxing by Meg had usually proved effective. Not now. Something had changed. Now her attempts to encourage him were having no success. Doing what was natural for a loving married couple was happening rarely, and if so, guiltily.

He was scared that his mother might hear, Meg had concluded, and accepted that having a family did not have to happen immediately.

Finding that she could actually be pregnant came as a surprise. Should she say? No, not yet, she decided, she'd wait until certain but it didn't stop her eagerly looking forward to telling him. He will be so pleased – our own baby – a proper family. We'll have to get another home, can't stay here with Phoebe, not when baby arrives...!

Several weeks later, when she was sure, the message passed silently between them as he read her lips and understood. The reaction was not as Meg expected. "What... me? ...A father? Oh no..." He was genuinely shocked, and Meg was sadly disappointed – then shortly afterwards discovered the reason!

Someone else had become important in Hamish's life – a certain Bella Roberts: loved by Hamish – but very quickly hated by his wife, and his mother. 'That floozy – Bella Roberts!' became the expression used – if they deigned to talk about her.

Once again, the die was badly cast in the Findlay family game – a child developing in Meg that would soon become obvious, a child that would be destined to enter life like its male parent – fatherless, thanks to Bella Roberts. She stole the dad – the floozy!

Bella Roberts, like Hamish, was deaf, and had secretly been teaching him sign language. Now, as everyone knows, that means a lot of hand-usage but, with them, the hands had strayed in unexpected and very enjoyable ways. For them, it was definitely the 'language of love'...

When Hamish told them, Meg found it hard to believe; his mother was even more shocked. He could not remain sharing the house with them – that was obvious, and so, taking the few items of clothing that he had at his mother's house, Hamish said goodbye to an irate and tearful Meg, and went to live with Bella.

Not far to walk because her home was just along the road and round the corner, and maybe too close for comfort and, sure enough, there was more than one occasion of screaming and shouting in the street, when Bella accidently met the ever-expanding Meg, or Phoebe Findlay. Bella could not hear the vile things they said to her, but she got the message.

Staying so close could not continue. Someone would be murdered!

"They'll be goin' soon and it's to be Australia, I've heard," was the gossip picked up by Phoebe from someone along the road. "They say ye can get there on the cheap..."

It was clear to Hamish they would have to go somewhere – anywhere – far away from his wife, and mother. Luckily, a pal at the shipyard knew 'a man', but it would take a little time to sort out. A place in Govan was coming up, for rent. Meanwhile, Bella Roberts and Hamish Findlay took great care each time they left their house, and kept a careful watch over their shoulders...

The day after their departure, Meg heard that they had gone – no longer around the corner. Off they had skipped, to where was not said, but gossip now had it that they were somewhere on the other side of the city, Govan maybe, but no one was certain. Others claimed Australia... The shocking part – they'd left in the middle of the night! Now, that was not on!

"Aye, they have scarpered all right, an' them with the rent not paid! Would ye believe it – a moonlight flit?"

It was not a salubrious district they'd left behind but, poor or not, there were standards to maintain.

That pair had let the area down, and 'Tut, tut, tut...' went the tongues.

Meg and Phoebe heard it all. "An' you should be glad they've gone," they were informed. "We're all better off without them..."

The neighbour's heartfelt comments, that were denigrating Hamish and Bella Roberts with such sincerity, certainly did something for Meg's morale.

That support generated a grim little grin – grim, because at that moment not much remained of her short marriage. The most that she was able to total up was – a baby on the way, her mother-in-law as her landlady, a left-behind copy of Treasure Island ...and a set of useless bagpipes!

15

2009
A big dig...

It was a lovely feeling for Tom to wake up, having slept well, and find himself lying next to his dear wife still snoozing away beside him – and be in no rush to get up. They were in their own warm bed, it was a Saturday morning in October, and it was not a working day. He stretched himself and counted his blessings, content to lie there mentally checking that all parts were continuing to function.

The electrical business was successful and it was quite a happy team that worked for him. His son David was one of them. Most of the others had been with him for years and it was unusual for anyone to want to leave. Also, he was surviving the credit crunch and, if nothing too dramatic came along, it looked as if he would be able to keep going comfortably.

When David joined the business from school Tom had been both surprised and delighted, but apprehensive. Was it wise for father and son to work together? Well, so far, so good!

Deliberately, their habit was to work in different locations and, at the end of the day, compare notes at home as if they were in different professions. That way they were less inclined to annoy each other.

But there was a wobbly one on Tom's horizon and that was what to do about pensions. He had difficulty understanding exactly what the best way was of dealing with these schemes. What he had seen, and not understood, was the losses that pensions systems currently incurred. They were apparently worsening every year, which caused his uncertainty. His was a small business. Was it only the big companies and their enormous schemes that expected the problems? Could it affect him?

What the heck – it's Saturday!

As he lay, hands clasped behind his head, gazing at the ceiling – that for the last two years was promised a fresh coat of emulsion that never happened – he repeated the Treasure Hunt clue in his head. No obvious answer yet, but today was the day and it seemed clear where they should be starting. In a couple of hours they would be together in his parent's garden, playing at treasure hunting, and, of course, working at loft clearance – if there was time.

How long will it take to clear that loft? Will we actually ever manage it? But more importantly, what are the chances of finding some more goodies up there, like last weekend?

He glanced at the clock.

Time to get up?

No, not yet.

But mustn't lie too long, could be a busy day.

...Another five minutes. Could tonight turn out like last Saturday night?

After last Saturday evening's meal, because he'd had no plans to meet his mates, and because his chasing after females was having little success, David decided that, for him, it could be a lazy night and he would stay at home. There were some cans of beer in the fridge, he had things to read, and he could maybe do something on the computer – but that wasn't how it turned out...

The records that had been gathering dust in that overcrowded loft for decades, that they brought back earlier, were now in their own front room, and during the meal, his father had talked almost non-stop about them. He was getting quite enthusiastic about his 'finds'.

David had settled comfortably in the front room, sitting with his magazine and reading an interesting article, beer within easy reach and his mother sitting across the room on the settee, knitting. A scene of peaceful tranquillity – until his father appeared.

"Have to see if these still work," he said. He was carrying the two pieces of electrical equipment they'd brought back earlier, the Dansette record player and the tape recorder. "Hope you don't mind."

David had been against his dad bringing home all that stuff. Was this the start of him going the same way as Gran and Grandad? Was he himself about to become a hoarder, and fill his own house with Gran and Grandad's loft rubbish? Now a screwdriver and a plug were in his father's hands. That's when David realised that there was a very good chance that he was about to be subjected to his grandad's ancient and abandoned record collection being played on a dodgy device by a nostalgic father.

Earlier that day at Bearsden, when it was time to stop and David was about to climb down the loft ladder, his father had shouted "Hold on a second, David," and carried over a record player, a tape recorder, and a stack of records.

"...And before you ask," he'd said, "I've been given permission to remove these. I'll take the tape recorder, if you can manage the rest. I'd drop them if I tried."

"Surely you are not taking all of this stuff!" was David's reaction as he was handed the record player with a stack of records sitting on top. They turned out heavier than he thought they would be, but he cradled them in an awkward one-arm grip, and stepped onto the ladder. He grabbed the rail with his other hand and started carefully downwards.

"Just a moment, the records, I'll take these," Tom offered, and reached for them. "You are bound to drop something."

"No, it is all right, Dad. I can manage. I'm a big boy now." David took another careful step downwards, but his father was insistent.

"Look, let me take some of the... Oh! ...Sorry!"

My Old Man's a Dustman was the unfortunate

one that slipped off and smashed at the foot of the ladder. Lonnie Donegan, no more!

"I'm sure you would have really liked that, David," said his grandad, at the foot of the steps picking up the remains.

David smiled – but silently thought... That would have been highly unlikely.

And what a Saturday evening it turned out to be ...well, for Tom.

His objective after the meal at home was simple – to attach a plug to the cable for the Dansette, to dust off the records, and select which was to be the first disc to prove that the machine still worked.

Gillian smiled tolerantly at her husband's boyish enthusiasm. David was apprehensive.

"Right, this is it," declared Tom and switched on the machine. Pride of place on the turntable was the very first record he'd ever owned, 'The Funky Gibbon'.

Was it the Dansette machine having an over-used stylus? Was it *The Goodies* themselves? For Tom it was a let-down. Surely, that record used to sound so much better! That had been his own choice a long time ago because he thought it was great, bought by his father and given to him for successfully passing an exam. The Goodies had lost their magic...

David was unimpressed.

"No matter, there are lots more," Tom enthusiastically informed the other two, and there were...

Thinking that he knew songs heard when he was

a boy, he was adding vocals to his father's old favourites but most times with nothing like the correct lyrics – but it was making him happy. It was Singalong Tom time.

For David, it was irritating.

Trying to blank it out by having a can of beer and reading his magazine was unsuccessful, so he sat hoping that the motor for the Dansette would burn out. It should have with the amount of use it was getting – and clearly the well-worn stylus was not helping the sound quality of any of the ancient pop-tunes.

The Dansette had been Grandad's, as were the records and they were all very old. Tonight, his dad was handling them reverently, as if it were his own well-loved collection! Jim Reeves, Herb Alpert and the Tijuana Brass. Who had heard of them? There was even a very young Cilla Black. It was tough for David...

However, he brightened up when his father put on 'Good Vibrations'. The Beach Boys had a reputation. He knew them. They'd created classics. So had Abba, and the Bee Gees. They were played next, and he reluctantly had to admit it – to himself only, of course – that this music had become – alright. It had improved so much that he was almost going to suggest that his dad should buy himself a new and better quality record player – but he stopped himself.

The worn stylus! The records were now ruined...

After a second can of beer and Queen on the turntable, followed by Blondie, David accepted that the evening was turning out not too badly after all and one thing was certain – tonight's music was a big improvement on the Punk Rock his father used to be mad on...

When samples had been heard from most of the records, Tom decided it was time to change to the Tape Recorder.

David became involved.

He volunteered to add a plug to the cable.

"This was my Mum's machine – the tape recorder," Tom told him. "She bought it before they married. Dad said today that it has sentimental value, and that he wants it back, and still working – or I'd have to answer to Mother! He said it doesn't matter about the Dansette."

As a reward for fitting the plug, Tom declared that David should choose what to play – provided the recorder still worked, but David did not recognise a single title on any of the tapes. He passed the honour to his mother. Her way of deciding was to dip her hand into the plastic bag, and...

'The Ying Tong Song...' was the result.

"The what?"

"The Goons..." Tom told an ignorant young man, "...just you listen. It is great ...and the proof of the pudding is in the hearing."

David grimaced at the mixed metaphor, but more disturbing was then to see his parents with smiles on their faces listening to this stupid song. They even knew the words and joined in – they were loving it! Oh, my goodness... Why was that popular?

"And I thought Lonnie Donegan would be bad," commented David. "Maybe I should have gone out."

Tom wondered if his son was being sarcastic last Saturday...

Another few minutes... he told himself. I will rise at eight, and he turned over.

Last week The Goons tape surprised him. He had not bought it, and it was not the sort of music that his mum or dad would choose either – certainly not Dad because he had no sense of humour back then – just books, books and more books...

Sad that Dad's memory is going. Starting to stumble over facts now. I just wish he'd laugh more. Now, when he laughs – it's because Mum gives permission! No, that is unfair, she only acts at being a battle-axe!

Then Tom realised – the Goons' tape – Granny Meg! It's been her choice! She liked stupid stuff. Always fooling around – like us last Saturday night!

...Can't lie here all day though! Should I waken Gillian? Of course, I should, and if I do it in the usual manner, bouncing around as I get out of bed, I'll manage to...

"Don't do that, Tom! Why do you always...? It is just to annoy me isn't it? And you've succeeded."

Ah well, she was awake...

There had been some negative thinking at last night's meal...

"Well, I hope that tomorrow we have as much success as last Saturday," Gillian had said, as she brought through the plates of delicious looking food. "You did well, David, to find the clue."

David gave a modest grin.

"Rubbish," said his father. "He didn't find it. It was his clumsiness and it found him. Anyway, I would not be surprised if this turns out to be one of Meg's leg-pulls! If we do solve the clues, will there actually be treasure?"

"Oh Tom, how could you suggest that?" said Gillian. "Granny Meg was not like that."

"Yea... That's being daft, Dad, of course there will," David had added, but not too convincingly.

However, Tom had planted the seed, and so, each went to bed with some doubts.

It was new day.

Rising mid-week was so different. Then it was for work and it was tough, but this was Saturday! David was up. For that young man, a normal Saturday used to begin with a long lie in bed, but that was before the Loft. It was all changed now. Early, yet wide awake and eager to go and it was all Granny Meg's fault! No denying it... he was into treasure hunting, but it was not something to chat about in the pub!

Sometimes it could be a strain for David and Tom to be on the same job and generally, if they could, they avoided that, yet here they were getting stuck in together at weekends, and enjoying it. The calendar didn't require marking – Saturday was pre-booked. It had become the day for either loft clearing or treasure-hunting, whatever took their fancy, and it was turning out very different and much more enjoyable than real work.

Tom was up too and needed no note to remind him of today's objective. Standing staring at the unshaven face in the bathroom mirror, the clue had become a permanent piece of poetry in his head after the many times he'd read it – and he desperately wanted to solve it. David had found the first clue – he wanted to be the one to find the next.

He recited Meg's rhyme aloud once more.

> *"Pass the time with a little rhyme.*
> *The clue you'll see underneath this tree.*
> *Do not be fooled, there's only one,*
> *But searching's such a lot of fun.*
> *It's a tree for gullible people..."*

"Get a move on, Dad, and quit talking to yourself," came from the one-man queue forming outside the door.

Tom was feeling confident. By the end of today they would have the solution, and be working on another clue. We can do it. No! *I can do it*, he decided. He was determined not to let his grandmother, or David, get the better of him, so he kept repeating the rhyme...

With a hearty cooked breakfast inside them, any doubts from last night's conversation faded. They were ready for the challenge – a Team Game, a concept that the males were slowly getting used to, and with a common wish – that they would be successful locating the next clue.

Although Gillian and David found Meg's challenges invigorating and took them in their stride, Tom found them very exhausting, physically and mentally. They would be going hard at it very shortly, and it was guaranteed he would be the one who'd come home tired. That's why he had already decided that tomorrow, and each Sunday in future, would be for doing absolutely nothing!

Sharp on ten o'clock, Gillian, Tom and David arrived at the old Findlay family home. The males were prepared for something physical. Gillian would be settling for observation only, though if it came to a push, she would supervise – she was good at that and knew that, in all probability, at some point they would need pushing.

"At least they look enthusiastic this morning," commented Beth, looking out the kitchen window. Angus nodded in agreement as he struggled to remove the sticky mess on the bottom of the breakfast porridge pan.

Tom and David stood together in the back garden, each holding a garden fork, and with a spade sitting available to grab at the correct moment. Their target was to locate a clue, buried beneath a tree: 'a tree for gullible people'.

As simple as that – but which tree in this miniature orchard was it going to be?

Gillian's observation point was the French windows. There she stood, hoping her males would benefit from first time luck – preferably with Tom the one to find something first. He'd seemed particularly eager to get here this morning. Was he trying to impress his mother?

Though they were standing in the garden

grinning at each other and appeared eager to start digging, neither Tom nor David felt overly confident. The creator of their Treasure Hunt, Meg, had had the chance to hide clues anywhere...

Meg passed away in 2006, aged eighty-six, in her son's house.

Before she died, she was still able to get about, though not as freely as she would have liked. She had the usual aches and pains – but was sharp in mind. Then she took ill – seriously ill. Elderly and unwell, it should not have been a shock, but it was – and only a bout of influenza.

The reason for joining Beth and Angus, for what turned out to be her last year, had not been ill health nor a confused mind. It was more a question of her wanting and needing the company of people she knew.

The flat she left in Glasgow had been hers for a long time – forty-six years almost. Very convenient for shops in the busy cosmopolitan Byres Road, with an easy stroll to the Botanic Gardens, and great for public transport.

She lived there, on her own, after Angus left to marry Beth in 1967 and at that point, revelled in the freedom of having responsibilities for no one other than herself. She could come and go as she pleased – and she did – thoroughly enjoying life. Then she calmed down and each day became more of a routine.

Visits of Beth and Angus with little Tom were a special delight for her.

Having a toddler about the house was wonderful, even if he did keep her on her toes when she took the role of babysitter. He would reach for every ornament and managed to smash a few, but she did not mind. Each breakage became another tale for a proud granny to pass on to anyone who would listen. Once a week she performed that role when he was little.

"Oh, no bother," she would tell an apologetic Gillian. "He keeps me young."

'Little' Tom grew up. He became a bit more independent, and the visits fewer, but appreciated even more by her when they did occur. He was a good grandson and she enjoyed his company, whenever she saw him.

However, at eighty-four years of age, for her, life became physically tougher. She was no longer able to wander about outside quite so freely – the pain in her hips and her feet saw to that. The people she had known, good neighbours for a long time, passed on or moved away, and she somehow could not feel comfortable with those who took their places. The newcomers tended to be younger and concerned with their own lives, and that she could understand.

No one seemed to want to make the acquaintance of the old woman in the middle flat who was becoming housebound. It was so different from when she was younger...

Gradually, much to her own annoyance, she recognised that if it had not been for going out with Jean, Beth's mum, she could easily drift into becoming a recluse. So the offer made by Angus and

Beth to go and live with them, was jumped at – not literally, she was too stiff for that – but it was certainly accepted with gratitude. There was plenty room in their house to let her have freedom to do as she wanted, when she wanted.

...And she retained her mischievous streak all the time she lived with Beth and Angus.

Angus was certain that the inspiration for the Treasure Hunt happened at their house, probably as a timewaster for his mother, but her having total freedom and access to almost all parts of the house and garden – a large area, could mean that finding clues could be difficult.

"Have you thought that her clues might not even be restricted to this property...?" asked Angus.

Tom and David grimaced and decided working on this one clue would be sufficient for starters. To keep digging until they found what they were looking for was the intention, and where to start, was the question. There were five trees in the back garden, and though none of them were overly large they had been sitting in those positions for a long time. Two apple trees, one pear tree, a plum, and a cherry – a fruit unwanted by Beth and left on the grass.

"If we each do an Apple tree?" suggested Tom, and their task began. "It won't be buried deep," he said with confidence. "She was old."

They did a shallow dig – without success. Going around again, but a little deeper was next, but again nothing. Contending with well-established roots was both awkward and tiring.

"What if Grandad's right, and it isn't even in this garden?" David asked hesitantly, a question Tom chose to ignore – it has to be here, he told himself.

As Tom moved to the base of the plum tree he suddenly had a flash of his childhood. For a moment, he was a young boy again, triggered by a sound from the other side of the wall – the rattle of a box of matches, followed by the rasp of one struck, sucking noises, a sigh of exasperation, and then another match struck – successfully this time. The familiar aroma preceded the cloud of tobacco smoke that drifted over the wall, a sort of chocolaty smell that he had liked ever since he was old enough to recognise what it was – and it caused an automatic response.

"Good morning, Uncle George!"

"Good morning to you, young Tom," and a head appeared, "...and I see you have a very capable helper with you. Hello David, and how are you today?"

"Very well, thank you, Mr. Sampson." David liked Uncle George, but he never felt comfortable calling him that. This old man was never his dad's proper uncle.

Uncle George was barely tall enough to see over the wall when he stood on his tiptoes. Today, it was the old routine – the box – so the whole head was visible! He was of a height that normally permitted only the top of his shiny, bald, head to show above the wall.

Tom, when he was small rarely saw the head and

communication was shouted, unless one of them found something to stand on, but he had always been aware of Uncle George's presence by the smell of the tobacco.

George and Mary Sampson had been there as long as Beth and Angus.

George had smoked a pipe since he was a young man and did not conform to the belief that it would eventually kill him. At seventy-one, he had decided that he would just 'wait, and let the Good Lord Above decide what will take me away.' He liked his pipe. Always the same brand of tobacco. It was obvious to Tom that he intended to share 'MacBaren Aromatic Choice' with the neighbourhood – whether they liked it or not – until he snuffed it!

This freedom to ignore medical recommendations was only by special dispensation from his wife – provided he was out of doors – conforming strictly to house rules laid down by her, ten years before. Indoors, his wife Mary dominated, so, here he was outside, the only place permitted for puffs.

The old, warm, tweed jacket that hung on the back door hook, ready for use especially in winter, had become his outdoor smoking jacket. Even he could smell it when it was just hanging there – sort of kipper-like.

"Nice to see you giving your old father a help with the garden," Uncle George said.

As his 'age complex' kicked in, for a moment, Tom thought Uncle George was talking to David, but no, he was talking to him.

"I don't suppose Angus is so able these days, like me. Ground is not too hard, I hope, Tom. There was a bit of a frost last night."

"Oh, we're not really helping Dad," replied Tom. "We're actually looking for treasure."

"Right," said Uncle George. "I hope you have success soon because I think it might change to rain. The forecast says it will."

That was when Aunt Mary came out, ready to walk to the shops. She was slightly taller than her spouse and did not have to stand on tiptoe to see over the wall.

"Good morning, Tom, and good morning, David. My goodness David, you are a big boy now. I remember when you used to run about in nappies. Seems no time at all since then," and she continued towards the gate.

David coloured slightly. Tom smiled and, naughtily enjoyed his son's discomfort.

"Must get going, got a lot of shops to visit," said George. "I am sure you'll need your wellies shortly."

Uncle George caught up with Aunt Mary and held open the gate for her.

"It is nice to see the younger people helping Angus, isn't it?" she said to her husband.

"Oh no," said George. "You've got it wrong, Petal. They are not helping him, they are digging for treasure."

"George! I wish you would stop that silly talk. I never know whether you are trying to be funny, or just being sarcastic. You are always the same."

Uncle George stopped in his tracks as his wife went on ahead. He was seventy-one, had been married for over fifty years, and still got it wrong. Ah well, his father had warned him. 'You'll never win, son,' he had said all those years ago.

Tom and David were not downhearted – yet. They still had a pear tree, a plum tree, and a cherry to dig over before that would happen, but overhead the clouds were darkening.

Tom had the plum so David went for the pear tree and it was David's fork that hit metal. They looked at each other.

No, it wasn't the next clue.

"Would you believe it!" said David. "I lost these nearly nineteen years ago."

It was David's toys – two little Corgi Cars, James Bond Specials. At last, recovered but with both of the little favourites dented by the fork. David felt bad about that but, by the look on his face, his dad obviously felt worse.

"I remember them costing me a ruddy fortune," said Tom. He had grudged the price of them at the time, he remembered, but he had given in and bought them for a begging son. "And you've gone and put the flipping fork through them! I wish you would take more care of your toys!"

At twenty-two years old and over six feet tall, when did he last play with his toys? "Sorry," was David's grinned response.

Unfortunately, so far that was the only find and there was only one tree remaining – the cherry – the only place left to dig. The clue must be there.

That's when the rain began. Only a few drops at first but George had predicted correctly and, in no time, it was heavy but Tom would not stop – he was on a mission.

David did not want to stop either, but he was sensible, and did. The sensible one went indoors.

Gillian had been watching the pair of them become more and more dispirited and saw Tom stupidly continuing to dig. The rain was becoming very heavy so, she grabbed a large umbrella and rushed into the garden and held it caringly over a determined husband. It was probably more good intention than practical support because, by the time she had reached him, Tom was already well and truly soaked. The ground had become muddy, but he carried on until he had carefully checked all the base of that cherry tree – twice.

The only things found – were cherry stones...

"Now, don't sit on the good sofa," his mum had yelled at him, as he entered the room via the French windows, "And look at the mud on the carpet... Oh Tom... Go into the kitchen!"

He felt foolish before but now, well and truly chastened – a ten-year-old again. He removed the muddy shoes and stood in his stocking soles, attempting to remove all the soil.

Beth fetched an old tartan shirt and gave it to him to wear.

"Just keep it," she told him. "Your father hates it."

Tom disliked it too, but it was dry and warm at

least. His father found him an old pair of his trousers, which were a near-enough fit, while his own were put at the boiler to dry.

Only when he had on his dad's clean trousers and no trace of mud was on the shoes did he dare to return to the sitting room. As he stepped on the carpet he checked that he was leaving no marks and went quickly across the room and sat on the sofa.

His mother was still in the kitchen. His father and David were talking about old magazines and did not notice him come back, but Gillian made a sympathetic face, then grinned. Tom suspected that she was enjoying his discomfort.

Then refreshments appeared, brought in by Mother – and only for Tom! There was a choice of jams, hot scones, and a mug of fresh coffee and all on a tray, which she carefully placed on his knees. Tom felt slightly uncomfortable.

"Sorry I shouted at you, Tom," she said and tweaked his cheek. "It's become a habit." And for him, that made the day a little brighter – a rare moment of displayed affection. The 'battle-axe' could care!

"Thanks, Mother," he mumbled through a mouthful of strawberry-smothered-scone.

"...But don't do it again!" came the sharp response, as she made a dramatic exit and returned to the kitchen. Tom just smiled.

It had been very disappointing for the two diggers, and as a result, everyone felt deflated. Could it be that 'A Tree for Gullible People' was growing elsewhere?

"If it's not in our garden, could it be in someone else's? Maybe she buried it under a tree next door," Beth shouted from the kitchen. "George and Mary have more than us."

That did not help. The others agreed it was very possible but, if not in this garden, it could be anywhere!

To re-motivate them, Gillian repeated the clue out loud from memory but that just brought quizzical looks?

Nothing! They were beaten and demoralised.

Outside, the rain continued...

From then on, even though the intentions were good, the day sort-of went downhill. Rather than have it totally wasted, Tom and David returned to the loft.

They found an old fire extinguisher – ten years beyond the recommended date for use. Tom carefully passed it to David, who in turn, carefully carried it down the ladder and handed it to Angus. Angus carefully carried it downstairs and into the back garden, but stumbled and dislodged the pin, or something, and the white powder shot out, going everywhere. The rain did them a favour by dampening it down, transforming a large part of the garden into a white soggy mess.

Tom knocked over a brass candlestick, which to be fair to him had been sitting precariously. When it dropped, it was onto a glass-framed fading print of The Hay Wain by Constable. The glass shattered. He cut his finger while clearing up the glass, but the wounded soldier carried on...

"Mother..." Tom shouted down through the opening, "Are you there?"

"What is it, Tom? Hurry up. I'm busy even if you are not."

"The old knitting machine is taking up valuable space just sitting here. Do you still make use of it?"

"No, I don't..."

"Would it be ok if we throw it out then?"

"Certainly not!"

"Right..."

Tom and David moved that piece of equipment to a different place – in the loft.

An old jigsaw in its box, when lifted, turned out to already have been open at the other end. The pieces poured onto the new flooring. David picked up all that he could find hoping the pieces that bounced into the insulation would not be important, or missed.

The final straw was Tom accidently walking into the loft indoor digital aerial and knocking it for six. Having had considerable trouble a couple of years ago finding a signal to pick up all the channels, and then having had difficulty securing the aerial in that position, Angus was not pleased – it was a poor reception area. It took Angus, Tom and David, quite a time to obtain the optimum signal once more and even then it was not as good as it had been.

When it was time to leave, there was little doubt – the day had turned out to be a massive failure!

16

1944 - 1957
It is not funny...

Meg had a bouncing baby boy and she called him Angus – for no particular reason other than she just took a fancy to the name. The exciting event of the new baby's birth had taken place with the help of Phoebe and the local midwife, and all had gone well.

Sadly, Granny Phoebe enjoyed the pleasure of her little grandson for only a year, and then passed away, leaving a huge gap in her daughter-in-law's life. Meg had become really close to Phoebe and relied a great deal on her for help and moral support, both of which had been essential since Hamish departed.

Missing her greatly, now and again Meg would bring out the rolled-up portrait of the young Phoebe in a theatre ticket office, the treasured drawing done by Alexander. She found it comforting just to sit looking at it. Odd that this was the only drawing that the long-gone artist ever did of his wife but Meg could sense the feeling that went into each pencil stroke. Gazing at it helped, but only a little.

Meg was not naturally a sad person. When younger, she was the one who played the joker and started everyone else giggling but, after the departure of her errant husband, that spirit seemed to have totally left her. Losing Phoebe had made it worse.

So, she created a little ritual one day, not long after Phoebe's demise, to boost her morale and confidence. Standing in the middle of the room she would look to the north, then the east, then south and finally the west, repeating each time, "I can stand on my own two feet". The only person listening to her, though not understanding a single word, was a tiny Angus. It helped. She repeated the chant several times each day, for a week, until eventually she believed that she had told the world. It strengthened her resolve. From then, if she felt down, she imagined the words, and had no need to speak them aloud.

As time passed, she found that she gradually became stronger and coped better with life. She was on her own but, looking on the bright side, at least she had Phoebe's home to live in, there was a roof over their heads and the war was over – and she'd started to smile again.

Meg wanted the best for her Angus but rationing was still on the go, so she was thankful for whatever she could get. The small amount of money that Phoebe had somehow succeeded in saving had been left to Meg. For that, she was very grateful. That money was spent sparingly and done while thinking of a lovely woman.

The kind neighbour across the landing proved a great help. Wee Mrs Gray, a much older woman than Meg, had been a widow for many years and lived on her own. On the night of heavy bombing of Clydebank early in the war, she had lost the few relations she'd had. Though never having had youngsters herself, she loved children, especially little Angus. When Meg mentioned the need to search for a job, Mrs Gray offered to look after the very young child. Part-time work for Meg in an office in town was the result.

Initially Wee Mrs Gray refused payment for minding little Angus, but using her neighbour's help with no recompense was not acceptable to Meg. A little money was eventually accepted, and, now that Meg could afford to buy it, some extra food. It was a good, friendly outcome for both.

Meg could hold her head high. Earning a living comforted her, and enabled her to help and guide her boy. She had great hopes for him. Of one thing, she was certain: it may be a long way off, but Angus would not be doing a manual job when he left school. She encouraged him to study hard for everything, and he sailed successfully through any exams he had to sit. He wanted to make his mother proud of him – and she was.

Then she went a stage further. She became 'pushy'. He tried even harder – and became the classroom 'swot'. He listened earnestly to his mother's advice, and acted on most of it – most of the time.

One exception – he refused to try the bagpipes.

No one at school did that, why should he? That was for old men and anyway, in class they already made fun of him.

And so, Grandad Alexander's pipes lay there, untouched, getting older. Meg had never looked in the box. Angus certainly would not. Therefore, the bagpipe case remained unopened in 'Phoebe's house' – as Meg still thought of it – and under the bed, the place it had rested for years. Twice a year, without fail, when Meg did a major cleaning she dusted the top of the box and – without fail – replaced the box in exactly the same position.

Angus became a grown-up quite suddenly.

Receiving the door-key for the house was a major event. He became an official front-door key-holder, and, conscientiously in case he lost it, kept the precious item on a string around his neck.

Mrs. Gray still played a role when he moved from Primary to Senior School. He was becoming bigger and more self-sufficient, but she was always there for him. "I'll just keep a wee eye on him," she'd say, but often now, it was Angus who helped Mrs Gray!

The young man took on the responsibility for shopping. When his mum had the chance to go 'full time', he shouldered other tasks with confidence. During this period in his life, he actually developed a flair for cooking. He would search and find recipes to prepare for his mum's delight when she came home from work and after a tiring day, she could normally look forward to arriving home to a hot meal, and relaxing afterwards. As she entered the close, she could usually tell by the lingering aroma what was about to be on her plate.

Sometimes, unfortunately, the disappointing smell of 'burnt offerings' would greet her, if her studious son had become over-engrossed in his homework. On these occasions, she was grateful he had not burned down the house and both would settle for a simple sandwich.

Meg was ambitious. She wanted to improve both her lot and her son's and, as she was now earning reasonable money, a house move had become possible. She searched and found a larger place at an affordable rent and in a more salubrious district. A step up in the social scale – Hyndland – a first floor flat and a close with a front door at the entrance. Not only that, a fully fitted bathroom.

Both Meg and her son, for the first time ever, felt posh. They experienced a real 'come up in the world' confidence as they entered *their* close, climbing a stair with tiles on the walls, tiles that were always clean and shining.

Wee Mrs Gray was able to visit them. She was suitably impressed by 'the place where the toffs lived'.

Meg had a few boyfriends or, men-friends would probably be more descriptive. She had taken a liking to slightly older males. Annoyingly though, very often they turned out to be married and had removed a wedding ring before entering the dance hall. Finding that out on many occasions meant an immediate end to the affair. Hamish's departure with Bella Roberts hurt her deeply so, she would not be the cause of other wives suffering the pain she experienced.

Meg had many flings but none of the males involved proved to be the right ones. Her son was the important male in her life.

Angus obviously had a good brain. He also had the ability to concentrate, memorising facts and figures with ease, and he could use sound logical reasoning to prove theorems and principles. However, there was one thing he lacked, and it disappointed Meg. He had not inherited her sense of humour and mischief. In fact, in those early days, Meg was convinced that his elbows did not even know what a funny bone was.

...But he can't have everything, she told herself philosophically.

Of course, moving home to the other side of the city meant changing school for Angus but give him his due, within weeks at the new school he had settled in – and almost immediately stood out as a star pupil again. However, being a newcomer, this, to his classmates made him seem like a show-off...

At least once each week, during his first month, something odd would happen at school. He would arrive home, sometimes with his tie tightened in such a knot that he would have to spend ages loosening it, or he would be minus a gym shoe that would mysteriously appear again a week later, or with shoelaces, that had vanished some time during the day, requiring replacement.

One day he arrived home with a sign on his back that he had not realised was there. It said, 'Look! My head's up my bum!'

Meg threatened to go to the headmaster about it.

"No, Mum, please don't do that! I am not being bullied," he told his mother. "They just like to annoy me at times. It is only a game for them," he insisted.

He didn't mind, he claimed, but she knew that wasn't true.

She tried reassuring him.

"The others are jealous because you are a 'brainbox,'" Meg told him, "I'll leave it be and we'll see over time if they get fed up. Anyway, meantime, just you laugh it off!"

Having said that, she immediately wished she had not. It was quite the wrong thing to suggest to Angus. Laughing was way beyond his capabilities...

17

2009
Getting clued up...

Absorbing stuff. David was holding it open in front of him. 'Harmsworth's Universal Encyclopaedia', published 1921. The title alone was a mouthful! And who would have believed it? He was actually reading it and enjoying every word.

Granny Meg, what are you doing to me? Laughing your head off, no doubt. Saturday night, and again I'm missing a couple of pints because of you, and I'm reading this because my grandad recommended it. I wonder if the guys will even notice I haven't appeared...

It had been a most disappointing Saturday. They'd left Bearsden feeling quite frustrated at having found nothing. Gillian had felt quite sorry for the males. So, to compensate, she conjured up a delicious meal when they arrived home, and their mood improved. Eating was a gentle recuperation for them, thanks to her skill in the kitchen.

Now, David was lying sprawled out on an easy chair in the living room – just like his old man – and, this evening, loving it! At my age, he thought. How sad...

His mates had told him he'd been missed last weekend – and here it was happening again, although for another reason this time. He wondered if Maureen, the barmaid would miss him. She was nice. Yes, a Saturday night felt great when he had a female hanging on his arm whispering in his ear that he was a wonderful guy – even though it usually meant her glass was empty. Not Maureen though. It was different with her. Pity she was always on the other side of the bar, working. Have to do something about that, soon.

Being at home last week felt strange, yet here he was again, sitting chilled out, drinking cider donated by a kind-hearted mum because there was no beer in the house, and he was getting pleasure from reading Grandad's encyclopaedia magazines. Starting to feel sleepy, though, just like the old man. Now that was worrying! What would his mates say about that?

Probably mock me senseless! Well, I will not be telling them – as if they cared....

Having no permanent girlfriend had some benefits, for instance, not having to rush off somewhere to be given the usual lecture, followed by his profuse and obviously insincere apology, for being late. His last girlfriend said goodbye after only four weeks because of that.

David turned another page...

What he was reading was obviously out-of-date in many cases but he found it intriguing, like an archaic Wikipedia on paper – ancient, but probably more accurate! David glanced across the room. The computer was lying idle – like his father over there who was out-for-the-count, snoring.

Pretends he wants to use the computer. "...But any time I want to have a go on the laptop, who's playing on it, eh?" he'd say.

David was getting used to that comment.

It is Dad's computer, yes, but if he was so eager he could buy another. Complains I hog it – and then soft-soaps me into doing stuff for him. It'll be the family tree next!

"What do we know about the Findlays?" Tom had asked, and then supplied the answer. "Nothing, I tell you! Our family... our ancestors... Do you know where we come from? No... Were we saints, or sinners? Do you ever wonder? You know, David, that sort of thing can be found on the internet – instead of all those silly games, or ...whatever."

David had heard it all – and would his father do anything practical about it himself? No! All mouth – but claiming he was the one who wanted to research his ancestors. Ha... ha...!

"Been my intention for ages, but of course, if you're using the PC..."

What a load of... It is obvious he will expect me to do it!

Anyway, Grandad had warned him. "David, you are about to be conned!" It hadn't happened yet! His father lay, open-mouth, snorting away, still fast asleep.

David lifted the next section of the Encyclopaedia, no longer dozing. He was bright as a button again, and eager to continue reading. Sitting at the side of the chair was the bundle brought back today. Quite a few to get through. Discovered and brought down from the loft last week. At the time, David presumed that they would be thrown out, but he was wrong. They were immediately grabbed. Grandad wanted them – all sixty-three separate sections – and started reading immediately. The seven he'd finished were given to David this afternoon.

"They might come apart in your hands," David was warned. "Rust is holding them together." Rust, that over ninety years ago began life as staples.

"*Phowafurr...*" The noise came from the depths of the seat opposite, followed by a more normal snort, as Tom changed position, in a deep sleep.

This afternoon's physical effort, and the disappointment at discovering zilch in the garden, had taken its toll on the old fellow. It had been all physical – in the garden and then afterwards back in the loft, more activity moving stuff, but the clearance was going really slowly. The amount of rubbish warranted a skip, but Beth's rate of acceptance for disposal was dead slow and stop! If they hired a skip it would sit in the driveway for months.

Tom tried suggesting that she could leave the choices to him and David, and proposed some items he'd selected, but that wasn't a good idea. He suffered another lecture before returning chastened to the loft.

Even David had to admit to tiring. Rummaging

about up there, climbing up and down the ladder carrying an item down, then being told, 'Oh no, keep that!' to have to take it into the loft again. That was tiring – and frustrating. Only slightly to a young man like him, and he would recover easily, but it was apparently proving much worse for the old fellow.

Sprawled out in the easy chair, Tom was now snorting gently in a deep sleep, comatose ever since he sat down after the meal.

This afternoon, Gillian had been helping too and should have been exhausted, but women were obviously made of sterner stuff. She was now standing ironing shirts. David would have offered to help but, when he tried previously and did a poor job, she finished-up ironing them again. So thanks, but no thanks, would have been Gillian's reaction – if he had offered!

Grandad could not recollect where the encyclopaedia came from. He doubted it was his family; they never had two spare pennies to rub together, he said. Couldn't afford magazines. Could have been from his in-laws, or, more likely, from next door. George's family had been well off for generations. They could afford them, but they wouldn't have been bought by George or his father – neither were born when the booklets went on sale. Were they second-hand? Or maybe they came from one of George's relatives?

"How did they get into your loft then?" David asked.

"No idea – can't remember."

"And you've never read them?"

"No ...at least I don't think so... Church Jumble Sale maybe?" He was still trying to remember, but he gave a shrug. "It's all very vague."

Anyway, it didn't really matter where they came from, Grandad concluded – there they were, waiting to be read and it gave him the urge to do some serious reading again, a habit he'd appeared to have lost. A nice result, David thought.

They included a lot about World War One and large sections were on the subject of the various battles. The booklet on David's lap showed early tanks in action.

"And at least Alexander came back alive," Grandad had murmured, and in the same breath, "Have you started the family tree yet?"

"...The family tree? Me?"

"Your dad said you would. Have you not?"

"Hmmm... No, not yet! But you mentioned Alexander..."

And the chat had progressed.

David's great-great-grandfather was a war hero, according to Angus, mentioned in despatches; a foot soldier in 'The Great War', as this encyclopaedia called it. The page sitting open in front of David showed a promise made by politicians all those years ago. "War will never be tolerated again!" David thought of all the current conflicts. *Will never be tolerated* didn't carry much weight, did it? Never believe a politician!

It saddened him, the emphasis given on the pages to the glorification of the fighting. Portrayed as a wonderful victory – implied it had been worth it –

with all the gory details shown, events that ended only a few years before publication. A bit morbid, he concluded. Shouldn't people have been trying to forget?

He'd seen bits of real film of that war on television and internet and they'd horrified him. Soldiers climbing out of trenches being shot down immediately; groups of men with eyes bandaged, making their way along a waterlogged trench, clinging fearfully to the shoulder of the person in front, victims of mustard gas and barely able to breathe; bodies hanging grotesquely from barbed wire in a muddy landscape.

No, nothing glorifies war, and yet we all go on fighting...

Maybe it was a good thing that filming was for specialists back then. Official photographers recording events limited what the public saw – not like today. Mobiles, smart phones and the internet, absolutely nothing of life missed. Most of it better not recorded in the first place...

Whoa! Dad says things like that! Oh no, I am turning into my father!

This was nothing like the raucous Saturday nights of many weeks ago. A sign of ageing, perhaps – in one so young? Only twenty-two and, this evening, he was becoming even more morose than his dad was. But, at least he was still awake. His dad slept on. His mum had gone upstairs.

He turned the pages very carefully.

'Pigeons', it said, 'used for communication during the war.' It was amazing how information circulates around the world now, he thought philosophically, and so much changed in a short time. Now, who doesn't have a mobile phone in a pocket? He tried to visualise walking around with a carrier pigeon tucked in his back pocket – but his imagination could not cope...

David sat for a moment gazing into space realizing how little he knew of his family background. A War Hero in the family that no one had mentioned. Meg would have, she would have told him everything, if he had thought to ask. It was her father-in-law.

Too late for questions now...

Oh, oh! His father was starting to wake up – a slow process and not necessarily a pretty sight. To avoid watching, David made himself useful. A mug of coffee was called for in recovery situations like this. He went to the kitchen and produced three and, by that simple deed, on his return became a family favourite – for a short time.

Tom was properly awake and Gillian was back beside them, ironing again. She stopped and sat down for a moment to drink the coffee. Only five more shirts...

All three were more subdued than the previous Saturday. Failure to solve Meg's clue had hit them hard and, of course, prevented them moving forward to the next clue presuming that, somewhere hidden, another existed.

"I'll bet Meg is sitting up there, laughing her head off," said Tom, his first words in two and a half hours.

"Solving it shouldn't be an impossible solution with our combined brain-power," said Gillian. "We managed the first two."

"Three mugs, that's what she will be thinking," contributed David. "Three mugs that she has succeeded in beating – once again."

That made the other two feel even less optimistic, and there was a gloomy silence as each sat with their own thoughts.

"Mugs! Three mugs! Tree mugs! Mug tree! I've got it!" Tom was shouting, suddenly becoming lively. "A tree for gullible people... Mugs? Not us. Real mugs – for drinking coffee! A gullible person... That's me! It's you! It's us! A tree for gullible... Yea..."

He had become rhetorical, excited, as the other two sat, not following. "Must phone Mum," and he went for his mobile.

It was ringing at the other end but there was no answer. He looked at the phone in his hand to check he had used the correct number. Try again. "Why don't they lift the phone? I hope they are all right... Come on – talk to me..." The answer service gave him the chance to leave a message, which he did. "Phone back – urgently – very urgently!" he demanded.

"Tom, would you like to explain, please?" requested Gillian.

He did, slowly and patronisingly. What they should have been looking for was not under real live garden trees – *obviously!* The clue would be under the Mug Tree – the one in his mother's kitchen. She'd had that for years, and, it would have been easy for the clue to have been hidden there.

"A mug tree? Is that what it is called?" said David.

"Well, even it is not, that's the name I remember Meg used to call it – the stand where the mugs are stored."

The other two were not totally convinced but without any other ideas, they would run with this one, but they could run nowhere until Beth Findlay phoned back.

Half an hour later – the call was still not returned.

"There must be something wrong. I am going round. I'll take the van. They could be ill. Are you coming David?"

Tom was getting agitated.

"Tom, sit down" Gillian instructed ...and the phone rang.

Tom immediately demanded to know why his mother had not been quicker to phone back, he had said it was urgent.

"You are so self-centred sometimes, Tom," was the response. "It can't always be about you, you know..."

She was not at all apologetic. Tom realised that very quickly and prudently stayed silent.

"It was the final episode," she curtly explained, "and we didn't want to be interrupted. You don't watch BBC4 of course. Anyway what do you want?" she demanded, "and why are you getting so excited?"

"Mum, the stand you use for the mugs – in the

kitchen."

"Yes ...you mean the mug rack?"

"Ok, the mug rack. Would you please remove the mugs from it and bring the stand to the phone."

"Tom, do you realise the time? We should be in bed. Why do you...?" She had no idea why she was doing it, but she did as requested, grumpily.

After a moment, the phone was lifted again.

"Right, Mum. Turn it upside down. On the bottom, is there a piece of paper, or a little package?"

Was he correct? Moment of truth? He was willing her to say yes!

"Hmm... There is a folded piece of paper stuck onto the base. I wonder how that got there. Angus... Where are you? Do you know how this...?"

"Mum! What does it say, please?"

"Just a minute – I'll have to put on my specs."

It seemed a very long minute.

"It says, '*I can't help droning on about this. It can be torture for some, but heaven for others. Keep it in the family for when they have a tart an' tea but it's not food and drink.*' What is this all about, Tom?"

"Mum, you are wonderful" he exclaimed and meant it. "Read it out again please, but slowly this time."

She did, and as Tom repeated, Gillian and David each scribbled the words on whatever they could grab...

"Thanks Mum. You have been a great help. Sorry to bother you so late. We will pop over tomorrow. See you then... Bye."

At the other end, Beth was holding a phone that was no longer connected. "Angus, I don't think I'm going to sleep well tonight," she grumbled.

As predicted, both Beth and Angus lay awake; that programme, it ended with a dramatic explosion, and on top of that Tom's emergency phone call. How could anyone sleep?

Gillian, Tom and David were up late, well and truly re-motivated. They had the next clue – and they did not sleep either...

18

1955
Loving it...

There was a period in her life when Meg Findlay decided to control Cupid.

It was before they moved to Hyndland. At that time, Angus was still at Primary School, and Meg and her son were living in the house near Argyle Street, in Anderston, the one she took over when Phoebe died.

Due to her circumstances, having been married, and lost a husband to another woman – that floozy Bella Roberts – Meg Findlay reckoned that she knew it all. She could write a book about the rights and wrongs of how to make the correct choice of soulmate.

Affairs of the heart became her forte.

The unpleasant experience in her love life should not have to happen to someone she knew, or even to someone she did not know. She was always on the lookout for anyone who might need her assistance – whether help was wanted, or not.

What had happened to her had been a hard

lesson from which she had learned a thing or two and, it meant that Angus was growing up without a father. That to her mind was not right, and though there was a possible solution to her own dilemma, she struggled to face it.

To try for another bloke – should she, or shouldn't she?

Any man who would take her on, or more importantly, that she would take on, could only be a partner, not a husband. He would be a bidie-in, as everyone in Scotland knows. He could not be a real father to Angus. How would her little boy feel, knowing that she had another man in the house who was not his real dad? Getting married again was out of the question – not without a divorce, having a husband still alive as far as she knew. A divorce would cost a fortune, a fortune that she did not have. She never actually approached a lawyer to find out how true that was; someone at work told her, and she was prepared to believe it.

The easiest option, if she had been brave, would have been to have found the right man, married him, and hoped that none of her neighbours noticed – in other words – bigamy! But she did not think she would get away with that. Anyway, there never was a man she loved enough to make her want to go that far. It was much easier to care about her neighbours, and their love lives.

Susie Thompson lived with her parents on the top floor, third landing, and two above Meg. She was old enough to get married but had not found the right boy yet. At least, in Meg's opinion, Willie Stevenson was not the right boy, but this was not something that Meg felt able to justify. She could not just stop young Susie in the street, and say so. That would be rude, and anyway, it was none of her business – but that was not going to stop her 'helping'!

A reputation very often goes ahead, and Meg had heard of Willie Stevenson. That he was playing around with several of the local girls was common knowledge. The moment another took his fancy he had no qualms about abandoning whoever had been the previous favourite. One time, Meg heard, it was even after getting some poor girl in the family way.

Meg liked Susie. She did not want her to be hurt, so, could she stand back and do nothing? In Meg's mind …no!

It was blatantly obvious that a lot of canoodling was going on between Willie and Susie in the pitch-black darkness of the back green, not far below Meg's window. Living on the first landing, how could she avoid hearing? The sounds travelled vertically.

Lately, over the last few dark nights, Meg could not help but hear the "Oohs…" and "Ahhs…" that she recognised as progressing to very serious canoodling.

If she was going to save Susie, she would somehow have to bring this romance to an end quickly, she decided. She hoped she would not be too late. Not a moment to lose. To stop it, she would have to act now! A visit to the middle of town was called for.

'Tam Shepherd's Trick Shop', was just up from Argyle Street. Meg was no stranger to the place. It was where she obtained the various little bits of magic and tricks that she had fun dabbling with, generally to other people's annoyance.

That evening, Susie, and Willie Stevenson were at it again, "Oohing" and "Ahhing" with gusto so, 'Plan A' was put into action, a simple one, involving itching powder.

It was a still evening. The powder would fall exactly where she wanted it, Meg reckoned. She had partially opened the landing window earlier, so her simple task would be to tiptoe down to the half-landing and empty the powder gently from the packet, onto the pair doing the heavy smooching, just below. It was dark enough for Meg not to be seen.

Success! With the packet emptied, and confident that the powder found its target, it was mission accomplished. Unfortunately, the following evening it was obvious that the deterrent had failed. From the 'Oohs...' and 'Ahhs...' they were still enjoying themselves much too much again...

It would have to be the same routine; maybe it would be more effective the second time but again, Meg was disappointed. The performance recommenced the next night, so, a change of tactics was necessary.

Meg felt a little put out with herself – 'Plan A' should have had more effect but, no matter, she would just move on a stage.

A simple solution would have been to pour a

bucket of cold water over the pair of them – like for dogs. For certain, the "Ahhing" would have stopped, but that was not in the least subtle. No, they would just go somewhere else, and probably Susie would never speak to her again.

Meg thought it through, carefully.

'Plan A' was never a certainty to work anyway, she knew that. That is why she purchased another product at the same time. A back-up – one that had been useful before. She could apply it with confidence – stink bombs!

She opened her door quietly, and with the three pellets in her hand, she crept halfway down the stair. Again, using the landing window, already opened just enough, Meg dropped the little capsules, being very careful not to hit the frolicking couple.

One, two, and three! The capsules burst silently as they hit the flagstones and the aroma released. There was little doubt of that – the smell reached her at the half landing.

Disturbingly, the pattern continue for another three nights: the canoodling, the "Oohs..." and "Ahhs...", and the stink bombs. Meg was beginning to suspect failure and then, on the fourth night – nothing.

Had she succeeded? Had the big split occurred as planned?

With the backcourt remaining silent on the fifth and sixth night, the answer had to be a resounding, 'yes'.

Meg 'just happened' to bump into little Susie on the stairway a few days later, and conversed politely. She, again, 'just happened' to say, innocently of course, "I haven't seen Willie Stevenson around here for a wee while, Susie. You are still going steady with him, aren't you? Is everything alright, my dear?"

Susie burst into tears.

"No, I'm not, Mrs Findlay. It's awful kind of you to ask, but no, we're not going steady, in fact we're no' going out at all..."

"Oh dear, whatever happened, love?"

"We had big arguments, him and me. When I said he had given me fleas, he said it wisnae him, it was me – that I had given them to him. Oh... an' I... I... I got real mad..."

"Oh dear, Susie, what a thing for him to say to you, and what a way to have to end it..."

"Oh no, Mrs Findlay, that wisnae the end – it was the wind..."

"He had wind, oh my, I can understand," Meg smiled. "A man that suffers from wind can be a big problem, especially after you get married – then they just don't care..."

"So, ah told him, that wis it... Ah couldnae be doin' with a man that had bad wind like he had, and had never even once said an 'excuse me'..."

"Quite right dear..."

"...But when he said it wisnae him, it was me that caused the smell, well, ah just lost it. He called it silent fartin'. Me, that's never farted in my life! He said he could put up wi' the fleas – they could be killed off, but he couldnae see how he could control my fartin'... An' that's when I hit 'im!"

Susie started serious sobbing.

"Come here, pet," said Meg, and gave her a wee cuddle.

"Oh, Mrs Findlay, it is awfy good to talk to someone like you. You understand these things..."

"Och, away ye go ...but anyway, it's probably for the best, ma wee darlin'," said Meg, and smiled, contentedly.

19

2009
None shall sleep...

It can be disappointing, suffering from an over-active brain. At this time of night and after a long day, relaxing into dreamland would have been nice.

She had lain down in the bed she shared with Tom, hoping to drop off quickly – but it was not happening! She should have been fast asleep by now. Was it that celebratory drink? When Tom solved the clue, what else could they do? They *had* to drink a toast to him, surely.

It was not as if I drank too much cider. Hmm... maybe? ...And surely, a ham sandwich with mustard at two in the morning should not be preventing sleep at three! Of course not... Ok, who am I trying to kid. I am Mum. I should have known better – but it tasted great!

Tom, beside her, was having no problem and had no need to use the 'wall' tonight. She suggested that method to him when he lay awake a while ago, although she suspected the cause for him not sleeping at night, was his regular evening snooze in the chair.

A simple procedure... "Close your eyes and imagine a brick wall," she often told him. "You can either simply gaze at the blankness, or count the bricks. I go for the blank wall. It is always great for me – asleep in no time." But for some reason, not tonight! She had closed her eyes and tried a moment ago, but someone had added a poster to her wall: MUGS ARE GULLIBLE...

What! No, no, that should not... It was her wall after all. She was the one who controlled it! She tried again. Eyes closed...

Oh, no! It was graffiti this time: GULLIBLE MUGS HAVE CIDER UP A TREE...

What is going on? Did Tom have a spray can?

Obviously, that post-midnight feast had not helped, nor the cider... It could be a long night. She sat up and looked to her side. Why was he not suffering?

"I can't sleep, Tom," she whispered. There was no reaction – Tom was dead to the world.

David was also lying awake, tossing and turning in his bedroom, with exactly the same problem as his mother. Sleep was very far away for him too.

He could see out of the bedroom window. He rarely pulled the curtains so that he could fall asleep gazing out at the stars or the moon or – being Glasgow – at raindrops rolling down the glass. It was still dark outside.

Is it nearly daylight yet?

It seemed as if he had already been lying awake for most of the night.

Open the window!

That should have helped. Fresh air, a sure thing to help you get to sleep.

Persevere...

For what seemed like a very long time, the window stayed open. He was now frozen. It was not working! He got out of bed and closed the window.

At least he was not stupid enough to have coffee with the food. Obviously that keeps you awake and would have been really silly. He'd taken the option of another two cans of cider, strong stuff, stronger than he thought it would be – how could his mother drink it?

He should go for a piddle in a moment, he realised. He did not want to get up, he was warm again and comfortable – but awake...

Lying on her other side might help, Gillian decided, and turned over.

Think of something nice, something that would be soothing and sleep inducing, something like ...what? The new cardigan, bought yesterday, yes, she could think about that, that would be nice.

A bit more expensive than planned, but lovely and worth every penny. A shame that it cannot be worn for a while, and having to put it in the drawer for a few weeks to keep it hidden away. If Tom, for once, actually notices when it is worn and asks if it is new, I can honestly say, "Oh no, I've had it for weeks. Don't you recognise it?" That will shut him up. But this was not putting her to sleep at all. She turned over again.

Tom lay snoring.

Life was not fair. Gillian could not understand how he could eat as much as she did and drink three cups of coffee, and sleep soundly in his chair for two and a half hours earlier in the evening – yet come to bed and go straight to sleep!

"Tom," she said in his ear, wanting a little sympathy. "Tom, I can't sleep."

Why does he snore like that? It is very annoying, and probably what is keeping me awake!

"Tom!"

...But Tom snored on...

"Two hundred and three... two hundred and four... two hundred and..."

Perhaps, there were better ways to get to sleep than counting aloud the numbers of woolly animals, David decided.

What time is it? Goodness. That's something I should not bother about if I am trying to sleep. He turned the illuminated clock the other way – then kept wondering what the time was!

Was the bed facing the correct way? It should be facing north – or was it south? Which way was north anyway?

At least we solved Meg's riddle, well Dad did, and with three of us present, we can all claim a little credit. What is the next clue again? Blooming heck, I can't remember. Where did I leave the piece of paper? What did I do with it? For goodness sake – why can't I sleep?

Gillian was currently contemplating if a jury would convict her if she placed a pillow over Tom's face and smothered him.

Might chance it – at least it would stop his snoring.

At last, she was feeling drowsy ...and then the mobile began to sound at the other side of the bed. Tom's phone – the irritating xylophone sound, over and over!

Thank you very much, whoever you are.

It sounded incredibly loud and startled her, just as she was about to drop off. Isn't that just like the thing!

"Tom. Tom... Tom!"

She was wide-awake again, but he was not, and, to stop the phone she had to stretch across his prostate form to grab it.

"Hello... Mum? ...It is you. Are you all right? ...Oh goodness. ...Dear, dear, not again! Have you contacted the doctor, or an ambulance? ...No? ...then I'll do that for you, right away. You lie down and take it easy until we arrive. Have you taken the tablets? ...Yes? ...Good, then sit and relax. Help is on its way."

"Thomas Findlay – bloody wake up!" and the manner in which it was said this time made certain that there would be no possibility of his continuing to enjoy the land of nod.

"Mum's unwell again. I'm phoning for an ambulance. Get on your clothes and get the car ready. We are going over..."

Closing the curtains, so that no light whatsoever could enter the room, had at last been the remedy for David and, thankfully, he was now asleep, totally oblivious to all of life's little fiddly problems and about to enjoy sweet dreams...

He thought afterwards, how easily one could be disturbed.

...Difficult to avoid waking – when a bedroom door bursts open to let a bright light pour in and temporarily render a person blind – and be followed by a voice bellowing down from a great height.

"David, are you awake? We're on our way to Granny Walker. She's had another of her attacks and I've phoned for an ambulance. We'll take the car. You can have the van if you need it. We'll call you later and let you know what's happening, but you don't have to bother. Just you go back to sleep! Bye!"

Right, ok then. "One sheep ...two sheep ...three sheep..."

20

1957
A surprise letter...

Meg Findlay did not normally receive many letters
in the post but, a few moments ago, she heard the
clatter of the letterbox. It could mean this was one
of those special days, although of course, the rattle
of the letterbox did not necessarily mean it was the
postman – or a letter – but then again what else
could it be? It was so much easier to sit
contemplating than to actually do something about
it.

She felt lousy ...absolutely lousy. There was no
other way of putting it. Her dearest wish was to sit
in that chair and feel sorry for herself all day. Her
head was throbbing – kept her awake for most of the
night. How she longed for an Askit Powder,
convinced that she could have managed to go to
work if there had been one in the house. That
remedy worked every time.

Not even dressed yet – she was in two minds
about returning to her warm bed. Too late now but
she wished that she'd asked Angus, before he left, to

pop down to the shops for that magic powder.

It was now well after breakfast time.

Angus sorted out his own food this morning, and eagerly went off to school half an hour ago. She admired his dedication and enthusiasm. Being into the third month, he seemed settled at his new school. A good boy, but she was glad to see the back of him this morning. The way she was feeling, everything he did sounded so noisy.

He took out a bowl for the cornflakes and clattered it on the table, and then the spoon clattered in the dish – even the cornflakes sounded like thunder as he poured them – and he kept talking to her!

The cup of tea, that he took time to make for her and although well intentioned, had caused her head unnecessary suffering too. Eleven times the spoon hit the side of the cup when he stirred in the sugar – and then she was unable to summon up the energy to drink it.

She loved her son but, today, it was nice when he went out... Peace!

Most unusual for her, having a day at home, off work, sick, but she had not been feeling too bright for most of yesterday either. Sleeping very little last night had not helped. Luckily, Monday was a quiet day so she would not be missed too much in the office. They should cope without her.

She wanted to go and check if it was a letter, but could not engender sufficient enthusiasm to move. She was certainly under the weather. The usual tingle of anticipation she had when a letter arrived was missing. Neither was there any enthusiasm for the guesswork game, the game always played on receiving a letter.

Good news? A nice surprise? Or a final demand?

For her game, she had to guess before she opened the envelope, but guessing was out today; too much bother even thinking... Anyway, if it were a letter, it would not run away, she would get it in a moment, when she could summon up the energy.

...And she fell asleep.

What? She woke, startled, as the banging came at the door.

"Yer coal's here!" was the shout. "Urr you there, Missus?"

Two coalmen were on the stair landing, at her door.

"She aye leaves the money an' the key under the doormat if she wants it. Is the money no' there?"

"No', it's no' an' she's no' in. Will the key no' be with the neighbour or somethin'? Ah told ye we shouldnae have carried them up, not without checkin' if she's wantin' it first... Ah don't want to have to take this bloody sack doon them stairs again – it's heavy! You had me doin' that at the last close an' I am not doin' it again – right? Ahm no' comin' out wi' you again. Could we no' just leave it at the door."

"Naw! Ah'm sure she'd love us fur that. Ah can just see her takin' it in her hoose, lump by lump, for the next two weeks.... Look, I am the driver, so I am the one that says whit you are goanie do, an' you will carry it doon them stairs again if I say so – right?"

Her first thoughts were that the noise outside her door would be wakening all her neighbours, then she realised it was late morning and they would all be up. She was probably the only one in the building still half-asleep...

With not feeling well, she completely forgot that this was the day for the coal delivery. She would have to let them in. They would want to pour the coal into the bunker and take away their empty sacks. There would be peace and quiet again once they'd gone...

Earlier, it had been the postman right enough. A letter was lying on the lobby floor. Without looking at it, she picked it up to prevent dirty feet walking over it. She opened the door and let the two men enter the small hallway to where the coal-bunker sat, and lifted the lid. It wasn't completely empty, but not far off it.

"Sorry, hen. Were ye havin' a long lie this mornin', an' this gommeral woke ye up? If he did I'm awful sorry. D'you want two bags as usual?"

As the coalman spoke, he poured the contents of the sack into the bunker, creating the usual dusty mess that she would have to clear up later. The second man came in with the other sack and emptied it, causing even more dust, and she paid them.

"See ye in two weeks again then, hen. All righ'?"

She would not. She would be fit and well again, and back at work, and in two weeks' time she would remember to leave the key and the money under the mat as usual. That was the easiest way for her because, with her working full-time, she had not had the chance to get to know her neighbours. Of course, there was no Wee Mrs Gray across the landing nowadays to help out in emergencies. She had always been there – but that had been a while ago, at the old place. How Meg missed that dear old lady.

The fellow across the landing here did not seem at all friendly. She hoped that when she got the chance to say hello properly, the people upstairs or in the close would turn out to be more so.

The dust from the coal delivery lingered in the air and started settling around the house as she went back into the kitchen. She flopped down again on the chair, and...

The letter! What happened to that letter? She'd lifted it from the floor. It was in her hand. Where had she dropped it? What if it had fallen into the bunker – before they poured in the coal!

She pushed herself out of the chair again, still feeling terrible. Oh, what she would have given for just one Askit Powder. The envelope, it was white. What would it be like if it was in the bunker?

Ah, there it is, on the floor.

Although covered by footprints it was still obviously a white one; she disliked brown envelopes, they usually turned out to be official and officialdom usually heralded a bill, which she liked even less than the brown envelope.

She picked it up, shook the dust from it, turned it over, and went through her normal routine. Who sent it? And no cheating.

I must guess without opening it, even though I am ill... The writing first of all...?

It was not recognisable, and made more difficult by the fact that it had been re-directed. The first line of the original address, printed carefully by hand, still showed 'Mrs Meg Findlay'. The lines underneath were neatly printed too, but had been scrawled out by somebody at the Post Office, no doubt, and the correct address added.

It had been sent to her old address... Now, who would do that?

The stamp... That was another clue, well, not the stamp itself – the postmark. As usual, on the stamp, the young Queen Elizabeth was looking serenely out, doing her bit for the country. Meg always thought that people would buy more stamps if the dear Queen Liz was smiling a wee bit, or, better still, if she had shown a cheeky wee grin...

The franking of the stamp was showing 'Dundee 11.30 a.m. 8 Feb. 57' and, though a little smudged, she could make that out easily enough. Posted last Friday, but that did not really help, and, from Dundee?

No, it wasn't working. As to who sent it, she had no idea! Maybe the fact that she was not feeling well was slowing down her perceptive powers, she told herself; she was usually better than this. Not getting enough letters to keep her in practice – that could be the problem. Sadly, it was not working for her today.

Defeat admitted – she would have to open it.

The flap was well sealed. A knife, she needed a knife, but not that one – jam on it. She took a clean one from the drawer and carefully slit the top edge of the envelope.

Inside were several pages of poor quality paper. Like sheets torn from a school jotter and with pre-printed lines on them. Someone obviously wrote this with care. There was an address at the top corner, but she knew no one who lived there. The writing, and it was real joined-up writing, was in blue ink, and smudged here and there.

The very first line caused her to sit down in surprise as she realised.

'Dear Meg, my very dear Meg...'

"My God ...it's him. After all those years..." She felt a bit dizzy. No wonder she did not guess the sender; never, in a month of Sundays, could she have guessed this!

'Dear Meg, my very dear Meg,
It has been nearly thirteen years since we were together, I know, but I haven't ever stopped thinking about you.
I hope that you are well and that our son is growing up to be as good a man as his father is. (That was meant as a joke, as I know you'll think that I'm a scumbag.)
I have never said I was sorry for what I did, regarding you and our son, or rather – before you correct me it should be – what I didn't do and still haven't done.'

She stopped reading for a moment. Well, she had to stop. Tears blurred her eyes. She wiped them dry, took a deep breath, and continued...

'You'll remember I did try at first and sent some money to you to help, several times, but that had to stop when life became a bit harder for me, and I apologise for that. I am very sorry – very, very sorry – and would like to come back home. I know now that I should never have left you in the first place and realise the hurt it caused you.'

She stopped again and gazed around the room. She had difficulty accepting this was happening, but the letter was in her hand, it was real. She continued...

'I know it will seem silly to you, me being just on the other side of the country, and feeling homesick, and after such a long time too. Homesick for you, for the son I've never seen, for Glasgow, and the people in it.

I am in Dundee. I lost my job in the yard at Govan, and because Bella had a few relatives in Dundee, we moved here in the hope of me finding work. I've had jobs in the shipyard here, but after each ship is finished, pay-offs are made until more work arrives, and then they take people on again and you hope you're going to get another chance of a job. It's not looking so good though at the moment.

You'll be pleased to know that Bella (and I know you'll hate even seeing her name mentioned), that her and me have parted. She's gone back to Glasgow to her mother, and good riddance.

Life's been hell living with her recently and I'm glad she's gone.'

"Oh Hamish... It took you long enough..." Meg sighed.

'In Dundee I feel like an outsider. It might have been wiser to have gone to Australia as we'd planned all these years ago, and then I would have had a good reason to feel homesick, but Dundee...
I hope you can feel it in your heart to give this deaf old fool another chance – we are still married, so that would be all the more reason. This letter is being sent with deep feelings of regret.
Your not-too-distant and ever loving husband, Hamish xxxx'

She held the envelope and the letter close to her chest. After all that time, her Hamish, her foolish but lovable idiot Hamish. It was strange the effect a letter can have, particularly one out of the blue like this that was so unexpected and sad.

A tear was there again, she just could not avoid it. She checked the date. Yes, it did say 8 February, and no, it was not an 'April Fool's Day' joke!

Suddenly she jumped up, tore the pieces of paper into little bits and threw them into the empty grate.

"It'll help light the fire later," she grimaced. "He wants to come back, does he? Bella's gone home and left him, has she? Aw the shame... Does he think I came up the Clyde in a banana boat?"

She felt a lot better now. Her headache had gone. She would put on some clothes – it was nearly dinnertime already.

"No use going into work now. It's time for a nice walk in the park," she smiled, "... and to get on with my life..."

21

2009
A little bit of delving...

The hospital waiting room at four in the morning was not a particularly comforting place. As he sat there beside Gillian, he wondered to himself if anything could improve it. The lighting was fine, the colours on the walls and ceiling seemed all right; chairs were well cushioned and with arms, and were spaced out in a reasonable way. So, what was wrong?

Could it simply be the expressions on other people's faces? The anxious will-they-be-alright looks of doubt that are hard to hide, as relatives sit worrying about the person they know is unwell. Yes, it could be. Could I help by doing a song and dance, or a joke or two? Certainly not! Random thoughts going a little haywire...

Tom reopened the two-year-old tattered copy of the Reader's Digest, picked up from the table. He had already read the article on page sixteen: 'Handy hints to help when you can't get to sleep'. Must be terrible for anyone with that problem at night, he told himself – probably caused by a bad conscience...

Gillian's mum had made it to the ward so there was not a lot more they could do, other than wait until they assessed her condition.

'...and the best time to plant them is when the ground is dry and warm.'

Tom's eye reached the bottom of the page before realising that he was taking nothing in. He had read it but had no idea what he had been reading about... He closed the magazine.

Is that a crack in the ceiling? His mind wandered very easily. Oh, oh – is it getting larger? Great place for spiders...

He spent some of the time observing others sitting in the large waiting room: observing, without it being obvious – the benefit of darkness outside and light inside. Clear reflection from the glass. There was a mixture of expressions, some faces obviously showing concern, some with eyes closed and dozing, others looking fed-up. After all, it was the middle of the night.

Look – the woman in the green coat, she's starting to yawn! She is still yawning... hope she doesn't start me off...

He looked away, stood up to stretch his legs, and gazed out of the windows through glass that was being well-washed by the heavy rain streaming down. The view was into an unusually quiet car park, near the hospital front entrance.

It looked as if the Saturday night into Sunday morning emergency casualties had eased off.

Ambulances zooming up the tree-lined driveway with blue lights flashing, sometimes followed by police vehicles with blue lights flashing too, had become fewer in the last half-hour. To him, looking through the rain-splattered window into the wet night-darkness, each one approaching with flashing lights had looked menacing – but that could be due to his own mood, and a dislike of hospitals.

Mutual gloom was the feeling both he and Gillian had since arriving. It was the uncertainty, not knowing how firm a grip her mother had on life. Feeling low is unavoidable when someone close to you is seriously ill, particularly when you know you are powerless.

Tom reached out to Gillian. "She'll be alright," he said.

She returned the comment with a sad look. "It's the worst she's been. I wish someone would give us a progress report. Do you think if we asked the nurse, she would know yet?"

It was another two hours of sitting, walking around in circles, fetching and drinking liquids from the vending machine and looking at the same magazine over and over, but not seeing it, before the nurse came to tell them the good news. Getting to the ward and reaching the bedside, to find her mum sitting up and able to chat, made Gillian feel so much better.

Tom did not think she looked too healthy, but as Gillian's mum herself said, "Being in the hospital is the best place to be, especially if you are no' weel..." Mrs Cath Walker would be staying for tests, and could even require an operation. Duration of stay to be decided later.

They left her at the hospital and made their way back home.

It was now after seven a.m. and gradually getting lighter. The rain had stopped. The clouds were breaking up. As they drove along, they felt the tension reduce. Tom started to sing. "One, two, three o'clock, four o'clock rock..." gently at first, then a little louder, "...Five, six, seven o'clock, eight o'clock rock..." and that is when Gillian joined in. Making the noise certainly helped ease the tension, but the song would have sounded so much better if both had been singing in the same key!

Gillian suddenly recalled they'd promised to keep David informed, but they were almost home, better not to wake him.

"He's such a grump if he doesn't have a good sleep," Tom added.

They arrived, and decided to leave their son in the dark for a little longer. Anyway, he was sound asleep when they looked in, although it was difficult to see in the pitch black that he had succeeded in eventually achieving in his room. They were not to know that he had fallen asleep barely an hour before they returned, still mumbling about sheep. It was very fortunate that they let him be.

Good to be home. They relaxed and had a cup of tea, tea made using their very own kettle and real tea bags, with real milk and real sugar, and they drank it out of real cups, sitting at their own kitchen table with a nice bright tablecloth – a table that did not wobble!

...So much better than the Hospital Waiting Room and the vended fluids that they survived on.

Gillian wrote a note for David, the essential facts about her Mum's condition, left it propped in front of the kettle – and then it was back to bed.

Almost instantly, Gillian dropped off to sleep.

Tom, meantime, could not. At first, he did not mind in the least, because he knew what to do. In addition to Gillian's old advice about 'The Wall', he had new tips spinning around in his head to help him – noted from the Reader's Digest and, as the morning became lighter, Tom found that he'd had plenty opportunity to test them all...

None worked!

It was ten o'clock when David woke, turned over, and went back to sleep, Sunday was not a day to rush at.

It was shortly after eleven before he raised his head again, decided he had slept enough, and declared himself ready to begin another day but with the silence in the house, he thought his mum and dad were still at the hospital. Must be serious if they had to remain. Gran Walker could be in a bad way.

Downstairs, he found the note and was pleased to learn his gran was 'comfortable', and that his parents were back, upstairs and in bed.

It was almost lunchtime, but cooking was not his thing. He made do with tea, toast and cheese, and that wakened him properly. He was the only one up and eager to do something. And last night's new clue could be a challenge. He could try and solve it – but what had he done with the piece of paper? He'd noted it down as his dad read it out and taken it...

Upstairs, to his own bedroom – on the bedside table!

Must get it!

His father, now being asleep, missed the spectacle of his son taking the stairs two at a time, grabbing the piece of paper and, without stopping, descending in the same manner, to plonk himself back in his seat – without being in the slightest out of puff! Tom would have been *sooooo* jealous.

Paper in hand, David decided that he would solve the clue on his own this time. He could not let 'Old Avacare!' beat him, so he sat and racked his brains, reading and rereading the scribbled words... 'I can't help droning on about this. It can be torture for some, but heaven for others. Keep it in the family for when they have a tart an' tea but it's not food and drink.'

This family is not overly smart and Granny Meg knew that. Surely she would not have made it too difficult. It must be something obvious, or easily accessible, and in Gran and Grandad Findlay's house ...or in the garden, or... somewhere else!

Fifteen minutes later, he was still desperate for inspiration, sitting staring at the scrap of paper. His mother and father could appear soon and he needed something that he could suggest, but no... Granny Meg was winning – yet again!

Maybe if I did something different, and didn't concentrate solely on the clue, it might suddenly click! The family tree! I could have a go at that, secretly, without Dad knowing though I just wish he would try himself. He's all talk, but never actually has a go. It should be easy for him but he's scared of the internet. Scared of making an error, or being caught out by a scam, or of someone finding his password and him losing all his money because he pressed a wrong button. He believes the scaremongers.

My dad is chicken. That's sad!

My great-great-grandad was a hero! Imagine that, a hero, in our family – *a man that faced enemy fire!* But how would he have coped with computers? Might not have been any braver than my old man! I wonder... and what about this family tree? If I set it up for Dad, would he have a go?

I could start with great-great-grandad Alexander...

Genealogy was becoming popular, and David was aware that there was lots of information becoming accessible on line, but he spotted another deterrent for his father – it would cost him!

'Scotland's People' was David's choice. It would have been unpatriotic not to have given that a wee peek, and it looked as good as any. Still to be paid for, but it seemed simple enough to use. His father should cope. He started the process, but the search for Alexander Findlay gave a long list. A common name.

More clues were needed and help was required.

I know a man, thought David, and he is only a phone call away.

"Hello. Grandad?"

Angus thought that the call was only to pass on the message about Cath Walker's hospitalisation and for David it was tricky switching the topic over. It took a few reminisces from Grandad about Gran Walker, before he managed.

"Dad still hasn't asked me yet – about doing the family tree, but I've made a start and I need help. You are the man. What can you tell me about your Grandad, Grandad?"

Asking questions that tested Angus's memory could be a chancy business; remembering facts and names was becoming difficult. It might work if he was given time, or if he was being asked on a good day. He could probably remember, but sometimes it could take days before it clicked, and then, clear as a bell.

Today was a good day...

"Alexander Findlay died 1919, shortly after returning from active service, but which month? Now, was it spring or winter of that year? His father and mother lived all their lives in Aberloudie – I know that – and he had a lot of brothers. The wife's name? What was it again ...Phoebe? Not sure, David."

Although it was his grandmother, Angus had never used her first name. She was always Grandma Findlay, even to Angus's mother, as far as he could recall. Never having known the woman – she had died when he was barely a year old – his knowledge of her was all second hand. To David, everything was useful – and Angus was warming up. "...Alexander's birthplace? Aberloudie; and he moved to Glasgow, Anderston district; from the quiet of the countryside to a street full of tenements."

Anderston was where his mother, Meg, was born. That much Angus recalled easily and with confidence. She'd moved to live in her mother-in-law's house, where she gave birth to Angus, and the pair of them had lived there for many years after the old lady died. Then frustration for Angus...

He could picture it: the place he lived when young, but the name of the street eluded him.

"The name of an English town..." Then it came suddenly! "*Dover*, yes, Dover Street! No chance of the number of the close. That would be pushing it... but my birth certificate will show the address. Hold on a moment, David..."

David was scribbling down notes like mad at the other end.

"Beth, where are you?" David heard him shout.

"Ah, you're there. Beth, where is my birth certificate, please – I need it now?"

"How in heaven's name am I supposed to know that?" David's grandmother's replied.

"Hmm! Right then. Sorry, David, that's it, I'm afraid..."

Grandad's contribution may not have been a lot, but it was a start and David was grateful, and so, to the next stage – to find what the internet knew of

Alexander Findlay.

Computerised records were wonderfully easy to access, providing they existed in the first place. In seconds, a hard-copy of his great-great-grandad's death certificate was in his hands – and Grandad got it right. Survived the trenches of the Great War, on 1st March 1919, then in peacetime, knocked down by a vehicle in a busy Glasgow street and killed. Cruel!

David stopped and listened.

No sound of movement from upstairs yet. Mum and Dad still sleeping. Might as well continue... A birth certificate?

Key facts: Alexander Findlay, male, Aberloudie, born before 1900. That was input. Ah... Not so lucky this time. It did not magically appear. Why would that be? Parents not registering the birth, or a dozy registrar's poor record? Or poor inputting information perhaps?

Had he run out of luck? Perhaps he just lacked the magic touch – that had been Granny Meg's domain!

Was there another approach... newspaper headlines? If Alexander Findlay was a hero, did newspapers report it? Glasgow newspapers had nothing as far back as 1919. Another blind alley.

"Well, I tried," he murmured under his breath, about to give up but then, "...just a moment!"

Some enthusiast had done a project: GLASGOW AT PEACE. A web site – dedicated to the period after World War One. Selections from newspapers, with photographs. Almost two hundred screen pages. It must have taken months of hard graft to complete. Only someone really crazy about Glasgow could have done it – an overly dedicated Weegie, David decided.

Anything for 1st March? But it wasn't in date order, which made it a little less attractive. He would have to look through all the pages but realised, that the date he was looking for might not be included. Get on with it! It would be a hard slog, he decided.

But it was not.

There was all sorts of news, not all earth shattering but interesting.

'Rangers beat Celtic on 18 October.' That would have pleased his father. 'An airship crossed the Atlantic, from Scotland to America, for the first time.'

'A Scottish revolution in the centre of Glasgow fizzled out.' David read some detail of this one. Could have been serious. English troops in George Square on stand-by because their Scottish mates were threatening to join the rebels. David wondered if his Dad knew that...

It could have been Home Rule way back then – a Red Revolution in Glasgow! The SNP should think themselves lucky – we might all have been Commies! Dad would have loved that – not! Learn a little every day – and there is more...

'The Kelvin Hall, an Exhibition Hall to compete with the best – an anonymous donor gave £6000 towards the cost of the next exhibition.' Wow! Who would do that now? Serious money in those days –

way before Lotto!

He was looking for a particular story, but he could not resist these snippets. His fingers were still crossed when he reached screen page102 of 200 – and here was something! The date he was searching for.

'The weather: very cold. Thick fog that has blanketed Glasgow for many days, to lift by Saturday, to be replaced by sleet and occasional snow showers.'

Hmm, winter refusing to leave – though at least fog is rare nowadays. He looked at the headline. CITY JEWELLER ROBBED AT GUNPOINT. It was not what he was searching for but he scanned the story. A jeweller attacked, in his Argyll Arcade shop, and uncut diamonds stolen. He'd given in and handed over twenty-five diamonds, after being kicked and beaten almost unconscious by the armed thief. The police had not caught anyone. The jeweller might have to sell the business, ruined, a broken man. He could not possibly continue...

Interesting, but unfortunately not about Alexander... Then he opened the next screen – and found it!

It felt strange reading the report of Alexander Findlay's accident.

It had happened a long time ago, but he felt involved, and saddened, and even though he knew little of the man, he could visualise it so easily. In his mind, David was standing at the scene, in a part of the city he knew very well, witnessing a catastrophe of long ago.

UNTIMELY DEATH OF WAR HERO.

Traffic in Argyle Street was disrupted yesterday morning due to a fatal accident in the region of the Hielanman's Umbrella. All road traffic was diverted, and the tramcar system, for the length of Argyle Street and adjoining streets, temporarily halted until the body of a man was removed to the City Mortuary and the Police Department had investigated the cause. The individual died at the scene after being struck by a moving tram.

Central Police would like to speak to anyone who witnessed the accident. Witnesses are asked to contact them at the Central Police Station. The male fatality was later identified as Mr Alexander Findlay, a resident of the Anderston District of Glasgow.

Mr Findlay's tragic death leaves behind a grief-stricken wife, who is expecting their first child.

Mr Findlay fought in the World War for the total duration, and was the proud recipient of a medal for heroism.

He had been severely injured twice, during the conflict, but, on each occasion when his leg injuries had barely healed, he returned to the bloody fight.

He had a nickname, during the conflict, chosen by his comrades, 'The Jammy Devil' and was one of the few pipers to actually survive the war.

The Commanding Officer at Maryhill Barracks said 'All who had known him and fought alongside him would be saddened by his unfortunate passing. He had been a very brave soldier.'

David was glad to be alone; he had tears in his eyes.

It was late afternoon before Gillian and Tom wakened. They appeared downstairs still looking woozy with no thoughts of the treasure hunt. They had enough on their minds with Granny Walker.

David made no mention of what he had been doing. There would be a more appropriate time to talk of his search but he reckoned he had achieved something and his day had not been wasted. He felt hooked already. The search for a family member had begun and it could blossom into a Family Tree.

Tomorrow, Monday, meant back to the daily grind, but it could delve a bit more in the evening – then it occurred to him – The family tree! He was doing exactly what his old man wanted... Damn!

22

1960
Golf clubs? Oh….

Meg would never forgive Hamish Findlay, but at least she was over the worst of the pain of her husband leaving her for 'that floozy Bella Roberts'. She was back to being her bright and mischievous self, enjoying her youthful energy and her cheery approach to living, but she knew it could not last forever, even for her.

Angus was growing up and, growing older, and becoming even more studious. His growing older caused mixed feelings for Meg; she was progressing at the same rate.

She did not relish ageing.

It was altogether a different sort of problem for her son...

Angus had reached fourth year, still at school, still a brain-box, and still displaying a dull persona. The teasing that happened when he arrived at the new learning establishment died out after those first few weeks.

His classmates decided to accept him for what he was – a bore.

To be fair, that was how his male classmates felt. As far as the females in his class were concerned, it was worse – he was a non-event. He was there, yes, he was nice, yes, but that was it, full stop, but then, for a string of reasons, and thanks to Elizabeth Smith and her dislike of maths, for a limited time only – Angus became a '*Love God*'.

Mathematics was the one class that Miss Elizabeth Smith found driest and liked least. Surprisingly, with her lack of interest, the necessary grades to permit continuation in that group were still achieved. There was no question though that during the lesson her mind would wander.

Angus, also in that group, was attentive and wide-awake, interacting with the teacher, as was his habit. His over-attentiveness happened in other classes too – so annoying for his classmates.

Elizabeth had a close friend, Grace. They often played 'I dare you!' during the break, with the challenge being to see who could come up with the most outrageous dare. The two girls were in total agreement that this was a much more productive way of using time during a tedious lesson. During today's maths class, a new dare came into the wandering mind of Elizabeth. Grace would learn of it shortly.

Elizabeth would be daring Grace to get Angus Findlay to go on 'a date'. An addendum was to be that she must have 'her wicked way' with him; go 'all the way' as they say.

The maths teacher, if he had glanced in her direction, might have wondered why a smile was on the face of someone who obviously detested his class.

Elizabeth was onto a winner, quietly confident that her pal would refuse this challenge. Everyone knew that as far as Grace was concerned, Angus was a wimp...

It was great being a girl. Girls could talk to one another with true feelings uncovered, but only with real girlfriends. That was how Elizabeth related to Grace. All of each other's private thoughts, shared, plus the added bonus in the relationship – Elizabeth knew that Grace would never tell her lies...

The maths lesson continued with Elizabeth's mind thinking of everything except the work going on in the classroom. Her mind was revolving around, *shhh* ...S. E. X.

Saying the word out-loud was something that neither she, nor Grace, ever did. There was no need to be crude and on that they always agreed. 'It' always sufficed in any girly discussions, but there was nothing against thinking about, *shh* ...s.e.x.

She glanced around the room and convinced herself that none of the girls in her class had ever truly experienced 'it!' She certainly had not, although there had been a rumour that Molly Davis ...but, it was only a rumour. No, none of her classmates would ever have gone 'all the way'. She would have been very disappointed if any of them were to admit that she was making a wrong assumption about them. My goodness, at fifteen-years-old, of course that would not happen: all too young for that sort of thing. In her mind, they were all as sweet and innocent as she and Grace – so this would be a first in the class – if Grace would be willing to 'dare'...

To Elizabeth, 'it' tended to be thought of in a romanticised and dreamy way, and often with a certain youthful and curling-lipped Cliff Richard figuring in the dream. He was number one in her imaginative cavorting. Each night she'd lay her head on the pillow and, as the music began inside that sleepy head, she'd looked forward to the pleasure of being Cliff's 'Living Doll' on yet another night...

Yes, Elizabeth dreamed a lot – particularly in the Maths class.

A little later, after class, when the two girls were on their own, she came out with today's dare.

"No, that's not a fair dare," said Grace reacting sulkily. "It has to be something that is achievable."

She said that, and meant it at the time, but Grace would prove braver than her friend had ever thought, and her rising to the challenge was not a decision taken lightly, especially with her opinion of Angus. If she was feeling generously spirited her reaction was normally, "Angus? Oh ...him?" Anyway, being a well-brought-up young girl, she was aware of protocols and in this case that boys were supposed to do the asking! ...And he would never ask her! So, what was she to do?

It was fortunate that Elizabeth was there to keep her right!

"He doesn't have to. Not this year," her friend was pleased to point out. "Have you forgotten this is a Leap Year? You can ask him..."

Grace forced herself, and asked – and was accepted by Angus, but in a nonchalant way, as if it were a common thing for a pretty girl to approach him and invite him to go out.

"Go to the cinema – with you? Yea," he replied. "You'll be paying, of course ...because you did the asking, ok?"

"Oh, right..."

Unfortunately, not the reaction she expected. She had been about to offer to share costs, but should he not have insisted on paying it all? That was certainly how she understood it. Hadn't every other boy paid in the past? Was it to do with Leap Year? She struggled to appear unfazed, but was worried. If she was to be paying, where would the cash come from – Mum, or Dad?

"Where are we going, then?" he continued. "There's a good film in town, at Greens Playhouse – The Brides of Dracula."

Ooh, sounds really romantic, thought Grace.

"How could we get there?" she asked, it was a good distance away.

"By bus, obviously," said Angus. "This outing, it'll cost you a fortune!"

"Doesn't matter," she heard herself mutter, and

wished she hadn't, and then had a brilliant thought, "Is it not showing somewhere nearer than in the city centre?"

"The Tivoli, I suppose, in Partick. It'd be a shorter bus ride," he compromised.

"Super choice..." said she, wondering if fulfilling this 'dare' was really worth it, but she had started so she might as well carry on. If that is what it was going to take, she was up for it.

"It's a great film – very artistic, I've heard," said Angus.

"Whatever turns you on," she smiled.

"Turns you on? What do you mean?" he replied.

Sadly, his mind was innocent, and sincere, she realised. He really was a wimp. This could be a tough dare – and a lousy date!

"Thursday, then?" she confirmed.

"Yea, OK. When will you be round for me?"

Came Thursday, and, as agreed at quarter past six, Grace knocked on the door at Angus's home. His mother answered and seemed surprised. It was such a pretty-looking girl standing on her doorstep ...and for her son?

"You must be Grace, then?" said Angus's mum, and added with the hint of a mischievous smile, "Do you collect all your boyfriends from their doorsteps?"

Grace coloured a little, and did not quite know what to say, and at that moment would have preferred to have vanished under the doormat. Then

Angus appeared, but he did not look anything like she expected!

This fellow looked 'hot'!

Greased hair slicked back, wearing a leather jerkin and tight jeans, and suede shoes. It was almost as if he had modelled himself on – The King. She caught her breath. Would he speak like Elvis too? Better still, would he perform like Elvis when the moment was right? He really looked the part.

...And who was about to be going out with this hunk of real manhood? She was... and she was delighted! This promised to be some evening...

But no – it wasn't!

"That was really good," he said, as they left the cinema afterwards.They walked down the cinema steps as two separate individuals. Grace was peeved – he behaved impeccably all during the film. He had not even try to cuddle her, never even tried to feel her...

He sat with his arms folded and enjoyed the film – the whole film...

What a disappointment! She felt like slapping him, not for anything he did, more for what he failed to do. He did not even try to kiss her. It had been pitch black in there. Anything could have happened!

Her wandering hands and her attempts to create at least a little excitement failed. He was totally in control, her hands gently pushed back onto her lap as he refolded his arms, and concentrated on the film.

Everyone around them was snogging and goodness knows what else. Was there something wrong with her? How embarrassing! What sort of behaviour was that? Why did he not take advantage? She wanted him to! Dressed like a real rocker, but behaving like a blooming monk!

How disgusting!

...And what was she going to tell Elizabeth tomorrow?

For Grace, 'tomorrow' arrived too quickly.

"He was hot stuff," she claimed next morning, before going into the history class and, as she said it, she felt so guilty. This was her friend she was talking to...

"You are kidding me," laughed Elizabeth. "Admit it, you failed the dare. You did not go out with him at all, did you? You'll have to do a forfeit!"

"No, no, he was really hot! Looked like Elvis and acted just as wild. Not like when he is at school at all. Ask Jean Allison, she saw us!"

Jean did not need asking. She had been entering the cinema as they had arrived. She saw a gorgeous bloke – with Grace. Jean started the gossip the moment she arrived at school that morning, and the word quickly went round an excited group of girls. "Grace has been out with an Elvis lookalike!" Everyone wondered where she found him, and who he was. They were very interested, and a tiny bit jealous...

Elizabeth accepted it. Her friend had been more

successful than expected. As well as being astounded, Elizabeth was jealous too.

Although he thought it was a smashing film, Angus Findlay said nothing to anyone at school about his free cinema visit, not even to Grace. He even apologised when he bumped against Jean Allison going into class, but no comment passed between them. Imagine, not recognising that she had rubbed against the much-talked-about Elvis lookalike! He'd been given the usual 'Oh, Angus, it's only you,' glance.

Poor Grace. She felt guilty about the lie. It seemed so much bigger now that all the girls were aware, but as far as she was concerned it was not over yet. She was not going to give up quite so easily on Angus Findlay. It was galling for her but if something were to develop, it would be entirely up to her.

It was Grace who phoned Angus at home and invited him to meet her in the park. She had a plan; they would slip into the bushes and...

Impossible to fail that way, she'd decided.

"Why?" he enquired, when she phoned.

"Well ...well ...ehm ...it would be to discuss the finer detail of the film, of course. We didn't do that last night, did we?" she spluttered out.

They met in the park, and... Guess what Angus talked about? The producer, the director, the gruesome make-up used, the dialogue, the costumes, the lighting; all analysed, much to a frustrated young girl's disappointment. The 'dripping blood' title sequence was even carefully dissected by Angus – as he theorised on ideas that could have improved the startling effect.

The bushes figured not at all in any action!

Grace made several attempts the following week, without moving very much farther along the path to achieving her goal, but she was determined to succeed with the dare, come hell or high water. She would have her wicked way with him – it was a dare, after all.

One evening, she decided to go full at it.

Resorting to the very short mini-skirt seemed a good idea at the time, but now she was not so sure, and was it wise to go bra-less? She felt very self-conscious about that. When she saw her mirrored reflection – the teddy bears' noses effect – she almost chickened out, but hers was a nicely developing young body-shape, and not one easily ignored. Though she could admit that to herself, and be proud of what she saw, she usually kept certain parts hidden.

There was no question about it, he certainly noticed the long bare legs; she was delighted about that. She could see he had noticed, and looked several times at her top half too, her little bears' noses: an effect that by now she felt braver about and a little more confident about displaying. Yes, she looked all right and this was going in the right direction... She could relax. She was halfway there.

She awaited his comment, her lips pouting

seductively at him.

"Aren't you (cough) cold, dressed like that?" he enquired, nodding knowingly towards her little protuberances... "It certainly looks it!"

I must strike him with something really heavy! That was all she could think!

Grace went home in a foul mood.

Her behaviour, during the previous weeks, disturbed her parents. Her father, particularly, was beginning to get a little worried about a daughter who seemed to be throwing herself at some dangerous male.

All fathers are suspicious of any fellow going near a daughter and Grace's dad was no exception. She was way too young to be involved seriously with boys, he reckoned, especially one that looked a bit like that ne'er-do-well, Presley. She was becoming besotted with the lout. He tried not to think what might happen to his sweet innocent little darling but... before anything did, it had to end!

Grace's mother had already tried dissuading her, "...only a silly infatuation," but without success. Grace was a determined girl.

Invite the boy for tea, her parents decided. They would meet her 'young man' and deal with him on home territory but, whereas her mum thought this would a chance to get to know him, her father had other ideas. He could see a spade as being what it truly is. He knew what boys were after at that age – he remembered – so, his was a simple strategy: after tea, take this so-called boyfriend outside, and get tough. Having done some amateur boxing when he was young, he reckoned he could still handle himself pretty well.

The boy arrived.

As they sat eating, for her father, doubts crept in. There was no tough-guy underneath the Elvis clothing, he decided. No need for violence with this one, he would fall over in a strong draught. This bloke's interest lay in studying and learning, quite unexpected. By no stretch of the imagination would he ever be a threat to his dear little Grace. He was interested in one person only – himself – and not a danger after all. However, he was a male, and males get daughters into trouble, therefore disposal was still necessary!

For his daughter's sake, there was a change of plan – a bribe could be the answer. A quick think while he ate... How could I buy him off? Cash? No, too crude.

The meal finished, a smattering of polite conversation followed, and then an invitation...

"Step this way a moment, Angus," and outside the two males went.

Grace was suspicious, then uncomfortable, especially when she heard her father speak. He could ruin everything.

"Look, I want you to stop seeing my daughter!"

"But she's the one that always wants to see me," Angus responded truthfully.

...My little Grace wants him! I do not believe that!

Was he being unfair, he wondered, what harm could this bloke do? No! Underneath he is still a male!

That strengthened the resolve...

"Tell you what I'll do. I'm a reasonable man," he said. "I'll give you my very own set of golf clubs if you stop seeing my daughter."

Already having supplied a free meal was very kind, but Angus felt that her dad was perhaps taking generosity a bit too far.

"If not, there is an alternative: if you don't stop meeting her – I'll beat the living day-lights out of you. In other words, I am telling you to bugger off. Do you understand?"

This was said nose to nose, calmly, and obviously without putting any undue pressure on young Angus, but Grace had been listening at the back door and rushed out.

"Oh Dad ...how could you?" she wailed.

He was ruining her chance of fulfilling 'The Dare'.

"Angus..." She gazed into his eyes, seductively, and moved up closer. "You are not going to listen to my silly old father joking like this, are you?" She pulled him towards her. "You want me, don't you – desperately..."

He looked at her and smiled, and she knew everything was ok – but no! Angus smiled because when she whispered in his ear, it tickled!

With his next words, "How many clubs are there and is a golf bag included?" Grace realised she would have to think fast.

When he added, "Oh ...are the balls and tees thrown in as well?" she knew it was time to give up.

Next day at school, Grace was quick to ensure that Elizabeth became aware that it was over between her and Angus. Elizabeth heard it directly and personally.

"I had to tell him that I can't carry on. No more – I'm exhausted!" That is what she told her best friend. "He's a sex fiend you know. I could never satisfy him..."

Of course, that was readily believed by Elizabeth – because they were best friends, and you do not lie to a best friend.

Word got around.

Elizabeth could not keep it to herself and the girls got to know that 'Angus' was the subject of Grace's story. Of course, they were disbelieving at first, but eventually accepted it to be true, and the story grew arms and legs.

The boys in the class were kept in the dark, but it was noticed and seemed strange to them that girls were regularly sidling up to that twit, apparently desperate for a date.

Grace and Angus never spoke to each other again, nor did Angus tell anyone about Grace and her dad and the golf clubs, but from that day on, the girls in the class treated Angus differently – not that he noticed. Poor young innocent Angus never quite understood what it was all about – that they all wanted an experience with 'The Love God'.

He continued to be a true gent and never mentioned Grace again – ever. Over the remaining months of his school term, though the temptations of 'free love' came on offer many times, he behaved like a saint (or, depending on your viewpoint – an idiot) because he never went out with any of these other girls.

Happiness, for him, was simply having a free set of golf clubs – he would get round to using them, one day...

23

2009
Three, two, one...

"Tom, are you remembering the tape recorder?" said Gillian. "Your father said he wanted it back, didn't he, and now it is gathering dust in this house. Shouldn't you return it tomorrow?"

"Yes, yes..." Tom had forgotten. It was Friday evening and some tapes left in the bag had not yet been played.

Meal over, David left the room to the strains of Simon and Garfunkel. They sounded a bit tinny, he thought, but recognisable. He liked that duo and went upstairs in a good mood. A change of clothing was in order, for this would be a night with his pals, possibly Tracy too. He hadn't realised that she fancied him, but according to Gordon, that was the case.

Wonder if Gordon could be taking the piss?

He had not seen any of them for a while and it would be good to get out again and leave Dad and Mum to play whatever music they liked without him sitting criticising in the corner.

When he came downstairs again, shiny and clean, Simon and Garfunkel had ended and been replaced by another recording. It was a tape randomly taken from the bag, and had surprised Tom and Gillian. It had an old sticker 'Me and Angus'. Tom had thought at first that it was just a blank tape that he could fool around with, then he discovered it was already used.

David stopped to listen – and was impressed.

"That is never Gran's voice... She was good. I didn't know she could do that."

Gran Beth, singing songs and playing guitar, expertly. His grandad was singing solo too and though his mum and dad were appreciating it, David was less sure about his grandad's performance. Angus Findlay was doing impressions of various performers, stars who had been big in bygone years but, in most cases, were now dead and buried. Tom and Gillian could recall the originals and said he was mimicking them extremely well.

"I wonder when they recorded this?" said Gillian.

"Will they even remember it?" asked Tom.

"Will they want to?" added David.

It was now routine, Saturday morning and the loft team had arrived at Angus and Beth's but, today was different. Tom had smiled broadly at his mother as she opened the door; he'd carried the tape recorder and borrowed tapes, ceremonially, into the house; he had then smiled at his father, and added a big wink for both his parents.

An unsettling start for them – this was not their normal Tom.

The recorder was placed on the dresser. Their son then invited Beth and Angus to sit down and get comfortable. More disturbing – not like Tom at all! The recorder was plugged in, and switched on.

It was a female voice, and immediately familiar to Angus and Beth, and it sounded beautiful. Tears came to Beth's eyes. They'd been transported back almost forty-two years.

Gillian noticed and went over. She put her arm around her mother-in-law as her performance ended and a young Angus began his.

"Where did you find this?" a slightly embarrassed Angus asked in the midst of his various voices. He remembered the time and the place of that 'most beautiful day', and wondered what else could be recorded. He could not recall checking the tape afterwards and, if it had continued running...

He heaved a sigh of relief when it ended without causing further embarrassment.

"Sorry, but we didn't mean to shock you. It was meant as a pleasant surprise, to see if you could remember making the recording," said Gillian.

"Oh yes," said Beth, "...a surprise right enough, and I do remember that moment, so I think we pass the test."

"It was in the bag of tapes Dad took from the loft. Hits from the sixties," said David, "...and I want to know, Gran, do you still have the guitar?"

"The guitar... Oh, I don't know, David, but I don't remember it being thrown out; Angus, do you?"

"Let me guess where it might be," said Tom, who until hearing the tape had not known his mother even owned an instrument, never mind been able to play one. "...It's got to be in the loft, right? Everything else is."

Tom received a look from both parents – he was much too chirpy today!

Beth stood up, the tape apparently dismissed and, going over to the sideboard, lifted a folded piece of paper and opened it.

"Last Saturday evening," she said, giving Tom one of her glares, "...you phoned late! Why the panic? You scared the life out of both of us. This was obviously another clue. Have you solved it yet?"

"Not a chance," said Tom, the chirpiness gone. "We've had no time – been back and forward to see Cath Walker. Gillian's mum is still in hospital. I think she's hoping you'll pop in to see her."

"We will, next week. Remember that, Angus! Now, we have something to tell you three. We've solved this clue – we think," and she said that a little too cockily for Tom's liking.

"It'll be interesting to see what my dear old mother has concocted for the final prize," Angus chipped in. "She was a fan of 'Three-Two-One', or 'One-Two-Three' – or whatever it was called. She loved it. I hated it. Can't remember the compere's name. Didn't find him funny. Anyway, at the end of the show he always read a conundrum that nobody could understand, and Dusty Bin appeared. Now, bearing that in mind, and knowing my mother, I ask you, what surprise do you think might it be?"

A dustbin? That would be one heck of a disappointment, Tom thought.

"But, you think you've solved this clue, Mum?"

Angus jumped in again, a chance to prove that his memory had not gone completely, and repeated the clue without needing the piece of paper. "I can't help droning on about this. It can be torture for some, but heaven for others. Keep it in the family for when they have a tart an' tea but it's not food or drink."

"So, Angus dear, tell them the answer," said Beth.

"It can only be ..." and, much to Tom's annoyance and David's admiration, the pause came exactly in the manner used in TV talent shows ...

Five-four-three-two-one:

"...Bagpipes!"

"Of course it is – the good old bagpipes," Tom repeated, with a bit less of the drama. Was that better than a dustbin?

"What bagpipes?" asked David.

Gillian was standing, only half-listening, still trying to remember the name of the compere on 'Three-Two-One' – she had never liked him either.

"The bagpipes that belonged to your great-great-grandad Alexander Findlay," said Angus. "The one I was telling you about."

"Our War Hero..." said David.

"The very one indeed, he was a piper, and when

he died, his wife..."

"Phoebe..." David chipped in again.

"That's the name ...as we said, well, she vowed that the pipes would stay in the family, to be passed down and played in honour of Alexander. They certainly stayed in the family, but, since he died, no one has even tried playing them."

"That's a bit spooky," said Gillian, who'd failed to remember the compere of 'Three-Two-One', and was listening to the story.

"I wouldn't mind trying them," said David.

"Oh!" exclaimed Tom "Is that it then? Could that be the prize? It's just to encourage someone to play them?" He immediately thought of the noise, and how sleeping in his chair in the evenings could quickly become past history. "But shouldn't we find them first? Perhaps there is another clue? Anyway, where could they be?" he asked.

"*Up in the loft, of course...*" came noisily and confidently in unison from the other four. Tom smiled. This was teamwork in action. They were now picking on him. He did not mind. He could take it because, strangely, at that moment he was feeling happily and pleasantly mature.

Then Gillian suddenly yelled out, "Ted Rogers!"

A set of bagpipes should not be hard to find so, up to the loft went David and Tom. Gillian stayed downstairs with her in-laws. Beth had got over the shock of hearing the old tape recording, and was enjoying a glow of self-satisfaction, and delighted that young David had complimented her. Angus had forgotten that he used to do the impressions!

Up in the loft, Tom ruefully remembered how this began – the jelly-pan. It seemed ages ago. Had there been progress? Only a little. Some useless junk had been removed but, the space after each item went seemed to be swallowed up again by something else. Could his father have been sneaking up with more stuff?

Tom had resigned himself to making only slow progress, not now sure which was more important – loft clearance or treasure hunt?

Restacking items to be kept, in front of unchecked stuff, had not been a clever move. If they worked this way during the week, there would be no business, but they did not let it bother them. Treating it as a pastime rather than a task made it much more pleasurable. No rush, was there? Plenty time... so, each new piece discovered was discussed and perused.

"Ah..." said Tom.

"The bagpipes, you have found them already?"

"No, but what would you say to a black and white television...?"

"Rubbish!" came out automatically, and movements continued.

They slogged on but, of the bagpipes, there was no sign. They were confident about some items selected as scrap, like the broken ornaments with little bags attached containing the chipped bits. Was repair likely? No chance! "Not worth asking," said

Tom, but they took the precaution of quickly hiding them, in case the person that they should have asked found out!

Tom could not understand why all this stuff had accumulated in the first place. Little of it was worth keeping, and as neither parent could safely climb the ladder nowadays, almost all of it must have been dumped there years ago. Yet the photo album with the clues that started it all was up there?

A yell of delight came from David. "Look what I have found!"

There was no mistaking the shape discovered in the pile. It was not bagpipes, but it was an instrument case, an old solid guitar case, dusty but undamaged. David carefully lifted it from the stack, and opened it.

The guitar! He wanted to hear his grandma play this!

"Time for a rest break," he immediately declared, and eagerly and triumphantly made his way to the ladder and downstairs.

Perfect timing. In celebration, coffee and scones filled with thick, homemade, raspberry jam appeared as if by magic.

Beth attempted reluctantly to tune a guitar that had lain dormant for all of her son's life. This she did with great care, and successfully without breaking the old strings. She hesitated, before attempting to play, finding it slightly awkward even holding the instrument again after such a long time.

"Ouch!" She had forgotten how tough the tips of

her fingers used to be to play this. It was more than forty years since the last time. "Sorry David, but I am a bit out of practice."

"I hope you will teach me," said David.

"Of course I will, but you'll have to give me time to get to know it again. Tell you what though. If you can find Alexander's bagpipes, why not have a go with them. You learn how to play the bagpipes, while I relearn the guitar? Make it a competition."

"Agreed..."

Odd, thought Tom, David agreeing to learn to play a set of bagpipes that they might never find?

"Dad, the pipes – could they have been put anywhere else?" asked Tom.

While they were upstairs Angus had had time to think, and the loft was now less certain. He could remember the pipe-case, long and narrow, a dark-brown, varnished wooden box, badly chipped in parts. Yes, he could visualise it clearly – but he could not remember where he put it.

"I'm sure that when Meg left Hyndland I brought them over," he said – then had a second thought. No, it was later, after she moved to stay with them. All Meg's selected belongings were removed from the house when it was vacated, they'd thought. It was when the charity people were clearing the large unwanted items of furniture that they discovered the bagpipes, still in their case and still under the bed.

Angus explained that he'd driven over and collected them.

"Just a moment," said Gillian, "They couldn't possibly be under the bed in this house, in the room Meg used, could they? Out of habit? Has anyone looked?"

Tom and Angus went hurriedly to check, but no, they found only dust balls. In all homes inhabited by the Findlay's the place to keep bagpipes was under the bed – except here, obviously...

"The garage!" exclaimed Angus. "Somewhere in the garage – that is where they'll be!"

That had been stated with total conviction, but his Dad's latest revelation did not fill Tom with confidence. His father's memory could again be playing up; and secondly, the garage must be a mess. The car was never in there nowadays.

"Are you sure, Dad?"

"...Absolutely, Tom."

Tom and David exchanged glances.

"Do you know exactly where, Dad?"

"...Oh no, Tom. You might have to look for it..."

The tea break was over, so, to the garage.

24

1958 - 1962
Up in the world...

Hyndland proved a somewhat different environment to Meg's old stamping ground of Anderston. The people she knew back there had been more open and friendly, although admittedly, she had stayed in that old house for a long time. She would have to accept that after thirteen years of living in each other's pockets at the old place, it maybe could take a wee bit more than ten months to feel accepted as a native of this area.

Yes, Hyndland had been her home for ten months. It seemed longer somehow. She had hoped by now to have made more friends and got to know the neighbours a wee bit better. They seemed more self-centred here; standoffish almost, not inclined to speak without a proper introduction. At least, to her, that was the way it seemed.

To Meg's ear, they even talked a special type of Glaswegian too. Not quite Kelvinside posh, but posh nonetheless, she considered. To her, her own voice sounded heavy by comparison, although by no means did she have a broad Glasgow accent.

When she considered the neighbours, the old fellow across the landing was the first to come to mind. He hardly gave the impression of wanting to be friendly.

Her next-door neighbour at Anderson, Mrs Gray, used to be in and out of her place regularly, and she used to be in and out of Mrs Gray's too. The relationship became quite close. By caring for young Angus in the early days, Mrs Gray had allowed Meg to do part-time work, work that progressed to become full-time and her help was very much appreciated. As time went on, she became like a grandmother to the young boy.

When Angus was a bit older, and Meg working full-time, taking the chance of earning real money, Mrs Gray used to take the boy into her home each day when he returned from school. She made sure he had some food to keep him going until Meg arrived back to prepare an evening meal. Of course, that was before Angus took over that duty.

When it came to his homework, ensuring that he did it conscientiously was an easy job for Mrs Gray. Angus was an unusual child who worried if he was prevented from doing it. For him extra reading and studying was normal whenever he arrived back from school.

Angus was certainly not teacher's pet! Probably the opposite, because he irritated them! Requesting extra homework was most unusual, and they produced it for him, specially. It was always extra work when they wanted go home. No other child ever asked for more. If his teachers had been a little more sensible, they would have anticipated and prepared it in advance, because he never failed to make the request. They considered him a little swot and, in addition – a damn nuisance!

Meg was delighted that her friendship with Mrs Gray continued after the house move. Mainly, it was the older woman who popped over to Hyndland to see her and Angus. This happened only at a weekend when Meg was not working, but the visits were regular and, if prearranged, not missed – until Mrs Gray died.

It was weeks after the funeral that Meg remembered something as odd.

At the burial of Mrs Gray, Meg, sitting at the funeral service, learned for the first time of her old friend's first name ...Sadie ...Sadie Gray. In all the time they had known each other, she never heard it used. When she spoke to the other neighbours who attended, she found none of them had known her first name either.

That saddened her ...and from then on, to know and use first names became very important to her. She knew her friend's name now but would never be able to say it to her; dear old Mrs Gray – Sadie – it was all too late... and Sadie was not at all like her current next-door neighbour, thank goodness.

Mr McDonald – no first name for him! A strange fellow. If she met him on the stairs, from him no more than a furtive glance and a silent nod. As she went down to catch the bus for work, he would be coming up the stairs with a newspaper, timed regular as clockwork. Each occasion, it was as if he had never seen her before in his life, even though it had been the same routine for almost every weekday morning over ten months.

She had done her bit, trying to be friendly towards him.

"Good morning, Mr McDonald, how are you today?" said so many times.

"Huh..." would be the scintillating reply. It was that, or just, 'the scowl'.

He had never stepped over her doorstep, and she had no desire to step over his. She would be reluctant to go into his house – if ever invited – though that was extremely unlikely. The name Count Dracula came to mind when she thought of him. She had seen the films. She knew what could happen to a fair damsel in the castle– or even to an old damsel, as she was.

In the building, there were two levels higher than Meg's own flat, though going up higher than her own door was not a habit. Directly above was Mrs Molly McGivern.

She was always pleasant enough every time Meg spoke to her, and about the same age as Meg. Chatting usually occurred on the way to and from work; sometimes at the bus stop, sometimes on the bus, either direction. Molly worked full-time in town but got off, and on, at a different stop from Meg.

Molly, a widow for several years, had no family,

but she did have a man friend – Meg learned that surreptitiously – he was never mentioned by Molly. A fellow would arrive every weekend carrying a bunch of flowers. Meg suspected he stayed all weekend – unless he skipped passed her door without her spotting him. Now, it was not like Meg to be bitchy – well, there was not yet anyone here that she felt close enough to be bitchy with, but... Let's face it, he was a bit young for Molly?

On the opposite side, in the flat above Count Dracula's, was the Sutherland family.

Meg had failed to make much contact with them so far. The most she managed would generally be a smiling, "Hello, nice day again," on the stairs, and that was about it. Hughie and Sandra were either rushing in, or rushing out, and it always seemed to be the two of them together.

Molly told her that she heard they had a small general store over in Govan, and worked all the hours God gave. For them there never seemed time to stop and talk, but at least it was a friendly greeting as they rushed passed, not in the least like Dracula. Of course, all local information that Meg gleaned came from Molly McGivern.

The people who lived on the top floor, above Molly, were pleasant and friendly as well. Meg did not feel that she'd had the chance yet to get to know them particularly well either. That young couple had a very young baby, a girl called Louise, who was born shortly before Meg moved in. She felt sorry for the mother, having to bounce the large pram down three flights of stairs, and then take baby for a walk to the park every day, rain, hail or shine. Meg was glad to see that she always wore flat heels to come down all these stairs – much safer.

However, the mother rarely pulled the pram back upstairs. She would carry the baby in her arms, leaving the pram in the close. It would lie there until the father arrived back from his work; bouncing it back up again was his duty. With her mind on other things at the time, Meg had almost walked into it sitting in the passageway when she came home one day. To learn their name, Meg had to sneak up, and look at the nameplate on their door. Maisie and Archie Turnbull. Baby Louise was not on the nameplate.

On the opposite side to the pleasant young family, was an older couple, Doris and Bob Lindsay. They were nice but she saw them very rarely, mainly because they both used sticks to get about. They managed up and down the three flights with difficulty, and very slowly. Meg was convinced it would only be a matter of time before they would both be housebound.

She wanted to suggest that they should be looking for another house on the ground floor somewhere, while they were still able to keep moving. Would that be cheeky? Resisting the temptation to ask was with difficulty. Her hope was that they had close family who could guide and help them, but she never saw anyone visiting. It was possible that family called when she was at work that she did not see, but that did not stop her caring and worrying about them. One Saturday, she made a point of popping up to ask if they needed any messages.

"I'm on my way to the shops, and it would be no bother."

This approach they appreciated. The first time, she received a polite, "No thank you, we're all right, but thanks for asking," but the following Saturday when she nipped up again, a shopping list was handed to her, prepared in anticipation.

Afterwards, Meg was more relaxed about their situation. These two would feel they could call on her in an emergency.

Visits to Doris and Bob became regular, for a coffee and a chat. She learned that they had two sons. Many years ago both left home to go to Canada and married local girls over there. Both had young families. The old couple received letters regularly, so they appreciated the progress of their young grandchildren, but visits from them were rare.

Obviously, they had no one to talk to, to help or guide them, so Meg took the plunge. She apologised in advance, and broached the matter of considering a move. They took it kindly but, having spent almost all of their married life in that close they did not want to move away. This was home. But at least she'd said her piece, and continued with her Good Samaritan shopping.

She was making friends. When she took stock – a close relationship had developed with the older couple, she had a chatting relationship with the younger couple, and there was a gossipy contact with Molly. She was beginning to feel as if she belonged. She was getting somewhere.

What about Count Dracula though? Should she take up the challenge of forcing a friendship on her own neighbour across the landing?

Oh, no! She was not quite up to that yet. Maybe another day...

The girl below Meg lived on her own. She was about thirty, and although rather shy, seemed to enjoy bumping into Meg and having a little blether now and again. Her name was Carol, Carol Maxwell.

Directly opposite, was a male.

'David Brown' it said on the nameplate, and he was probably in his mid-thirties, Meg reckoned. He appeared to be single, but he was also either shy or did not want to know those around him in the building. He never talked comfortably with his female neighbour in the close, Meg learned. He certainly never spoke with Meg.

It was no skin off her nose and she accepted it. A least, he was better looking than 'Dracula' – but she had a worry about Mr David Brown. He might grow old – and become just like the old grump across the landing from her.

One day, she would have to do something about that...

It was Meg's valued judgement that these two on the ground level, in the close – that they were perfect for each other. She liked to think that she had a sixth sense for these matters. Affairs of the heart had been a success for her before, she told herself, and now here was another chance. The question – how should she approach it and, at the same time have some fun...

Meg was not alone in the flat. Angus still lived there with her, but any thoughts about their downstairs occupants were her own. She never considered discussing them with her son.

Angus worked in the shipyard, the same shipyard that his father worked in years ago.

"That's where your dad met that floozy Bella Roberts, so look what happens to people who worked there! It is a den of iniquity! No son of mine will ever work in that place..." That had been Meg's vow – before Angus went for the interview. Later, she had to admit, in Angus's case, there were slightly different circumstances.

Angus had been eager to leave school. With excellent reports and results, when he went for the job in the shipyard, his very first application and without his mother's knowledge, they grabbed him right away. Someone in the company immediately recognised that this youngster had great potential. His job would be in the drawing office, a white-collar job and very different from Hamish's. He would not return home with dirty hands, and, unless a bomb went off in the shipyard, he should not become deaf, plus... girls had never been an attraction for him as he was always too busy reading.

So, Meg had to accept that a drawing office position was a few levels more successful than his father reached, and also that there could be a future in it. It was obvious that shipbuilding was a good solid business, had been established for a long time, and would continue on the Clydeside, forever...

Angus, happy to be living at home with his mother, had no inclination to live anywhere else. It was nice and easy at home: a mother who cared and happy that he shared the house, although, and just as important – he did not earn enough to think of wandering off. He lived at home, spent a lot of time at work, and knew nothing of his mother's plan for the two innocent victims who lived below.

'The plan' began with a purchase by Meg of a ball of strong twine.

Meg had a theory that what was essential, to bind a community together effectively, was conflict and a common enemy. As far as Carol and David were concerned, she was about to become the common enemy – but anonymously. A little bit of harmless conflict was about to be created by her, and would very quickly prove her theory to be correct.

It was very simple. The good old game of tying two door-handles together. It had always worked well when she was young – knocking on both doors, and then running away. This would be the perfect reason, and time, to resurrect it. What could be more infuriating than not being able to catch who was doing it?

Meg was ready and about to cause mayhem....

Saturday morning. The campaign was about to begin.

Angus had gone into town, to a bookshop as usual. Little Louise's pram had been bounced down the stairs from the top flat, and because it was Saturday, both Maisie and Archie were doing the two-hour meander, pram-pushing together. Meg watched them leave the close, and was certain they had vanished up the road. She knew that Dracula had been to, and returned from, the paper-shop, as was his normal routine, and that Hughie and Sandra had bustled out early to open the store on the other side of the river. There was no chance of Doris and Bob venturing out, they said so yesterday, and she had confidence that Molly and her young man would not surface until late afternoon – a pattern established over many weeks of observation.

After a final wee peek to be certain no one else was about, and that both Mr David Brown and Miss Carol Maxwell were at home, with a heart thumping like mad she crept down the stairs.

The handle of Carol Maxwell's door was tied securely with one end of the string. She stopped and listened.

No sound.

Nothing was stirring. The string was stretched across the close to the opposite door handle and tied tightly. She took a deep breath and...

Ready! She would have to be quick! It was a pity she could not reach both doorbells at exactly the same time.

Her fingers were poised. The bells were pressed!

And back up the stairs she went, rapidly and silently...

With her door ajar, she heard the noises downstairs as both doors failed at first to open. There was a moment of silence: then a *bang* and a *twang* as one door closed, and the other opened suddenly as the twine gave way.

The person who pulled the hardest, a certain Mr Brown, fell back as his door shot open. Carol was able to open her door easily after that, but closed it again, gently – to avoid the sounds reaching her tender ears of the cursing from the flat opposite.

Mr David Brown removed the twine, looked up the stairs, saw not a soul, went to the close entrance, looked up and down the street, then to the back entrance, but could see no one to shout at. With a shake of the head and an annoyed scowl on his face, he went back inside. He said not a word, well, other than the initial surprised cursing!

Meg gently closed her door. Ah, well, she had broken the ice ...and, if Mr Brown and Miss Maxwell recognised that a prankster was targeting them both, it would surely encourage them to speak to each other.

It did not happen right away though. She could tell it would be taking a few attempts.

Meg left it for a few days to let the dust settle, anyway she was out at work, so, it was the following Friday evening, when the pram was upstairs and everyone settled, that she used the same ruse. She was on her own tonight. Angus had gone to the cinema on his own, to see a documentary about shipbuilding. Everyone else was at home, inside.

This time she used two strands of twine, a little stronger. It would still have to break, but not so easily. The door handles would come off otherwise!

She rang both bells – and slipped quickly back up the stairs, and listened, as she did last time. The twine held and doors stayed closed. He must have realised what was happening because the male voice said, "Not again. Bloody Hell! If I get hold of the little bas..."

With difficulty, Mr Brown succeeded in restraining himself as he realised Miss Maxwell was at her door too. He did not attempt to force it this time, but shouted to her, "I'll get a knife..." which he did, and cut the cord.

Meg could hear muffled talk down below. She gently closed the door quite happily. The plan had moved forward. At least, this time they did speak.

As she crept down the stair on the following Saturday morning with the twine in her hand again, she felt a slight unease. Angus had gone out. She could not put her finger on why, but there was a distinct reduction in confidence. Of course, it could have been the rushing of breakfast, a touch of indigestion, but...

She had to remind herself she was doing this for a very good reason. These two people belonged together and she was being the catalyst, encouraging a reaction.

It was a certainty that neither had left their abodes this morning, they were inside their separate flats. She knew that, so why the uncomfortable feeling? Could it be that Miss Carol Maxwell, and Mr David Brown, were both behind their respective doors, waiting, ready to whip them open and grab her?

Her ear went to one door, followed by her ear to the other. Not a sound. It was safe, but she could not relax...

Quickly the twine-tying was done using double thickness again, the doorbells pushed, and followed by a frantic run to reach the safety of her lobby. While struggling to gather breath, she listened at her slightly opened door. Did she get away with it again?

Was that a handle turning? Unsure.

It was very quiet ...and then she heard the mournful whistling. Someone was coming in the close. Oh no, not Molly McGivern's fancy man, not at this moment, please. Surely, she didn't missed him on the stair! He should be still in bed, upstairs, with Molly...

Then the noises that followed told her it was not him – it was her Angus! He was supposed to be away all morning...

Meg was aware that Mr David Brown was tall,

good looking and single. What she did not take into account was that he was also quite smart and agile. By coincidence, he had been behind the door the very moment she pressed his bell. He'd rushed to the back room, hurriedly climbed out the back window and came into the close by the rear entrance to catch the culprit red-handed – having missed Meg by a whisker, but just in time to grab the poor startled Angus.

"Got you," and he grabbed Angus's collar. "You are not getting away this time, you sly little bug..."

He stopped mid-sentence when he realised his female neighbour had joined him in the close. With a sharp breadknife, poked through the narrow doorway opening, she had successfully severed the twine, and saved Angus from some undeserved physical abuse.

"Don't hurt him," she implored. "He was only playing a game, obviously. It's Angus, lives with his mother, upstairs."

"Phone the police," Mr David Brown demanded of her.

"Ughhhh...' Angus tried to say something – but failed.

"Is that really necessary?"

"Just please phone!"

She did, and a big burly Glasgow police constable appeared, to find a choking Angus held by the collar and barely able to speak until his throat was released.

"What did I do?" Angus gasped.

When he was told what had been happening, the constable looked sternly at this guilty-looking bloke at the end of David Brown's arm.

Angus denied any knowledge and pleaded innocence, but the police notebook came out: a date recorded; names recorded; addresses recorded, and then Angus was marched upstairs.

His mother would require to be informed, the policeman told him.

"But I haven't done anything!" protested Angus, as he was marched up the flight of stairs to his own front door, and there, to stand suffering an arm-lock until his mother opened the door.

Meg felt all faint discovering Angus standing on her doormat between a big policeman and David Brown. Miss Maxwell was standing behind looking somewhat unsure about the whole affair, with a breadknife in her hand.

"It might be better if we talked about this inside, Mrs Findlay," said the constable, "...it could turn very serious."

In single file they followed Meg in – the guilty party, who was still baffled; the upholder of the law; the downstairs male; and Carol, still holding the breadknife.

Inside it was major decision time for Meg. Should she bluff it out, deny all knowledge and scold Angus for being naughty; or should she admit that she was at fault?

Not really a hard decision.

The policeman and Carol Maxwell tried hard not to

laugh as Meg explained it had been her having a little bit of fun, and nothing at all to do with her seventeen-years-old son. She refrained from mentioning the ulterior motive of bringing her two neighbours closer together.

The policeman's little notebook was brought out of the breast pocket, again, in a very officious manner. This was a middle-aged woman with a mid-life crisis, the bobby had deduced, but he liked her style. Is she maybe going loony, he wondered to himself? He had heard of that sort of thing before...

For the sake of Mr Brown, who was doing all the complaining, the policeman pretended to make notes as the story unfolded and tried to look serious, but was unable to avoid a slight smile on his face – and a blank notebook...

Mr. David Brown did not find anything funny – at all.

The policeman asked the two complainants to come back into the lobby with him. After calming the annoyed male, and asking the female to stop giggling, he suggested they accept it as a joke. "Surely you don't want it taken farther, do you?" he said. He assured both of them that he could guarantee it would not happen again.

"I can bet my size twelve boots on it!" he declared.

This was accepted, although reluctantly by David Brown, and off down the stairs they went. Carol Maxwell was now chattering happily to her neighbour. He was responding, but not happily – he was not going to admit that it was actually nice getting to know this pretty, young lady from next door, even under the odd circumstances.

Three remained upstairs...

Meg stood, totally humiliated, a failure. She felt tiny and mouse-like, being lectured by a big, burly, uniformed representative of Glasgow Constabulary who was probably only a few years older than her Angus. She was standing distinctly uncomfortably, whereas Angus, having recovered from the initial shock, was now sitting on a chair. A grin was developing. He was apparently enjoying his mother's discomfort.

Nervously she stood, hearing little of what the Constable was saying. "Not acting your age... behaving like a big wean... being a poor example... and a public nuisance..." Only odd phrases were being heard until he said, "...but, Mrs Meg Findlay, you have made my day!" His last statement was clear and said with a smile on the big man's face, and immediately removed all tension.

"Would you like a cup of tea, son?" automatically came out of Meg's mouth before she could stop herself.

After PC Stuart Wilson left, Meg was deeply embarrassed at the indignity of having to apologise profusely to her wronged son, especially when he just burst out laughing. He could not believe what his mother had done. He only returned for a forgotten key, and although it was uncomfortable at the time, he was glad he had not missed any of it.

She stood there amazed. It was hard to believe that her son, the one who had never appeared to have any sense of humour, had found that funny and, that he was laughing out loud – *at her expense!*

After that, Meg tried to avoid bumping into David Brown.

Carol made a point of chatting to her whenever she saw her. That was nice. She enjoyed the joke and held no grudges. As well as a pleasant neighbour, Carol became a good friend to Meg. David Brown was not quite so forthcoming, and continued for a long time to look at her with deep suspicion. For him, if they met for any reason, 'nutcase' was the word that popped into his head.

In the weeks that followed, it was obvious that Carol and David had taken a shine to each other, and a delighted Meg was one of the first to learn the news – her two neighbours were going to be married. David's house was the one they would live in.

After finding that out, Meg decided that what she had done had been totally justified. She even considered she could claim credit for the development of the romance, though she could not tell anyone, not even Angus.

She had seen the potential, and had taken the appropriate action, though she suffered the consequences, but all for a very good reason. Yes, the touch was still there – but she was not quite finished yet...

After contacting the building's factor, and successfully convincing him that he would become a wonderful person in her eyes if he did what she was asking, Meg obtained his agreement. Her idea was that Maisie and Archie could flit from their top-floor flat to the about-to-be vacated ground-floor one. It would be a sensible move, she suggested to them, and, as it turned out, she persuaded them easily.

It gave her a nice feeling inside.

Helping, persuading, interfering, manipulating of others; call it what you like, it was a skill that she still possessed – although it had been a little more difficult this time, she decided.

If she could have done it physically, she would have stood all day patting her own back, telling herself what a clever girl she had been. As it was, she settled for just walking around with a grin bigger than a Cheshire cat's. However, she decided that it might be wise to quit the matchmaking business for good, while she was winning.

...And she did.

25

2009:
Worth a search...?

Have my parents got no sense?

How many times over the years had Tom asked himself that? As he swung open the garage door, the question came again because, in the garage, lying unassembled and stacked near the inside wall were the parts for another self-assembly wooden shed that should never have been bought, and obviously had been purchased to give them yet more storage space – because they couldn't part with anything.

"If you don't need it, throw it out. That's what a dustbin's for. You can't store everything. Please stop trying to!" he'd tried telling them.

"Hmmm..." his mother had said then. His father had looked at the ceiling.

Last year they had listened to his advice to buy the first shed. He'd suggested that bits and pieces that they were not using, but felt they had to keep, could be kept in a shed in the garden.

"Save Dad climbing the loft ladder."

"A brilliant idea, Tom. Much safer," his mum had

agreed. "Just a short distance along the path, open the door, and in it could go, and be forgotten about... A shed would be perfect. You will help erect it, won't you, Tom?" and it had been in use at the bottom of the garden for a while and appeared to have done the trick.

They talked of buying a second one but Tom had said they would be wasting money – one would be enough. They'd listened, and been convinced – he'd thought.

This second shed saddened him, for even this 'extra storage' was being stored now! Incredible! What was mostly useless junk, in his opinion, was in the loft, in the shed at the bottom of the garden, and in this large double garage – and now they had this other shed on stand-by!

David was on his father's side

"The other one... surely that isn't full yet."

Tom took a deep breath.

"Looks like it, and the car sits in the driveway because there's no room in here. I thought your grandad was being too lazy to drive it inside."

His hope had been to just open the garage door and find the bagpipe-case sitting on a shelf, but the shelves were stacked with everything else. If the bagpipes were in the garage, to find them they would first have to empty the place.

"No, don't lift stuff out. We could go in, squeeze around gaps, and search that way," David suggested.

Yes, a good idea!

"I'll do this side, if I can squeeze passed this other

blooming shed. Ouch! I've got bloody skelves in my hands now!" Tom yelled, although he'd barely moved. It was painful. He held out his hands for David to see.

"You shouldn't have run your hands along the edge of the panel," David told him. "Any idiot knows that. It's what happens, Dad, when you do that over rough wood – you get splinters! What age are you?"

"Forget the lecture. Just pull the bloody things out! Ouch! Ouch!"

Spiders and cobwebs; Tom had never been comfortable with these – or mice, though mice weren't spotted, but the spiders were doing a great job, webs everywhere, sticking to hands and arms, it felt – *yugh* – horrible...

No sign of anything that resembled a bagpipe box, as far as he could see, though seeing was awkward, like the loft had been but worse. The single electric light bulb hanging from a rafter wasn't working, and the doors were open but none of the light was reaching the places they were trying to check. It was a large space, so David went back into the house to ask Grandad for a torch.

He returned grinning.

"Grandad says the only one's in the garage!"

Two rusty old lawnmowers took up valuable space. They'd been replaced years ago by a modern petrol-powered version, which was there too, but why keep the old ones? They had been sitting there since before Tom left home.

"Tut, tut!" came out – then he had a twinge of guilt. He was blaming his father for not disposing of these, but this was his fault! "Don't bother, Dad, I'll get rid of the old mowers," he remembered saying.

The old mowers sat in front of four snow tyres, bought and never used because of an enormous quantity of berries on the rowan tree one year. His mother convinced his father that it indicated a very severe winter. It wasn't, but the tyres were bought – just in case...

...And the bike, how old, he wondered? It had been in the garage since he was a boy.

Any of them would use it in his younger days, although he probably shouldn't have; for many years it had been much too big for him. Good job it was a female's type with the cutaway bar, or he would never have managed when he was young. He couldn't sit in the saddle, he remembered, had to stand on the pedals to get around; used to play about the streets on it too. Not so much traffic in those days though, not the sort of thing he ever let David do.

The bike tyres were flat – as they had been almost every time he went to use it when he was older. Repaired hundreds of times; probably more patch material on the tyres than original rubber. It could probably sell very easily at a car boot sale, old bikes being the 'in thing' – but I will leave it just now and come back to it later. God ...there I go again. Is there a Chinese proverb, 'Why do today that which can be left till tomorrow – or the next day?' If there isn't –

there should be!

David squeezed along the side of the old self-assembly MFI wardrobe – the one years ago that used to be in his dad's boyhood bedroom, and tried to open the door, and now he was stuck, having failed to notice the roll of chicken wire he edged passed. The back of his jumper had caught on the wire edges.

"Don't move," said Tom, and squeezed in beside him, "I'll loosen it for you," and, having done that, had to undo himself as well.

Standing on oil was not a good idea either. It was lucky David noticed his dad's footprints on the garage floor. He could imagine if his gran found oil on the house carpets...

It was a large space and there was so much stuff, but they'd completed the search without success and were about to start again. A shout from Grandad in the house stopped them.

"Found it, boys!"

A slightly peeved look passed between Tom and David. They went back inside.

Angus suddenly had had a flash of memory while fetching the Dyson for his Saturday morning vacuuming routine. Because the bagpipes were found after the rest of her belongings and later brought over from Meg's old house, he put them at the back of the large cupboard in the hall. They'd been dumped and lain there, untouched, ever since. More like a well-filled small room than a cupboard, so no wonder he had not remembered. Great storage area – particularly for items to be forgotten.

Boxes, at least many of them were empty, had to be shifted to reach the far end. David did that all by himself. With the bagpipes about to be his, he was the enthusiastic one today and there! Right at the back – the box.

He grabbed the handle and lifted it. Heavier than expected. He carried it solemnly along the hallway into the kitchen and placed it on the table. The other four heads gathered around, expectantly. The little flip-catches were unlatched. He paused then lifted the lid, and there they were – a war hero's bagpipes.

His four elders stood silent, awaiting his next move. Were they all expecting the ghost of Alexander to appear? He certainly was...

Silly! He reached out, but suddenly felt a chill run up his spine. Was there a piper's curse waiting to land on the first one to touch them?

"Do you want the honour of lifting them, Grandad?" he asked. "After all, you were the one who guessed the clue?" and he stepped back, then suddenly felt bad. What a wimp, landing Grandad with the problem!

"Ok," said Grandad and stepped forward, and reached, but not for the pipes. There was a paper wrapped round one of the drones, held in place by a piece of string. He had to untie a tight knot to remove it. He carefully unrolled it, and smiled – the next clue!

That changed the mood in the room immediately. The bagpipes were abandoned as Angus held up the paper to a round of applause. He took a bow.

No ghost! Of course, I didn't really expect one anyway, David thought bravely.

"Hurry up, Father. What does this one say?" pushed Tom.

"Glasses... I need my glasses... Gillian, you take it please."

She held it carefully, exposing Meg's clear and neat writing, and read aloud.

> *"You are doing fine, just take your time*
> *The scene is quaint, the scene I'll paint*
> *The wide blue sky, the paint is dry*
> *One day, such fun, new life begun.*
> *This tale untold; let it now unfold.*
> *Heroic fame, was that to blame?"*

There was silence as five brains worked furiously at the same time, until, "I'll put the kettle on," came from Beth and the pressure was off, and they all started talking at once. A cup of tea and Beth's homemade pancakes and jam – the thinking man and woman's way of dealing with a clue like this – at least, that was the way in this house.

The bagpipes, still in their case, lay forgotten in the corner of the room because, sitting around the table, the intrepid five had started bandying about various ideas.

Angus's seemed best. Obviously to do with a painting, he suggested, and could be one that Meg created herself. She was a novice. Took up painting while still living in her own house. A first attempt was 'Painting by Numbers', pre-packaged paints and brushes, with the numbers shown on a little printed canvas; a simple scene – a house beside a stream, with flowers in the garden. She enjoyed that experience and went a little further, to do her own thing.

For inspiration, she borrowed some books from the library, and copied stuff from them. Angus had thought at the time that it was very good for a first attempt by an older person. He squirmed as it came back to him about the books. His wife smiled as he told the others. She had enjoyed his embarrassment, she remembered.

He had returned the books to the library just before Meg moved home, the ones he found lying about. She'd taken them out three years previously and forgotten. The librarian had been very understanding. She said that as no one had asked for them she would overlook them being overdue, and that she had an elderly mother like that herself.

No fine was charged, but he was deeply embarrassed. Meg had found it highly amusing when he returned and told her – he had not!

Angus explained that his mother painted many more, but not all came with her, and there was no doubt as to what happened to the ones she chose to bring.

"I remember clearly... Over in Hyndland, I personally wrapped them with brown paper, tied them together, five, maybe six, in the parcel."

Angus sat with his eyes closed, picturing that day, talking out loud.

"I remember putting the parcel in the boot of the car, driving back here, lifting it from the boot, and carrying it into the house. And then, of course, I..."

"...*put them in the loft*," chorused the others.

Angus opened his eyes. "How did you know that?"

David remembered handling a heavy, rectangular, dusty, brown-paper parcel on his last visit to the loft. He hadn't opened it. He had lifted it aside, wondered about the contents and shoved it in a corner. It could have been the paintings. Had he put other things on top?

"I'll get it!" he told them and hurried upstairs and into the loft. He knew exactly where they were. He brought them down, very carefully, into the kitchen; carefully, because they could all be 'masterpieces'.

Beth cut the string and the contents of the brown paper parcel, wrapped by Angus six years ago, were exposed. There they were. Meg's works of art, six of them.

...Masterpieces? If they were, it was surprising that they survived the next ten minutes because each painting was lifted by five art critics who were behaving like Philistines – as they realised guiltily later. In their eagerness to find the next clue, each painting was manhandled roughly by the five of them and the subjects, carefully selected and painted by Meg, totally ignored because they didn't appear to help them. There was a clue to find! Even the wrapping paper was checked carefully, but without success.

So much for the inspired guess.

A collective sigh of disappointment as they sat back down.

Then Gillian lifted one, a still life. Her approach now a bit more civilised. It was very good, she considered, and I'd be proud if I could paint like that. Her only experience had been with an emulsion brush, and good though she had been at that, it could not compete with Meg's slightly daintier workmanship. Yes, this work of Meg's was being viewed in a more appreciative manner. The bowl of fruit sitting on a table with some loose fruit looked lifelike, if a still life was describable as that and the others, to Gillian's amateur's eye, seemed equally good, probably copied from a book, but good.

"I'd like a couple of these to hang in our house," she said, and put them aside.

The four remaining were wrapped up again for return to the previous resting place.

"Is the clue perhaps in the subject of the picture, something we have to interpret?" asked David.

Everyone thought that to be a very astute question and congratulated him for thinking outside the box. They all tried thinking that way too – but it did not help. They were still in the dark.

Gillian read the clue again.

> *"You are doing fine, just take your time*
> *The scene is quaint, the scene I'll paint*
> *The wide blue sky, the paint is dry*
> *One day, such fun, new life begun.*

This tale untold; let it now unfold.
Heroic fame, was that to blame?"

It still seemed to be about a painting, they all agreed, and one with the magic ingredients of a quaint scene, blue sky, fun, and new life... Had they missed something perhaps?

The clue did not appear to refer to the content of the two Gillian chose so the other four were unwrapped once again, and an attempt made to analyse and review them in a different way. They weren't modern, but to use the word quaint did not seem appropriate either. All four were landscapes with blue sky and fluffy clouds. Where was the fun and new life? Not showing on these, it seemed.

"Were any other paintings at her old house – maybe left behind, but relevant?" asked David.

"No, your grandad's correct, the clues would have been created when she was here. Anyway, the other paintings will be long gone."

"What about pictures hanging on the walls here? Could they hold the clue perhaps?" was David's next question. "She may not have painted them."

Again the other four heads nodded in appreciation. David was doing well today, and yes, it was possible, but then again – anything was possible, so, the heads swivelled around the room. Many photos and paintings of ships adorned these walls, reflecting the working history of Angus. Not in here then...

"Check each room," said Tom.

David made for the stairs, and, as usual, took

them two at a time. His father, who followed, didn't. They went together into each of the upstairs rooms. Each room had lots of pictures covering the walls and of an assortment of subjects, pictures that were normally not even noticed.

"Good grief," said Tom. "I've just realised. They never throw anything away, do they...? They've been hoarding pictures too."

"Could be worse," said David. "At least they are on the walls – they could've been in the loft!"

They looked carefully at them all but had to conclude that nothing appeared to fit the bill. So, they went back downstairs and followed Gillian and Angus into the front room.

Beth was already there, standing looking pensive. Pictures filled the walls of this room too, but one was more impressive than the others and that one had Beth's attention. An oil painting, large, with a small, engraved plate attached to the frame that simply said 'The Trossachs'.

It showed a blue-skied summer's day...

Beth looked at Angus, Angus looked at Beth, and a little light bulb above each head began to twinkle. Having fun, new life?

Tom, began life there – though he didn't know that.

Meg did ...and yes, the blue sky...

"Why don't you lift that one down, and check the back of it, Angus," Beth suggested, with knowingly raised eyebrows and the beginnings of a confident smile, and sure enough, it was the one Meg selected a long time ago to convey her message to her Treasure Hunters.

An envelope was tucked in the frame at the back. David had the privilege of first look this time, and inside were three pieces of paper...

26

1967
A beautiful mover...

Beth MacAndrew reckoned she had an excellent job. She worked in a company that was very obviously a male dominated organisation and populated mainly by males. Most of the work for them was physical, and much of it, heavy – in a shipyard.

She was not required to do heavy work, being the Assistant Cashier. At only twenty-two, she had done all right for herself. No chance of progressing to Chief Cashier however – that always had been and probably always would be a man.

It helped a bit that her dad was also an employee of the Company, a very well-respected manager, working in the yard where the real heavy work was done for the construction of the vessels, though these days he was not expected to do manual. His name, Jack MacAndrew.

With Beth being around the other managers and directors, in the canteen, or dealing personally with them when they collected expenses, she regularly heard the gossip. It was impossible for her not to hear it. The buzz was that her father's future was assured – earmarked to become a Director in the not too distant future. He was only forty-eight. To become a Director would be a very important promotion, but she also knew that gossip could turn out to be very wrong.

She avoided gossip herself, except to listen – she would never pass it on ...well, maybe occasionally?

Beth's own personal development certainly was not down to her dad. She had worked hard enough to succeed under her own steam – something she had to keep telling herself to maintain her confidence, especially each time Sandra Stevenson was in the vicinity. Disturbing when that jealous cow made sarcastic comments deliberately and loud enough for her to hear.

Working as a junior clerk for three years had been good grounding for Beth. Whatever special training the Company demanded of her over the years, she had done without question, on top of attending the obligatory evening classes and passing all exams with flying colours. She was satisfied that she deserved to be where she was, no matter what sweet, fat, Sandra said.

The responsibility of the small team of girls was hers. At times, the team had to work especially hard, for instance, when preparing pay packets. Getting that wrong could lead to a riot her boss had warned her. It happened to him a long time ago, he claimed, nearly strung up on the nearest lamppost by a maddened workforce; short in their wages and blaming him for the error. He escaped, but it had been a dangerous moment...

Beth doubted this having really happened. A ploy, to keep her and her team motivated, she suspected, but she did not permit anyone to attempt to prove it – she would have been the one blamed.

Changes were afoot for the Cash Office. As far as Beth was concerned, the sooner they introduced the new-fangled computer machines she had heard about, the better; it would take a lot of the unknown out of it. These computer things, as far as she knew, were enormous, the smallest being about the size of four elephants at least, and ate punch cards for breakfast.

If pushed, she readily admitted that hers was not exactly a smart technical description, but it was all she knew. Oh, and the other thing she heard was that people like her could be out of a job because of them. She did not want that.

Time for a visit to the Drawing Office; she had not been there for a couple of days and did not have to think hard for a reason – there was always something to justify it.

It was regularly done on any old pretext and felt good, walking right through the general drawing office area into the Chief Draughtsman's Office. In that office, it was males only – with tongues hanging out.

She was not the only female employed in the yard

by any means. The Tracing Office, next door to the drawing office, was where other girls were employed, females only in there, but they did not have the freedom to roam that Beth had appropriated.

The mini-skirt worked for her, but she knew, it wasn't just the mini-skirt that attracted attention in the Drawing Office. When walking in there, her body movement had an extra special wiggle, improved by each visit, and now nearly perfect. As she walked the long passage between the drawing boards, she was well aware, without having to look, that all eyes were on her bottom, gently jiggling side to side, in the practised manner. She could do it nowadays without a hint of embarrassment.

Her particular interest was towards the drawing board just outside the Chief Draughtsman's Office, easily observable through the half-glass partitions that formed the outsides of the Chief's office. Of course, her interest was not for the drawing board itself. Working at that particular post was the object of her contrived visits – Angus Findlay.

How annoying could that man be? He was the only one in the whole babble of gawking draughtsmen who continued to work and ignore her presence. The instant she opened the door and sashayed in, every other male downed pencil and ogled, and continued ogling, waiting for her return journey – except him. How could he ignore her when no one else seemed able? How dare he?

Every time so far it had been the same reaction,

or rather non-reaction, a total failure even to look at her during all of the six weeks that she had been interested in him, even though she recently doubled the number of visits per week.

She would have to be careful though, her boss was getting suspicious each time she said airily, "Just popping over to the Drawing Office," and sauntered off...

This was a young lady on a mission, determined to prove something for herself; she'd heard talk about his being a 'Love God'. It seemed unlikely. As far as she could discover, none of the girls in the company – not a solitary one – had had a date with him. Not engaged, or married either – she had checked – sooooo... Could he be, *hmm*, different?

She was determined to find out!

He was reputed to be dedicated to the job. If not actually designing, or discussing the project, he would have his nose in a textbook, even at breaks, keeping abreast of the latest technology. It was a well-known fact that he had never ever missed an evening class in the all the years of his apprenticeship – and that was serious studying. Most unusual in that office.

Everyone, particularly those who worked around him, and who were somewhat less conscientious, felt that his dedication was way beyond the call of duty. Of course, he could just be showing-off...

Yes, Angus was the attraction, Angus Findlay. She liked that name. She heard recently that his card had already been marked – full marks – and that he was almost certainly destined to be the next Chief Draughtsman. It was probably the reason for his position just outside the Chief's office. It would be an easy move, as soon as old Bob Fleming vacated the post – and everyone knew that Bob was quickly getting passed it...

Angus was the Senior Section Leader and not yet twenty-three. That was a faster career development even than her father's, and Angus looked in much better shape too.

Yes, she glanced again – he did look a bit of all right!

"Oh, yes, Mr Fleming. Just phone me when it's ready, and I'll collect it from you," was her comment as she was about to leave, "...no, it's no bother to pop over. It really is my pleasure," and as she said that, she gave him a sweet smile.

To the great amusement of all of his staff who could see every move through the glass partitions, Mr Fleming's cheeks coloured slightly. The poor man was embarrassed.

That surprised Beth. It never happened before and, now, having been seen by everyone – except Angus Findlay, of course – it was unfortunate. She felt slightly guilty. It was all her fault. They would probably mock poor Bob unmercifully afterwards, that is what they were like in the Drawing Office. As she left, she had a sudden thought – I hope old Bob doesn't think it's him I fancy... She shimmied back the way she'd come, gratified to observe that the dirty devils were all ogling her rear view again.

27

2009
Headline news...

David poured the contents onto the table. The envelope Meg had placed behind the painting had been used previously. A stamp was still attached, franked, a Christmas one and, with a closer look, the details were legible.

'Glasgow – 19 Dec 2005': eight months before Meg died. The clue must have been hidden behind the painting after that date. Helpful, and confirming what Angus suggested previously.

Three bits of paper fell from the envelope onto the table. Tom and Gillian each lifted one, obviously cuttings from a newspaper. They read silently. The third was hand-written. David lifted it.

"Ah, another rhyming clue..." he said.

They looked at each other. Tom and Gillian nodded for David to go first.

> *"The news is old,*
> *The pipes are cold,*
> *A case was made*
> *For them after parade.*

A medal, a gun –
Will you be the one
To find where they're concealed?
Soon all will be revealed..."

"She liked her little rhymes, didn't she?" said Tom. "Will I read this out and see if it helps? It's a cutting, tells of the accident in Glasgow: about Alexander Findlay, killed by a tramcar..."

David recognised all the words his Dad read, the same information that he'd found. He had more to add. In his pocket were a couple of pieces of paper that he had not yet shown to his parents. When his dad finished talking, he brought them out.

The death certificate had been David's first achievement, then later, the birth record. The official recordings of the start and end of the man's life, a man long gone but remembered as a hero, and pieces to add to a family picture.

"Did Granny Meg not talk about him?" David asked his grandad.

Angus shook his head sadly.

"The Findlays were not her blood relations – she only married into the family. Anyway, why should she have been proud of the Findlays? Hamish, my father, was the connection by marriage, but he left her – and for another woman! Abandoning a pregnant wife to go off with that floozy Bella Roberts? That was not an action anyone could consider noble. That man was certainly no hero to me, or my mother," he said. Unusual for him, Angus was displaying bitterness. "Sorry. I am getting carried away."

Gillian felt the tension.

"Should I read this part out now?" she asked.

"Yes, please, Gillian," said Angus. "I'm sure it wouldn't have been put in the envelope by mistake. It must be relevant."

The information she held had no date. She presumed it originated about the same time, and even could be from the same newspaper as that held by Tom.

"I can't see the connection, but here goes... The headline says –

CITY JEWELLER ALMOST KILLED."

"Mr Ivan Pilger, the well-known jeweller who has premises in Argyll Arcade, was confronted yesterday by an armed ruffian who tried to kill him. Mr Pilger told our staff reporter that he had been kicked and punched by this villain and had come very close to death. He had resisted handing over valuable jewels, clutching them tightly to his body until a gun was placed to his forehead. It was only the thought of the heartache his death would cause his wife and family if he were to be shot, that made him reluctantly hand over twenty-five uncut diamonds worth many thousands of pounds. Mr Pilger fears that he may have to end his business activities due to this enormous loss. He also has been told that he may never walk properly again and could be in pain for the rest of his life. Even while suffering his great distress, Mr Pilger is courageously attempting to ensure that his business remains open during normal hours Monday to Saturday. He tearfully explained that he would not want to disappoint loyal customers and prevent them purchasing his current bargains. He also requested it to be pointed out that his special cut-price sale is starting next week, no matter how much pain he might still be suffering."

The silence in the room when Gillian finished seemed to indicate that the others did not see the relevance of this piece of news either. David thought it odd. He had already discovered both these reports last week – joint headlines – the accident and a jewel robbery.

Was it just a coincidence?

Tom tried to move the thinking forward. "Perhaps we should concentrate on the clue," he suggested. "Pipes are cold... she says. Surely not the water pipes, it has to be the bagpipes again, no...? News is old... I can't guess where Meg would have obtained those pieces of apparently original newspaper, but these two extracts could be the old news, right?"

In the absence of any smarter ideas, they all nodded.

"...But 'a medal and a gun'? What's that about?"

"Been hidden, haven't they," David chipped in. "Wonder what kind of gun – a toy, a picture of one, or maybe even a real one? It could be a revolver, or a machine gun, or..."

"Dear me! Surely not a real one..." said Beth. "It is illegal to have an unlicensed firearm. You can be arrested for that sort of thing! Angus, did you ever see your mother brandish a gun? I hope she didn't bring it with her when she moved in with us. Anyway, where would she get such a thing?"

"My mother would have been terrified of a gun," retorted Angus. "She did get involved with the law, I remember," and he almost smiled, "...but that involved string and is another story."

"Could be hidden in the garden. Maybe we should start digging again, Dad," David joked, and received a glare from Tom.

They had acquired another clue, but further progress seemed unlikely.

"Is it alright for me to take the bagpipes home tonight, Gran? If I'm going to start, it might as well be right away. Have you been playing the guitar again? Can I hear you?"

Beth held her hands out for David to see that the fingers of her left hand were a bit tender – yes, she had started. She smiled and turned to look at Angus. David noticed it to be a loving look. That is nice, he thought – but it had been a sort of conspiratorial look as well, the kind that kids do when they have been up to something.

"I'm not ready to play yet, but why don't you ask your grandad to do some of his impressions?" suggested Beth mischievously. "He's very good..."

"What... No, no, I, ehm..." and Angus left the room hurriedly.

28

1967
A chance meeting...

She tried to think of a way to attract his attention without actually throwing herself at his feet.

To go on a date with Angus Findlay had become Beth's big aim in life, it was an obsession now, but a secret one. She certainly did not want that nosey cow, Sandra Stevenson, getting wind of it. That would be a catastrophe. If she were ever to find out, it might as well be printed in big headlines in the Glasgow Evening Citizen.

Beth McAndrew was still visiting the Drawing Office as regularly as good sense permitted, but somehow giving him the eye was not working. He appeared to be a cold fish and no mistake, but she was determined.

A new film that Beth would love to see was the latest James Bond movie, 'Thunderball'. It sounded very exciting mainly because she fancied Sean Connery, even more than she fancied Angus Findlay.

When I go out with Angus that is not something

to mention, she reminded herself. It was no longer '...if I go!' The poor lad did not know it yet, but Beth McAndrew had made up her mind.

Yes, he will be begging me and I'll see that film – if only she could think of a plan!

Getting a male to go on a date with her had never been a problem before. In fact, she regularly refused the approaches of a few others from the drawing office. Chic Davis, for example, with the ginger hair; she couldn't stand ginger hair – and his was curly too! Graham Steel was another who kept asking her, but he had very bad blackheads, and she would never go out with a guy with bad blackheads. *No sirree! Yughh!*

However, the best laid plans are not always successful, as everyone knows, and sometimes a plan isn't even necessary – things happen, and Beth's 'happening' was to be on a Saturday morning outside Marks and Spencer's in Argyle Street, where she would be shopping with her mum.

Jack McAndrew did not want to be there, shopping was no pleasure for him. His wife and daughter did it so much better without him. That he knew – they told him, but they kept insisting that today was different because it was his good fortune they would be celebrating. He had to be there. He just smiled and stayed at home.

He was now the Senior Yard Manager, a considerably up-graded position providing the luxury of a bigger salary. That is why mother and daughter were in the centre of Glasgow, and, thanks to Father, with extra money to spend. It was so wrong, and they knew it, his not being with them to have fun too but, however disappointing, they were coping – and spending his money for him. At least, he was in their thoughts...

Beth and her mother were waiting to cross the road. Shortly, it would be convenient to off-load their purchases into the car, which was sitting in a car park near the Clyde, but there was still the prospect of spending more on the other side of Argyle Street. Lewis's Polytechnic could be well worth a visit.

They stood patiently at the edge of the pavement.

In Beth's right hand was a large paper bag, containing some of their purchases: two sets of flimsy underwear, three blouses and a pair of brown casual shoes. Two Mars Bars were also in the bag as a special treat, both being sweet-toothed, for enjoyment when the shopping was definitely completed.

Beth's left hand held a largish box containing a portable radio/tape recorder, that she'd had her eye on for some time; under her arm was a new type of squeezie-mop, an unwieldy purchase made earlier in the day. After the demonstration, they had been unable to resist. It was much better than the one they had at home and, anyway, it was a bargain. Her mum was using both hands to carry the box of stainless steel pots, which was awkward and heavy.

Beth carried the mop with the long pole – under her arm: a lethal weapon.

Jean McAndrew became nervous when attempting to cross a busy road and Argyle Street was always busy. Crossing used to be so much easier when the trams were still running, she remembered; when they had been there, inevitably they had formed bottlenecks, and given pedestrians a fighting chance.

Eventually, a gap did appear in the traffic. Beth turned to her mother and said, "Right, let's go now."

Beth went to move with her mum, but a loud "Ouch!" came from behind her. The pole of the mop had hit something soft. An involuntary "Sorry," came out of her mouth, as she swung round to apologise to the injured party, almost striking him again in the process. Yes, she had hit a man – but not just any man. It was Angus Findlay. What a coincidence!

"It's alright, I'm ok," he said, backing off slightly in case she attacked again, but then he hesitated, and asked, "Err ...don't I know you?"

Beth felt slightly dizzy. She must have turned too quickly, she told herself, nothing to do with the person that she had fantasised about for weeks, standing in front of her, talking to her, no, no, no...

"Are you alright?" he asked, and reached forward slightly in case she needed help.

Meantime Beth's mother had succeeded, on her own, in crossing the road perfectly safely and was now standing on the other side of the busy street, waiting, with a puzzled look on her face, unable to signal to her daughter because of the heavy box in her hands. Who has she met?

"Yes, thank you," Beth replied, regaining some composure. "I'm so sorry I hit you with..." and then, suddenly realising that this might be her only opportunity, "...I'm Beth, Beth McAndrew. You might have seen me at the shipyard. I'm the assistant cashier..."

"Oh yes, you're ...eh ...the young lady who comes over to the office every so often. Ehm ...I am Angus, ehm ...Angus Findlay... You ...eh, (*cough*) you won't have noticed me, I know, but..." and he blushed, really blushed, a bright shade of red – but it did not stop him talking.

The next part came out in a rush!

"...And I've always thought you were lovely but never had the courage to ask you out so can I ask you now and will you go out with me – and please don't say no." A deep breath was essential after that.

"Oh yes..." she breathed back.

"Beth, I thought you were crossing the road with me." Her mum was back beside her again. "Did you change your mind? Oh hello, is this someone you know? Aren't you going to introduce me?"

"Mum, meet Angus..."

Beth's eyes did not leave Angus's as she spoke. This could get serious...

The chance meeting, that day, developed into the very first date for Beth and Angus, though it turned out to be a threesome. Jean, going along with her daughter and her 'friend' for a coffee to a newly opened up-market cafe in Queen Street, ensured that there was no chance of the two younger ones getting in any way personal.

Angus insisted on paying.

Later, Jean commented about that to her daughter, how impressed she was; how pleasant to have had coffee and cake with such a nice young man, so polite, and him insisting on having the bill – must have been expensive too. "It could be possible," she'd said, "that today we met the only gentleman remaining in Glasgow."

She did not consider what the older gentleman, back at home and who'd financed their day, might have thought of that comment!

It had been some day, bumping into her like that. Angus thought he had frightened her; she went all pale. Beth was lovely and – amazingly – she seemed to like him. So did her mother – especially when he paid for the coffees. He would have to hurry though if he was going to get back to town on time. He hoped she would not be late, or they would miss the start of the film.

"Mum..." he said, a little while later, after hurriedly gulping down his meal, "Ehm ...have you any money you could give me? Just as a loan. Mine seems to have vanished already..."

Love blossomed, but Beth's visits to the Drawing Office were not quite so often. She only went now when a genuine error occurred in a wage slip and it was truly necessary to go. She had achieved her goal and no need to push it. Angus belonged to her.

They went around together, and the word circulated. Everyone quickly became aware of a new romance at the shipyard – except poor Sandra Stevenson – she was well peeved to be one of the last to find out.

The film turned out to be an anti-climax for Beth. The James Bond film that she had been so looking forward to, it was good, very good in fact, but Beth discovered that Sean Connery was not as sexy as she had hoped; in truth, he could not compare with her Angus. Angus was real and right beside her in that cinema.

Beth had always been a good girl, well, as good as is reasonable to expect, and decided long before, that no matter how the young people of her age were supposed to be behaving, she was not buying into permissiveness. She would leave that to the likes of the groupies and suchlike to enjoy all the 'free love' that she had heard boasted about. She did not believe it was true anyway. As for smoking stuff that made your head go funny – no! That sort of behaviour was not for her.

She preferred being sensible, not drinking too much and behaving morally. Chaste was what she'd vowed to be – until she got married, although, now and again, she permitted herself the odd immoral thought or two – and enjoyed it.

Since they had been together, Angus behaved like a perfect gentleman, fitting her vision of what the man of her dreams was meant to be.

That was, until the day that they went to the Trossachs...

Beth was a privileged girl.

Her father had a car and paid for her driving lessons. She proved herself a very quick learner by passing her test and becoming a competent driver while young, and was permitted the use of the car when she wanted – except when required by her father or mother.

Since pairing up, Beth MacAndrew and Angus Findlay had been seeing a great deal of each other.

"Dad, could we go for a run – this weekend?"

The weather forecast was excellent, the car, available and earmarked on the calendar for them to use if they wished, so, they could go for a picnic.

...But where?

Jean had met Angus once, in town, but Jack had not. They thought it about time for them to get together as a family, in a formal way, to find out more about the young Romeo who had taken their daughter's fancy. They would invite him to their house for a meal.

Angus lived in Hyndland: Beth, in Bearsden. If they were to travel north, which was the most convenient direction to get them out of the city quickly and towards lovely countryside, it seemed better to start from Beth's place. The car outing was planned for Saturday. That meant inviting Angus for a meal with them on Friday evening and for him to sleep overnight at Bearsden.

The Drawing Office tom-toms started beating the moment Angus appeared at work on Friday morning, carrying a packed overnight bag. For Angus Findlay it was the first time this had happened.

"A dirty weekend, a dirty weekend, a dirty weekend..." began the office drums.

"No, impossible, not him, he isn't that sort," commented an unbeliever... "A dirty weekend... Angus...? No, never..." The drums hesitated...

"Angus Findlay? No... Are you sure?"

"Yes!" and the tom-toms sounded, louder and faster.

He reached his workplace.

"Angus is going for a dirty weekend. Angus is going..."

Bob Fleming was about to join the chant, and then thought it was not becoming for the Chief Draughtsman to behave like the natives, and resisted. He permitted the noise to continue for a short time, then went out and circulated. The chant continued a few more moments after he appeared, then the buzz of normal drawing office chatter returned. This meant, to Bob, that these lazy so-and-so's who called themselves draughtsmen, were back to doing very little as usual...

Sandra Stevenson was delighted to inform

everyone in her communication chain, "Have you heard about Beth and Angus... They are..." The important part, she whispered – Sandra knew that Beth would appreciate her discretion.

The raised eyebrows at the end of the day among the Drawing Office crew displayed a little tinge of jealousy. Angus Findlay was going to Beth McAndrew's home and, he was getting a lift from Jack MacAndrew.

You have to be someone to get a lift in Jack McAndrew's car; he is the Senior Yard Manager! The lucky sod...

29

2009
A learning curve...

David was impressed. Gran was away far ahead of him, and already playing her guitar again, but she had done it all before. For her it was just a refresher and much easier than starting from scratch. She knew what she was doing, he told himself. All that was required of her was simply to become proficient again. He, by contrast, had yet to begin...

The bagpipes were now his, carefully carried home in the wooden container last Saturday from Gran and Grandad's. To avoid tripping over the long box in the dark in his bedroom, the pipe-case had been placed under his bed.

The promise he made to her, that he would be learning how to play these pipes, he now wished he hadn't. It was Thursday, and he had made no attempt even to lift them from the box. What if she asked how he was getting on? Was there a good excuse? No ...but he had reasons.

Two of the nights, football was on telly, though disappointingly uninspiring games, and not a good time for starting anything new. One night he had been for a drink with his pals because he had not seen them for several weeks, and therefore, when he got home he had no energy or inclination to try and anyway, it had been too late to start. Not good reasons to have to admit to!

Hope she doesn't ask – I'd have to admit it. Everybody knows that 'ye canny kid your Granny!'

But as long as she did not phone in the next five minutes, he could do something about it. If he lifted them out immediately, he could truthfully say that he had started. He opened the lid, expecting the hinges to squeak, but they did not.

My bagpipes now... Yea! He looked at them, and smiled.

...But what's that?

Tucked down the side of the pipes was a rolled-up piece of paper, and it was somewhat squashed. Why was that not noticed before?

His eyes lit up, and his immediate thought – another clue and I found it, so yah-boo to you, father! A thought for a father who was not even in the house!

Carefully, he unrolled the paper.

It was not a clue at all. It was a drawing, done in pencil or charcoal, of a figure, a female and the face looked familiar. She was sitting inside a little office, or a cubicle, in what could be a theatre foyer, he guessed, although it should have been obvious to him – the sign. It said 'Ticket Office'. The bottom corner of the paper had folded over and hidden what the artist had carefully written, '*Lovely Phoebe* by Alexander F – 11 March 1914'.

Of course, he realised, it was familiar because Phoebe was in the photos they found in the loft, and the signature: Alexander F? Did his great-great-grandad do this? Then, he had another thought... 1914 ...ninety-five ruddy years ago! He looked at the drawing in his hand with amazement, and then at the instrument sitting in front of him. These pipes are really old – even older than my old man!

The drawing was placed carefully on the top of the bookcase – must not be damaged, and the pipes were cautiously lifted from the case. Being alone was probably good – no-one to embarrass him, because he hadn't a clue how to go about this. It was the first time he had held a set of bagpipes with the intention of playing, and it felt awkward.

He'd seen the Tattoo on telly, and watched the massed pipers doing their stuff. All very impressive and they made it look easy but all he knew was which end to blow into! That should have been rather obvious anyway, but he could tell when he lifted the instrument that something felt wrong. The bag ...it was not pliable. It felt like an enormous dried prune. There was no way that he could blow any air into it.

Obviously, these pipes had not been touched for a very long time. Could something be done with them or were they destined for the dustbin?

It was all a bit of a disappointment. Was his burst of enthusiasm to come to nothing? Worse still – it was Thursday evening! What would Gran say if she found out when he discovered the state they were in?

He needed help. Who could he turn to? Did he know anyone that played the pipes? No! His mother and father had gone to the hospital to visit Gran Walker. They had only just left, but it was unlikely that they would know what he should do anyway. Obviously, he could not speak to Gran or Grandad Findlay either.

Where's the laptop? In this technological age, he knew the answer had to be there for him – on the Internet! Someone was bound to have both bagpipes and a computer, and know something about both – and there was. In fact, there were many. A search for 'Bagpipes' gave him thirty-six pages. A mass of websites, and all with something to contribute to his learning.

Start at the top. Right... 'Where to buy a new set – Sale Now On!' No thanks. Well... not yet. 'Want a piper for a wedding, or bar mitzvah?' No thanks. 'How to contact the Red Hot Chilli Pipers.' No thanks again.

Keep looking...

The bag for the pipes, what was it made of? It would not be any sort of synthetic material. It was an old instrument. Can it be fixed, or will it have to be replaced?

Another search. Thank goodness for the internet!

...But what to ask? He tried, 'Inflating a sheep's stomach?' and he now had the addresses of local vets. Inputting, 'Bagpipes for beginners' gave another batch of pages, many repeating the original search.

Am I getting anywhere? He was being flooded with knowledge – knowledge that just confused him.

This website told him to forget about trying to play the actual bagpipes. He would have to obtain another instrument – a chanter. Where do I get one? I buy it ...on the internet, of course!

But, a chanter? What had that to do with bagpipes? He pictured India; dry and dusty and a hot sun beating down, flies all around, and, surrounded by excited chattering children, a little skinny wizened gent in a turban and loincloth sitting cross-legged. In front of him and slowing emerging from a tub-shaped straw basket, a snake, swaying hypnotically to the music that was being played – on a 'chanter'!

He opened his eyes, looked back to the computer screen. It was all sales pitches – a chanter was only the start. An instruction book was essential. Buy that – to learn what to do with the chanter ...and, after buying a chanter and an instruction book, he would want to play tunes, so, he would require sheet music. Yea, right! Pull the other one! For bagpipes? Sheet music! Who would believe that?

The internet was wonderful – but he was beginning to think that he had bitten off more than he could chew, especially when it emphasised his 'breathing'. Surely, he did not have to buy a book about that! He'd been doing that all his life.

Then the article talked about grace notes, and burling, and skirling, and... All this was making him dizzy! As for inflating a sheep's stomach, apparently, he was getting bagpipes confused with a haggis!

Ah, 'Seasoning', this is what he was looking for. To soften it, the bag had to have a treatment of a seasoning mixture, and that stuff would seal up the stitching too and stop air leaks – very technical... and where would he get that? ...On the internet!

He was fast becoming an expert. If someone asked him a question about bagpipes at this moment, he could bore them for hours. There was certainly an awful lot more to this than he had thought, but even more disturbing to find – they could make you deaf!

...So, he would need a chanter, an instruction book, sheet music, a seasoning mixture, deep breathing instruction, and ear-defenders! Might as well get a safety helmet, and bicycle clips while I am at it!

All this, to learn how to play five sticks poking out of a wee tartan bag...

A tartan bag...

That took him down another path, the tartan, on the bag cover, what was it? He did not recognise the pattern. Was there a Findlay family one, he wondered? He knew little about tartans – but he knew how to find out. So, back to the laptop! It could be another fact for the family tree...

There was not an actual Findlay design, he

discovered, but it was acceptable to use Farquharson or MacKinnon, but the cover on his bagpipes did not seem to be either of these. Maybe he was not seeing the true colours though, the bag looked rather tatty. If he asked his mum nicely, she would maybe wash the cover. The tartan might be more recognisable then.

He held his bagpipes in his hands. It was strange, but it was almost as if he could sense his long-departed relative being near. He put them on the table and looked in the box. It could do with a good clean, too.

Something glinted, a piece of glass. He lifted it out, but it was not just a piece of broken glass, was it? He put it down on the table with the pipes.

The case looked old and battered, almost as if it had been in the wars. He stopped, and smiled. It *had* been in the wars, for four years, and small wonder it looked battered, but it looked as if it had done its job well, protecting the pipes over all that time. The inside surface that went part way along the base was to support the drones, he presumed, but looked as if it had been altered after the box had been constructed.

The inside of the case was felt-covered, but the shelf was a slightly cleaner material. Was it only a shelf? Would a piper not always have to have spare parts with him, like reeds? These could get damaged, easily – according to the Internet. Could there be a compartment, underneath, for storing the reeds? No... not that he could see, and then he found a tiny clip that held a lid secure. It was not obvious. He released it and the flap opened. No reeds inside, but there were two packages, each wrapped in cloth.

The first he lifted was not heavy. He held it, trying to guess what it might be, just as he used to do at Christmas, or his birthday parties, trying to imagine what was inside a parcel before opening it. He guessed, and guessed correctly. It was a medal, a medal 'For Bravery'.

For the other one no guess was required. As he lifted it, the content was obvious. It had to be the gun, and it was...

David unwrapped it. He had never handled a handgun before and it was heavy. Bound to have been used. It felt uncomfortable thinking of how many lives it could have ended. What would it have been like to fire?

He could not resist. He held it in his hand, arm outstretched, finger on the trigger, pointing at the picture of himself when five years old, a photo that he hated.

As he took aim, there was a noise behind him and he swung round automatically – to face his mother entering, carrying a full cup of...

"*BANG!*" came out of his mouth. He couldn't stop himself, and hot coffee flew passed his shoulder.

"What the...?" screamed his mother. "David, what are you doing and where did you get that?" was asked in a shocked voice.

Tom appeared in a rush to see what all the

commotion was. As he stepped into the room and saw what David was holding, his jaw dropped.

"I've solved a clue," David said nonchalantly...

30

1967
The view...

Beth's mum had prepared a lovely meal. She wanted her daughter to be proud of her, but it was also was a chance for her to show off a little to the nice young man that she'd already met. She liked him, and wanted him to be impressed.

During the meal, intelligent chat from Angus was appreciated by Jack, and his mannerly behaviour appreciated by Jean. All-in-all, it was an enjoyable three-sided conversation over a wide variety of subjects, thanks to the knowledge Angus had gained from all the books he'd read over the years, and the studying he'd done at evening classes.

Jack was impressed. He had heard good reports of this young man at work, and meeting him confirmed it – he was right for the Company. Jean was impressed. She had already made up her mind when she met him before – he was right for her daughter.

Beth was not happy. She wished that she had gone with Angus to the Milngavie Fish Restaurant, just the two them head to head, with the aroma of vinegar in the air and a fish and chip tea in front of them. Maybe then, she would have had a chance to talk to her Angus...

During that evening, after the meal, it was a back seat for her in her own home and little chance to have a conversation of any length, or privacy, with her visitor.

Jack and Angus talked about work; ships, steel, staffing at the yard, world shipping markets, and future contracts – you name it, they discussed it.

"A beer, Angus, and you'll have a drop of the hard stuff too, I'm sure," suggested her father.

Angus nodded his head – he was sure too.

The two males sat and laughed and chatted – and drank more than they should have, of course. It was fortunate that Beth had shown Angus which bedroom he would be using and that he was able to find it, because when he and Jack went off to bed, it was long after Beth and her mum had given up on them.

The two males wished one another a pleasant sleep and staggered off towards the appropriate rooms, having consumed sufficient alcohol for each to consider the other to be really, and truly, the world's most wonderful person.

The destination for the day out was decided during last evening's meal. It would be the Trossachs – highly recommended by Beth's parents as a place of natural beauty, not too far to drive for a round trip, and with lovely places to picnic – perfect – provided it did not rain. The young couple accepted the suggestion graciously, although they had little to do with the choice.

Angus and Jack being closeted together more, or less, for the whole evening had left Beth and her mother to prepare a generous amount of food to take on the picnic. Without her husband's knowledge, Jean donated a bottle of an expensive wine that Jack had jealously hoarded, adding it to the other goodies in the picnic hamper. It he had known, he would probably have disapproved of the special wine's use for a picnic, especially as his daughter was driving. Jack had always told her, never to be silly about drinking and driving. He had seen the result of excessive drink too often.

Beth was up, bright and eager at seven o'clock, kettle on, bread in the toaster, and eager to go. Hot coffee was in the flask, and the picnic basket filled. Her mum and dad were still sleeping and would not rise until late. She was the only one moving around and trying to do everything quietly, waiting for Angus to appear – but he did not.

Knocking on the door of the spare room received no answer. Angus was still fast asleep.

She had to shake him quite hard. He wanted to turn over and continue his dream of building a cargo ship all by himself – hard work and he was currently covering the deck with a very thick paint, and the brush was very, very, heavy...

"The day hasn't started too well, has it Angus?" she said to the not-quite-awake-yet figure on her left. Beth's earlier enthusiasm had diminished somewhat but she told herself not to be silly, it could still turn out to be great...

Angus was sitting in the front passenger seat, dozing off and on, seeming less interested than he ought to have been in the beautiful scenery around them. He kept opening the window and saying that he felt unwell. Unsurprisingly, she felt no sympathy, which, incidentally, was almost the same feeling her Mum was having for the other male who'd over-indulged last night.

However, they reached Aberfoyle and wandered about a bit.

The walking helped Angus feel a bit better, until they began gazing in the windows of souvenir shops. The combination of seeing the displays of different brands of whisky, and how bad his reflection looked, made him feel very rough again. Whisky! Yugh!

A seat down by the river helped. Beth produced the flask and a cup of an excellent brew of coffee: that created some stimulus, and they started back on the road.

Along the Duke's Pass they went. They swung from side to side a little as Beth drove at a fine speed up the gradient. She was glad it was a dry road, and a quiet day for other traffic, but Angus was tense. He was gripping onto his seat, tightly.

"Are you all right?" she asked, but kept watching

the road.

The nausea felt earlier by Angus was returning, and getting worse with each bend in the road. "Do you always go round corners at this speed?"

She swung round the next with a screeching from the tyres, having stopped concentrating for a moment – maybe she had been showing off, she realised, so she slowed down a bit.

Beth knew where she was aiming for. A lovely spot that she visited with her parents a few years back. She remembered it as deserted, with a beautiful view over a loch and with a place off the road to park. A steep walk up the hill, admittedly, and then a path through thick undergrowth for a while.

They were almost there.

...And they had arrived. She stopped the engine. He felt so much better in an instant!

"Sorry if my driving disturbed you," she said, and they cuddled.

Angus regretted how, last evening, he eagerly accepted her father's hospitality and told her so. Beth heard out his garbled apology with a straight face, but she could not keep up the pretence – he looked so upset. A smile slowly developed and soon they were both giggling at his stupidity.

Today, just the two of them, at a remote spot in beautiful countryside. So much better than last night.

"At last," she sighed, "I have you all to myself."

What a lovely girl... Angus was relieved. He had

not spoiled her day.

They carried the picnic basket, a tartan blanket to sit on, plus her new radio-tape recorder, up the steep path to reach the targeted spot, and it was just as she remembered – but Angus saw it in a different way...

"The perfect place for a burial..." he said, gazing at the expansive view.

Beth looked at him. A bit morbid, surely, she thought. ...And then she froze, a moment of trepidation. Just two of them, him and her... alone in that secluded spot! Do I really know this man? Who is he thinking of burying...? Had she misheard?

"Spectacular," he added. "Yes, a perfect spot as a last resting-place."

...No, she had not.

Angus stood there grinning, delighted with life, and thinking nowhere in the world could be any nicer than this.

...She gave him a funny look. Was she standing beside a maniac?

Wait a moment! It is not a threat – he is being sarcastic! Getting at me – about my driving – the way I took the corners, and just because he has a sore head, he has decided to take it out on me! Huh! He was the one who drank too much! The cheek of him – and what a way to behave on our first outing together! If he thinks, that he can tell me...

...And before she could stop herself, "Well, you can walk back then, if that's how you feel!" she blurted out.

Angus's mouth fell open.

Why did she say that? What did I do? It's a very long walk!

"...I only... Umm... beautiful... Oh dear..." was all he managed.

Beth suddenly felt foolish, blushed and gave a shy smile. "Sorry, I am being silly. You have a strange effect on me. Come here..."

They cuddled, and kissed, lips lingering, eyes closed, each very conscious of the warmth and the contours of the other's body. It was isolated, they were standing on the hills alone, unseen by anyone, and they were tempted... A hot day – and getting hotter, so, both had a silent thought – *behave!*

"Food, let's have some food," Beth suggested, pulling herself away.

While she laid out the various goodies from the basket, Angus found something else to do: he played with her new tape recorder. There were only two tapes, and one of them was Beth's attempt at recording directly from the radio, an experiment.

When she tried recording at home, reception of the Light Programme was best. Lucky because that was the station broadcasting 'Pick of the Pops' on Sundays. On that first Sunday, the day after she'd bought the machine, she sat listening, pushing buttons, rewinding and restarting. With her first attempt, Alan Freeman's voice kept intruding into the music, not what she wanted and, for many records, she missed the start. It needed practise to know when to press the buttons.

She pronounced that attempt a failure.

By the next Sunday, she had become an expert, and surprised even herself with her success. Whole tunes from start to finish, and lots of them, clear as a bell, and with none of good-old Alan Freeman's *'All right, pop pickers?'* interrupting the flow. She did a very efficient job of filling the tape, she told herself.

The other tape was blank, well, except for the first ten minutes. On that, Beth had been experimenting with live recording – her own voice. She enjoyed singing and playing her guitar, and had become quite accomplished, but it was the first time she had heard herself. It sounded good, but she modestly classed herself as 'only reasonable' and left the effort on the tape. Inevitably, Angus found the result.

"You don't want to listen to that!" she exclaimed, but was pleased that he did and, hearing herself, as it played in the silence of the hillside, secretly, she was quite proud. Angus listened. When he said, softly, that she sang beautifully, he meant it.

"Could I try recording you?" he asked. "Would you sing for me now?"

She did – for Angus, *her* Angus, a little shyly to start but gradually she became more confident. She sang 'Scarborough Fair', perfectly to his ears, and then apologised – they were sitting hand in hand on a beautiful Scottish hillside – and it was an English song! Another was demanded, and a Scot's song it had to be, at Angus's insistence. A faultless unaccompanied rendition of 'Ae Fond Kiss' was the result.

"Your turn now!" she said.

He laughed. "I can't..." but he did, after a little pressure, persuaded because only Beth would be listening. She started the tape, and it was her turn to be surprised. He was singing in other people's voices; impersonating well-known performers, and she laughingly applauded his bravado.

Comfortable with each other and suddenly they realised, that for certain, this was love. There were no inhibitions now.

He had never before sung with anyone listening. In fact, Angus had only ever done impressions at home, for his own fun, and only with his mother out of the house. He surprised both Beth and himself by bursting into song, letting her hear him. Out came Elvis, and Sinatra, Crosby, then Frankie Laine, and Perry Como!

Enough! He leaned forward and pressed the stop button, but that was insufficient for his one-girl audience. She demanded more and restarted the tape. He obliged happily, with some home grown favourites: Doonican, Bygraves, Ken Dodd, Adam Faith, a little bit of each. He knew parts of many songs, associated with the singer, but there was one he knew really well, his best voice, Nat King Cole.

He sang, "When I fall in love" for Beth and genuine feelings poured out. Beth sang a harmony, and enhanced the recording.

"You are great!" she told him. "You ought to be on stage."

She said it, but knew he would never perform in public – that would take a different sort of courage. This was a once-only performance for her, and each knew it was a very special moment.

They kissed again – and were tempted again ...but there was food to eat and a few glasses of wine to consume. It was fun being together, just fooling around like this.

The wine made them feel drowsy and they lay back in the sunshine, sharing images seen in the shapes of little fluffy clouds. There they were, two dozy individuals, gazing at a beautiful blue sky, utterly content...

The tape deck was now playing the other tape, her successful recordings from radio. Together, they sang along with Cliff, he warbled '*Bachelor Boy*'. A little grin of satisfaction was on Beth's face as it ended on a fade-out that would have satisfied a professional and led, just as competently, into the bouncier musical sound of '*I like it*'.

"Bet you don't know who that is," she teased. Surprisingly, Angus did – he took his nose out of books sometimes...

He knew. "Gerry and the Pacemakers..." he told her. "Soon to be dropping out of the Top Forty, Pop Pickers," ...and it was Alan Freeman's voice! "...And, this week, sliding down to number twenty-nine."

They cuddled closer, and thanks to Beth's skilled use of the recording controls last Sunday, Gerry's cheery song segued beautifully into '*I'm confessing that I love...*'

Angus needed no prompting – he was enjoying himself. "And now we are listening to the smooth sounds of Frank Ifield," and the Freeman voice once more. "This song peaking at number one, this week, but ...how long it will stay there only time will tell, Pop Pickers. It's up to you."

She smiled at him, he smiled back, and the music continued...

The Searchers now bounced happily along. "Currently at number three, it's '*Sweets for my Sweet*' and a great choice of music – especially for all young lovers..." Mister Freeman's voice softly caressed these words, and gave an excuse to cuddle even closer.

The effect of the wine, the gentle easy-on-the-ear sounds playing in a background, the beautiful surroundings, and the warm sunshine; everything was contributing, as the music continued into a new song...

They turned towards each other.

This time, temptation won!

The perfect moment. Beth's hands wandered southwards, as Angus's went north to begin with, then south as well...

Wow, oh, wow...! This was heaven...

"Sweets for my sweet, sugar for my honey..."

For a moment, but only a moment, Beth remembered her old suspicion – of Angus, not liking women! How wrong she had been!

"Your first sweet kiss thrilled me so..."

It had become serious. Neither was an expert –

but it was all happening so naturally. The recorder though knocked over due to the tartan blanket being severely disturbed continued playing, and the song changed yet again, but neither noticed...

"She loves you, yea, yea, yea..."

Even the golden eagle, flying majestically over the hillside, a sight that should normally have caused considerable excitement, flew unseen today – something else was holding the attention of the young couple.

"Oh ...Angus... the music... it's... the last ...one... on the tape...

"She says she loves you and you know that..."

"Oh yes... yes... yes..."

Angus didn't seem to mind about the tape nearing its end – or that the Beatles had shot up the chart and reached number twelve in the Top Forty this week. These facts had lost their importance!

"...And you know you should be glad... Oooh..."

"Angus...!"

"What...! Yes... What...!"

For once, the young lads from Liverpool were not the centre of attention, but they were still singing, and using clever harmonies to bring their huge international hit to a subdued climax!

"...She loves you. Yeh, yeeh, yeeeh, yeeeeeeeh..."

A lovely ending...

...But a female voice continued; maybe not as musical, though there was no question – by comparison to the Beatles – the young lady sounded much more enthusiastic! She was giving it a lorra-

lorra welly...

"*Yeh, oh, yeeh ...ooh ...yeeeh ...ooooooh ...ANGGGG...GUS!*"

...And it segued beautifully...

For a long time they lay contentedly in the sunshine, arm in arm. Angus broke the silence. "Beth ...was that safe?"

"Don't worry Angus. You have to try many times before a girl can get pregnant..."

"...If you say so, Sweetheart."

"...Yes, trust me and don't worry, Angus... Just relax..."

However, a tiny Thomas Hamish Jack Findlay – as sometime in the future he would be destined to be called – was going to prove that once can be enough!

31

2009
Do not shoot!

When Gillian recovered from the shock of her son brandishing a revolver in their front room, and David had attempted, but failed, to properly clean the coffee stains from the carpet for which he was receiving full blame, and Tom had made more coffee, they all sat down to consider the latest development in the treasure hunt.

In addition to the gun, the medal, and the drawing of Phoebe, another item was at the bottom of the pipe-case – a sealed envelope. It was underneath the two wrapped packages in the compartment. A plain envelope...

Tom was the one who opened it carefully and took out the sheet of paper.

He read it – silently, and then read it again – silently. When it came to this sort of thing, he could be as annoying as his son.

"Oh, come on, Dad. We want to know too," complained David.

Tom read it once more, but this time, aloud.

"Well, have you guessed? The clues you've seen?
The clues were linked is what I mean.
You've reached this far but must do better.
It's written clearly in the letter,
A loved one's ears had learned the score,
For much was heard beyond the snore.
But where to hide the final clue?
I wouldn't want to needle you.
So, let's just knit it all together,
The machinations of a blether."

"The final clue? So, we have still to find it ...and I'd hoped this was it!" said Tom.

David heard the comment, but he'd stopped thinking. He decided he deserved a rest. Well, he found that clue, and the medal, and the drawing – and the gun. Enough excitement for one evening. He had done his bit, so he would take a back seat and leave it to his very capable parents to work this one out. They could have the glory. He had a set of bagpipes to worry about, and the bluffing he'd have to do when he next met his grandmother...

Gillian's mind was on other things too. "It's my bed-time and I suggest you two get to bed as well," she said. "Remember, you have work in the morning, whereas I... I might have a lie-in tomorrow!" After adding that, with a smirk on her face, she departed.

Tom laid Meg's poem down on the table. No attempt to decipher that tonight, he decided. Obviously the hunt was not over yet, but there was no rush, the clues had been waiting many years to be solved. If left to him, it might be a few more before it would happen.

"What's this, David?" Tom asked, and lifted the lump of glass from the table. "Did you put it here, or was it your mum?" He turned to look at his son, sprawled in the chair and obviously in a world of his own. "David!"

"Oh sorry! The bit of glass? I thought it had broken off something. I lifted it out of the pipe case. It was in the corner of the case when I took the pipes out."

Tom held it to the light. Unusual...

"Is it just glass?" He looked at it again, and turned it around in his fingers. "It doesn't look broken."

David shrugged, happy to let his dad play detective.

"David, have you ever seen an uncut diamond?"

David's eyes widened. He shook his head.

"Me neither, but... Could we find anything on the computer about uncut diamonds, do you think? Granny Meg may have left behind a real one!"

David grinned. "You think so? But you said there would be no treasure!"

He checked. A quick Google entry and... "Voila!"

What an assortment! Tom looked over David's shoulder at the images he'd found. They were seeing all shapes and sizes. None actually matched the glass in front of them, but they all appeared different to each other anyway. A second look at the screen easily convinced Tom. David grudgingly agreed.

"Looks real to me," Tom said, trying to sound calm but with excited fluttering in his stomach. "Value?" he asked. He had to remain casual in front of his son. "If it is, can you... *uhmm*... work some magic for its value?"

With a total lack of knowledge of diamonds, cut or not, that was not so simple. Lots of mumbo-jumbo about international markets, and, that only an expert could judge a value, was the best David could find.

A bit frustrating...

So, Tom decided, if it needed an expert opinion it was up to him to find that expert. Someone with the required knowledge could be found in the city centre, and he knew exactly where to look.

"I have work in town tomorrow, and after, I'll visit a jeweller. Don't mention this to your Mum just yet and let's hope it turns out to be a nice surprise..."

The electrical work in the Supermarket was straightforward and rapidly completed. Tom left his handwritten invoice and told them very politely that he would appreciate prompt payment, knowing full well that there was little chance with that mob. It was a national company, with headquarters somewhere down south – the big boys were the worst for paying.

He hurriedly drove farther into the city, hating the fact that he would have to use one of the multi-level car parks. Parking on double yellow lines in

Glasgow was suicidal, so he could not drive up and park outside the door. To reach the jeweller that he had in mind would mean a lengthy walk.

He checked his pocket, and yes, the potentially valuable piece of glass was still safe. The destination – Argyll Arcade. There, if he did not have success with one jeweller, there were another twenty or more from which to choose.

He reached Buchanan Street slightly out of breath, and decided on the one near the entrance: Pilger and Sons. Established 1894.

Might as well try there. They should know what they are talking about, they have been at it long enough... Pilger. Unusual name and seems familiar... Nope, cannot remember!

He entered, aware of looking a bit scruffy in his working clothes, and suddenly became conscious of CCTV cameras strategically placed around the shop. Could not get away with a robbery in here, he reckoned.

The person who came forward was wearing a smart, and obviously hand-tailored suit, an expensive-looking pale blue shirt and a yellow silk tie. Tom would have sworn blind if he had to, that the shoes had come straight out of the box that morning and, from the aroma of this bloke's after-shave, a bottle of that stuff probably was attacked every half-hour.

Tom shuffled around a bit, feeling decidedly uncomfortable, and then noticed that this smarmy git sniffed snootily as he came towards him. Cheeky sod – but as he needed this Muppet's assistance, he spoke nicely.

"Could you help me please? I have been given this as a gift by a distant relative, and I am suspicious that he might have been ...uhm ...pulling my leg. He said it was valuable." Tom had almost said, '...taking the piss,' but stopped in time. This pillock probably would not have understood.

"We do not do valuations without an appointment, *SIR*," said the smarmy git.

The overtly cultured accent grated on Tom's ears. In particular, the way he accentuated, 'Sir'. Tom wanted to give him a thump and walk out, but he needed help...

"I am very sorry, but I'm only in town for one day. I have to be back in Paris by tomorrow, and it is rather urgent. Could you possibly oblige?" As he spoke, he realised his accent had suddenly become toffee-nosed too – but he needed assistance and the Paris bit seemed to have had an effect. This bloke probably realised now that Tom was a multi-millionaire who dressed down.

"Well..."

"Thank you," Tom said effusively. "That would be wonderful."

The assistant lifted his eyeglass and looked. "At first glance, sir, it does appear to be the genuine article."

That's good! Tom noted the change in attitude, and the less superior way that the important little word 'sir' was said. "And the value?" he asked encouragingly.

"Obviously it can only be very rough, and it would have to be confirmed by laboratory testing, but it could work out anything between four and five thousand for a diamond of this quality and size, but only if cut well and polished, you understand."

Tom tried to avoid looking shocked, but to be told that he had won a few millions on the Lottery, could not possibly feel any nicer!

"You'd have to pay for the cutting, and the polishing, and for one of this size and quality, ehm …maybe about one hundred and fifty pounds; but could you excuse me a moment, sir, I think that is my phone."

Tom stood dumbstruck – up to five thousand pounds!

His phone?

I heard nothing!

Tom waited, but to him it sounded like the man was making a call, rather than receiving. With no-one else in the shop, other than him and the assistant, it was almost silent, so what was being said by the quietly spoken voice was almost able to be heard, but he had to listen very carefully.

"Hello, Inspector Mar... ...yes, Paris... ...that latest robbery... ...uncut... Yes... There is some... Indeed... trying to fence... Yes, could be... ...And he's here now. Looks a bit rough..."

That was as much as Tom heard, because he grabbed the diamond from the counter and was out the door and along the street at a fast pace, having to avoid those silly people window-shopping getting in his way.

That guy thinks I am pedalling stolen goods – what a bloody cheek!

He kept walking quickly, dodging along one street, along a lane, into another alley, and eventually found himself walking across the concourse at Central Station.

Why did he have this guilty feeling?

He could not stop himself glancing at the policemen standing there. He felt he was being watched.

Then he stopped and looked around at the people milling around the station concourse.

No one was following him. He had been too quick for that, and anyway, there would be no justification. He didn't steal anything. Why did he panic? He hadn't needed to rush off ...and that is when he realised his other mistake. How could he be so stupid? The car – in the car park...

He'd shot off in the opposite ruddy direction!

32

1967
A little surprise...

They had to get married ...well, maybe not essential, but it was decided to be the best solution for all involved.

A few months after the day at the Trossachs, Beth had confirmation, and the most beautiful day that both ever enjoyed became a little less wonderful. When Beth told Angus the 'good' news, he came mighty close to heart failure.

"But it couldn't happen the first time, the one and only time ...could it? You said..."

"Yes, I know I said it, but I was wrong – right? Because yes, it could, and yes, it did."

Not surprisingly, she sounded a bit rattled.

Angus smiled ruefully and gave her a hug.

Their most beautiful day ever had been in summer, hardly a cloud in the sky, Angus remembered. He often thought to himself afterwards, if it had rained that weekend, would life have been different?

With Beth certain, the dilemma for both was how to tell parents about an unexpected pregnancy? They would have to be informed at some point.

Beth's would be the first and it was praying on her mind. The previous night she had a dream, though a nightmare would be a better description – involving her and her father.

There she was, a fat belly and obviously displaying all the signs of having been pregnant for many months, kneeling in front of a stern Victorian father, pleading with him not to send her away. He was looking beyond her – no eye contact – grim of face and resolute, with a corporation almost as large as her belly (and not in the least like her father), tall and overpowering, arm outstretched and finger pointing out of the house. She could not actually hear words, but they were obviously: "Go – and never darken my doorstep again – and as for that scoundrel Findlay..."

Angus was not to be present when she would break the news to her parents, but after telling him of the dream, he suggested that he should be in the vicinity – waiting at the end of their driveway to carry her going-away suitcase.

To her relief, the response was a great deal better than feared. She told her mother in private, and she in turn called her father into the room to hear it repeated. Beth had found them to be anything but angry, in fact, they had both been downright sympathetic. Jack, her lovely, lovely father, even smiled wryly.

"It happens..." was his comment, perhaps remembering his own young days? "And what does young Angus think should happen now?"

Young Angus, earlier that day had been trying unsuccessfully to work at his drawing board, unsuccessfully because other matters were clogging his normally, highly absorbent brain. The masses of lines on the drawing in front of him looked a meaningless jumble, and the book, sitting open, could have been Chinese hieroglyphics.

At a loss as to which way to turn, because in his ordered life, this was not the way it was supposed to be. He loved Beth, he had a good job and was happy in it, but the money he earned was not yet at a level to be able run away with her, get married, and live independently in their own home with the responsibility of a little baby ...and the stigma!

Tonight, he decided, he would tell his mother.

That evening, standing in front of his mother feeling incredibly foolish, as his sad tale spilled out about how much he and Beth had enjoyed their day at the Trossachs, her reaction shocked him – she giggled! Meg thought it hilarious – she giggled, and giggled, and then had to apologise to a humiliated Angus.

"Well then, when's the wedding? I'm in the mood for a knees-up," were her words. In truth, she was worried, but hid it well. It was not a good idea beginning a marriage under pressure like this.

However, Beth had become a favourite.

Since she and Angus became friends, Beth had visited Meg at home many times and they'd had long and pleasant chats. Meg liked her a lot. In Meg's opinion, and decided long ago, Beth would make the perfect wife for her Angus. It was obvious to her that they were a capable pair. They could support each other very well and should marry as soon as they liked.

It did not take too long for a reasonable solution to emerge and it was Jack McAndrew's idea that sparked it. The Bearsden house was large and, if their daughter left home, it would feel much too big for just Jean, and him. Why shouldn't the two youngsters get married, more or less right away, a simple ceremony that Jack would happily fund, and they could live with them at Bearsden until they could afford their own home?

Even though it was his future father-in-law who provided this solution, Angus was relieved. He was also relieved when Beth happily accepted it too. He would make it up to Jack sometime in the future, no idea how, but that would be resolved at the right time.

Unfortunately, for Jack MacAndrew, the future was likely to be short term...

They would have the wedding at Bearsden, in the house where the happy couple would be living, and invite a few friends. Neither Angus nor Beth had close relatives other than their parents. Angus's father, Hamish, might be out there somewhere but, at Meg's request, he would not be receiving an invitation. Written out of her life as far as she was concerned and as for Angus, his son, that man was never in it.

In the very short time since they met formally, the relationship between Jack and Angus had warmed. For them it now was more like father and son. They felt close.

A few weeks before the wedding there was the usual whip-round by the staff at their workplaces in the Drawing Office and the Cash Office. Many workers in the yard who knew them also contributed and the money collected was given to the couple to buy something appropriate. They chose a painting, an oil painting of the Trossachs.

Just before the big day, at a ceremony in the Drawing Office, the gift was presented formally. The Chief Draughtsman, Bob Fleming, made a nice speech, complimentary to both for the jobs they did for the Company. He remarked how suited they were for each other. "And I'm sure you chose this lovely view for some personal reason. Am I correct?" he said, indicating the painting.

Angus only replied, "Yes," and gave no hints, but a little enigmatic smile was there as he looked at the scene. He could even have marked the exact spot with a cross!

All the unmarried males in the drawing office were envious of Angus's good fortune. They would have loved the chance with Beth – she had a beautiful wiggle, and even old Bob Fleming had a twinge of jealousy. With the many visits Beth made to the drawing office over the months, he had hoped that she fancied him – even though he was an old married man.

33

2009
Guessing correctly...

On the way home, Tom thought that he would be welcomed with open arms when he told Gillian and David what he'd learned – but now and again Tom could be wrong...

Gillian was shocked. "A diamond? And you found it ...in the pipe-case? What makes you think that it is your property?" she shouted at him, when she had taken in the value.

"David found it, so if it's not mine it's his, and it's worth a lot of money," he protested.

"Oh my God," Gillian shuddered "Oh dear me... No... This means...."

"What's wrong now? Are you alright?"

"That item about the jewellers and the robbery, you don't think that... Could Alexander have...?"

"No... Don't be silly..."

"Then why did your grandmother leave that piece of news?"

David said nothing. He stood there – wisely, just

listening.

Tom had stopped to think. He looked at the valuable piece of glass in his hand. "I suppose you could be right," he grudgingly admitted, "but let's not rush at anything. We will have to complete the next clue and maybe the answer will be there for us. I hope it doesn't say the wrong thing... Anyway Mum and Dad will think of something again."

That Friday night the sleeping patterns were unsettled. At about three am, after David had unsuccessfully tried some of the tricks he used before, he got up. He went into the kitchen, and was met by his mother. She had the same problem.

"Cup of tea?"

"Yup."

"Want a biscuit?"

"Yup ...please... You... Sleep?"

"Nope..."

Upstairs, the moment his head hit the pillow, Tom had gone out like a light. He was dreaming sweet dreams of limitless wealth.

Saturday morning again, bright, and early and they were on their way, though being bright this morning was not a claim that should be made for Gillian or David. They sat chatting and awake together from the early hours of the morning so, sensibly, Tom was doing the driving. There would be a lot to discuss when they arrived at Beth and Angus's, and reliance would be, hopefully, on the brainpower of the older couple.

"I can't wait. Dear old mother will have kittens when we tell her that you found a gun, David,' said Tom, grinning broadly.

"Don't tell her, please," said Gillian. "She doesn't have to know that yet."

They arrived and sat down together, as a happy family should, and small talk began.

"Good news," announced Gillian, "we've found another clue," and she looked to Tom as she said it, expecting him to present the vital evidence. There was a pause as it was realised that they'd failed to bring it with them. Committing to memory had not even been attempted this time, so the piece of paper was essential. Tom would have to go back to Jordanhill.

"Imagine forgetting to bring it. Don't know what's been wrong with you two this morning!" he grunted, as he left the room, grumbling about the inefficiency of wife and son. By the time he'd jumped into the car he'd absolved himself totally of blame.

Back at the table, as Tom was not normally an important contributor anyway, the small talk continued without him. Beth said she had been practising and brought out her guitar. She played a few chords, disguising the agony of her fingertips, and sang and played some tunes from memory. Then apologised for being rather rusty.

David smiled, because she sounded just as good as she did on the recordings!

He felt guilty. Her achievement made him feel worse. He could have tried harder, and would do next week, he promised himself. One day I'll get my own back, he resolved. I'll play them and deafen them – but that would be a long way away. At least, if pushed, he could claim that he'd made a start in learning about his instrument.

"I'm progressing... methodically," he said, hoping she wouldn't ask details. "You know... Ordering on-line. Seasoning for the bag, a chanter, and an instruction book – but I can't read music."

"Don't worry about that. I'll teach you, if you like. You can come over here each evening. Much better than going out drinking with your pals, or watching silly football, or chasing girls! We'll get on with it together."

"Oh! Uhm... Yes, Gran." Blooming heck! Am I that obvious?

"Good. I'll put on the kettle."

After they'd enjoyed tea and toast and homemade jam, Tom was back again, and it was down to real business – the treasure hunt.

"Found by me," said David, immediately claiming credit, "...this other clue. In a hidden compartment in the bagpipe case. And I found a medal too."

He smiled proudly. It was his moment.

"But ...wait for it... Guess what else was found?" said Tom. "This will get the party going!"

Oh no... thought Gillian. Not the gun!

"A diamond!" said David on a high, and then

cringed. Gillian relaxed again. David took the drama out of his father's build-up but, as usual, Beth and Angus were more interested to hear it coming from him anyway.

"...but Dad found out its value... Dad, tell them what it is worth."

The eyes swung back to Tom. He smiled, but said nothing. He started to count in his head to crank up the tension like the other two males did – and reached six...

"Come on, Dad, we're waiting!"

"...Almost five thousand pounds!"

"Oh..." said Beth, less than impressed. "Whose is it, then? And where did it come from?"

Tom hesitated. He could sense he was about to say the wrong thing – as usual, but much to his delight and relief, his father chipped in.

"Well, if it was in the bagpipe case, it was part of Alexander Findlay's estate, I'd say, and therefore belongs to the family."

"But how would it get there?" asked Gillian. "Alexander wasn't a rich man when he died, was he? And his wife surely wouldn't have been able to buy it."

"It could have been Meg's," Beth suggested. "Remember that it's her treasure trail we're following. Maybe this is the treasure."

"Ah..." David figuratively then threw a bucket of water onto that suggestion when he reminded them all, it could not be the treasure yet, because Meg had left another clue – a clue that still awaited solving.

"But it's not bad having a diamond for starters, particularly if there's more treasure to come," he added.

"Ah... yes, you'll want the clue," said Tom. He took the envelope from his pocket and handed it to his mother to read out.

> *"Well, have you guessed? The clues you've seen?*
> *The clues were linked is what I mean.*
> *You've reached this far but must do better.*
> *It's written clearly in the letter,*
> *A loved one's ears had learned the score,*
> *For much was heard beyond the snore.*
> *But where to hide the final clue?*
> *I wouldn't want to needle you.*
> *So, let's just knit it all together,*
> *The machinations of a blether."*

The one thing they all agreed right away was that Meg liked writing poetry – lousy poetry, but it did rhyme, however, the silence that followed showed inspiration to be in short supply this morning.

Beth did have an idea, but said nothing. She could not be certain, but at least it was a possibility. She smiled to herself. This might even be the final answer, so why rush it when I can savour the moment...

Anyway, Angus began talking.

"'The clues were linked'. Now what does that tell us? If it is the newspaper clues she's referring to, then it seems very likely that this jewel could have been stolen," he contributed, "but, by whom? 'A loved one's ears had learned the score, for much was heard beyond the snore.' Something to do with sleeping? Hidden under a bed?" he continued.

Angus had the floor now, and was permitted to lead. Beth hoped he would go in the same direction as her. She already had reached the next stage in her head.

"'I wouldn't want to needle you, so, let's just knit it all together.' Beth, could it be in your knitting bag ...or your needle box?"

Beth could see he was not going in the same direction after all. Had she guessed correctly, because she could think of only one thing now?

"What about her line 'These machinations of a blether'... If you add that to your other thoughts, Angus, what do you get?" she prompted.

Angus just looked blank.

"The tape recorder?" was David's sudden inspiration.

"Never thought of that, David," his grandmother said affectionately.

Now, if I had said that out loud, the slightly peeved son of Beth thought, it would have been, *Do not be so silly, Tom!*

"What about the knitting machine?" Beth continued.

"Didn't we throw that out?" said Tom.

"I would certainly hope not. If you did, look out because it was without my permission!"

Tom received the glare.

Tom and David went up the ladder – to find the knitting machine, and Tom remembered where it was. It had been carefully placed on the floorboards at the far end of the loft, but many large items were stacked in front of it. They could either move a whole lot of stuff to safely get it, or go round the edge – where there was no flooring and they'd have to step on each ceiling joist to gain access.

"Dad, shouldn't we move all the...?"

"No."

"But, wouldn't it be wiser then, if we used boards to...?"

"No!"

"But..."

Tom's look advised David not to continue to push him. Tom had had enough! Today it was: Good-bye, Old Avacare... Welcome, Mister Let's-Get-The-Damn-Job-Done!

The two males moved slowly round the outside, gently lowering each foot to feel the structure before stepping forward. No point in being *stupid* and accidently missing a joist.

The return journey, carrying the knitting machine, proved more awkward and costly and, guess what? They *were* stupid – because Tom's loss of balance caused both of them to miss the solid wood. Their feet did not go fully through the plaster – the insulation cushioned them. They struggled on, reached the safety of the solid flooring, and breathed a sigh of relief.

What was the damage? They climbed down the

ladder and looked into the spare bedroom – two bulges now existed about a metre apart on the ceiling. They didn't have to speak – just nodded. They knew if they said nothing and, if no one went into bedroom, they could get out of the house without a major telling-off – worry about it next weekend.

They climbed back up the ladder. The knitting machine now sat on a clear patch of solid flooring. At least the object of the exercise had been achieved. The box had nothing attached to the outside. The ends were taped closed, so they opened it, slid out the flat unit. With some satisfaction, there, held in the needles, they found another envelope.

"Wait a minute..." said Tom. "We are in the loft. How did Meg manage up that ladder to place the clue in the box?"

"Your very old granny was Wonder Woman!" said David.

It was later discovered that, Angus and George, from next door, had struggled to lift the heavy machine into the loft about three years ago. Until then it had been sitting unused in its box in the upstairs bedroom. Meg had not entered the loft – she had only been in the bedroom. So much for their powers of deduction!

Tom and David agreed it was unwise to encourage the others to come upstairs. They might go into the bedroom – and look up! So, they took the still sealed envelope downstairs for the others to open.

In the kitchen, Tom's hopes that they'd reached the conclusion of the trail were dashed because this envelope, when opened, contained two more envelopes. One was marked 'Read first' and the other 'Read last'.

Gillian was given the first, and opened it. The writing looked childish. It seemed as if written by someone who was not used to putting pen to paper, and was painstakingly done. Her eye went to the bottom of the letter. It was from Phoebe.

She began to read.

"Whoever sees this will be the one who has been given my dear Alexander's bagpipes. You will be close family because that is the way I asked it to be."

Gillian stopped a moment, and looked at the others. She had their full attention.

"No one else knows of this and no one outside our family must ever be told. It is a secret that I am taking to my grave. The husband I loved so dearly became a thief. He was a hero who fought a hard battle in his mind long after he left the army, but I have difficulty forgiving him for the wrong he has done. I know not what to do. He did not tell me of the misdeed and died not knowing I knew of his theft."

Gillian stopped again. She looked around the table. Each was listening intently because some of the previous facts were beginning to fall into place.

She continued...

"He had horrible dreams. I lay awake at night beside him hearing the pain he was suffering, hearing him talk as he slept, and the dreadful memories he had after being with all the dead around him. War is terrible. The night before he died, he was haunted by something different, something that he had done wrong on that day. The gun. He had used it and stolen jewels, precious stones, ten of them, and ran off with them. In bed that night he tossed and turned and kept mumbling, about his pipes and the terrible thing he'd done. He'd stolen something that he'd hidden. "Phoebe mustn't know... Phoebe mustn't know..." but I found them. I found what he hid, after he was dead. They remain hidden because I did not want anyone to know my hero husband was a thief. I know he did it for me but I cannot touch them and do not want them. They will stay hidden until you find them. You will know what is best to do, my dear relative. Written by Phoebe Findlay, loving wife of Alexander Findlay."

Each one sat silently, absorbing the pain of a long dead woman, a troubled woman who had adored her husband.

Gillian could see that her mother-in-law was particularly upset and was so glad that David and Tom hadn't mentioned the gun. That would have really pushed her over the edge...

34

1967
Cold tonight...

It was cold, very, very cold, and had been ever since before Christmas. The thermometer had not risen above freezing in all that time and was getting even colder at nightfall. It was too cold for snow, and any surface water was frozen solid. Even the edge of the river had frozen in places.

Jack McAndrew was just about to go back outside again.

He found it strange that, even though his life had almost always involved working in the open air, or at least in unheated places, he still disliked the cold and had never got used to it, but although it was warmer inside, he still liked working in the open air of the yard.

For the past hour, he'd been in his office tidying up the last of the reports and a few other documents. Office work was not his forte, he preferred 'hands on'. The shipyard was silent: exactly as it should be with the shift having ended for New Year a short while ago.

Total closure for two full days and he was planning another two in addition. Wonderful! This would be a chance for him to switch off.

Jack had always taken his responsibilities very seriously. The company appreciated his dedication over the years and now he was enjoying the reward: an excellent salary, although occasionally, he did feel the strain of the task. That is why it would be nice to relax over the next four days with his family and forget about work.

As the shift ended, and the men were leaving the yard, he had been down at the gate wishing them well, participating in the backchat that he so much enjoyed. He thought the men, his men, appreciated that sort of thing – and he was probably right, most of them did.

The heavy warm overcoat he wore in the winter did a good job of keeping out the worst of the cold, but underneath he also was wearing one of his wife's hand-knitted pullovers, lovely and warm, and heavy; he liked the weight. Just lifting it off the chair before even putting it on in the mornings, the bulkiness of it made him feel cosy. It remained on until he arrived home again at the end of a day.

He did have several pullovers in the same pattern and in varying shades, and was able to change them regularly. His caring wife would wash them, and in the cold weather, he would never be without one.

Jack could appreciate the tale he had heard of one old bloke in the yard, who apparently felt the same way as he did about the cold weather. There was a difference though – the old bloke had only one set of long drawers – kept on all winter. That man worked alone.

For Jack, even with hand-knitted thick woollen socks inside his working boots, his feet were never as warm as he would have liked, but the moment he stepped through his own front door he would be into cosy slippers. He had woollen gloves but only wore them occasionally. Hands in pockets were preferred. Not best for his posture, perhaps, but why care if the hands are warm?

Has it been mentioned? Jack did not like the cold!

It was New Year's Eve, so he slipped the small bottle of brandy into his pocket; not something he did normally, drinking while working, but this was different, it would be his last look around his place for the old year. There would be no one else around, and it was that special time of the year for a Scotsman.

He thought of this yard as 'His Place'. He grew up near here, and all his working life had been in the Yard. He had spent time in the Drawing Offices, the Plating Sheds, and the Engineering Workshops. He had been with the welders, the joiners, sheet metal workers, painters, with almost every trade, except the riveters and caulkers. He had dodged that, and consequently – he could still hear...

He stepped outside and locked the door – and the cold hit him. That night, he had to be careful as he stepped gingerly onto each tread of the stairs, holding firmly to the handrail.

Earlier in the week someone had been round spreading sand and salt to keep the stairs safe but, unsurprisingly, there was no-one to do it on that night, so they were frosting over. The old fellows who looked after the entrance gate, and took turns as night watchmen, still had to do their shifts no matter what the time of year might be, and if needed, they'd put sand down where slippery underfoot, especially if they were endangered.

These fellows had a large area to cover in their wanderings. Ice and frost were treacherous underfoot especially when it formed on the metal plates lying about the yard, so they would be wary wherever they went. They knew the terrain. It was their life, their work, just wandering around. He had not expected them to sand his steps tonight. After he left nobody would be up there over the next four days.

It would not be too unpleasant doing a watchman's duties, he thought – apart from the cold. Usually quiet at night. The yard cats leaping out at them – just being friendly – was the most excitement they would have on their rounds. At least, recently, they had not had to deal with any real trouble, like angry overheated strikers, for example, trying to make a point. You had to be ready to dodge a flying fist if it got physical, but that tended to be an expected hazard in those circumstances.

In the last few years, he successfully had

avoided that, but the problem had not gone away forever, not on the Clyde. The newspapers designated it 'Red Clydeside' about forty years or so ago, and that mood remained. Strikes... they were accepted as 'facts of life' in shipyards.

He put on his white plastic safety helmet, out of habit really. He sometimes asked himself why he wore it... It was not as if it would do any good if one of the fabrications dropped from the crane. Foremen, they traditionally wore bowler hats in the past, but that was because they tended to treat the workforce like slaves and were often disliked. How unfortunate if a block of wood, or a rivet, accidentally fell from the deck of a ship in the stocks onto the head of a passing foremen far below. It would have been painful to say the least, and there would be no hope in hell of catching who did it!

He never had worries like that. He had confidence in his workforce, and heaven help any of his managers, or foremen, if he caught them behaving like bullies towards their teams.

...But there was a good reason for automatically putting on the helmet. It was the woollen skullcap. Knitted for him by Jean as a joke, in pink and white stripes, but by God it helped to keep his head warm, and he used it – but not without the plastic safety helmet. He kept that colourful skullcap hidden from eyes that might mock.

As these thoughts went through his head he had been meandering along the normal route through the silent sheds. Not normal on that night though.

During the working day, everything happened: continual noises of metal on metal, flashing from welding, instructions shouted, and the piercing sound of whistles to gain attention of the isolated crane man, sometimes to wake him up.

The silence tonight was a little eerie, every breath reminding him how cold it was. He looked up at the Drawing Office windows, all darkness, only the odd light in corridors to permit safe movement for the night watchman.

One was coming along towards him. Well wrapped up too.

"Hi, Bill. Everything under control?"

"Aye, Mr McAndrew. A few places could be tidier, ah suppose. At Hogmanay ah like to see everythin' put in its place properly to begin a New Year, but a lot of the younger blokes dinnae go for the old fashioned ideas."

"I know what you mean, Bill. The important thing is that you have your high standards. Keep up the good work."

"G'nigh' Surr."

"Good night Bill." An old stalwart who had worked here longer than he had; the man's father had had the same dedication...

The Drawing Office being in darkness probably meant that Angus would be home already, the office closed with the rest of the yard. Lucky lad. He would probably be at home, having brought his own car that day. He'd be sitting back, slippers already on, in front of the roaring fire.

Angus had not been able to drive six months ago, but he was good. Beth had helped him with the lessons. He passed first time too...

God it is cold... He took the small bottle from his pocket and had a mouthful. The brandy burned his throat, and he felt warmer immediately, although maybe that was just his imagination.

Imagination or not, he did not care – it worked.

Jack liked Angus, his new son-in-law. He seemed perfect for his daughter. It had been an unfortunate start – him and Beth having begun a family unintentionally, but... What the heck! They are happy together aren't they? That is what matters.

All living successfully together in his Bearsden home, four of them, Jean, him, Beth and Angus, and soon to be five. It made him feel warm inside thinking of a little grandson being on the way. Well, they thought it would be a boy, but he'd be just as delighted if it turned out to be a girl.

He stopped for a moment. He was now in the yard looking towards the enormous shadowy hull of the partly constructed cargo ship sitting in the stocks. It was fairly well advanced and on target for launching early spring. Nice to meet targets, he thought, not nice to fail. That had happened several years back; a lightning strike – by the carpenters – stopped the launch.

It went ahead, eventually, the wife of the Ship's Owner performing the ceremony, but the bottle had not smashed until the third try. Made him a little jittery when that happened, but the launch had been successful. The chains swung the vessel round at the correct moment. They had to be accurate with that, the Clyde being quite a narrow river for launches.

It could go wrong, of course, and did so for one Clyde yard about eighty years ago. The Daphne: that ship turned over at her launch. One hundred and twenty-four workers died. That was on his mind at each of his launches. He always ensured the minimum of workers on board when she went down a slipway – and never failed to cross his fingers. He was not superstitious but he would have hated a disaster on his conscience...

Beth had been well, thank goodness, only another nine weeks to go until the baby's arrival. The house would seem strange with a young child in it. He hoped they would never ask him to get up in the middle of the night for the bottles and nappy changing – he was well out of practice.

He'd reached the fitting-out quay, a cargo vessel being finalised, floating gently, straining on the hawsers. He liked to see the workmanship of the rigger team.

Did they get it right? Not too much tension at high tide or at low, or too much slack allowing it to drift into the river? The watchmen would keep an eye on the vessel anyway. Many of them were ex-riggers. They still cared.

The tide had just turned. It was just after high water. There was quite a difference in the level of the river between high and low here, even though the shipyard was a good distance up from the river mouth.

It would be cold in that water tonight.

What he could see out there was not much. With most of the lighting off, the surface only glinted now and again reflecting the lights over the other side, but he could see a reasonable current from the bits of driftwood floating downriver.

'*Another little drink, and another little drink,*' he started singing in his mind. He would not dream of singing aloud – people would just laugh – at least his family always did. He removed the top on the bottle and sniffed, and took another sip. The mouthful warmed him. I could get to like this, he thought, as he stepped over the straining hawser.

What happened next was so quick!

He was at the edge of the wharf. The bottle was still in his hand and as he stepped over, but his boot slipped on a patch of ice, and his footing went.

He lost his balance – he grasped at the hawser but his hand slipped – the frosted rope was too thick...

He was going over the edge!

He could do nothing to stop himself. He was falling into the river! He grabbed the air...

"*Heeeeelp...*" but there was no-one to hear his vain and solitary cry as he hit the water – and sank – like a stone...

Bits of glass lay on the wharf where the bottle had smashed, the remainder of the warm brandy slightly melting the frosted surface...

It was not realised at the shipyard that the tragic accident had even happened until the phone call came from a worried wife. She had not been expecting him home on time, but this was very late. Angus had told her of his father-in-law's phone call to him earlier in the day.

"I'll be a little later than usual. I just want to check that everything is as it should be before I leave tonight. Oh, and tell Jean I love her and I'll eat the meal when I get back, even if it is dried up and burned."

The gatemen had changed over shifts at the usual time. The one who arrived had been to the Govan Arms before starting the shift. He had not been too eager to start. The other was rushing off to the same pub to catch up on his mates; they would have been drinking for an hour before him.

When they changed shifts, it was not realised that the boss was still in the yard. Even if they had realised, it would not have mattered, he was the Boss. He knew what he was doing...

When they looked, they found his car in the car park – the only one.

No sleep at Bearsden that Hogmanay, and it was not because of a wish to stay up for the bells – they were awake because they feared the worst...

Angus attempted to reassure his mother-in-law and Beth, that Jack McAndrew would be all right, he'd probably fallen somewhere in the yard. It would have been very icy there.

"He will be found shortly. He is in the yard somewhere, and be home soon. The worst thing could be that he slipped and knocked himself out. Stop worrying – they'll phone shortly and tell us that he is on his way..."

In his heart, he did not believe his own words. Somehow, he sensed how serious it had actually been and sadly, he was proved correct.

Jack's body was not recovered until many hours later, at daylight, a great deal farther down-river. It was judged that with the heavy coat, and the woollen jumper that he had been wearing, together with the heavy boots, he'd had no chance.

The family was informed.

Beth went into premature labour...

35

2009
Is this the end?

Beth asked for a toilet break. It was less a call of nature than a chance to dry her eyes and make sure she did not look like a silly old woman.

Angus was taking a breath of fresh air at the back door. He'd let all the heat out of the house by leaving the door wide open, causing Tom to think that for a clever man his father could be a right idiot sometimes. Tom got up and shut the door. His father, on the outside, wondered, was it something he'd said...

Gillian and David sat looking at the other unopened envelope. Curiosity, both realised, was great for making you forget the previous night's lack of sleep.

When everyone returned refreshed and all were seated once more, Beth asked Gillian to read the second letter, "Unless anyone else would rather..."

Only negative head wobbles.

This one was from Meg. Gillian felt apprehensive and hoped it would not be more sad news. She began...

> *"My dear Angus, Beth, Gillian, Tom, and David, You'll be wondering how I knew you would succeed, and how I would know it would be all of you, together? I knew because you are a family, my family. I had every confidence that a silly old woman who is on her last legs couldn't outwit the best brains in Scotland."*

"We'll never know if my mother was being witty, sarcastic, or genuine, will we?" sighed Angus. "With her, my guess would be tongue in cheek... Sorry I'm interrupting."

> *"You have reached the end of the trail and will have read the letter left by my mother-in-law, Phoebe Findlay. I knew nothing of this letter until recently, although – if any member of the family had decided to become a piper – they could have found it, no doubt. No one did and the poor old bagpipes became older and older with never a sound coming from them. Traditionally under the bed was the place for them, but now the more modern place, since I have been residing, gratefully, with Angus and Beth, is in the cupboard. As part of the search, you will have found the hidden compartment in the pipe-case, and you will now be the proud holders of a medal and a gun, or you would not be reading this."*

"A gun?" Beth sat up straight. "No one told me you found a gun."

"It's hidden at our place, Mum. Don't panic. We'll explain afterwards," said Tom.

Gillian paused a moment. Beth had accepted Tom's comment, so she continued...

"I found Phoebe's letter, and the other items, when I still lived on my own and that had been only due to me feeling nostalgic. All I had wanted was a look at a family heirloom – it is what you do when you get older. It was a struggle to move them from under the bed, but I was very glad I did. When I looked at the pipes in the case, I exposed an old secret."

Gillian stopped for a moment and tried to ease the tension in her shoulders.

"My mother-in-law left notes on top of the set of pipes, one of which you have seen. As you are aware, it hurt her severely to find out what her beloved husband had done. You will possibly not yet have discovered the spoils of the robbery. I know only because my mother-in-law left two notes, one that I memorised and destroyed, telling me about her stumbling on the hiding place, and you will have read in the newspaper clipping that the jeweller Mr Ivan Pilger stated he had lost twenty-five jewels..."

"What?" David and Tom both exclaimed, looking at each other.

"I only found one!" said David. "Mum, did you really say twenty-five? I remember that's what it said in the newspaper cutting, but we didn't know then what it was all about."

"If he stole twenty-five where are the other twenty-four?" This was Tom blurting out now. He was confused. "...Has someone else pinched them?"

Gillian waited patiently to continue.

"...Phoebe did not know where the robbery took place until she saw the newspaper report. You have read the cutting, but you will find only ten large uncut diamonds, because that is all that ..."

"Ten...? David?"

Tom and David looked at each other.

"Yes, I heard it, Dad. You did say ten, didn't you Mum?"

"Would you two stop behaving like silly little children ...please," requested Gillian, adding a threatening tone to her voice. "This is a difficult enough task as it is, without your constant interruptions."

"...because that is all that Alexander Findlay actually stole, and you will find them, ten large diamonds, hidden inside the bag of the pipes. Phoebe gleaned this from Alexander's ramblings in his sleep and, in his sleepy mumblings, she also heard him say, 'My Phoebe – must help.'"

Tom and David were fidgeting now.

"The jeweller, Mr Ivan Pilger, claimed to his Insurance Company that twenty-five gems had been stolen, and not ten, and instead of suffering

a loss, he would have made a handsome profit, so no sympathy is required in that direction. I leave it to you, my dear family, to decide the best approach in the circumstances. It is your choice. You could treat them as 'Treasure' and keep them, or return them to where they came from, which I do not think justified. Or you could always dispose of them by throwing them into a deep part of the dear old River Clyde, as I would have done if I had been fit enough – although I am not sure about that... I am going to my grave knowing at least that I have not disclosed my mother-in-law's painful secret to anyone other than family, though I do feel a little guilty at not taken positive action myself. I do hope you'll forgive me for leaving you with the task. Please do not be over-influenced by any of my suggestions. You are all big and ugly enough to make up your own minds (and I am joking). I am sorry not to be still with you, but I want you to know, you will be in my thoughts until my last breath.

From your Mother, Grandmother, and Great-grandmother – yours lovingly, Meg xxxxx

PS. I hope you enjoyed Treasure Hunting."

Gillian's hands were trembling. She succeeded in reading the whole letter as unemotionally as she could, which seemed the correct thing to do, but it had been a considerable strain. ...but, by God, she thought, the emotions are going to erupt any second.

She took deep breaths and noticed that the others appeared to be suffering the same way, until Beth took control in her highly efficient matriarchal manner.

"I think we need another break – cup of tea everyone? I have some freshly-made scones and jam just waiting to be eaten."

Everyone nodded an eager, "Yes!" and began to breathe normally once again.

36

1967-71
A fresh start...

The germination of Thomas Hamish Jack Findlay's little life had been an error. Of course, that was not his fault, and certainly the sad circumstances leading to his early appearance were of no one's choosing. However, the timing of his arrival into the world was similar in error.

Beth gave birth prematurely.

Happening on New Year's Day and being seen as a very special baby would have meant photographs in a newspaper, informing the world that his birth had been one of the first of the New Year, but that fame was not to be his – he was born on the second...

After an extended stay, both mother and new baby were able to leave hospital in a healthy condition and with no known complications – other than having to face a very painful fact that a stalwart of the family was no longer there.

The tragic circumstances of Jack McAndrew's departure had been a great shock, and all were in mourning, so the homecoming of the new mother and a new baby was not a joyful occasion.

Obviously, the people affected most by Jack's death were the ones who had been closest to him: his wife Jean, his daughter Beth, and his son-in-law, Angus.

It left a big gap in the shipyard too. It would maybe not be easy but, for certain, someone would be found to fill his shoes and, unfortunately, at the yard, remarkably quickly Jack would become a fond but hazy memory. "That bloke McAndrew? Aye, he wuss a nice big fella, wuss he no'? Whit wuss his furst name again?"

It would be harder for his family. For Jean, Beth and Angus, life was so different. For them he would never be replaced, or forgotten. Jack would have been a great grandad. He would have loved little Thomas!

It took a long time to come to terms with the fact that the big, bluff, friendly husband and father would not be coming breezily in the front door each night, expecting to be forgiven at being late for the meal, as usual... but life moved on.

Angus took the lead role in the household after Jack's death. He also took on an important position in the shipyard when dear old Bob Fleming went, retiring early due to ill health. Angus became, as had been predicted by all, the Chief Draughtsman.

Jean valued having her daughter and son-in-law around to comfort her but living together had its advantages for the young couple too. Recognising whether little baby Thomas was genuinely unwell, or simply having a tantrum, could be difficult for the new young mother to recognise, so having her mother around to turn to for advice was greatly appreciated. A situation of mutual benefit, but Jean recognised that it could not continue forever that way.

Jack had been a prudent, but generous man, and a caring husband and father. His glass was always more than half-full and life to him was for living happily. He had never liked to contemplate death. He knew it would come to him sooner or later, 'preferably later,' he used to joke...

Not surprisingly, it was only when he had been promoted to his senior role, and realised that time was flashing past, that he got round to doing something about the future for those he would leave behind. If anything untoward were to happen, heaven forbid, he would be able to tell himself that at least the family would be 'comfortable'.

Life Insurance he had for many years. That had been an almost automatic purchase, due, many years ago, more to a persistent, insurance salesperson than smart planning on his part. Now, with the new job, he could afford to increase his premiums dramatically. At least Jean and Beth should have no worries if the worst happened, but I've no intention of going, he told himself. Really... I am still a youngster.

Fate had other plans...

In the Will, Jack divided his worldly-goods equally between wife and daughter. Jack – who must be in heaven and able to rest in peace – had done them proud because when his end did come, Jean and Beth had few financial cares. The results from his Life Assurance were overwhelming!

It was time...

Yes, a flat of my own, somewhere nice, and near Meg, would do me perfectly. That would be practical. Less to clean, but large enough for living on my own – and having Meg within walking distance would be great.

In the three years that had passed since the accident, the memories of Jack had become less painful and Jean McAndrew was the one who decided to change. She felt it wrong that Angus and Beth always felt obliged to have her opinion on whatever was being discussed or decided, and it shouldn't be like that. It was pleasant living together and there had never been any fall-outs but, they were young and had their baby, and their requirements were quite different to those of an older woman. Anyway it could work both ways. If she moved out, the house would be theirs to do whatever they wanted with it, and she could choose what she wanted to do, and when she wanted to do it, without consulting them.

Jean and Meg had become very close friends, after Beth and Angus married, and visits one to the other became regular occurrences. As Jean had not worked since her marriage to Jack, and Meg only worked part-time, they had many opportunities to meet.

After Jack's death Meg was a staunch ally and support. She encouraged her friend to be active, and as a result, Jean spent a lot of time at Meg's home in Hyndland. Those visits gave Jean a taste for the area.

She liked the variety of choices – botanical gardens at the top of the road, easy access to regular transport, and the added appeal of the great assortment of shops. There was a general bustle about the place, and yet, the adjoining residential areas could be quite tranquil.

It would be subject to the correct choice of flat, of course. They were expensive – but she knew that Jack would not have minded her spending the money.

Meg loved where she lived and welcomed the possibility of her friend being nearby. Jean no longer wanted anything large, so the pair of them sought out suitable flats currently on the market. The search became their combined time-consuming hobby. It did not take long. The perfect one was found, and in Jean moved, to her new home in Hyndland.

The Bearsden house, now without her mother, felt uncomfortable for Beth. With only the baby for company when Angus went to work, the place was cold and empty, and too big. She preferred going outside for walks with the pram.

She was now eager to leave the house, but not the area, and on her wanderings with baby Tom, she saw it. Two houses side by side, both with a 'For Sale' sign in the front gardens.

The one on the right! That is the one! It has great character.

No words of dissent from Angus when he arrived home from work that evening, even though it had been a difficult day. He consented to going back out again on foot with her – the meal would be late. He was pushing the pram this time and Beth eagerly guiding. It was only a fifteen-minute walk.

Disappointingly, in the duller early evening light, the outside did not look quite as lovely to her as it had in the spring-morning sunshine, but it still looked good. Angus agreed but, two days later, seeing the inside was an anti-climax. With the previous owners having been an old couple, the decor was not exactly modern, and as for the kitchen units...

"We could make it ours," said Beth. Angus nodded – but wondered who would be doing the making? He was useless at that sort of thing.

By co-incidence, another young couple, also potential buyers were on a return visit to the house next door. Conversation over the dividing wall led to introductions.

This was Mary and George. A little older, and they had no children. After much searching, they had found their dream palace, and were about to finalise the sale and buy it.

"...In excellent condition," said George. "We could move in right away."

Hmm, thought Beth, perhaps choosing the house with 'external character' had not been the wisest option.

That first meeting was with each couple standing in what was about to become their own back garden, with George on tiptoes to talk, and struggling to reach over the wall to shake hands. His wife was taller and could look over easily. They were both very nice, said they loved children, and already had a name for their home. It was to be 'Shangri-la': a peaceful place.

Unwise to commit to that name, thought Angus, particularly if they were to become neighbours – little Thomas could grow up and make them regret it! However, meeting them, liking them, having coffee together in a local café and enjoying the company, clinched it for Beth.

"It will be the perfect house for us," she enthused, "after renovations..."

"But..." said Angus, in a panic. To his relief, the renovations would be by contractors – not him!

They could look to a new future with confidence. Little Tom would play in a big garden with lots of fruit trees and, though the house had many more rooms than required, both were in total agreement that it was wise going for it. Experience told them, accidents could happen. Baby Thomas could finish up with a few wee brothers and sisters.

...Better to play safe this time!

37

2009
It is getting serious...

For the five people round the table all the facts were there. No more clues were required. Lying in front of them – three pieces of paper, mugs that were now empty, and plates with only the remaining traces of jam.

Had the tea break engendered inspirational thoughts? No, because what was needed now was action!

Tom and David were now chomping at the bit. Meg's letter had stated there were more diamonds – another nine, and worth a lot of money – so they were desperate to get back to Jordanhill to prove it!

Would they still be in the original hiding place? If so, it was no use being at this kitchen table, when the bagpipes were sitting on another one – at Jordanhill!

"Let's get going," said Tom, to a wife who appeared to have become deaf.

"Come on, Mum," said David, getting to his feet and full of enthusiasm that his mother obviously did not share.

Beth and Angus also refused to become excited, minds already made up, it appeared. For them, what they had learned so far was becoming a dilemma. Whether only one diamond, or ten of the blooming things, they could see only trouble ahead.

Gillian would not be rushed. She was not caring about whatever might be rattling about in a set of old bagpipes. Her mind was on the letters. They had touched her. She found them extremely emotional. Hand-written documents created by two women, both seeing death to be close, but each so different in attitude. Phoebe: sad and regretful of a husband who went wrong. Meg: informative, cheerfully facing the prospect of her death, and having fun teasing them with this treasure hunt.

Gillian wanted to just sit and talk about them, and started to, with Beth, deliberately ignoring her husband and son, who were becoming a bit short-tempered. They swithered on going without her, but eventually did succeed in getting her to stop and she was reluctantly ushered out of her in-laws kitchen, and into the car, and then they were off!

Tom and David had a date with a set of bagpipes!

The drive home was hair-raisingly fast!

Back at Jordanhill in record time because, at Anniesland Cross, Tom beat the traffic lights for a change by having his foot down and stopping for nothing, ignoring the blasts of horns as he scraped through each traffic light that had already changed from amber to red!

"Yea!" said David encouragingly, beside him.

Gillian, in the back seat, sat horrified and numb, expecting any moment to be chased by the police. She gave a sigh of relief as her husband screeched into their own drive way.

Then the key would not unlock the front door quickly enough.

And there they were – the bagpipes, sitting on the table, exactly where they'd been left.

Gillian's tummy felt decidedly funny. "The loo!" was her shout as she rushed upstairs.

Tom and David moved forward quickly to the table.

"I'll take them apart..." declared Tom, and reached to lift the bagpipes, but stopped when David's arm reached out in front of him.

"Dad. This is a skilled job – for a piper. Remember, they are mine."

His words came out with a sudden surge of jealous pride and more aggressively than David intended, but the pipes, they were his – it was *his* instrument! Then, he remembered the jewels.

"Sorry, that wasn't said nicely, was it? And I didn't mean the stuff inside," he apologised. "It wasn't a claim for the treasure."

"Of course, it wasn't," said a dad who was not sure if that was true, but David seemed to know what he was doing. Very carefully, but not quickly enough for Tom, the chanter was removed.

"The reeds must not get damaged, Dad," David

explained, putting fresh knowledge into practice even though his father did not want to know. The reed from each of the three drones was then tentatively removed while Dad fidgeted about, standing close, but far enough away to avoid the blame for any damage, and to escape getting a black eye from the unwieldy movements of his son and the swinging drones. With the last drone removed, a couple of diamonds fell on the floor.

"Promising..." said Tom, lifting them, with the start of a smile.

Now they had three... They looked at each other, eyebrows raised expectantly. David gently worked the bag and was not disappointed, as another four rolled onto the table.

"Seven..." said Tom expectantly, but no more dropped out.

David felt the bag. There was one lump, and another two lumps... Not quite there yet, but close. It took a little patience to move these three from a position they had been in for more than ninety years, and were obviously quite happy to remain. A little more gentle persuasion and...

Now there were ten!

Tom washed them clean. These little bits of glass, lying on the table in front of them could be worth a great deal of money – but why were they not elated? They should be feeling incredible – but they did not!

"Ah, Gillian! Look, the ten diamonds!"

Gillian had recovered slightly, and came over to look, but she became almost as unexcited as they were. The treasure hunt was pretty much over, but it seemed to have gone flat.

"Right," said David.

"Hmmm..." said Tom.

"I'm going for a lie down," said Gillian.

David decided it could be unwise to leave uncut diamonds sitting on the kitchen table. It would be just the thing if, for the first time in their lives, the house was burgled! Into the hidden compartment they went, and the lid was closed. He then carefully reassembled his bagpipes, placed them on top of that now very important secret place so that the compartment was hidden again, closed the container and then, as a final precaution, hid the very precious pipe-box itself ...

Where? Under the bed, of course!

Dutifully, Tom phoned his parents.

"We have found them," he said. "They were in the bagpipes, as expected. We now have a total of ten sparklers."

"Hmm... Good!" was his father's response.

It occurred to Angus as he put down the phone, that "Good!" was a curt reply to give Tom, but he had a bigger concern.

Moments before, Beth suggested that her mother – dear old Jean McAndrew – should come to live with them, and who could dispute the need? Her mother was now eighty-seven and becoming rather frail. In those circumstances, what could he do – other than accept it philosophically?

They had managed reasonably well while his own mother was with them – as far as he could remember. They'd all got on well. That had been at his suggestion, but this time it was at Beth's, and it was her mother.

"Oh well, here we go again," he'd sighed.

...And if Beth thinks she can cope, who am I to argue? Might be different with her own mother though – both getting a bit short tempered. Ah well, such is life! We will soon see ...then a grin came to his face.

"Hope she doesn't bring bagpipes!"

It was later that week, on Thursday, when Gillian found an item in the Glasgow Herald; something she had to read out to her husband and son; something that could have ramifications for their situation, and it disturbed her. It made them sit up straight.

A woman was arrested for having an old unlicensed pistol that the police found under her mattress, a pistol that her father brought back after fighting in World War Two. He was long dead, but she had kept the gun. Yesterday, her trial had ended and she was being sent to prison for five years.

"We could all go to jail if the police raid us!" Gillian said, genuinely perturbed. "We've got a pistol in the house!"

"She must have been up to something else as well," said Tom dismissively. "Probably into drugs or something."

"Doesn't say that here." Gillian looked worried.

"Anyway... We could say it is David's gun!" said Tom.

His joke fell flat.

That would be something else for the family committee to consider on Saturday. However, for the three around the Jordanhill breakfast table on that Thursday morning, it was a foregone conclusion – the gun – they would have to get rid of it. They had never dealt with guns before, never mind disposing of one, so, 'How?' was the big question.

There was certainly no denying it; since they began Meg's Treasure Hunt, life had created a fair number of new, and unexpected experiences for them all.

38

2002
Changes in the close...

Meg looked out of her front room window. As usual, cars parked one behind the other for as far as she could see. No spaces if Angus and Beth came to see her this afternoon, but it could change as the day progressed, of course. It was handy for people who shopped in Byres Road to dump their cars here for a short time.

She had never been able to drive. Never had a car – never had the need, or else she might have done something about it. Public transport had been good enough, and she liked a good walk – not too far nowadays though.

The sun was shining and she was glad because she had an outing planned with Jean for this morning. She was two years older than her dear friend, but her hips had lasted better and she could walk a little further and faster, but then again she had not had a pacemaker fitted. Jean had.

They would aim for the Botanic Gardens, the usual planned destination. It did not matter if they did not reach it. The intention was always there, but they rarely bothered to go that distance, nowadays. There were many coffee shops to choose from if they became tired, or if it looked like rain, or if they just fancied it. It was not unknown for their chat to start, and the day to vanish, while they were still in the original shop but today, she would have to be back by lunchtime in case Angus and Beth did come over.

It was nice having conversations with her son and daughter-in-law. They were good company, and it was even nicer when Tom and Gillian were there too. It was a comfortable family, a happy group.

Days when young David came over with them were even better, though it didn't happen quite so often since he became a teenager. What age is he now, she wondered, fifteen – or is it sixteen? They used to enjoy telling each other silly jokes and playing tricks on each other when he was younger but, of course, she was younger too. It had been the same with Tom, even further back.

Ten years has made a big difference! I used to consider myself a young thing...

It was comforting that the same old neighbours were still in the building. Wait a moment, what was she thinking?

I lie! Old Dracula next door went into a home, years ago, probably kicked the bucket by now, and Doris and Bob, they are away too, passed away that is. Maisie and Archie, still on the top flat but getting on a bit. Young Louise, she turned out a lovely young woman. Married with her own youngsters.

Comes to visit her folks regularly; popped in to see me too ...nice girl, and there's Carol downstairs. She did well bringing up the two boys on her own.

That had disappointed Meg. After her bringing them together, what a shock to learn five years later, that David ran off with another woman. Poor Carol, left on her own with the children.

Yes dear, Meg remembered. Unfortunately, it happens...

Molly, upstairs, had moved away. Meg wondered if she stayed with that young man. He would be called a 'toy boy' nowadays, and how could she have been bothered with all the shenanigans? Maybe kept her fit though!

...And the other couple, what was their name again? They had the shop. Och, never mind, it will come back to me later...

She wondered sometimes if she had outlasted Hamish, not that she really cared, but... Should she have answered his letter all those years ago? Women in two generations of this family had had to manage on their own. She hoped that Beth and Angus would continue to be as happy as they appeared. They had always been well suited.

Meg had been thinking a lot about Phoebe this week, and there was a bit of nostalgia when she decided to have a wee peep at the bagpipes. That was a shock.

The pipes were still where they'd always been – under the bed. Sad that no one had ever attempted to play them, but Angus had been adamant that bagpipe playing was not for him. He was much more interested in his books and reading, but that turned out to be the best thing for him. He had done well for himself, even after leaving the shipyard.

For Meg, dragging the pipe-case from under the bed had been awkward, dust covered as usual. It had been an odd feeling opening it, with the inside not having seen the light of day for about sixty years. Phoebe must have put the letters inside shortly before she died.

Though Phoebe had been her mother-in-law, Meg had been closer to her than to her own mother – she realised that on reflection, but she had forced herself to think of her as a distant but much loved friend, and that seemed to make the deep and sad feelings seem a little less painful, but reading the letters brought these feelings flooding back.

Why did Phoebe never confide in me? Felt ashamed perhaps. Didn't want me burdened too, perhaps.

Now that she had found out, it did feel a burden, and what to do about it? What could she do? She did not want to say anything to Angus, although that is exactly what she felt her mother-in-law should have done with her. Was doing nothing the acceptable alternative? Of course not!

I'll think of something...

Angus and Beth had very kindly offered to have her live with them at their home in Bearsden, and she was giving it serious consideration. It would mean not being so close to Jean, but they could still talk on the phone. Jean visited Bearsden regularly – not under her own steam, mark you, because Angus behaved like his usual gentlemanly self, collecting and returning her by car.

It is really quite simple, she decided... Angus could take the two of us down to the little coffee shop at Bearsden Cross – save our energy and give us more time to chat. Just like now, except it would not be Byres Road, and I have the mobile phone, so when the shop is shutting, I could phone Angus to collect us. Angus won't mind. He probably won't be doing much anyway...

Yes, she was getting to like the idea a little more but, imagine, leaving this house – after forty-eight years. She almost felt attached to the place.

Good not to be paying any more rent though. Must have bought this place fifty times over.

It had not been so easy to get to know the new neighbours these days. They tended to be in and out and stayed no time at all, as if they were just after making a profit buying and selling the flats.

But, where would the young lad downstairs get his extra money – he did her shopping. He would have to find another source of income if she goes. She used to do that for Doris and Bob all those years ago – for nothing.

Suddenly, an idea came to her – about the bagpipe problem. Perhaps it would be shirking her responsibilities a little, and she might not be around to see the fruition – but after I've gone, they could...

Teamwork is something that is pushed as a good

way to have a job done, isn't it, and who would make a good team? My family would! Yes, they would support each other. It would not be one person shouldering the burden – and they are a smart bunch, and when they get to the end of the trail, they could have the prize, if they want it... Yes. If not, they would be strong enough to decide collectively what would be best...

The idea was a bit cockeyed at that moment, but she would work on it, could do that when she moved to Beth and Angus's. The clues could be hidden there. It's a big house. Anyway, there will be plenty of time to fill in the details.

She was getting excited about this... and yes, she would definitely take up Beth and Angus's offer and move in beside them. There'll be plenty to do when she gets there. Already, in her head, the hiding places were beginning to be decided.

Yes! I will create a Treasure Hunt!

39

2009
A family decision...

It had been a busy week. David had been working hard wiring a new house and, though the job he was doing was absorbing, even challenging at times, by the end of each day he could not wait to finish and return home to the laptop. The internet was proving very helpful to him – dangerously compulsive. His father was convinced that he was becoming an addict but, if he was, David didn't care – it was fun.

Friday evening and engrossed by the display on the screen, David was swithering over which tartan to choose. He was now convinced that when playing his bagpipes he should be wearing a kilt.

He could visualise himself – the star, swaggering up and down Sauchiehall Street on a Saturday afternoon, breeze blowing, kilt swirling, and the crowds yelling for more. He could not wait to get started ...but then he had a slight doubt. Would ordering the kilt be a wee bit premature? Should he maybe first learn how to play his pipes?

Indecision remained about all the bits and pieces

that he was going to buy. The important item, the chanter was on order but seemed to be taking rather a long time to arrive. He had thought it would be next day delivery, probably coming from somewhere like Inverness, or Fort William – somewhere that sounded 'teuchterish', but he was beginning to suspect the internet company could be in India, or China. The 'dotcom' address did not say!

However, thanks to the internet, he had discovered that Scotland had a National Piping Centre. A 'national' centre – it made it sound important. They must know everything about bagpipes there; and, one thing was certain – it was not in India or China! It was in Glasgow, and he could even visit the place. Their web site showed that they stocked chanters and instruction books. He could have bought his stuff over the counter! He would go into town on Saturday, after the family meeting, and check it out, maybe take the pipes with him and get their advice.

Yes, roll on Saturday! Thank you, Internet...

Saturday had arrived and there they were again, five heads round the kitchen table at Bearsden, but this time determined to reach definite conclusions – maybe... Being gathered around that table had become a Saturday-morning habit but, today, they were not chasing back and forward searching the loft for clues – they had all these. Today was for serious discussion.

Tom and David sat a bit shame-faced. They'd

come in, all bouncy and smiles, expecting to be welcomed by the usual cup of tea and scones, with home-made jam.

"I went upstairs yesterday – to do some dusting," Beth said in a very unwelcoming voice, that David recognised as trouble – but Tom didn't.

"Nice to know you're keeping yourself busy, Mother," he commented, with obvious condescension. "It's good to keep active."

David suddenly guessed what was coming, but it was obvious that the penny had not dropped for his father.

"Went into the front bedroom..."

"Uh-huh..." said Tom, with a slightly amused expression. "I know where that is."

"A lot of white plaster on the carpet..."

Tom and David looked at each other. Last Saturday's mishap! For David – he'd been busy, and could blame the internet and bagpipes. Tom? He had just totally forgotten!

"I looked up and... Well," said Beth icily, "I'd never seen molehills upside down on a ceiling before. Hmmm... Not smiling now, are you..."

Gillian hadn't been aware of this. She gave her two males a dirty look. There would be words afterwards...

Both were deeply embarrassed, apologised and promised they would be back tomorrow, Sunday, to fix the mess, provided they could buy some materials.

So, the meeting began with father and son feeling

sheepish, rather than their normal mouthy selves.

"Beth and I have talked this over," said Angus, "...and we can only think of one way to deal with what Meg's clues have helped us discover – ten uncut diamonds, one handgun, and one medal for bravery."

Angus did not say what the 'one way' was, even though everyone sat expectantly. He leaned back and waited for one of the others to speak, and they could not help but fill the silence.

For the benefit of Beth and Angus, Gillian repeated the story she read about the woman keeping her father's gun under the mattress, but although Angus and Beth had already heard it on the local news earlier that week, they were too polite to stop Gillian from telling her version. Anyway, she told a good story, they always thought.

"So, the gun? Does anyone want it?" asked Tom. "Should we sell it at a car boot sale, or simply bury it in the garden?"

Tom nodded towards the area he had already dug under the trees on an earlier visit.

"Neither, thank you!" was Beth's reaction. "You are not being very smart. What would George and Mary think if they saw you burying a gun?"

"I wouldn't be doing it," said Tom. "I was going to ask David!"

"Tom, if you can't talk sensibly..." was the reprimand from Gillian.

"Why not just take it down to the River Clyde, as Granny Meg suggested, and throw it into the middle of the river?" was David's contribution.

"I'll go along with that," said Angus.

"Me too," said Beth.

"Good idea, David," said Gillian.

Tom just nodded, wary of saying anything.

"Now, the medal?" asked Angus.

"In the river...?" Tom offered.

"Tom!" ...said his wife.

Her idea was much more sensible. Keep it in Beth and Angus's house, displayed in a picture frame, with the 'Hero' newspaper clipping included. It would look good hanging on the wall. It could be mounted and framed professionally and that way, it would remain in the family – handed on at some point, of course. Her suggestion received general approval, except from Tom, who sat in a huff.

"Excellent!" declared Angus and continued. "Now a tricky one ...what to do with the diamonds?"

"They could be worth a lot of money," said Tom, who could not sit and just listen. "We could invest in having them cut and polished, and then sell them, or, we could have two each, and do our own thing. Ten divides nicely by five."

"I'm not happy doing that," said Beth. "I feel it would be on my conscience if the results of stolen goods came back to me."

"I wouldn't want that either," agreed Angus. "It's not as if they were left to us legally, like in a will, and especially if my grandfather obtained them dishonestly."

"Yes, they could really be someone else's

property," Gillian chipped in.

Tom did not think this was going the right way at all, although he guessed he was about to become a minority of one.

"Whose property is it then?" he asked. "It can't be the jeweller's because he reclaimed more than double his loss. Nor can I imagine walking into the Prudential Insurance Offices, or whoever was the Insurer, and saying, 'These belong to you. My Great-grandad pinched them from a crooked jeweller!'" Tom rested his case, and was then shot down, as expected.

No one wanted to think they could be party to the proceeds of theft, including David who was really only interested in keeping his great-great-grandad's bagpipes – legally.

"Why don't we throw the jewels into the Clyde as well," offered Beth.

"But, they are... What a waste..." Tom muttered under his breath.

"What was that, Tom?"

"Nothing, Mother..."

...And so, it was decided!

The following Saturday at ten a.m. precisely, they would meet on the walkway near the Finnieston Crane, have a little memorial service for Alexander, Phoebe, Meg, and Jack McAndrew, and throw the handgun and ten large uncut diamonds formally into the middle of the River Clyde.

Even though, in the ceremony, they would be commemorating Jean's husband, Jack, Beth's mother would not be invited. They decided that for her it would be too emotional and over-taxing. She was rather frail and – she would have found out about the diamonds!

Angus had an additional reason to exclude her that he didn't divulge to the others. After the ceremony he would be collecting that self-same woman, his dear mother-in-law, and bringing her back to start her new life residing with them. He had only a few more days to feel he did not run an old folk's home. He liked the woman, but wanted to delay the start just a little longer. She could be with them for a long time, he reckoned. That woman had some of the same qualities as his mother.

Yes, he knew that Jean was a game old bird...

40

2009
No loose ends...

One minute to ten o'clock.

They decided to move – the two Glasgow down-and-outs who were sheltering from the cold wind blowing up the river, and about to share an early morning drink from a bottle of fiery liquid hidden in a brown paper bag. Being of no fixed abode, they were used to mobility, so another hundred yards downriver would make little difference and the booze would still taste delightful, provided they did not drop the bottle. Experience told them that the couple that had appeared nearby, dressed very soberly for a Saturday morning, could be Jehovah's Witnesses, or maybe even Salvation Army in disguise – and guess who they would target immediately!

It was a chilly morning.

Standing at the side of the River Clyde, near the Finnieston Crane, on a dreich November day was not the most comfortable of positions, but at least Beth and Angus had made sure they wore the correct clothing. It was cosy in the car. Now they definitely felt the contrast.

Perfect timing was normal for them. If a time was stated, then that was when it should be happening. Younger ones were not quite as good at it, were they...?

"There they are," said Angus.

Gillian and Tom were hurrying along.

"Sorry, sorry, we got stuck in a jam at Partick – traffic lights acting up," said Gillian. "Hope we're not late. David not here yet? Ah, here he comes now."

It was two minutes past ten. Incredibly good timing for us, Tom thought – brilliant for David.

Hugs, kisses, and 'good mornings' were shared, with hot breath steaming around them. Not the sort of morning to hang around unnecessarily.

"Well, if we are all ready. I have prepared a little ceremony – and I wrote it down in case I forgot it. Memory's not perfect these days, I'm afraid."

Stating the obvious, Dad, Tom thought.

"You have the... uhmm... gun, David?"

"Yes Grandad."

"And, Tom, you have the diamonds?"

Tom nodded, and tapped his pocket assuredly.

"Are you alright, ladies – yes? Then we'll make a start." Angus coughed to clear the throat for his big speech, put on his glasses, and brought out the sheet of paper.

Tom admired how his old man could rise to an occasion and speak with confidence in public when required. Quite different from the normally quiet, slightly shy person he was in most of his private life. He remembered his gran telling him, that meeting and marrying his mother had had a tremendous influence on his dad's confidence, helped him relax and enjoy life more. She had even encouraged him to appreciate a joke and laugh. It had never stopped him working conscientiously though.

"If we all bow our heads for a minute and just have our own personal thoughts of the loved ones we are here to honour," requested the man in charge.

Beth was thinking of Dad. The people who had known him always said, 'Good old Jack McAndrew,' but he had not been old. Life could be so unfair at times. Back then, she'd been worried for her unborn baby, but he'd turned out all right. He's a fine lad is our Tom, though I do not tell him that often enough I suppose... Looks a bit like grandfather McAndrew too, yes indeed, across the nose...

At that precise moment, the thought going through David's head was that he should have put on a jumper as his mother suggested. "I don't feel the cold," he'd claimed. His mind wandered to the bagpipes, and that helped him forgot about the lousy weather. Thanks, Alexander Findlay. I'll try not to think of you as bad because I am sure what you did was for the right reasons. I will look after the pipes for you. They are mine now, but I'll play them for you... even though you were a rogue! Sorry... Shouldn't have thought that! Big date tonight... *Goodness! What is her name again?* Oh yes, Maureen... Mustn't be late.

Gillian had loved Tom's grandmother. Meg had been wonderful with young David when he was growing up. If I reach old age, I hope I'll have her sort of energy... and what a sense of humour she had too. She was a bright and breezy woman – even burdened by her mother-in-law's secret. Wish I was like her. What am I thinking? Me? Bright and breezy? No, no chance of that. And poor sad Phoebe... Glad I have a good husband. Yes, I do love you, Tom – with all your faults...

Angus was nervous. He kept telling himself he was with close family, but... it was time. He looked down at the paper in front of him and began to read aloud. "A great river like this has witnessed many events, some have been wonderful. Many, tragic. Today we remember one of the tragic ones, the death of Beth's beloved father and my dear father-in-law, a man to whom I felt very close..."

He is not speaking in his normal voice. Why not? Sounds like ...like ...Cary Grant, or is it Tony Curtis? Tom always got the two mixed up if he did not see the face.

"...and became one of the very sad events. As a relatively young man, being overly caring of the job he..."

He is doing it deliberately, Tom realised. I have never heard him do something like this before – other than on the old tape.

You are doing fine. Beth willed Angus on...

"...because he was no jerk, no sirree! Jack McAndrew had a very special talent for working with people, real people and they missed that guy. It was not just us that loved him, an' felt the pain. Oh, no – this guy had lotsa..."

Gillian was looking slightly quizzical, but with a little smile developing. That voice, I can't quite place it...

David had not really been listening to what was being said about great-grandad McAndrew. It was ancient stuff, way before his time, in the distant past. Like history at school. Boring... He had always drifted off in that class...

"...happened years ago but just seems like yesterday. Then, we have a hero, a hero with flaws, Alexander Findlay. This was one guy that just couldn't stop himself..."

The American accent – it had been James Cagney, now it was Jimmy Stewart. Tom recognised it right away. David wondered why his grandad was not speaking normally. He now was listening, and hearing, and it was his benefactor being talked about – the bagpipe man.

"...And, like many, he suffered after-effects of battle, recognised nowadays, but not back then. This guy was a hero, a hero that returned to the fight twice after injury, something that could not have been easy. He wouldn't have thought of himself as a hero but..."

Hope the Piping Centre is open Saturdays! David could not get on the laptop to check before leaving, because his father had been searching for lost relations!

"...and, the secret that dear Phoebe kept close to her heart..."

Tom and Gillian were smiling – Winston Churchill. Even David recognised the voice – from War documentaries. You could not possibly mistake it.

"...and a gun, brought back after all the fighting had ended. A sad memento and used in the wrong manner in peacetime by Alexander Findlay. David, do you have it? Would you please do your duty and dispose of it as we have agreed."

David suddenly heard his name – and remembered. He brought the pistol from where he had tucked it under his belt, and, holding the barrel, threw it into the middle of the river.

"Aw yea! Goan yersel, wee man! Did ye all see tha' then? Whit a throw! Aye well, anyway, ah jist hope that wee gun'll vanish deep intae the mud, jist like ma wellies used tae..."

An excellent Billy Connolly impersonation – but Tom suddenly had a horrible thought. Across the river was Pacific Quay and a big building – BBC Scotland. What do they use as a backdrop for each news presentation from that building?

Heck! It's where we are standing! The camera

always pointed at the Finnieston Crane. Did they use a live background for the broadcasts? Goodness! What if they are on air at this moment and we've been seen by the whole of Scotland – throwing a gun into the river?

Tom stood expecting to hear a police siren and to see blue lights flashing and a carload of coppers coming rushing at them.

Angus was now mimicking the Reverend Ian Paisley, very recognisable; and it was about Phoebe. Tom's mind had been elsewhere so he missed most of it.

"...the pain of finding what a devoted husband was willing to do for her. She decided to keep that a secret until she died and it must remain a family secret. She did not try to spend the ill-gotten gains her husband left behind, and passed away knowing her conscience was clear. She did not benefit from them. When eventually her daughter discovered..."

He'd changed to another, much softer, Irish accent. David recognised it immediately, good old Sir Terry Wogan.

"...of great spirit, wit and inventive mischievousness. Hence our reason, as a tight little band of relatives, for standing here now. Tom, you are ready?"

Tom nodded and reached into his pocket, carefully grasping all ten objects at the same time. In a swift movement, he threw them into the River Clyde, in the same efficient way David had done.

Even though it was a dull, cloudy day, each one

of the five, watching in the freezing cold, saw ten sparkling portions of conscience, survivors from several generations ago, splash and vanish into the murky depths.

"Thank you, Tom. That was very brave, and to finish off, as Meg might have said, if she had been still with us, 'Good game! Good game!' and now all our consciences can be clear. The game is over. Yes, my loves, good game, good game..."

The 'Brucie' voice ending Angus's speech had been perfect and not surprisingly, the family members gave him a deserved round of applause. Two slightly inebriated fellows sitting farther downriver now wished they had stayed a bit closer to hear it all. They did not have much in the way of free entertainment...

"Bravo, Angus. I told you that you could still do it," Beth said and gave him a big hug.

There were handshakes and kisses again as they parted to do their own things, glad to be escaping the cold wind, each feeling much relieved that their special little ceremony, and Meg's Game – both – had ended. The hunt was over but... the loft clearance was not. It would now continue at a leisurely pace.

"See you next Saturday, as usual?" called Tom.

Beth clung close to Angus for some extra warmth as they returned to the car. Angus realised, now that he could relax after his little performance, he was actually looking forward to having his mother-in-law to stay. It was the right thing to do. That was always important – applying good simple family values to living.

As the other three walked towards their vehicles, David said cheerio and left on his own, driving the van. He was going to visit a national bagpipe centre. He felt he had done his bit today, in fact, everyone had. It was a great family and he would make them prouder.

...But when I can play my pipes, should I perform first at the Argyll Arcade, or the Hielenman's Umbrella? Hmm... an extra bonus tonight – Maureen... That is her name isn't it?

Gillian was wondering what to make for the evening meal. Something not too complicated, but the boys deserved a nice one. They behaved well and did not let her down. On Monday, her Mum would be out of hospital, but it looked as if she would have to go back in for some sort of operation. As usual, she had not really understood what the surgeon was proposing, so Gillian would have a chance to ask him herself on Monday.

Tom was smiling as he entered the car. Everyone was happy.

If David organises lessons and concentrates on learning the pipes, the laptop will be free for me to use – get the family tree underway. I have been meaning to do it for a while. Honest! I'll prove to David that his old man is not useless, but if I get stuck, I can always ask number-one-son for help!

"You know, Gill, I never did manage to figure out how the photo album got into the jelly pan in the first place. It bugs me. Meg wasn't capable of..."

"Oh. Didn't I say? It was your dad. He put it up in the loft for her. He told me. You should have asked me, Tom. I've known that for ages..."

"Oh..."

As he drove along he could not resist feeling his emptied pocket once more, with a smile. Job done! ...But there was a lump! He tentatively reached in and found that he still had one of the little beauties. By mistake, he had thrown away only nine. He brought it out cautiously, so that Gillian would not notice...

Her mobile sounded and she answered. Her mind was elsewhere.

As he drove along the expressway, he glanced quickly at his hand. What to do with it? He opened his window slightly, and received a puzzled frown from Gillian, as noise increased and the cold air came in.

"Just clearing my head a little," he told her.

She turned her head away again and, with a quick flick, his hand was empty. He wound the window back up. He was confident that the piece of glass would shatter immediately it hit the road, or eventually be crushed by the continuous stream of traffic. That is what glass does – it shatters!

So, what was sitting at the bottom of the River Clyde?

The other nine pieces of glass, of course!

There had been some good and some stupid ideas from the meeting last week and throwing the potential of more than fifty thousand pounds into the River was a stupid one. So... he bought the cheap glass necklace, removed the imitation gems and...!

Before, he had been unsure about managing on his pension – but not now. The little jewels were going to be his personal insurance, a nice little supplement. Anyway, the pension question would probably sort itself out.

He had not been into his own loft for a long time. When they got back home, that is where he would be hiding the *real* little beauties that were held safely in the other pocket. Exactly where to put them, had yet to be decided, but it would be up there in a dark and dusty place – though he might have to tidy it first!

If he could manage without having to sell the diamonds, his conscience would be clear. It could become David's problem in the future – him and his offspring, if he ever gets round to settling down.

Yes, thank you Meg, for your treasure hunt! It was a great game but, when my turn comes, will I cope with rhymes and clues...? Hmm...

mac black

www.macblack.info
and
www.uppbooks.com

and for the kids...

www.ingramcontent.com/pod-product-compliance
Lightning Source LLC
Chambersburg PA
CBHW070832260626
47170CB00007B/2348